THE PRINCESSE DE CLÈVES

MADAME DE LAFAYETTE was born Marie-Madeleine Pioche de La Vergne in 1634; her father was a member of the minor nobility. In 1650, she became maid-of-honour to the Queen; she also began to acquire a literary education from the writer Gilles Ménage. She married François, Comte de Lafayette, in 1655, and left Paris to live with him on his country estates. In 1657, she established a friendship with Mme de Sévigné, and in 1659 returned to Paris, where she organized a salon and began to take part in court life. She made the acquaintance of leading writers such as Huet and Segrais, and in 1662 published *The Princesse de Montpensier*. This was followed in 1669–71 by the Hispano-Moorish romance *Zaïde*, published under the name of Segrais but reliably attributed to Mme de Lafayette. She formed a close (some would say amorous) relationship with the Duc de La Rochefoucauld in the 1660s, and this continued during the 1670s, when it seems that she was working on *The Princesse de Clèves* with La Rochefoucauld and Segrais. The novel was published anonymously in March 1678 and was an immediate success, although it also provoked considerable controversy. The death of La Rochefoucauld in 1680 was followed three years later by the death of her husband; she herself died in 1693. Several other works have been attributed to her, although they were not published until long after her death: these include memoirs of the French court for 1688–9, *The Comtesse de Tende* and the *Histoire de Madame Henriette d'Angleterre*.

TERENCE CAVE is Professor of French Literature in the University of Oxford and Fellow of St John's College. He is also a Fellow of the British Academy. His previous publications include *Recognitions: a study in poetics* (Oxford, 1988; paperback 1990).

OXFORD WORLD'S CLASSICS

For over 100 years Oxford World's Classics have brought
readers closer to the world's great literature. Now with over 700
titles—from the 4,000-year-old myths of Mesopotamia to the
twentieth century's greatest novels—the series makes available
lesser-known as well as celebrated writing.

The pocket-sized hardbacks of the early years contained
introductions by Virginia Woolf, T. S. Eliot, Graham Greene,
and other literary figures which enriched the experience of reading.
Today the series is recognized for its fine scholarship and
reliability in texts that span world literature, drama and poetry,
religion, philosophy and politics. Each edition includes perceptive
commentary and essential background information to meet the
changing needs of readers.

OXFORD WORLD'S CLASSICS

MADAME DE LAFAYETTE

The Princesse de Clèves
The Princesse de Montpensier
The Comtesse de Tende

Translated with an Introduction and Notes by
TERENCE CAVE

OXFORD
UNIVERSITY PRESS

OXFORD
UNIVERSITY PRESS

Great Clarendon Street, Oxford OX2 6DP

Oxford University Press is a department of the University of Oxford.
It furthers the University's objective of excellence in research, scholarship,
and education by publishing worldwide in

Oxford New York

Athens Auckland Bangkok Bogotá Buenos Aires Calcutta
Cape Town Chennai Dar es Salaam Delhi Florence Hong Kong Istanbul
Karachi Kuala Lumpur Madrid Melbourne Mexico City Mumbai
Nairobi Paris São Paulo Singapore Taipei Tokyo Toronto Warsaw

with associated companies in Berlin Ibadan

Oxford is a registered trade mark of Oxford University Press
in the UK and in certain other countries

Published in the United States
by Oxford University Press Inc., New York

Translation and editorial material © Terence Cave 1992

First published as a World's Classics paperback 1992
Reissued as an Oxford World's Classics paperback 1999
Reissued 2008

British Library Cataloguing in Publication Data

Data available

Library of Congress Cataloging in Publication Data

Data available

ISBN 978-0-19-953917-8

10

Printed in Great Britain by
Clays Ltd, Elcograf S.p.A.

CONTENTS

INTRODUCTION

In 1679, there appeared in London a book entitled *The Princess of Cleves. The most famed Romance. Written in French by the greatest Wits of France. Rendred into English by a Person of Quality, at the Request of some Friends*. This extremely free translation of *The Princesse de Clèves* was licensed in 1678; since the original had been published in March of that year, it appears that the fame of the new 'romance' had spread rapidly.

The title also shows that the work was ascribed not to a single author but to the collaboration of a group of 'great wits'. It had in fact been published anonymously (see the publisher's prefatory note), and no subsequent edition of the period attributed it to Mme de Lafayette. In a famous letter of 13 April 1678, she herself denied all part in the composition of the novel; some thirteen years later, another letter (of which the authenticity has been questioned by at least one critic) contains a phrase which may be interpreted as an admission of authorship: when asked by her old friend Gilles Ménage whether he may attribute the novel to her, she replies, 'To you, what would one not confess!'[1] What is undisputed is that *The Princesse de Clèves* emerged from Mme de Lafayette's most intimate intellectual and social milieu. During the 1670s, two of the greatest wits of France visited her house regularly: these were the Duc de La Rochefoucauld, whose *Maximes* had been a *succès de scandale* in the preceding decade, and Jean Regnault de Segrais, an established writer of prose fictions. Both of these have been put forward as candidates for the sole authorship (even though Segrais left Paris for the provinces in 1676), but it seems

---

[1] The letters referred to here are to be found in André Beaunier's edition of Mme de Lafayette's correspondence (see below, Select Bibliography). The letter to Ménage is of uncertain date, but Beaunier proposes Sept. 1691 as a plausible conjecture.

more likely that, as the English version claims, it was in some sense a collaborative exercise.

The question remains a critical one for modern readers. Was *The Princesse de Clèves* written, wholly or in part, by a woman? In the absence of conclusive external evidence, what is the evidence of the text itself? What about *The Princesse de Montpensier* and *The Comtesse de Tende*, both traditionally attributed to Mme de Lafayette although their claims to authenticity are by no means equal? The question of authorship will be addressed again later, but for the moment one may simply note the appearance of a theme with wide ramifications: the theme of secrecy, of a truth never fully confessed, a name suppressed.

Whoever wrote *The Princesse de Clèves*, its appearance was certainly a landmark in the history of the novel. In the letter of April 1678 mentioned above, Mme de Lafayette, having cleared herself of any imputation that she might have an interest in the matter, gives her judgement of the work's merits:

I find it most agreeable, well written without being extremely polished, full of wonderfully fine things that even merit a second reading. What I find in it above all is a perfect imitation of the world of the court and of the way one lives there. There is nothing of the romance, nothing extravagant in it. Indeed, it is not a romance: it should properly be regarded as a memoir. That was, I have been told, the title of the book, but it was changed.

The French phrase 'Aussi n'est-ce pas un roman' looks as if it means 'it is not a *novel*', a claim that might seem paradoxical given the general agreement that *The Princesse de Clèves* is the first work of prose fiction written in Europe which may unambiguously be assigned to the genre of the novel. It has joined a canon where it may be seen to bear a clear family resemblance to, say, Laclos's *Les Liaisons dangereuses* and Constant's *Adolphe*, as well as to the novels of Jane Austen and even Henry James.

The point, of course, is that the canon did not yet exist; what did exist was the *roman*, which in seventeenth-century French meant 'romance', that is to say a fictional narrative of considerable length depicting the extraordinary adventures of heroes and heroic lovers. A wide variety of works of this kind were written and read up to about 1660 in France, and they constitute a major point of reference for any new writer wishing to establish herself (or himself) on the scene. Thus, for example, in *The Princesse de Montpensier*, the sudden luminous vision of the princess in a boat, seen from the bank by a group of noblemen, appears to them like 'something out of a romance' (p. 164) and they speculate on its potential love interest.

What one notices first, then, is the negative emphasis: 'it is *not* a romance'. It implies, first, that readers might have come to *The Princesse de Clèves* with the wrong expectations and even misread it; secondly, if this new work must initially be defined by saying what it is not, rather than what it is, there can be no ready-made category waiting to receive it.

It is perhaps not surprising, then, that as soon as *The Princesse de Clèves* appeared it provoked a vigorous literary controversy. It had been an instant success; the Paris booksellers rapidly sold out; readers in the provinces had to wait months before getting a copy. The question was therefore posed with considerable urgency and publicity: what *was* this new phenomenon? Was it to be approved or rejected? The debate was pursued in salon conversations and at court, in private correspondence, and then in print: Valincour's *Lettres à Madame la Marquise *** sur le sujet de la Princesse de Clèves*, which analyses in detail—often critically—the novel's formal structure, its representation of the characters' feelings, and its language and style, appeared in the same year;[2] Donneau de Visé, the editor of the fashionable monthly *Le Mercure Galant*, ran a kind of opinion poll on the question 'Should wives confess to their husbands their passion for other men?'; the Abbé de Charnes (possibly ghosting for Mme de Lafayette herself) produced a defence of *The Princesse de Clèves* against Valincour in his *Conversations sur la critique de la Princesse de Clèves* (1679).

Seventeenth-century French society loved literary quarrels: there had been major furores over Corneille's *Le Cid* (1636) and Molière's *L'École des femmes* (1662–4) and *Tartuffe*

---

[2] A modern facsimile reprint is available (see below, Select Bibliography).

(1664–9), to mention only the most notorious; several of Racine's tragedies also provoked controversy. It is no doubt symptomatic of a potential new direction that this time the quarrel concerns prose fiction rather than the consecrated genres of tragedy and comedy. Heroic and pastoral romances had provided plenty of material for polite conversation since the 1620s at least, but prose fiction was none the less regarded as a 'low' genre, designed mainly for consumption by women readers.

The Princesse de Clèves marks a turning-point; yet it did not appear out of a void. Prose narrative had gradually begun to establish its credentials on new ground in the previous twenty years. The erudite bishop Pierre-Daniel Huet wrote a substantial *Traité sur l'origine des romans*, which was published as the preface to the first volume of *Zaïde* (dated 1670, printed in 1669), a Hispano-Moorish romance usually attributed to Mme de Lafayette. More directly relevant to the conception of *The Princesse de Clèves* is the work of Segrais, the writer who was to share Mme de Lafayette's literary favours with La Rochefoucauld. *Zaïde* was originally published under his name, and it is certain that he at least played a significant role in its composition. As early as 1657, he had produced a collection called *Les Nouvelles françaises*, in which his fictional mouthpiece, Princesse Aurélie, makes an important distinction between the romance (*roman*) and another genre with a long history, now becoming fashionable again, the *nouvelle*. The *nouvelle* is a short prose narrative, which might be as short as what we call a short story or as long as a novella. Aurélie defines the difference as follows:

we have undertaken, in our stories, to present things as they are, not as they ought to be ... one may say that the difference between the romance and the *nouvelle* is that the romance is written according to the rules of decorum and in a poetic manner, whereas the *nouvelle* must remain a little closer to history and devote itself to representing things as we see them happen in ordinary life rather than as we imagine them to be.[3]

---

[3] Jean Regnault de Segrais, *Les Nouvelles françaises, ou les divertissements de la Princesse Aurélie*, ed. Roger Guichemerre, vol. 1 (Paris: Aux Amateurs de Livres, 1990), p. 99.

The phrase 'ordinary life' here has little to do with social realism in the nineteenth-century sense; the representation of the everyday life of ordinary people was restricted to the comic and the picaresque novel in this period. It also turns out that the difference between *roman* and *nouvelle* is not always evident in the stories themselves. Yet the revival of the short prose narrative form is a significant event, and it is perhaps not irrelevant that Segrais invokes as a model Marguerite de Navarre's *Heptameron*, a sixteenth-century collection of stories which in turn claims to imitate Boccaccio's *Decameron* but with one difference, namely that the stories should be true. The *Heptameron* was first published in 1558, the year in which the narrative of *The Princesse de Clèves* begins; it is in fact specifically mentioned in the novel (see below, p. 61). The sixteenth-century setting, the claim to imitate life, the preference for a concise, sober narrative form, are all characteristic of the re-emergence, in the 1660s and 1670s, of the *nouvelle* and its development into something very like a novel.

The *Comtesse de Tende* and *The Princesse de Montpensier* are *nouvelles* in the sense defined above. Neither would have seemed generically or thematically strange to Marguerite de Navarre. Both are terse narratives of a passion that, despite efforts to control and hide it, breaks out disastrously; both are morally serious, and *The Princesse de Montpensier* even ends with a formal moral 'lesson'. Yet there is a different emphasis in the post-1660 *nouvelle*, an emphasis conveyed by the epithet used to characterize the genre from about this time: it is the 'nouvelle *historique*', the '*historical* story', which sets the fashion, and *The Princesse de Montpensier* (1662) is an early example of this genre. When Mme de Lafayette says that *The Princesse de Clèves* should properly be regarded as a memoir, she is invoking a contemporary taste for quasi-historical narratives which purport to describe the private rather than the public aspect of historical events; memoirs record the intimate personal passions and intrigues that are glossed over by the official record. The *nouvelle historique* invents private lives and feelings for well-known historical figures, or invents fictional characters who act out their drama amid historical figures and events, or both; it deals in what is secret, in what history censors.[4]

The historical sources for the three works, and particularly for *The Princesse de Clèves*, in which the memoir element is much more prominent, are known in considerable detail.[5] They include sixteenth-century works like Brantôme's colourful, and much embroidered, portraits of great men and women, which appeared in a new edition in 1665–6; the writings of seventeenth-century historians—Mathieu, Mézeray, Le Laboureur; and, for the description of court ceremonials and the like, the works of Père Anselme and Godefroy. The fact that certain of these sources appeared during the mid-1670s helps to clarify the somewhat vexed question of the date of composition of *The Princesse de Clèves*.[6]

In its opening pages, *The Princesse de Clèves* seems to promise the spectacle of a magnificent court and the story of illustrious love affairs: the novel begins, then, as a memoir. It becomes a novel at the point where the invented figures of Mme de Chartres and her daughter appear on the scene, inaugurating a 'private' story that no history or memoir could have told. Thereafter, the figures of Diane de Poitiers and Marie Stuart, the references to the Treaty of Cateau-Cambrésis and the weddings and other celebrations that accompanied it, offer a kind of counterpoint to the thread of that narrative; at the same time, the secret quarrels described within the fiction are shown to motivate the public destinies of characters like the Vidame de Chartres and the Chevalier de Guise. *The Princesse de Montpensier* dramatizes the amorous inclinations of such great men as Henri, Duc d'Anjou (later Henri III), and the Duc de Guise; it also relies on the

---

[4] On the relationship between memoirs and women's writing in 17th-century France, see Faith Beasley's *Revising Memory* (listed below, Select Bibliography); I am also indebted here to the unpublished work of Elizabeth Guild.

[5] See the articles by Chamard and Rudler (listed below, Select Bibliography).

[6] A reference by the publisher Claude Barbin in 1671 to a book entitled *Le Prince de Clèves* which he was planning to publish has led to speculation that the novel was already in progress at that date, but the evidence is far from conclusive.

Massacre of St Bartholomew for part of the denouement; and it takes its central couple from a family so illustrious in the seventeenth century that the publisher (acting perhaps as a mask for the author herself) felt obliged to defend the work in a prefatory note (see below, p. 158). Yet the amorous intrigue itself is fictional and the figure of the 'unrequited lover' is invented. Although *The Comtesse de Tende* refers to no major historical events, it bears a clear family resemblance to the other two works: the story takes place in the same historical period and concerns characters from the same royal and noble circles; one of the central figures (the Chevalier de Navarre) is invented, while others are historical.

At this point we must return to the question of authorship. To cite *The Comtesse de Tende* as belonging to this group is tendentious, in so far as it was neither published, nor ascribed to Mme de Lafayette, nor even publicly mentioned, until well into the eighteenth century. Some conjecture that it was written by another hand; some, that Mme de Lafayette wrote it towards the end of her life; others again, that it had been in her bottom drawer since the early years of her experimentation with the *nouvelle*. Of course, one can also argue plausibly enough that a later, inferior author was attempting to take advantage of the successful formula of *The Princesse de Clèves*. Yet its existence proves at least that the formula was both successful and powerful, and it is not unreasonable that it should be allowed its share in posthumous glory, like a painting from the school of a great master.

The Princesse de Montpensier is a much clearer case. It was first published in 1662, and there is plenty of evidence that Mme de Lafayette herself wrote it, aided, it seems, by her writer friend and former tutor Gilles Ménage. It thus supplies, as we have suggested, a convenient historical link between Segrais's experiments and *The Princesse de Clèves* itself. One link, it is true, does not make a chain. The publication of *Zaïde* in 1669–71 shows that longer, more complicated, and more fantastic fictions were still marketable in these decades, and that Mme de Lafayette herself probably tried her hand at one. But other writers took over the

form of the *nouvelle historique* and developed it in original
and successful ways: the best known of these was Mme de
Villedieu's *Les Désordres de l'amour*, published in 1675, which
was widely discussed, thus helping to create the fashion on
which the *succès de scandale* of *The Princesse de Clèves* was
based. It even contains a marital confession scene, which led
some contemporary critics to claim that the *pièce de résistance*
of the later novel was stolen property.[7]

It was in fact the confession scene in *The Princesse de Clèves*
which caused the greatest furore. This was because it provided a test case for plausibility in the expanded *nouvelle
historique* or fictional memoir.[8] Extraordinary and exotic
things can happen in romances, but the claim to be in some
sense historical entailed for the seventeenth-century reader a
submission to common experience and common opinion.
The confession, while undoubtedly intriguing, was judged by
the majority of readers canvassed by *Le Mercure Galant* to be
wholly implausible. Wives just don't say such things to their
husbands. Likewise, fortuitous incidents—again common in
romances—are censured by Valincour (the two episodes, for
example, in which the Princesse de Clèves chances on
Nemours again after the death of the Prince).
   One may find these judgements naïve, and argue that the
novel may legitimately exploit accident and test experience
at the limit of plausibility; yet they show what pressures—
mostly invigorating ones—were exerted on literary texts in
the seventeenth century by their transformation into material
for passionate conversation. Readers of that period were not
naïve; their habits of reading and interpretation were simply
different from our own. In this particular instance, we are

[7] The rather implausible reply, issued by the novel's defenders, was that
the author had conceived this scene before *Les Désordres de l'amour* appeared
and that she had in mind a scene in Corneille's Christian tragedy *Polyeucte*
(*c.*1640) where the chief female character Pauline confesses to her husband
Polyeucte that she loves another man (Pauline's behaviour is impregnably
chaste and the confession unarguably above-board).

[8] On the question of *vraisemblance*, with particular reference to *The
Princesse de Clèves*, see the excellent essay by Gérard Genette listed below,
Select Bibliography.

also witnessing a challenge to those habits, a shifting of agreed boundaries: hence the generation of so much controversy and interest. Whatever the objections, the novel was a sell-out, which means that readers were perhaps quicker than critics to change their preconceptions.

Another line of attack on *The Princesse de Clèves* was that the opening historical panorama is superfluous and that the various secondary narratives interrupt the central thread; these issues are still debated. The intercalated stories are as follows: what one might call the public histories of Marie de Lorraine (pp. 17–18), of Diane de Poitiers (pp. 26–31), and of Ann Boleyn (pp. 60–3); and the private stories of Sancerre and Mme de Tournon (pp. 42–51) and of the Vidame de Chartres and Mme de Thémines's letter (pp. 74–81). The very brief biography of Marie de Lorraine is often omitted from this list, leaving four major 'digressions'.

They may be regarded as descendants of the complex multiple narratives of romance; they also recall the way in which, in collections of *nouvelles* like the *Heptameron*, storytellers recount to each other interesting case histories, stories which exemplify a given proposition or situation. They all occur within approximately the first half of the novel, which already suggests that they have a functional role connected with the exposition and development of the story: if they were merely digressive prolongations, they would be found throughout. The aftermath of the last story moves the action directly towards the confession scene, after which the narrative flow proceeds with undiminished urgency. The earlier stories are in the main 'memoir' fragments, extending the opening survey of court figures with the loves of illustrious royal women.

A detailed study of these stories would show that they are linked in many other ways both to the main action and to the predominant themes of the novel. One of their functions is certainly to inject a heady dose of amorous intrigue at a point where the primary narrative is still predominantly decorous; indeed, they bring into a story of unconsummated passion the narrative force and seduction of consummated passion. But this is not just a strategy to keep the reader

interested: the Princesse de Clèves herself listens to all the
stories and cannot help imbibing the dose. She is also the
recipient of the prince's remark, made in passing as he tells
the story of Sancerre, that he would wish his wife to confide
in him if she were threatened by a passionate entanglement;
this is one of a series of cleverly placed anticipations of—
and motivations for—the confession.

The position of the Princesse de Clèves as a 'reader in
the text' is in this way a dynamic one, relaying the examples
and counter-examples of the secondary narratives—
examples of the disastrous intermingling of love and power,
of the unhappiness caused by love affairs, of jealousy, of
duplicity—into the primary narrative. These extend the
lessons Mme de Chartres attempts to give her daughter (she
herself tells the story of Diane de Poitiers) and provide a
complex body of instructive materials which the extremely
young princess has to try to assimilate in order to survive the
corrupt world of the court. Yet there is no crude didacticism
in *The Princesse de Clèves*. There are plenty of moral judgements, stated and implied, but no suggestion that the path of
virtue is smooth. And the princess signally fails to assimilate
any of the messages embedded in the stories until her own
experience has led her to learn for herself, a much more
painful and dangerous process.[9]

The telling of stories by characters in the novel means, of
course, that the narrative perspective shifts a good deal.
Overall, the narrator knows what the characters themselves
may not know, even about their most private feelings: when
the princess reads Mme de Thémines's letter and assumes
that it is addressed to Nemours, she attributes her distress to
Nemours's knowledge of her love for him: 'But she was
deceiving herself. This pain that she found so unbearable
was in fact jealousy with all its attendant horrors' (p. 72).
After the confession, we are given the meditations first of the
princess, then of Nemours. Yet this omniscience is tempered
by discretion: with the exception of a few maxim-like gen-

---

[9] On the complex question of 'example' in this novel and in *Zaïde*, see
John D. Lyons's *Exemplum* (below, Select Bibliography).

eralizations, and the moral conclusion of the early *Princesse de Montpensier*, the narrator is habitually non-interventionist. The narrative voice moves smoothly between external, impersonal descriptions of historical characters and events and the inner world of the principal characters, recording both as if from the point of view of a privileged but detached observer.

One of the reasons why the compositional technique of *The Princesse de Clèves* is so interesting is that it shows the impact on prose narrative of a conception of dramatic economy promoted above all, in the 1670s, by the tragedies of Racine. In a famous preface to *Bérénice*, published in 1671, Racine speaks disparagingly of tragedies which bristle with 'incidents', and advertises the virtues of extreme simplicity. The tragedian must hold the audience for five acts 'by means of a simple action, sustained by the violence of the passions, the beauty of the sentiments, and the elegance of the expression'. This shift from external action to what we should now call psychological action, where the narrative is carried forward through shifts in the thoughts, feelings, and perceptions of the characters, will have a long and illustrious future: indeed, we now habitually relegate 'mere external action' to an inferior category and regard 'psychology' as indispensable.

There are, of course, external events in *The Princesse de Clèves*, but the story is plotted not through them but through their impact on the princess's changing awareness of her situation and of her own feelings. External incidents and events—like the secondary narratives—are thus made the object of a continuous activity of assimilation and interpretation. The theft of the portrait, the Duc de Nemours's riding accident, Mme de Thémines's letter, the silk-merchant's reference to an unknown stranger, are treated in this way; another particularly graphic instance is the scene where, having heard from the Reine Dauphine that the secret of her confession is out, the princess hears Nemours come in and hides her face while he is interrogated by the Reine Dauphine. Much of the narrative is in fact constituted by a series of percussive shocks to her consciousness.

The princess interprets, but she is often wrong; she has no reliable access to other people's feelings, nor even to her own; most of her conjectures are provisional. She does, it is true, progressively acquire lucidity, but always too late: when it comes, it only shows her the walls of her labyrinth and the broken thread of her will. The prince, too, who manages to draw a correct inference concerning the identity of his wife's would-be lover, subsequently draws from Nemours's nights at Coulommiers a false inference which proves fatal to him. He sees at last that he may have been wrong, but the recognition comes too late to save him.

There is good reason to believe that this aspect of *The Princesse de Clèves* derives from a conception of human fallibility which became widespread in cultivated circles in France in the later seventeenth century and permeated—even inspired—many of the masterpieces of the period, from La Rochefoucauld's *Maximes* to the tragedies of Racine and La Fontaine's *Fables*. This pessimistic view of man as a fallen creature blinded by self-love and self-interest and led into error by his passions was vigorously promoted by the theology of the Jansenists, a religious sect which had considerable influence on secular society through intermediaries such as Pascal and through its seminary at Port-Royal, where Racine was educated. This does not mean that writers such as La Rochefoucauld, Racine, and Mme de Lafayette were themselves Jansenists or were particularly concerned with religious issues; it means that the Jansenists' view of man's moral and psychological nature proved to be detachable from their theology of grace and to be readily adaptable to secular contexts. Above all, it proved to be extraordinarily fertile as an imaginative resource for writers. It provided them with a cogent and complex account of human behaviour in which conscious intention was seen to be constantly belied and undermined by dark, partially unfathomable motivations: what makes things happen is something we can't quite see, or don't see in time; we live in a world of signs and clues which we must interpret but which are never reliable enough to provide certainty. Modern literature—especially French literature—has thrived on such a view, enhanced by an increasingly elaborate secular psychology; the family resemblance, mentioned earlier, to novels from *Les Liaisons dangereuses* to Henry James has a good deal to do with this theme. *The Princesse de Clèves* is a forerunner not only in its narrative economy and its authorial discretion but also in the implication that our moral lives as well as our happiness are flawed by something unknowable, a blur or patch of darkness lying deep in our consciousness.

Thus, in *The Princesse de Clèves*, characters constantly deceive both others and themselves. They are subject to error, unease, and confusion: words denoting these states of mind recur incessantly throughout the novel. The confession scene, which might at first sight seem a triumph of moral purpose over the forces of passion, turns out on closer inspection to be nothing of the sort. The princess embarks on the confession without specifically intending to, and she refuses to divulge one essential item, Nemours's name. Her state of mind afterwards, when she tries to assess what she has done, is ambivalent, lurching from horror to a sense that she might possibly have done the best thing. And the exercise is undermined by the secret presence of Nemours, which unseals the perfect confidentiality between husband and wife, turns it into a confession of love to Nemours, and releases the story to be retold, disastrously, in the public domain. Nemours almost comes to symbolize here the dark, unseen motives (self-love, passion, perhaps also a prurient curiosity) that distort even the most idealistic of gestures. Likewise, at the end of the story, the princess's renunciation requires at least two motives (duty towards the memory of her husband; her own peace of mind), as if a single moral imperative were not enough: that an aura of doubt hangs over this denouement is attested by the critical debate it has aroused. Uncertainty is so pervasive that, in the end, it affects even the novel's readers: one is left with a real complexity, a knot only partly untied.

This view of the novel is widely accepted, and has in the main supplanted a reading which stressed the exceptional, even heroic ability of the princess to resist her passion. In that reading, her ultimate rejection of Nemours is a triumph

of duty and reason over passion, comparable to the acts of
heroes in the dramas of Corneille; the confession, although
tragic, is also sublime. Mutually exclusive as these interpre-
tations may sound, they should perhaps not be regarded as
wholly incompatible. Mme de Lafayette spent many forma-
tive years in salons where a more optimistic view of human
nature was promoted, and she had the closest connections
with *précieuses* who attacked marriage, claimed independence
and education for women, and believed that love could be
founded in esteem for the virtue of the beloved (and thus be
morally enhancing). She may have remained attached to
some of these views even when she had moved into different
circles in the 1660s, as the prevailing climate of sensibility
changed; though her relations (the social and intellectual
kind) with La Rochefoucauld seem to have become intimate,
it is not essential to believe that her views were identical with
his.[10] One could perhaps at least say that the clash between
the two conceptions allowed the point of the novel to be
sharpened. The princess seems nostalgic for a world where
will can be imposed on circumstance and passion can be
contained, a world personified in her mother; but the mother
dies, leaving only a pale shadow of her values behind. Dissimulation and intrigue are endemic, the princess herself is
infected; she seeks the utopian security of Coulommiers—
an echo, again, of the idyllic settings of pastoral novels such
as the *Astrée* of Honoré d'Urfé—but encounters there, on
two decisive occasions, the fatal shadow of Nemours.

The Princesse de Clèves is not the only work of this period
to subject dated idealistic fictions to a critical rereading.
Molière's Alceste, champion of sincerity, spouts quasi-heroic
rhetoric in an environment wholly unsuited to it; Racine's

---

[10] In two letters of 1663, preserved by La Rochefoucauld's friend
Mme de Sablé, Mme de Lafayette declares herself to be shocked by La
Rochefoucauld's excessively negative view of human nature; these remarks
need not be taken quite literally, but they do indicate the unwillingness of
Mme de Lafayette at that time (i.e. not long after the publication of *The
Princesse de Montpensier*, but fifteen years before *The Princesse de Clèves*) to
identify herself with the moral implications of the *Maximes*.

Titus, in *Bérénice,* is an ironic inversion of Corneille's self-confident heroes. But the question of exactly how one should read *The Princesse de Clèves* is deeply interesting in a special sense because it is bound up, once again, with the question of authorship. The hypothesis of a collaboration between 'great wits' is valuable because it suggests that the strands of the novel may indeed be multiple, reflecting the convergence and conflict of rival conceptions in contemporary society. At the same time, there is no reason to assume that, if there *was* a single author, the picture would be different: literature thrives on its ability to dramatize unresolved conflicts. As we have seen, Mme de Lafayette's social and cultural career would have given her the resources to conceive such a work, and *The Princesse de Clèves* is much closer to the one other fictional narrative we know is hers— *The Princesse de Montpensier*—than it is to the moral writings of La Rochefoucauld or the fictional writings of Segrais.[11]

But is the perspective of the novel recognizably that of a woman? Feminist readings make this claim, but in most cases they start from the assumption that Mme de Lafayette did write it—perhaps for the good political reason that a woman may for once be allowed the benefit of the doubt. In the writing itself there is one tiny clue, a single grammatical form, which seems more reliable as hard evidence than any more general argument based on theme or narrative voice: at the moment when the princess first sees Nemours—the *coup de foudre*—she is 'surprised'; the participle in the French sentence has an impersonal subject, but the writer has given it a feminine ending ('surpris*e*').[12] It is extremely unlikely that a male writer would use the marked feminine form in these circumstances: is this then Mme de Lafayette's— doubtless involuntary—signature?

The other reliable clue is the anonymity itself. Male authors of the seventeenth century sometimes preferred not

[11] For a recent comparison between *The Princesse de Montpensier* and the later novel, see the article by Roger Duchêne listed below, Select Bibliography.
[12] See also the note on the passage in question, below, p. 210.

to declare themselves on the title-page—novels in particular were often published anonymously—but they usually allowed their authorship to become public in other ways. *The Princesse de Clèves* is the only really striking case of unresolved anonymity in this period, and that makes it a great deal more likely that the author was a woman moving in the highest social circles. Women *in those circles* were not supposed to write for the public, still less to admit that they did; and Mme de Lafayette is the only plausible candidate.

One may therefore read *The Princesse de Clèves* as a woman's novel without the inconvenience of a circular argument. It is a major undertaking: so many readings have turned the author into another Corneille or another La Rochefoucauld or another Racine that the implications of her being none of these are disconcertingly rich. Historical caution is needed again here, of course, since seventeenth-century feminism is quite different from modern varieties of feminism; but that simply makes the issue more complex and more fascinating. In the present context, only a few indications can be sketched in: it is up to the reader to do the rest.

A good place to begin—because it draws on the cultural experience of seventeenth-century readers—is the role of chivalry in the novel. In the historical period of the action, the tournament was already a survival from an earlier feudal age; in the seventeenth century, it was still a public spectacle which the novel's first readers could themselves have attended, but it was rapidly becoming an archaic reconstruction rather than a living tradition—which is why the reader is treated to a precise technical description of the tournament at the end of Part III, not a first-hand description but one borrowed by the author from a historical source. In tournaments, gallant, handsome men are supposed to do battle for the honour of the women whose colours they wear; Nemours's display of personal attractions and accomplishments on this occasion is so successful that, despite the reasons the princess has for suspecting his good faith, she is impressed. The old formula proves that it can still work. Yet the way the scene as a whole is presented allows the reader to see that chivalry is a fiction and a decoy: it is merely the public face of a war between the sexes in which idealism and heroics are not greatly in evidence.

This much would be easy to translate into the general terms of one of La Rochefoucauld's maxims. But the exact pathos and irony of Mme de Lafayette's dramatization depends on the position of a vulnerable female spectator exposed to a display of gratuitous masculine power. The seventeenth-century women who defended their own sex also applauded (and sometimes wrote) heroic literature because it gave a privileged position to women as the object of a morally enhancing love; *The Princesse de Clèves* gives that view a tragic twist, showing that the moral enhancement may be minimal and that the woman may well be crudely exploited in the process. It would not be difficult to read a number of other episodes in a similar light: the gallant or *précieux* conversation pieces, for example, in which Nemours's wit enables him to exert leverage on his women listeners. One should bear in mind that the princess is extremely young (15 to 17 until the last paragraph of the novel) and thus extremely vulnerable.

The Comtesse de Tende demonstrates in the starkest possible way the exercise of another kind of power, that of husband over wife. Within the first paragraph, we are told that the Comte de Tende, finding his young wife insufficiently passionate, casually takes a mistress; at the end, he accepts with relief the Comtesse de Tende's death as a solution to the problem caused by her own infidelity. Does the story take the double standard for granted as a grim fact of life, or does the antithesis have an ironical function? The narrative certainly takes us into the increasingly desperate world of the young wife as she realizes her pregnancy and attempts to attract her husband's sexual attention in time to hide the cause: the sexual facts of this sequence are all clearly apparent despite the euphemistic language, and we read them from her angle; the husband remains a cipher.

The Prince de Clèves himself often displays what would nowadays seem to be a reflex assumption of male superiority—unsurprisingly, in an authoritarian society where everyone was conditioned to play a certain role within the hierarchy. It would not occur to him, of course, to give his wife the freedoms that men enjoy: her confession is a desperate attempt to escape the pressure imposed on her by the behaviour he prescribes. It is true that he avoids the Comte de Tende's crude double standard, in that he takes no mistress (his wife plays *that* role by virtue of a kind of paradox much savoured by seventeenth-century readers), but he finds the sexually promiscuous Mme de Tournon 'incomprehensible' as a woman because she can keep two lovers on the boil at once; and it is he who dies of his wife's supposed infidelity, as if someone has to die of such a monstrous act, leaving her to suffer the guilt of having caused his death. On the other hand, the portrayal of the tense marital scenes between the confession and the prince's death is one of the finest achievements of the book: for once, in this world of arranged marriages and formal relations between husband and wife, real tenderness breaks out, real pain, real marital perplexity. Valincour himself notes with approval the extraordinarily eloquent silence that falls between the couple at the end of one of their passages (p. 103). These scenes could be said to represent, for the first time in modern literature, the domestic tragedy of marriage, and they represent it with a remarkable lucidity and imaginative sympathy. Readers who become exclusively preoccupied with Nemours's voyeuristic excursions to Coulommiers, or with the denouement and its motivations, would do well to look again at the marital dialogues and ask what is entailed, ethically, in the contrast between these and the princess's dialogues with Nemours: on the one hand, a claustrophobic winding through a labyrinth of wit and allusion; on the other, a painful striving after some genuine human contact.

That such scenes should have been conceived by a woman whose own marriage seems to have been a sedate affair and who—like other so-called *précieuses*—steered clear of passion, is by no means a self-contradictory supposition. Elsewhere in the novel, it might well be the presence of strong women that best indicates the gender of the narrative. These are the women who manipulate their men: Diane de Poitiers, though much older than her royal lover, keeps him permanently on a string; Mme de Tournon loses her brilliantly executed game with Sancerre and d'Estouteville only because she dies in the hour of triumph; Mme de Thémines arranges her strategic retreat with no less brilliance and then, as the final stroke, describes it to her ex-lover in a letter of almost Jamesian intricacy; Catherine de Médicis imprisons the Vidame de Chartres in a tightly drawn verbal contract, so that when he fails her he is lost. The men use power as a matter of course: that is their *métier*. The women use it with a more conscious sense of contrivance, of 'beating the system'. They make their plans and carry them out with all the perseverance, all the artistry, and all the secrecy of an anonymous woman novelist.

This analogy between the novelist and her surrogate characters is neither a mere conceit nor a biographical reduction (it seems highly unlikely that Mme de Lafayette behaved remotely like any of these women). It bears rather on the position of a woman who is intelligent, imaginative, informed, socially well placed, but who has no access to the *public* exercise of power. For such a woman, secrecy, confidentiality, anonymity, privacy is the only regime possible; the effects she creates come from some inner chamber, from that little room called a *cabinet* to which she withdraws to meditate or where she may arrange an occasional tête-à-tête. Many of the key scenes in the novel occur in such secret places—a curtained bed, a pavilion in a country garden—and are contrasted with the great public scenes, the marriage-feasts and the jousting. Sometimes a character only needs to drop his or her voice in order to create a moment's confidentiality in a crowded salon.

The princess gropes her way through this claustrophobic landscape, desperate for air, for the open expression which is denied her. Ironically, when at last her secret breaks out, it is corrupted, hijacked, misread by an unsympathetic public: such is the fate of women's most intimate language. No wonder this scene was so controversial, so widely condemned, yet so fascinating to readers: it transgresses the very norm by which women are kept in their place, the rule that relegates them to the private rather than the public domain. No wonder, too, that the author wished to remain anonymous: the last transgression of signing her work would not only have been scandalous, it would have deprived her of the one place from which, as she clearly saw, a woman could exercise power.

The notion that the princess, by her final renunciation and disappearance, *triumphantly* escapes the constraining conventions of genre and gender, is I think a retrospective construction by modern feminists. For the character, the void in which her personal life and happiness are swallowed up is a traditional retreat, the exemplary convent. Although she has gone far beyond the moral perspective of her own mother, the princess cannot see the future liberties of which her fictional daughters will eventually avail themselves. If *The Princesse de Clèves* celebrates the reassertion of privacy at all costs, then one has to admit that the cost of privacy in the seventeenth century was high indeed. The real triumph must surely be the author's. We know that her novel troubled readers, that it produced *trouble*, confusion, emotional and moral uncertainty. It belongs to a 'new' genre; it portrays situations almost unthinkable in its day.[13] Perhaps, in the late seventeenth century, such a novel work could have been produced only by a woman.

Language, Style, and the Problems of Translation

Popular opinion, reinforced by the literary histories of an earlier generation, has it that the seventeenth century in France was a golden age of order, harmony, and symmetry, a period when the French discovered their national genius for *clarté* of thought and expression and forged a language at once precise and elegant. This myth has been so potent and so enduring that it has shaped the very way the French think about themselves; for centuries, it has influenced not only their literature, but also their education, their institutions,

---

[13] One might thus see the novel as distantly prefiguring (though with much less fictional and historical self-consciousness) John Fowles's *The French Lieutenant's Woman*.

and even their laws. It is thus by definition not an illusion: like any other form of publicity or propaganda, it has created its own reality. Yet it ought not to be taken at face value. Recent work on the style and semantics of French neoclassicism has shown that the meaning of words and phrases central to the self-conception of the age—*esprit, mérite, honnêteté, galanterie,* to name only a few—is shifting, even shifty; abstraction, far from connoting conceptual lucidity, goes hand in hand with ambivalence.[14]

The problem, difficult but fascinating when one confronts the original texts, becomes excruciating in translation. Many individual lexical items have no single equivalent in English: *galanterie,* used in the very first sentence of *The Princesse de Clèves,* may be taken in the general sense of 'courtly manners', but it also evokes the social codes of flirtation and seduction; *admiration* might easily, for a seventeenth-century reader, have a meaning closer to 'wonder(ment)' than to 'admiration'. Sometimes one can tell from the context; more often one can't be sure. And the problem is compounded by the frequent use of such words throughout the novel in senses which patently shift. When analysing the original text, one may well want to follow the itinerary of such key words as they mark out domains of meaning which are unfamiliar to us: these are the isobars of a seventeenth-century sensibility conditioned by beliefs and social institutions radically different from our own. In translation, however, and for that very reason, a given French word cannot always be rendered by the same English equivalent. *Repos* may sometimes be simply 'repose'; elsewhere 'tranquillity' or 'calm' may make a better fit with the context (and the rhythm of the sentence).

One may, I think, argue that things are made somewhat easier by the fact that these key words themselves tend to form lexical clusters: *admiration* belongs to a group where one also finds the near-synonyms *étonnement* and *surprise;*

[14] See the article by Peter Bayley referred to below, Select Bibliography; also the glossary in Peter Nurse's edition of *La Princesse de Clèves,* and the 'Introduction à l'étude du vocabulaire de la *Princesse de Clèves*' (together with the glossary) in Émile Magne's critical edition of the novel in the Textes littéraires français series.

repos alternates with *tranquillité*, forming a nucleus which is further defined by its antonyms *trouble, agitation, inquiétude, confusion, embarras; galanterie* belongs with *honnêteté*, but also with *liaison* (which doesn't quite mean 'liaison'), *inclination, attachement, engagement, passion*, and the like (seventeenth-century French has almost as many words for types of amorous attachment as Eskimos are reputed to have for snow); *mérite, vertu, honnête*, and *honnêteté* (again) are all terms which seem to imply intrinsic (moral) worth, but somehow turn out in the end to be inextricably linked with social criteria, with appearance. One way of translating these words without grossly betraying the original is to make use of equivalents in English which, while not wholly archaic, survive from a parallel cultural tradition familiar to literate readers through, say, eighteenth-century English texts or the novels of Jane Austen. I have thus used 'merit' and 'inclination' freely, together with 'wit' for *esprit*. Elsewhere, I have built up my own groups of synonyms, and sometimes used two words to bring out the nuances of a single French equivalent. And finally, I have provided explanatory notes in instances which seemed difficult and significant enough to require commentary.

The style of *The Princesse de Clèves* and its siblings also defies the neoclassical myth in that it is hardly a model of elegance, lucidity, and symmetry. It is true that, overall, the novel is more soberly organized than its romance predecessors: it is, for example, divided into four almost exactly equal parts, although the divisions do not always correspond with pauses in the narrative flow and may have more to do with marketing techniques than with neoclassical aesthetics. Despite the 'digressions', the narrative is also consistently functional; self-indulgence is not apparent even in the set-piece description of the tournament, which is in fact quite brief and brings to a climax the external history within which the private love-narrative is set. The aesthetic focus, in other words, is firmly controlled, and this is a major achievement.

At the level of the sentence, however, the style is often tortuous and repetitious. One can of course defend these features as part of the expressive means by which the reader is led through the psychological labyrinth; they connote confusion and uncertainty in the characters, and perhaps also obsession (the insistent, over-insistent, preoccupation with how things are *seen* is the most striking and famous instance). But the intricate and extended use of subordination can still seem awkward to the plain English ear, especially where it is combined, as it often is here, with a general tendency to hyperbole. One of the most common structures, sometimes repeated in successive sentences, is 'the princess was so beautiful/astonished/confused ... that she ...'; and such constructions are regularly combined with secondary subordination (inserted relative clauses and the like). Seventeenth-century critics noted how often the author uses the conjunction or relative pronoun *que*, and it is all too easy in translation to find oneself using 'that' four or five times in a sentence. I have avoided the extreme solution of systematically unpacking the subordinate clauses and punctuating more firmly. It seemed important to leave enough of the syntactic detours in place to preserve their expressive function. On the other hand, I have attenuated some of the more awkward instances, reordered certain sentences, and introduced shorter units occasionally in order to let in a little air and light where nothing crucial seemed to be lost thereby. For similar reasons, I have sometimes introduced paragraph divisions where there are none in the original.

As I have already indicated, one of the most insistent aspects of the novel's style is what one might call the rhetoric of appearances. The words *paraître*, *sembler*, *voir*, and their synonyms are used with a frequency that borders on the obsessive; the same is true of words denoting a character's mental processes ('elle trouva que', 'elle jugea que'). This feature is not too difficult to handle, since a way out—if one is really necessary—is provided by synonymy. More awkward is the use in French of indirect pronouns, which, according to the rules of French grammar, are usually tucked away neatly before verbs with no obtrusive prepositions: 'il *lui* parut que'. In innumerable instances these provide the precise angle of vision, the way in which an appearance or phenomenon or utterance is received, and are thus crucial to the effect. When they are unpacked, however, as they must be in English, the result is often heavy and repetitious. I have elided them only when they may be easily inferred; otherwise I have left them intact, sometimes adjusting the word order somewhat to make them less obtrusive.

Similar considerations guided the rendering of direct speech. No one doubts that the sensibility and manners represented in *The Princesse de Clèves* are those of the seventeenth rather than the sixteenth century, and the way the characters speak may be seen as a literary transposition of polite conversation at the court of Louis XIV. We can't be sure that people spoke like that, but the formality, the display of wit (in its various senses), the slightly mannered or rhetorical gesturing conform to a common ideal attested by other contemporary texts. Likewise, internal monologue, or the narrator's representation of violent emotional response, is often couched in an exclamatory rhetoric ('What reflections was she not obliged to make . . . !'). It seemed wrong to transpose these passages wholesale into a familiar twentieth-century idiom: the touches of *préciosité* are part of the aesthetic effect, as are more mundane things such as titles and forms of address, where the French form has normally been retained.

I have throughout attempted to achieve a balance between fluency and readability on the one hand and a degree of defamiliarization on the other, to remind the reader that these texts open a window on to a different culture, a different society, and a different taste. The best way of internalizing that alien sensibility is of course, in the end, to approach the French text direct. Ideally, one would have liked to produce a bilingual edition with the translation on a facing page; but those who have at least a basic knowledge of French should find, if they obtain a copy of the original text, that the translation is literal enough to serve as what used ignobly to be called a 'crib'. I would prefer it to be regarded as performing, in written form, the work of a discreet interpreter.

NOTE ON THE TEXT

As I have already indicated, an English translation of *The Princesse de Clèves* appeared as early as 1679 (London: Bentley and Magnes). Two further versions were published in the eighteenth century (1720 and 1777). The late nineteenth-century translation by Thomas Sergeant Perry in two volumes (London: Osgood, McIlvaine & Co., 1892) is based on an 1889 French edition and contains the same rather romantic illustrations and the same liminary material (including a preface by Anatole France).

Of modern versions, the soundest is no doubt H. Ashton's (London: Routledge & Sons; New York: E. P. Dutton, 1925; reissued in London by the Nonesuch Press, 1943): Ashton was a competent seventeenth-century scholar whose biography of the author, *Mme de La Fayette, sa vie et ses œuvres* (Cambridge: Cambridge University Press, 1922), has always been well regarded. Other versions include Walter J. Cobb's in the Signet Classics series (New York: New American Library of World Literature, 1961). Nancy Mitford's translation, first issued in 1950 (London: Euphorion Books), published in a revised edition by Penguin Books in 1962, and then reprinted in Penguin Classics from 1978 with further revisions by Leonard Tancock, is the only version still widely available. It is full of clever and idiomatic renderings: Nancy Mitford has all the skills of a professional writer. But it is also unreliable: many errors have survived the various revisions to which it has been subjected. Furthermore, in order to achieve fluency, the translator indulges in drastic reductions of Mme de Lafayette's intricate syntax—at times whole phrases and even sentences are swallowed up in something approaching paraphrase. In Mitford's translation, the novel seems lighter, less serious, more like the consumer historical novel. Some readers may prefer this, but it largely disqualifies the version as a means of approaching the original text.

The text of *The Princesse de Clèves* poses few editorial problems, in that there are no manuscripts and no significant variant versions. Modern editions are based on a copy of the first edition (Paris: Claude Barbin, 1678) preserved in the Bibliothèque Nationale in Paris, which contains a small number of contemporary manuscript corrections, usually attributed to the publisher Barbin. Manuscripts of *The Princesse de Montpensier*, on the other hand, offer a considerable number of variants, and there is at least one interesting variant reading at the end of *The Comtesse de Tende*. For all these works, I have used the text given by Émile Magne in the Classiques Garnier series (see the Select Bibliography), since this is the most convenient and accessible edition. However, I have indicated in the notes a few variants which seemed especially interesting, and commented in one or two instances on textual problems.

Acknowledgements

In preparing this translation and its Introduction, I have been greatly assisted by the wit—and the astringent judgement—of Gillian Jondorf, who suggested innumerable improvements; Angela Scholar, too, deftly touched up some renderings in *The Princesse de Montpensier*, and her comments on the Introduction included a sentence which I liked so much that I incorporated it word for word. I offer them my warmest thanks. The translation as a whole is dedicated, with great affection, to Caroline Friend.

SELECT BIBLIOGRAPHY

The Text

THE most convenient edition of the French text of all three stories, together with *Zaïde*, is to be found in Mme de Lafayette, *Romans et nouvelles*, ed. Émile Magne (Paris: Garnier Frères, 1961; reissued in 1970 with a new introduction and other material by Alain Niderst).[†] The standard critical edition of *La Princesse de Clèves* is still the one by Émile Magne in the Textes littéraires français series (Paris: Droz, 1946 and later printings). A scholarly edition of *La Princesse de Montpensier* and *La Comtesse de Tende*, taking account of manuscript and other variants, is available in *Histoire de la Princesse de Montpensier sous le règne de Charles IXème roi de France; Histoire de la Comtesse de Tende*, ed. Micheline Cuénin (Geneva: Droz, 1979).

Two editions of the French text of *La Princesse de Clèves* with introduction and notes in English may be recommended:

1. ed. K. B. Kettle (London: Macmillan, 1967).
2. ed. Peter H. Nurse (first published in London by Harrap, 1970; issued in Walton-on-Thames by Thomas Nelson and Sons from 1984).

Studies in English

The following general studies are useful introductions:

Raitt, Janet, *Madame de Lafayette and 'La Princesse de Clèves'* (London: Harrap, 1971).

Scott, J. W., *Madame de Lafayette: La Princesse de Clèves* (London: Grant & Cutler, 1983).

Articles worth consulting include the following:

Bayley, Peter, 'Fixed Form and Varied Function: Reflections on the Language of French Classicism', *Seventeenth-Century French Studies*, 6 (1984), 6–21.

Brody, Jules, '*La Princesse de Clèves* and the Myth of Courtly Love', *University of Toronto Quarterly*, 38 (1969), 105–35.

Levi, Anthony, '*La Princesse de Clèves* and the *Querelle des anciens et des modernes*', *Journal of European Studies*, 10 (1980), 62–70.

Scott, J. W., 'The "Digressions" of the *Princesse de Clèves*', *French Studies*, 11 (1957), 315–22.

There have been many recent studies (books and articles) drawing on modern—and especially feminist—critical approaches. Among these are the following:

Beasley, Faith E., *Revising Memory: Women's Fiction and Memoirs in Seventeenth-Century France* (New Brunswick and London: Rutgers University Press, 1990).

DeJean, Joan, 'Lafayette's Ellipses: The Privileges of Anonymity', *Publications of the Modern Language Association of America*, 99 (1984), 884–900.

Hirsch, Marianne, 'A Mother's Discourse: Incorporation and Repetition in *La Princesse de Clèves*', *Yale French Studies*, 62 (1981), 67–87.

Lyons, John D., *Exemplum: The Rhetoric of Example in Early Modern France and Italy* (Princeton, NJ: Princeton University Press, 1989).

Miller, Nancy K., *Subject to Change: Reading Feminist Writing* (New York: Columbia University Press, 1988), ch. 1: 'Emphasis Added: Plots and Plausibilities in Women's Fictions'.

Moriarty, Michael, 'Discourse and the Body in *La Princesse de Clèves*', *Paragraph*, 10 (1987), 65–86.

Studies in French

A helpful review of the history of the French novel in the seventeenth century is provided by Antoine Adam in his Introduction to *Romanciers du XVIIe siècle*, Bibliothèque de la Pléiade (Paris: Gallimard, 1958). On the *nouvelle* in the seventeenth century, see Frédéric Deloffre, *La Nouvelle en France à l'âge classique* (Paris: Didier, 1967). The following give sound—if now somewhat dated—introductions to the life and work of Mme de Lafayette:

Dédéyan, Charles, *Madame de Lafayette* (Paris: SEDES, 1956).

Pingaud, Bernard, *Mme de La Fayette par elle-même* (Paris: Éditions du Seuil, 1959; repr. as *Mme de La Fayette*, 1978).

Recent introductory studies on *The Princesse de Clèves* include:

Malandain, Pierre, *Madame de Lafayette: 'La Princesse de Clèves'* (Paris: Presses Universitaires de France, 1985).

Niderst, Alain, *'La Princesse de Clèves' de Madame de Lafayette* (Paris: Nizet, 1977).

For a substantial new biography of Mme de Lafayette, see Roger Duchêne, *Mme de La Fayette, la romancière aux cent bras* (Paris: Fayard, 1988).

The historical sources of *The Princesse de Clèves* and the way they are handled in the novel were determined in a series of articles by Henri Chamard and Gustave Rudler which appeared in *Revue du XVIe siècle*, 2 (1914), 92–131 and 289–321, and 5 (1917), 1–20, 231–43. These are still cited as definitive in recent studies.

For a recent article providing up-to-date perspectives on the question of authorship and the relationship between *The Princesse de Montpensier* and *The Princesse de Clèves*, see Roger Duchêne, 'Les Deux *Princesses* sont-elles d'un même auteur?', in Roger Duchêne and Pierre Ronzeaud (eds.), *Mme de La Fayette, 'La Princesse de Montpensier', 'La Princesse de Clèves'*, Supplément 1990 de Littératures Classiques (Paris: Aux Amateurs de Livres, 1990).

The following critical essays are outstanding:

Genette, Gérard, 'Vraisemblance et motivation', in *Figures II* (Paris: Éditions du Seuil, 1969), 71–99.

Rousset, Jean, *Forme et signification* (Paris: Corti, 1962), 17–44.

Additional Seventeenth-Century Texts

A facsimile of the *Lettres à Madame la Marquise *** sur le sujet de la Princesse de Clèves*, attributed to Jean-Baptiste-Henri Du Trousset de Valincour (usually known simply as 'Valincour'), is available (Tours: Université de Tours, 1972); this provides direct evidence of the critical reception of *The Princesse de Clèves* when the novel first appeared.

Mme de Lafayette's *Correspondance* has been edited in two volumes by André Beaunier (Paris: Gallimard, 1942). Mme de Lafayette is also said to be the author of a historical work often known as *Histoire de Madame Henriette d'Angleterre* and edited by Marie-Thérèse Hipp under the title *Vie de la Princesse d'Angleterre. 1720* (Geneva: Droz, 1967).

Finally, it is helpful to compare *The Princesse de Clèves* with Mme de Villedieu's *Les Désordres de l'amour* (1675), available in a modern edition by Micheline Cuénin (Geneva: Droz, 1970).

---

† The following edition, which appeared after the present translation was completed, contains a wider range of texts and up-to-date information on the question of authorship: Madame de La Fayette, *Œuvres complètes*, ed. Roger Duchêne (Paris: Editions François Bourin, 1990)

A CHRONOLOGY OF
MADAME DE LAFAYETTE

1634   Baptism, on 18 March, of Marie-Madeleine Pioche de La Vergne; her father was a member of the minor nobility.

1649   Death of Mlle de La Vergne's father.

1650   Her mother marries Renaud de Sévigné, uncle of Mme de Sévigné. Mlle de La Vergne becomes maid of honour to the Queen, Anne of Austria, and begins to take lessons in Italian and Latin from Gilles Ménage.

1652   Renaud de Sévigné is compromised in the Fronde and exiled in Anjou, together with his wife and step-daughter.

1654   Ménage sends Mlle de La Vergne the latest fashionable heroic romances by Madeleine de Scudéry.

1655   On 15 February, Mlle de La Vergne marries François, Comte de Lafayette, a widower some eighteen years older than herself. She accompanies him to his estates in Auvergne and Bourbonnais and assists him with his legal and financial problems.

1656   Death of her mother.

1657   Mme de Lafayette establishes a friendship with Mme de Sévigné.

1658   Birth of Mme de Lafayette's first son Louis.

1659   Birth of her second son René-Armand. She settles permanently in Paris, where her salon is a success, and begins to participate in court life. Close relations with Huet and Segrais, major figures in the contemporary development of narrative fiction.

1662   Anonymous publication of *La Princesse de Montpensier*; Molière's highly successful and controversial comedy *L'École des Femmes* first performed.

1664   First edition of La Rochefoucauld's *Maximes*.

1665   Close friendship established between Mme de Lafayette and La Rochefoucauld.

1666   Molière's *Le Misanthrope* first performed.

1667   Racine's *Andromaque* first performed.

1669–71   *Zaïde* published in two successive volumes under the name of Segrais.

1673   Death of Molière.

1674   Publication of Boileau's *L'Art poétique*.

1675   Mme de Villedieu's *Les Désordres de l'amour* published. It is likely that Mme de Lafayette, assisted by La Rochefoucauld and Segrais, was already working on *La Princesse de Clèves* by the mid-1670s.

1676   Segrais leaves Paris.

1677   Racine's *Phèdre* first performed.

1678   *La Princesse de Clèves* published anonymously (March). Publication of Valincour's *Lettres à la Marquise* (December).

1680   Death of La Rochefoucauld.

1683   Death of the Comte de Lafayette.

1684   Mme de Lafayette renews relations with Ménage, now an invalid.

1688–9   *Mémoires de la cour de France* for these years, possibly written by Mme de Lafayette, will be published posthumously.

1692   Death of Ménage.

1693   Death of Mme de Lafayette.

1718   Anonymous publication of *La Comtesse de Tende* in the *Nouveau Mercure*.

1720   Publication of the *Histoire de Madame Henriette d'Angleterre*.

1724   Publication of *La Comtesse de Tende*, attributed to Mme de Lafayette, in *Le Mercure de France*.

The Princesse de Clèves

Publisher's Note to the Reader

Much as this story has been applauded by those who have read it so far, the author has not felt able to declare his identity; he was afraid that his name might diminish the success of his book. He knows by experience that literary works are sometimes condemned because the author is held in low esteem; he also knows that the author's reputation often confers lustre on his writings. He has therefore decided to remain in his present state of obscurity so that the reader's judgement will be as free and equitable as possible; he will nevertheless declare himself* if the story is as pleasing to the public as I trust it will be.

PART I

NEVER has France seen* such a display of courtly magnificence and manners* as in the last years of the reign of Henri II. The King was chivalrous, nobly built, and amorously inclined; although his passion for Diane de Poitiers, the Duchesse de Valentinois, had begun more than twenty years earlier, it was none the less violent and he advertised it no less openly.

He devoted a great deal of his time to bodily recreations, in all of which he excelled. Not a day passed without hunting parties, tennis games, ballets, tilting at the ring, and other similar diversions; Mme de Valentinois's colours and monogram* were to be seen everywhere, and she took care to adorn herself no less brilliantly than Mlle de La Marck, her granddaughter, who was at that time of an age to be married.

Her appearance at court was sanctioned by the Queen's presence. The Queen* herself, though no longer in her first youth, was a beautiful woman; she loved grandeur, pomp, and pleasure. The King had married her while he was still the Duc d'Orléans, his elder brother being the Dauphin until he died at Tournon—a prince who had seemed destined by his birth and by his noble qualities to be a worthy successor to his father François I.

The Queen had an ambitious nature and delighted in her royal rank. She seemed to suffer the King's attachment to the Duchesse de Valentinois lightly, and she never showed any jealousy, but she had such a profound capacity for dissimulation that it was difficult to guess her true feelings; political self-interest obliged her to keep Mme de Valentinois close to her person in order to draw the King himself closer.

The King enjoyed the company of women, even of those he was not in love with. Every day, at the hour when the

Queen held her circle, he was to be found in her apartments,* where the flower of court society, both men and women, gathered without fail. No court has ever brought together so many beautiful women and wonderfully handsome men: it seemed as if nature had bestowed her finest gifts on fair princesses and noble princes alike. Mme Elisabeth de France, who later became Queen of Spain, was beginning to display an astonishing wit and the unparalleled beauty that was later to be fatal to her. Marie Stuart,* Queen of Scots, whom they called the Reine Dauphine because she had just married the Dauphin, was a paragon of wit and grace; having been brought up at the French court, she had acquired all its most exquisite manners, and she had been born with so much natural feeling for things of beauty that, despite her extreme youth, she loved and understood them better than anyone. The Queen, her mother-in-law, and Madame the King's sister, also loved poetry, music, and the theatre. François I's taste for literature, both verse and prose, lived on in France, and his son loved bodily recreations, so that every kind of pleasure was represented at court. Yet what gave the court its splendour and majesty was above all the infinite number of princes and great nobles whose qualities surpassed the common measure. Those I shall name here were, in their different ways, the ornament and wonder of their age.

The King of Navarre commanded universal respect, both for his high rank and for his noble bearing. He excelled at the arts of war; wishing to emulate the Duc de Guise, he had more than once renounced his position as general in order to fight beside him as a simple soldier in the most perilous engagements. The Duc de Guise had indeed displayed such remarkable valour and won so many victories that even the greatest captains among his peers looked on him with envy. His valour was sustained by every other noble quality: his mind ranged far and deep, he had a noble and lofty soul, he understood political affairs no less than he understood war. His brother the Cardinal de Lorraine* was endowed from birth with an overreaching ambition, a penetrating wit, and an extraordinary eloquence. He had also acquired a vast store of learning; this he used to enhance his reputation by defending the Catholic religion, which the reformers* were beginning to attack at that time. The Chevalier de Guise, who was later known as the Grand Prieur, was a prince loved by all: he was nobly built, sharp of mind, skilful at arms, and famous throughout Europe for his valour. The Prince de Condé had not been well endowed by nature, but in his stunted body was contained a proud and lofty soul and a wit that made him attractive even to the most beautiful women. The Duc de Nevers, who had covered his name in glory by his deeds in war and the high offices he had held, was no longer young, but he was none the less an ornament of the court. He had three sons, all of the most noble bearing: the second, who was known as the Prince de Clèves,* was a worthy successor to his father's renown; his courage and generosity were accompanied by a discretion one rarely finds in young men. The Vidame de Chartres,* a descendant of the ancient house of Vendôme whose name had been borne with pride by the princes of the blood, was equally distinguished in war and in courtly manners. He was handsome, charming, valiant, bold, open-handed; what is more, all these qualities shone out in him with a special lustre. He was the only man worthy of being compared to the Duc de Nemours,* if anyone could have been compared to him. But M. de Nemours was nature's masterpiece. He was the most handsome and the most nobly built man in the world; but those were the least remarkable of his qualities. What put him above all others was an unparalleled valour, together with something pleasing in his turn of mind, his expression, and his gestures, the like of which has never been seen. He had a light-hearted manner that was attractive to men and women alike, an extraordinary dexterity in all forms of exercise, and a way of dressing that always set the fashion yet could never be imitated; there was about his whole person a special air of distinction that made it impossible to look at anyone else when he was present. There was not a lady at court whose pride would not have been flattered to see him at her feet; few of those who had had that honour could boast of having resisted; there were

even several among those to whom he had given no sign of
passion whose passion for him was none the less ardent.
He was so kind-hearted and had such a natural inclination
for amorous affairs that he could not refuse to pay some
attentions to those who tried to please him; thus he had
several mistresses,* but it was difficult to guess which he
really loved. He often went to the Reine Dauphine's apartments; her beauty and kindness, her desire to please everyone, and the special esteem she accorded M. de Nemours
had often led people to believe that he had dared to cast his
eyes even in that direction. The Guise brothers, who were
her uncles, had greatly increased their credit and authority
by her marriage; they were ambitious enough to aspire to
be on equal terms with the princes of the blood and to
share the power of the Connétable de Montmorency. The
King relied on him for the conduct of the greater part of
the affairs of state and treated the Duc de Guise and the
Maréchal de Saint-André as his favourites; but those whom
favour or the affairs of state brought close to the King's
person could only retain their position by deferring to the
Duchesse de Valentinois; although she was now neither
young nor beautiful, she governed the King with a power so
absolute that one may say she was mistress both of his
person and of the State.

The King had always liked the Connétable; as soon as he
had succeeded to the throne, he had recalled him from the
exile* into which François I had sent him. The court was
divided between the Guise family and the Connétable, who
was supported by the princes of the blood. Each faction had
always sought to gain the protection of the Duchesse de
Valentinois. The Duc d'Aumale, a brother of the Duc de
Guise, had married one of her daughters. The Connétable
aspired to a similar alliance, not content with having married
his eldest son to Mme Diane, a daughter of King François
by a lady of Piedmont who took the veil as soon as she had
given birth. This marriage had encountered many obstacles
because of the promises M. de Montmorency had made to
Mlle de Piennes, one of the Queen's maids of honour;
although the King had overcome them with great magna-

nimity and patience, the Connétable still felt that he was insufficiently supported if he could not be sure of Mme de Valentinois and if he did not separate her from the Guise brothers, whose power was beginning to make her uneasy. She had delayed the marriage of the Dauphin with the Queen of Scots as long as was in her power: she could not tolerate the beauty and precocious intelligence of the young Queen, or the ascendancy that the marriage conferred on the Guise brothers. She particularly hated the Cardinal de Lorraine; he had spoken to her harshly, even contemptuously. She saw that he was in league with the Queen, and in consequence the Connétable found her disposed to join forces with him and cement the alliance by the marriage of her granddaughter Mlle de La Marck to M. d'Anville, his second son, who later succeeded to his father's office in the reign of Charles IX. The Connétable had no reason to believe that M. d'Anville might make any objection to such a marriage, as M. de Montmorency had done; yet, although the reasons were hidden from him, the difficulties were scarcely less great. M. d'Anville was desperately in love with the Reine Dauphine; however little hope he might have that his passion would be returned, he could not make up his mind to enter into a commitment that would divide his attentions. The Maréchal de Saint-André was the only man at court who had not taken sides. He was one of the King's favourites, and the favour he enjoyed depended only on his own personal qualities. The King had been fond of him while he was still the Dauphin; since then he had made him Marshal of France at an age when few have yet thought of aspiring to the lowliest offices. The King's favour bestowed on him a lustre which he sustained by his many good qualities and his pleasing personal appearance, as well as by the great refinement of his table, the taste with which he had furnished his apartments, and a display of wealth no other private individual had ever matched. The King's liberality provided for this expenditure: for those he loved, he would go to the point of extravagance. The King did not possess all the great qualities, but he had many; in particular, he loved war and understood it. Thus he had had some notable successes: except for the Battle of Saint-Quentin,* his reign had been nothing but a series of victories. He had won the Battle of Renty in person; Piedmont had been conquered; the English had been driven out of France,* and the Emperor Charles V had seen the end of his good fortune outside Metz, which he had besieged in vain with all the armies of the Empire and of Spain. None the less, as the misfortune of Saint-Quentin had reduced the prospect of conquest on our side, and as fortune had since then appeared to be evenly divided between the two monarchs, they found themselves almost without intending it in a position where it seemed desirable to make peace.

The dowager Duchesse de Lorraine had begun to propose such a peace at the time of the marriage of M. le Dauphin;* since then, some secret negotiation or other had always been going on. Finally Cercamp,* in the Artois region, was chosen as a meeting place. The Cardinal de Lorraine, the Connétable de Montmorency, and the Maréchal de Saint-André were the King's representatives, the Duc d'Albe and the Prince d'Orange spoke for Philip II, while the Duc and Duchesse de Lorraine acted as mediators. The principal clauses of the treaty were the marriage of Mme Elisabeth de France with Don Carlos, the Spanish Infante, and of Madame the King's sister with M. de Savoie.

Meanwhile, the King remained on the frontier, where news was brought to him that Queen Mary of England had died.* He sent the Comte de Randan to congratulate Elizabeth* on her accession, and she received him warmly: her rights to the crown were as yet by no means securely established, so that it was to her advantage to be recognized by the King of France. The Comte de Randan found she was well informed about the interests of the French court and the merits of those who belonged to it; in particular he found her absorbed with the reputation of the Duc de Nemours. She mentioned him so often and with such enthusiasm that, when M. de Randan returned and gave the King an account of his journey, he told him that there was nothing M. de Nemours might not hope for from the Queen, and that he was certain she was capable of marrying him. The King spoke to Nemours about it that very evening; he got M. de Randan to repeat all his conversations with Elizabeth and advised him to try his fortune in this great matter. M. de Nemours thought at first that the King was speaking in jest, but, seeing that he was quite serious, he said:

'At least, Sire, if I embark on such an extravagant adventure on your Majesty's advice and in your service, I beg you to keep it secret until success justifies my ambition in the public eye. I would not wish to seem vain enough to suppose that a queen who has never seen me should wish to marry me for love.'

The King promised to speak of the plan to no one but the Connétable; he even considered that secrecy was necessary if it was to succeed. M. de Randan's advice was that M. de Nemours should go to England on the pretext that he simply wished to travel, but Nemours could not make up his mind to this. He sent Lignerolles, a clever young man and a favourite of his, to discover what the Queen's feelings were and to attempt to establish some kind of relationship. While awaiting the outcome of Lignerolles's mission, he went to see the Duc de Savoie, who was just then in Brussels with the King of Spain. The death of Queen Mary had put serious obstacles in the way of peace; the conference broke up at the end of November and the King returned to Paris.

There appeared at court* in those days a young woman so beautiful that all eyes turned to gaze upon her. Peerless indeed her beauty must have been, since it aroused wonder and admiration* in a place where the sight of beautiful women was commonplace. She was of the same family as the Vidame de Chartres and one of the foremost heiresses in France. Her father had died young and left her in the safe keeping of his wife Mme de Chartres, a lady of extraordinary wealth,* virtue, and merit. After losing her husband, she had spent several years away from court; during this retirement, she had devoted herself to the education of her daughter. She sought not only to cultivate her wit and beauty* but also to make her love virtue and be virtuous. Most mothers imagine that one need only avoid speaking about amorous entanglements in front of young girls in order to preserve them from contamination. Mme de Chartres believed the opposite. She often gave her daughter descriptions of love; she impressed on her how attractive it can be in order to convince her more easily of what she said about its dangers; she spoke to her of men's insincerity, of their deceptions and infidelity, of the disastrous effect of love affairs on conjugal life; and she painted for her, on the other hand, the tranquillity that a woman of good reputation enjoys. She told her how much brilliance and distinction* virtue bestows on a woman who is beautiful and well-born; but she also taught her how difficult it is to preserve virtue except by an extreme mistrust of one's own powers and by holding fast to the only thing that can ensure a woman's happiness: to love one's husband and to be loved by him.

This heiress was one of the most eligible in France at that time; despite her extreme youth several proposals of marriage had already been made. Mme de Chartres, who was exceptionally proud and ambitious, considered almost nothing worthy of her daughter; so, when she was in her sixteenth year,* she decided to take her to court. As soon as they arrived, the Vidame came to see her. He was astonished at Mlle de Chartres's great beauty, and with good reason. Her white skin and fair hair gave her a lustre no other girl could equal; all her features were regular, and her face, her figure, were full of grace and charm.

The day after she arrived, she went to match some stones* at the house of an Italian who traded in jewels throughout the world. This man had come from Florence with the Queen and had become so rich through his trade that his house looked more like a lord's than a merchant's. While she was there, the Prince de Clèves came in. He was so taken aback by her beauty that he was unable to hide his astonishment, and Mlle de Chartres could not help blushing when she became aware of it. She none the less recovered her composure without betraying any other interest in the Prince's behaviour than was demanded by the rules of civility towards a man of his evident distinction. M. de Clèves gazed at her in amazement, wondering who this beautiful young girl could be whom he had never seen before. Her manner and the attendants who surrounded her told him clearly enough that she must be a person of the noblest rank. Her youthful appearance led him to believe that she was unmarried; yet her mother was not present, and the Italian, who was not acquainted with her, called her 'Madame', so that he did not know what to think and continued to regard her with amazement. He became aware that she was embarrassed by his stare, unlike most young girls, who are usually pleased to see the effect of their beauty on men. It even seemed to him that he was the cause of her impatience to leave, and in fact she went out quite soon after. M. de Clèves drew some consolation for her disappearance from the hope that he would now find out who she was, but he was surprised to learn that no one knew her. He remained deeply moved by her beauty and by her modest behaviour, and it is not too much to say that he conceived for her, from that very moment, a passion and esteem beyond the common measure.

That evening, he went to visit Madame the King's sister, who was highly considered because of the credit she had with her brother, a credit so great that the King, in concluding the peace, had consented to cede Piedmont so that she could marry the Duc de Savoie. Although she had always wanted to be married, she had never wanted to marry anyone but a sovereign; she had for this reason refused the King of Navarre when he had been the Duc de Vendôme. She had always desired a match with M. de Savoie, for whom she had felt an inclination ever since she had seen him at Nice at the interview* between King François I and Pope Paul III. As she was a woman of great wit and taste, she attracted everyone in good society, and there were times when the whole court was gathered in her apartments.

M. de Clèves went there as usual. He was so preoccupied with Mlle de Chartres's wit and beauty* that he could speak of nothing else. He openly recounted the story of his chance encounter and never tired of praising this woman whom he had seen but did not know. Madame told him there was no one like the person he was describing: if there had been, everyone would have known her. Mme de Dampierre, her lady-in-waiting and a friend of Mme de Chartres, over-heard this conversation. She approached the King's sister and whispered to her that it was doubtless Mlle de Chartres whom M. de Clèves had seen. Madame turned back to him and said that, if he would come and see her the next day, she would show him the beautiful woman who had made such an impression on him.

Mlle de Chartres did indeed make her appearance on the following day. She was received by the Queens with every imaginable courtesy and was greatly admired by everyone present: she heard nothing on all sides but praise. This she accepted with such noble modesty that she seemed hardly to hear it, or at least to be moved by it. She went next to see Madame the King's sister, who complimented her on her beauty and then told her how she had disconcerted M. de Clèves. A moment later, the Prince himself came in.

'Come and see', she said to him, 'whether or not I have kept my promise. Let me show you Mlle de Chartres: do you not see in her the beauty you have been looking for? You ought at the very least to thank me for having told her how much she has already aroused your admiration.'

M. de Clèves was delighted to see that the beauty of the woman to whom he had been so strongly attracted was matched by her position in society. He approached Mlle de Chartres and begged her to remember that he had been the first to admire her, and that, without knowing her, he had felt for her all the respect and esteem she deserved.

He left the company of Madame together with his friend the Chevalier de Guise. They were at first unstinting in their praise of Mlle de Chartres; but it eventually occurred to them that they were going too far, and neither said any more about what he thought of her. Yet, in the days that followed, they were obliged to speak of her again wherever they happened to meet. The newly arrived beauty long con-tinued to be the subject of every conversation. The Queen sang her praises and held her in exceptionally high regard. The Reine Dauphine made her one of her favourites and asked Mme de Chartres to bring her to see her as often as possible. The King's daughters sent for her to take part in all their amusements. In a word, she was liked and admired by the whole court, with the exception of Mme de Valentinois. This was not because she resented her beauty: she knew too well from long experience that she had nothing to fear as far as the King was concerned. Rather, she so hated the Vidame de Chartres, whom she had sought to draw into her circle through the marriage of one of her daughters* but who had instead joined the Queen's circle, that she could not look with favour upon anyone who bore his name and for whom he openly displayed his affection.

The Prince de Clèves fell passionately in love with Mlle de Chartres and ardently desired to marry her, but he feared that Mme de Chartres's pride might be wounded at the thought of giving her daughter to a man who was not the eldest son of his house. Yet it was a noble house, and the Comte d'Eu, who was the eldest son, had recently married a person close to the royal family; M. de Clèves thus had no real reason to be afraid: he was simply shy, as lovers usually are. He had many rivals: the Chevalier de Guise seemed to him the most formidable because of his high birth, his merit, and the brilliance that royal favour lent to his house. The Chevalier had fallen in love with Mlle de Chartres the first day he had seen her; he had noticed M. de Clèves's passion, as M. de Clèves had noticed his. Although they were friends, the estrangement that occurs when two men pursue the same object had prevented them from discussing the matter; their friendship had grown cold without their having the courage to enlighten one another. That he had by chance been the first to see Mlle de Chartres seemed to M. de Clèves to be a happy omen and to give him some advantage over his rivals; but he foresaw that his father the Duc de Nevers would put obstacles in his way. M. de Nevers was on very intimate terms with the Duchesse de Valentinois; she was an enemy of the Vidame, and this was sufficient reason to prevent the Duc de Nevers from allowing his son to have thoughts of marrying the Vidame's niece.*

Mme de Chartres, who had made such efforts to instil

virtue into her daughter, did not desist from taking the same precautions in a place where they were so necessary and where dangerous examples abounded. Ambition and love affairs were the life-blood of the court, absorbing the attention of men and women alike. There were countless interests at stake, countless different factions, and women played such a central part in them that love was always entangled with politics and politics with love. No one was tranquil or indifferent; all thoughts were on seeking advancement, gaining favour, helping, or harming; boredom and idleness were unknown, everyone was kept busy by pleasure or intrigue. The ladies had particular attachments to the Queen, to the Reine Dauphine, to the Queen of Navarre, to Madame the King's sister, or to the Duchesse de Valentinois, attachments which were created variously by inclination, by reasons of social decorum, or by sympathy of temperament. Those ladies who had left their first youth behind and who professed the most austere virtue belonged to the Queen's circle. Those who were younger and sought gaiety and the pleasures of love courted the Reine Dauphine. The Queen of Navarre had her own favourites; she was young and had power over her husband the King of Navarre: he was allied to the Connétable, and in consequence enjoyed great credit. Madame the King's sister still preserved some of her beauty and attracted many ladies to her circle. The Duchesse de Valentinois could draw any woman she deigned to look at, but few women were to her taste; other than a small number who were on terms of intimacy and trust with her and whose temperament bore some relation to her own, none were received except on days when it pleased her to have about her a court like the Queen's.

A state of rivalry and mutual envy existed between these different factions. The women of whom they were made up were also jealous of one another's social advantage or lovers; it often came about that the interests at stake in the form of ambition and advancement were connected with the other sort of interest, less important perhaps but no less strongly felt. In this way, there reigned at court a kind of orderly unrest which made life very enjoyable but also very dangerous for a young girl. Mme de Chartres was aware of the peril and was constantly wondering how to protect her daughter from it. She begged her, not as a mother but as a friend, to tell her if anyone ever talked to her of love, and she promised to guide her behaviour in the sort of situation where young people are often at a loss.

The Chevalier de Guise displayed his feelings and intentions towards Mlle de Chartres so openly that no one was ignorant of them. He saw none the less that what he desired was all but impossible. He was well aware that he could not be a suitable match for Mlle de Chartres because his wealth was insufficient to meet the demands of his social rank; and he was aware, too, that his brothers would not want him to marry for fear of the decline that the marriage of younger sons* ordinarily brings about in the fortunes of a noble house. The Cardinal de Lorraine soon showed him that he was right: he condemned the Chevalier's attachment for Mlle de Chartres with extraordinary vehemence; yet he did not give him the true reasons for his opposition. The Cardinal nourished a hatred for the Vidame* which was secret at that time, though it became known afterwards. He would rather have allowed his brother to enter into an alliance with anyone but the Vidame, and he declared so publicly how far removed he was from giving his consent that Mme de Chartres was deeply offended. She took the greatest care to make it apparent that the Cardinal de Lorraine had nothing to fear, and that she had no thought of any such marriage. The Vidame adopted the same policy; he resented the Cardinal's conduct even more than Mme de Chartres because he was better informed of its cause.

The Prince de Clèves had given no less public indications of his passion than the Chevalier de Guise. When the Duc de Nevers heard of it, he was not pleased. He believed none the less that he had only to speak to his son to make him change his mind, so that he was not a little surprised to find that he had the firm intention of marrying Mlle de Chartres. He expressed his disapproval, lost his temper, and was so unsuccessful in hiding his anger that the reason for it was soon common knowledge at court, eventually reaching the

ears of Mme de Chartres herself. She had never doubted
that M. de Nevers would think it to his son's advantage to
marry her daughter; she was astonished that the houses of
Clèves and Guise should fear an alliance with her own
rather than desiring it. Her resentment led her to think of
finding a match for her daughter which would put her above
those who believed themselves to be above her. Having
reviewed the field, she singled out the son of the Duc de
Montpensier,* who was known as the Prince Dauphin. He
was at that time eligible to be married and was the greatest
match to be found at court. Mme de Chartres was a clever
woman; she had the support of the Vidame, who was
extremely well regarded; furthermore, her daughter was in
fact an excellent match. She handled the affair so skilfully
and successfully that M. de Montpensier himself appeared
to desire the marriage, and it seemed as if no difficulty could
be placed in its way.

The Vidame, who knew of M. d'Anville's inclination for
the Reine Dauphine, nevertheless believed that he should
also make use of the power that the Reine Dauphine had
over this gentleman to persuade him to further the interests
of Mlle de Chartres with the King and the Prince de
Montpensier, who was a close friend of his. He spoke of the
matter to the Reine Dauphine, who entered into it the more
gladly because it concerned the advancement of someone for
whom she had great affection. She revealed her sentiments
to the Vidame, assuring him that, although she knew she
would displease her uncle the Cardinal de Lorraine, she
would gladly pass over that consideration because she had
reason to complain of his conduct and because he was
always espousing the interests of the Queen against her own.

Women who enjoy affairs of the heart are always pleased
to have a pretext for speaking to a man who is in love with
them. As soon as the Vidame had left Mme la Dauphine,
she commanded Chastelart, who was a favourite of M.
d'Anville's and knew of his passion for her, to go and
tell him on her behalf to call on the Queen that evening.
Chastelart accepted this commission gladly and respectfully.
He came from a good Dauphiné family, but his merit and

wit surpassed the advantages of his birth. He was received and well treated by all the greatest lords at court, and the favour shown him by the house of Montmorency had forged particularly close links between him and M. d'Anville. He had a handsome figure and was skilful in all kinds of exercise; he sang agreeably and composed poetry, and his amorous and passionate nature so pleased M. d'Anville that he confided to him the love he felt for the Reine Dauphine. This confidence brought Chastelart closer to the lady, and it was in seeing her frequently that he began to fall prey to the ill-fated passion* that deprived him of his reason and finally cost him his life.

M. d'Anville did not fail to call on the Queen that evening. He thought himself fortunate to have been chosen by Mme la Dauphine to give his aid in bringing about something she desired. He promised to obey her orders to the letter, but Mme de Valentinois, who had been informed of the intended marriage, had taken great care to place obstacles in its way and had influenced the King against it, so that, when M. d'Anville spoke to him about it, he made it clear that he did not approve of the plan and even commanded him to say so to the Prince de Montpensier. It is easy to judge what Mme de Chartres felt about the collapse of a plan that meant so much to her, especially as the disastrous outcome of the affair gave so great an advantage to her enemies and was so damaging to her daughter.

The Reine Dauphine intimated to Mlle de Chartres in the most friendly way the displeasure she felt at having been unable to help her:

'You can see', she said, 'that my power is modest indeed. The Queen and the Duchesse de Valentinois so hate me that they cannot but cross me, either themselves or through those who depend on their favour, in all the things I desire. And yet', she added, 'my only thought has always been to please them; they hate me solely because the Queen my mother* once caused them disquiet and jealousy. The King had been in love with her before he fell in love with Mme de Valentinois, and in the first years of his marriage, when he had no children as yet, although he loved the Duchesse de

Valentinois, he seemed almost ready to have his marriage dissolved so that he could marry the Queen my mother. Mme de Valentinois was afraid the beauty and wit of a woman he had been in love with before might diminish her own favour, and joined forces with the Connétable, who also did not wish the King to marry a sister of the Guise brothers. They won the late King over to their side; he thoroughly detested the Duchesse de Valentinois, but he was fond of the Queen, so he gave them his support in attempting to prevent the King from having his marriage dissolved. In order to put out of his mind any idea of marrying my mother, they arranged for her to marry the King of Scotland, who had recently lost his wife Mme Magdeleine, the King's sister. They did this because he was the party readiest to conclude the marriage, and thus failed to honour the commitment that had already been made to the King of England, who very much wanted to marry my mother. There was even a serious threat that the broken promise would cause a rupture between the two kings. Henry VIII could not be consoled for not marrying my mother; when other French princesses were proposed instead, he always said that they could never replace the one who had been taken from him. My mother was certainly a great beauty and it is remarkable that, although the widow of a mere Duc de Longueville, three kings* should have wanted to marry her. Unhappily for her, fate gave her to the least of the three and sent her to a kingdom where her life is full of sorrows. They say I look like her, and I fear I may resemble her too in her misfortunes. Although I appear destined for great happiness, I cannot believe that I shall live to enjoy it.'

Mlle de Chartres told the Reine Dauphine that these gloomy forebodings were quite unfounded and that she would soon be forced to abandon them; she must not doubt that her happy prospects would be fulfilled, as every appearance indicated.

No man now dared cast his thoughts in the direction of Mlle de Chartres, whether for fear of displeasing the King or of not succeeding with a woman who had hoped for a

prince of the blood royal. M. de Clèves was deterred by
neither consideration. The death of his father the Duc de
Nevers,* which came about at that time, left him entirely
free to follow his inclination and as soon as the proper
period of mourning was over all his thoughts turned to the
question of how to marry Mlle de Chartres. He considered
himself fortunate to be able to make the proposal at a time
when events had removed the other contenders and he could
be virtually sure that he would not be refused. The only
thing that marred his joy was the fear that she might not like
him enough. He would have preferred the happiness of
knowing she cared for him to the certainty of marrying her
without her love.

The Chevalier de Guise had to some extent provoked
his jealousy, but as this feeling was founded rather on the
Chevalier's merits than on anything Mlle de Chartres had
done, he devoted himself to attempting to discover whether
by good fortune she approved of his feelings for her. He
only saw her when the Queens received or in public
assemblies; it was difficult for him to have a private conversation with her. None the less, he succeeded in contriving
an occasion and spoke to her of his intentions and his
passion with all the respect imaginable. He begged her to
let him know what her feelings were for him and told her
that his own were of a kind that would make him eternally
unhappy if she obeyed her mother's wishes only out of duty.

As Mlle de Chartres had a noble and upright spirit, she
felt genuinely grateful to the Prince de Clèves for the way
he had approached her. Her gratitude lent her replies and
her words a certain gentleness which was sufficient to give
hope to a man as desperately in love as the Prince was. In
consequence, he flattered himself* that he had achieved at
least part of what he desired.

She reported the conversation to her mother, who told her
that M. de Clèves was so distinguished and so full of good
qualities, showing a wisdom beyond his years, that, if her
daughter felt an inclination to marry him, she would gladly
consent. Mlle de Chartres replied that she had perceived his
good qualities, that she would even marry him with less

reluctance than another man, but that she felt no particular attraction for his person.

The very next day, the Prince had the proposal delivered to Mme de Chartres. She accepted it, and was troubled by no fear* that she was giving her daughter, in the Prince de Clèves, a husband whom she could not love. The contract of marriage was concluded, the King was informed, and the engagement became generally known.

M. de Clèves found that he was happy without, however, being entirely contented. It greatly distressed him to perceive that Mlle de Chartres's sentiments did not go beyond esteem and gratitude; he could not flatter himself that she was concealing any that were more gratifying, since the terms they were now on allowed her to reveal her feelings without affront to her extreme modesty. Hardly a day passed on which he did not complain to her about it.

'Is it possible', he would say to her, 'that I should marry you and not be happy? Yet it is true that I am not. All you feel for me is a sort of kindness which cannot satisfy me. You are neither impatient, nor restless, nor troubled;* my passion affects you no more than would an attachment based only on the advantage of your rank and fortune rather than on the charms of your person.'

'You are unjust to complain,' she replied. 'I have no idea what you can expect beyond what I am doing, and it seems to me that decorum forbids me to do more.'

'It is true', he replied, 'that you give me some apparent favours with which I should be satisfied if there were something beyond. But, far from holding you back, it is decorum alone that makes you go as far as you do. I am unable to touch your affections or your heart, and my presence neither pleases nor disturbs you.'

'You cannot be in doubt', she returned, 'that I am glad to see you, and I blush so often in your company that you also cannot doubt that the sight of you disturbs me.'

'I am not taken in by your blushes,' he replied. 'They come from a sense of modesty, not from a movement of your heart, and I only take from them what little advantage I can.'

Mlle de Chartres did not know what to reply, these distinctions being beyond her comprehension. M. de Clèves saw all too well how far she was from having the kind of feelings that would satisfy him, since it seemed to him that she did not even understand what they were.

The Chevalier de Guise returned from a journey a few days before the wedding. He had been conscious of so many insurmountable obstacles in the way of his plan to marry Mlle de Chartres that he had been unable to flatter himself that he might succeed. The sight of her becoming the wife of another man was none the less a grievous blow to him. The pain failed to extinguish his passion and he remained as much in love as before. Mlle de Chartres had not been ignorant of the feelings that the Chevalier had had for her. He let her know on his return that she was the cause of the extreme sadness that was visible on his face, and his merit and charm were so great that it was difficult to make him unhappy without feeling some pity for him. Accordingly, she could not help pitying him, but this sentiment gave rise to no others. She told her mother how sorry she was that the Chevalier was so fond of her.

Mme de Chartres marvelled at her daughter's great frankness, and with good reason, for it was unmatched in its spontaneity. But she marvelled no less that her heart should remain untouched, especially as she saw clearly enough that the Prince de Clèves had touched it no more than her other suitors. In consequence, she took the greatest care to strengthen her attachment to her husband and to make her conscious of what she owed to the inclination he had had for her even before knowing her, as well as to the passion that he had demonstrated by preferring her to any other match at a time when no one dared think of her any longer.

The wedding took place. The ceremony was held at the Louvre, and in the evening the King and the Queens came to take supper with the whole court in Mme de Chartres's apartments, where they were received with extraordinary magnificence. The Chevalier de Guise dared not draw attention to himself by failing to attend the ceremony, but once there he was so incapable of mastering his sorrow that it was easily detected.

M. de Clèves did not find that Mlle de Chartres had changed her feelings when she changed her name. The status of husband gave him greater privileges, but the place he held in his wife's heart was no different. It also came about in this way that, although he was her husband, he did not cease to be her lover, since he always had something to desire beyond possession; although she accepted their life together perfectly well, he was not entirely happy. She continued to arouse in him a violent, restless passion that disturbed his delight. Jealousy had no part in this unease: no husband has ever been further from falling prey to it, no wife from giving rise to it. She was none the less in an exposed position in the midst of the court: she was present every day when the Queens and Madame received. All the handsome young men saw her in her own apartments and those of her brother-in-law the Duc de Nevers, whose house was open to the whole of society; but her manner inspired such respect and seemed so far removed from affairs of the heart that the Maréchal de Saint-André, though a man of great boldness who enjoyed the King's favour, was moved by her beauty without daring to make his feelings known to her except by his attentions and constant service. Several others were in the same case; and Mme de Chartres reinforced her daughter's own good behaviour with such an exact respect for all the proprieties that she finally succeeded in making her appear unassailable.

The Duchesse de Lorraine, while working to secure peace, had also been working for the marriage of her son the Duc de Lorraine, which had now been concluded with Mme Claude de France, the King's second daughter. The wedding had been fixed for February.*

Meanwhile, the Duc de Nemours had remained in Brussels. He was wholly preoccupied with his plans for England, continually receiving couriers from there and sending others back. His hopes grew stronger every day, and Lignerolles finally let him know that it was time to go in person and conclude an enterprise that had been so well begun. He received the news with all the delight that may be expected of an ambitious young man who finds himself raised up to a throne by his reputation alone. His mind had imperceptibly become accustomed to the idea of this great fortune; whereas he had at first rejected it as something unattainable, the difficulties had been erased from his imagination and he no longer saw any obstacles.

He sent post-haste to Paris to give all the necessary orders for a magnificent train so that he might appear in England with a brilliance proportionate to the design that drew him there, and he hastened to come back to court himself to attend the marriage of M. de Lorraine.

He arrived the day before the betrothal ceremony. The very same evening, he went to inform the King of the present state of his undertaking and to receive his orders and advice for what still remained to be done. He then went to call on the Queens. Mme de Clèves was not there, so that she did not see him and was unaware even that he had arrived. She had heard everyone speak of him as the most handsome and agreeable man at court; Mme la Dauphine above all had described him to her in such a way and had spoken of him so many times that she had made her curious and even impatient to see him.

She spent the whole of the day of the betrothal at home dressing for the ball and royal banquet that were to take place that evening at the Louvre. When she arrived, her beauty and the brilliance of her costume caused a great stir. The ball began* and, as she was dancing with M. de Guise, there was a loud noise over by the door of the ballroom as of people giving way to someone coming in. Mme de Clèves finished dancing, and while she was looking round to find someone she intended to take as a partner, the King called to her to take the person who had just arrived. She turned and saw a man who she felt at once could be no other than M. de Nemours stepping over a chair to make his way to where the dancing was. He had such presence that it was difficult not to be taken aback on seeing him when one had never seen him before, especially that evening, when the care he had taken to dress elegantly added still more lustre to his appearance; but it was also difficult to see Mme de Clèves for the first time without being amazed.

M. de Nemours was indeed so taken aback by her beauty that when he was close to her and she curtsied to him he could not help betraying his admiration. As they began to dance, there arose in the hall a murmur of approval. The King and the Queens recalled that the couple had never seen one another before and found it somewhat strange to see them dancing together without being acquainted. They called them as soon as they had finished dancing, without giving them time to talk to anyone else, and asked whether each was not eager to know who the other was and whether they had not already guessed.

'As for me, Madame,' said M. de Nemours, 'I am not in doubt. But, as Mme de Clèves lacks the reasons for guessing who I am that I have for recognizing her, I should be glad if Your Majesty would be so kind as to tell her my name.'

'I am sure', said Madame la Dauphine, 'that she knows it as well as you know hers.'

'I assure you, Madame,' rejoined Mme de Clèves, who appeared rather embarrassed, 'that I find it harder to guess than you think.'

'You are perfectly capable of guessing,' replied Mme la Dauphine; 'and it is even quite flattering* to M. de Nemours that you should not wish to confess that you recognize him without ever having seen him.'

The Queen interrupted them in order to allow the ball to continue; M. de Nemours took the Reine Dauphine as his partner. She was a woman of the most perfect beauty and M. de Nemours had seen her as such before his journey to Flanders; but this evening he had eyes for no one but Mme de Clèves.

The Chevalier de Guise, who still worshipped her, was at her feet, and what had just taken place caused him the sharpest pain. He took it as an omen that fate meant M. de Nemours to fall in love with Mme de Clèves. Whether her face had really betrayed some inner turmoil* or whether jealousy had caused the Chevalier de Guise to see more than was there, he believed that she had been affected by the sight of the prince and could not prevent himself from telling her that M. de Nemours was a lucky man to make her acquaintance by means of an incident that had something so romantic and remarkable about it.

Mme de Clèves returned from the ball with her mind so full of everything that had happened there that, although it was very late, she went to her mother's room to give her an account of it; she sang M. de Nemours's praises in such a way that Mme de Chartres entertained the same suspicion as the Chevalier de Guise.

The next day, the wedding ceremony was held. Mme de Clèves saw the Duc de Nemours there; his grace and charm were so extraordinary that her astonishment was still greater.

On the days that followed, she saw him in the company of the Reine Dauphine, she watched him playing tennis with the King, she saw him tilt at the ring, she heard him speak; but, whenever and wherever she saw him, he so surpassed all others and so dominated the conversation by his bearing and by his pleasing wit that he soon made a deep impression on her heart.

It is true, too, that the violent inclination M. de Nemours felt for her gave him the engaging, amusing manner that flows from the first impulse to please the beloved; he was thus even more charming than usual. In consequence, since they frequently met and recognized in each other a perfection unequalled at court, it was difficult for them not to be infinitely attracted to one another.

The Duchesse de Valentinois went to all the parties held at court, and the King behaved towards her with no less vivacity and attentiveness than when he had first fallen in love with her. Mme de Clèves, who was still young enough not to believe it possible to love a woman if she is over 25, was astonished by the King's attachment to Mme de Valentinois, who was a grandmother and who had just married off her granddaughter. She often spoke of it to Mme de Chartres.

'Can the King really have been in love with her for so long?' she would say. 'How can he have become attached to a woman much older than himself who was his father's mistress and who, they tell me, continues to be the mistress of many other men?'

'It is true', replied her mother, 'that it was neither Mme de Valentinois's merit nor her fidelity that gave rise to the King's passion and has maintained it ever since, which is also why he cannot be excused; for if she had been as young and beautiful as she was high-born, if she had had the merit of never having loved a man before, if she had loved the King with the most scrupulous fidelity, for his personal charms alone, with no self-interested regard for rank or wealth and without making use of her power for any but decent ends or for ones the King himself approved, it must be confessed that one could hardly help praising him for his great devotion to her. If I were not afraid', continued Mme de Chartres, 'that you might say of me what is said of all women of my age,* that they love telling stories of their own day, I should explain to you the beginnings* of the King's passion for the Duchess, together with some other matters concerning the late King's court which are in fact quite closely connected with things that are happening at present.'

'Far from accusing you', rejoined Mme de Clèves, 'of repeating stories of the past, I may justly complain that you have failed to instruct me in the affairs of the present and to explain the various interests and liaisons of the court. I am so ignorant of them that, only a few days ago, I believed M. le Connétable to be on intimate terms with the Queen.'

'Your opinion was quite the opposite of the truth,' replied Mme de Chartres. 'The Queen hates M. le Connétable, and if she ever has any power* he will be made all too aware of it. She knows he has told the King repeatedly that, of all his children, the only ones who resembled him were the illegitimate ones.'

'I should never have suspected her hatred', interjected Mme de Clèves, 'after seeing how scrupulously the Queen wrote to M. le Connétable while he was in prison,* how happy she appeared on his return, and how, no less than the King, she always calls him "my good friend".'

'If you judge by appearances in this place,' replied Mme de Chartres, 'you will frequently be deceived: what you see is almost never the truth.

'But to return to Mme de Valentinois: as you know, her

name is Diane de Poitiers; she comes from an illustrious house, being descended from the ancient lineage of the dukes of Aquitaine; her grandmother was a natural daughter of Louis XI; in short, every drop of her blood is of noble origin. Her father Saint-Vallier found himself compromised in the affair of the Connétable de Bourbon,* which you have no doubt heard of. He was condemned to be beheaded and was taken to the scaffold. His daughter, who was wonderfully beautiful and who had already attracted the attention of the late King, succeeded—who knows how—in obtaining her father's life. His pardon arrived just as the death-blow was about to fall; but he was so overcome by fear that he was no longer conscious, and he died a few days later. His daughter appeared at court as the King's mistress. The Italian expedition and the King's imprisonment* interrupted the course of their passion. When he returned from Spain and Mme la Régente went to meet him at Bayonne, she took with her all her maids of honour, among whom was Mlle de Pisseleu, who later became the Duchesse d'Étampes. The King fell in love with her. She was Mme de Valentinois's inferior in birth, wit, and beauty; her only advantage was extreme youth. I heard her say more than once that she was born the day Diane de Poitiers was married, but hatred rather than the truth made her say it: unless I am much mistaken, the Duchesse de Valentinois only married M. de Brézé, the Grand Sénéchal of Normandy, at about the time the King fell in love with Mme d'Étampes. Never was there such great hatred as there was between those two women. The Duchesse de Valentinois could not forgive Mme d'Étampes for stealing from her the honour of being the King's mistress. Mme d'Étampes was violently jealous of Mme de Valentinois because the King maintained his liaison with her. He was never absolutely faithful to his mistresses; there was always one who enjoyed that title and the honours that went with it, but the ladies known as the "little set" shared his favours, each taking her turn. When his son the Dauphin died at Tournon, some say of poison, he was deeply affected. For his second son, the present King, he felt less natural warmth: he found him neither bold nor vivacious enough for his taste. One day, he complained about him to Mme de Valentinois, and she replied that she wanted to make him fall in love with her: it would, she said, make him a livelier and more agreeable man. As you see, she succeeded. Their passion has lasted for twenty years; it has been diminished neither by time nor by any obstacle.

'The late King opposed her plan from the outset. He may still have been sufficiently in love with Mme de Valentinois to be jealous; or he may have been influenced by the Duchesse d'Étampes, who was in despair at the idea of M. le Dauphin being attached to her enemy. Whatever the truth of the matter, it is certain that the sight of their passion made the King bitterly angry: not a day passed without some sign of it. His son was not afraid of his anger or his hatred, and nothing could make him reduce or conceal the strength of his attachment: the King was obliged to endure it as best he could. The Dauphin's stubborn resistance to his will drove them farther apart and brought the King closer to his third son, the Duc d'Orléans. This son was handsome, nobly built, full of fire, ambition, and youthful ardour; he needed a restraining hand, but he would have become a prince of great stature had he lived to a more mature age.

'The Dauphin being the elder son and the Duc d'Orléans the King's favourite, there existed between them a kind of rivalry that came near to hatred; it had begun in their childhood and continued ever since. When the Emperor passed through France,* he gave his preference unreservedly to the Duc d'Orléans; M. le Dauphin was so offended that, when the Emperor was at Chantilly, he tried to make M. le Connétable arrest him without waiting for the King's command. M. le Connétable refused. The King subsequently blamed him for not following his son's advice, and the incident was one of the main reasons why he later exiled him from the court.

'The quarrel between the two brothers gave the Duchesse d'Étampes the idea of seeking the Duc d'Orléans's support to further her cause with the King against Mme de Valentinois. She succeeded: the prince, although not in love with her, espoused her interests hardly less than the

Dauphin had espoused Mme de Valentinois's. Two factions were thus formed at court, and you can no doubt imagine what they were like; but these intrigues were not limited to women's quarrels alone.

'The Emperor, who had remained well disposed towards the Duc d'Orléans, had on several occasions offered to make the Duchy of Milan over to him. In the peace proposals that were discussed later, he raised hopes that he would give him the seventeen provinces* and his daughter's hand in marriage. M. le Dauphin wanted neither peace nor the marriage. He made use of M. le Connétable, whom he had always regarded as his friend, to impress on the King how important it was not to give his successor a brother as powerful as a Duc d'Orléans in league with the Emperor and backed by the seventeen provinces. M. le Connétable entered into M. le Dauphin's plans the more willingly because in that way he could thwart those of Mme d'Étampes, who was his declared enemy and who very much wanted to see the Duc d'Orléans raised to a high position.

'M. le Dauphin was at that time in command of the King's army in Champagne and had brought the Emperor's forces to the brink of utter destruction; but the Duchesse d'Étampes, fearing that too great an advantage on our side would make us refuse peace and the Emperor's proposed alliance with the Duc d'Orléans, secretly sent a message to advise the enemy to surprise Épernay and Château Thierry, which were full of food supplies. They did so, and in this way saved their entire army.*

'She did not enjoy the fruits of her treachery for long. Shortly after, the Duc d'Orléans died at Farmoutier of some kind of contagious disease. He was in love with one of the most beautiful women at court, who also loved him. I shall not name her, for her life since then has been blameless and she has even taken care to conceal her passion for him: her reputation deserves to be protected. By chance,* she received the news of her husband's death the very day she heard of M. d'Orléans's; thus she had a pretext which allowed her to hide her real distress without being put to the trouble of suppressing her feelings.

'The King did not long survive his younger son: he died two years later. He recommended M. le Dauphin to use the services of the Cardinal de Tournon and of the Amiral d'Annebauld, saying nothing of M. le Connétable, who was for the time being in exile at Chantilly. None the less, the first thing his son did* when he became king was to place the reins of government in the hands of the Connétable.

'Mme d'Étampes was driven out and was as badly treated as she could expect to be by an all-powerful enemy; the Duchesse de Valentinois took her revenge in full, both on the Duchesse d'Étampes and on all those who had displeased her. Her power over the King's mind appeared more absolute than it had been while he was the Dauphin. The King has been on the throne for twelve years now, and she has throughout that time had sovereign authority in all matters: she bestows offices and manages affairs of state as she will; she has had the Cardinal de Tournon, the Chancelier Olivier, and Villeroy sent away from court. Those who have sought to open the King's eyes to her conduct have been ruined in the attempt. The commander of the artillery, the Comte de Taix, who disliked her, could not refrain from commenting on her amorous intrigues, and especially her affair with the Comte de Brissac. The King had already become extremely jealous of M. de Brissac; none the less, she succeeded in having the Comte de Taix disgraced. He was relieved of his office, and—one can hardly believe it—she contrived to have that same office given to Brissac, after which she made him Maréchal de France. The King's jealousy became so intense, however, that he could not bear the Maréchal to remain at court. Jealousy is usually bitter and violent, but in the King it is gentle and moderate because he respects his mistress so much; in consequence, not daring to send his rival away without a plausible reason, he made him governor of Piedmont. Brissac spent several years there; last winter, he returned on the pretext of asking for troops and other necessities for the army he commands. The desire to see Mme de Valentinois again and the fear that she might forget him were probably the real motives for this journey. The

King received him with the utmost coldness. The Guise brothers, who dislike him but who dare not show it because of Mme de Valentinois, used M. le Vidame, who is his declared enemy, to prevent him obtaining any of the things he had come to ask for. It was not difficult to do him harm: the King hated him, and was made uneasy by his presence at court. The result was that he was obliged to return empty-handed to Piedmont; his only meagre consolation was that he had perhaps reawakened in Mme de Valentinois's heart feelings which absence had begun to extinguish. The King has certainly had other grounds for jealousy, but either he has been unaware of them or he has not dared to complain.

'I do not know', added Mme de Chartres, 'whether you will not think I have told you more than you wished to know.'

'Any such complaint, Madame, is far from my thoughts,' replied Mme de Clèves. 'If I were not afraid that you would find it tiresome, I should ask you to acquaint me with many other details I am ignorant of.'

M. de Nemours's passion for Mme de Clèves was from the very beginning so violent that it spoilt his taste for all the women he had loved and with whom he had maintained relations during his absence; it even erased them from his memory. He did not so much as take the trouble to seek excuses for breaking with them; nor could he find the patience to listen to their complaints or reply to their reproaches. Mme la Dauphine, for whom his feelings had been quite passionate, could not hold her place in his heart against Mme de Clèves. Even his impatience for the English expedition began to diminish and he was no longer so eager to hasten the arrangements which were necessary to his departure. He often went to see the Reine Dauphine because Mme de Clèves was often there, and he was not sorry to let people continue to believe what they had previously thought about his feelings for the young queen. Mme de Clèves seemed to him to be so rare a prize that he resolved rather to fail to give her any signs of his passion than to risk making it known in public. He refrained from speaking of it even to the Vidame de Chartres, who was his close friend and from whom he hid nothing. He behaved so cautiously and kept himself under such close observation that no one suspected him of being in love with Mme de Clèves, except the Chevalier de Guise. It would have been difficult for her to detect it herself had not the inclination she felt for him made her particularly attentive to his behaviour: she was in fact unable to doubt it.

She found herself to be less disposed* to tell her mother what she thought about the Duc de Nemours's feelings than to speak to her of the other men who were in love with her; without deliberately intending to hide anything, she said nothing about it. But it was all too evident to Mme de Chartres, as was her daughter's liking for him. The knowledge was acutely painful to her. She well understood how dangerous it was for her daughter to be loved by a man as handsome as M. de Nemours to whom she was also attracted. Her suspicions concerning her daughter's inclination were fully confirmed by an incident that occurred only a few days later.

The Maréchal de Saint-André always sought every opportunity to display his magnificence. On the pretext of showing him his house, which had only just been completed, he invited the King to do him the honour of taking supper there with the Queens. The Maréchal was also gratified* to be able to parade before the eyes of Mme de Clèves an expenditure so lavish that it bordered on extravagance.

A few days before the date chosen for the supper, the Dauphin, whose health was not good, had been unwell and had received no one. His wife, the Reine Dauphine, had spent the whole day at his side. Towards evening he felt better, and summoned into his chamber all the persons of quality who were in the antechamber. The Reine Dauphine retired to her own apartments and found there Mme de Clèves and certain other ladies who were on particularly familiar terms with her.

As it was already quite late and she was not dressed, she did not call on the Queen. She let it be known that she was seeing no one and had her jewels brought to her so that she could choose some for the Maréchal de Saint-André's ball and some she had promised to give to Mme de Clèves. As the ladies were thus occupied, the Prince de Condé arrived. His rank was such that every door was open to him. The Reine Dauphine asked him what was happening in the Dauphin's chamber, since he had doubtless just come from there.

'They are arguing* with M. de Nemours, Madame,' he replied, 'and he is defending his cause so vigorously that it must be his own. I believe he has a mistress who makes him uneasy when she goes to a ball, for he insists that it is disagreeable for a lover to see the woman he loves at a ball.'

'What!' rejoined Mme la Dauphine, 'M. de Nemours doesn't want his mistress to go to a ball? I certainly thought husbands might prefer their wives not to go, but it never occurred to me that lovers might be of that opinion.'

'M. de Nemours takes the view', replied the Prince de Condé, 'that there is nothing lovers find harder to bear than a ball, whether or not they are loved in return. He claims that, if they are, they endure the mortification of having less of their lady's love for several days, because there is no woman whose concern for her appearance does not prevent her from thinking about her lover and at such times all women devote themselves entirely to their appearance. He maintains that they want to look their best for everyone's sake and not merely for their lover's; that, when they are at the ball, they seek to please every man who looks at them; and that, when they are satisfied with their beauty, they experience a pleasure to which their lover's contribution is small. He also says that when a man's love is unrequited it is still more painful to see his mistress at a party; that the more she is publicly admired, the unhappier he is to be excluded from her love; that he is constantly afraid her beauty may kindle some other love better rewarded than his own. And finally, M. de Nemours maintains that there is no suffering equal to that of seeing one's mistress at a ball except that of knowing she is there when one is not there oneself.'

Mme de Clèves pretended not to hear what the Prince de Condé was saying; but she listened to him attentively. She had no difficulty in guessing her own contribution to the opinion put forward by M. de Nemours, and above all to his remark about the mortification of not being present at a ball attended by one's mistress, because he was not to be at the Maréchal de Saint-André's ball, the King having given him orders to go to meet the Duc de Ferrare.

The Reine Dauphine joined in the Prince de Condé's laughter and refused to endorse M. de Nemours's opinion.

'There is only one occasion, Madame,' said the prince, 'on which M. de Nemours would consent to his mistress's going to a ball, and that is when he himself is giving it. He says that, last year when he gave one for Your Majesty, he believed his mistress was doing him a favour by her presence, although she appeared to be there only as your companion. According to him, it is always a compliment to a lover if his mistress participates in an entertainment he is giving, and it is agreeable to him if she sees him playing the leading role at an occasion where the whole court is present and acquitting himself successfully as host.'

'M. de Nemours was right', said the Reine Dauphine with a smile, 'to approve of his mistress going to the ball. At that time, there were so many women to whom he gave that distinction that, if they had not been present, there would have been hardly anyone there.'

As soon as the Prince de Condé had begun to relate what M. de Nemours thought about balls, Mme de Clèves had felt a strong inclination not to go to the Maréchal de Saint-André's. She had no difficulty in sharing the view that a woman should not be the guest of a man who was in love with her, and she was gratified* to have a stern moral reason for doing something which was a favour to M. de Nemours. She none the less took away the jewels the Reine Dauphine had given her; but that evening, when she showed them to her mother, she told her that she had no intention of using them. The Maréchal de Saint-André, she said, took so much trouble to advertise his attachment to her that he doubtless also wanted to make everyone believe that the entertainment he was to provide for the King was also meant for her, and on the pretext of doing the honours as master of the house he would pay her attentions by which she might perhaps be embarrassed.

Mme de Chartres opposed her daughter's opinion for a while, as though finding it capricious; but, seeing that she clung to it stubbornly, she gave in. She told her that she would have to feign illness as a pretext for not going: the real reasons would not meet with approval, indeed it was essential not to let them even be suspected. Mme de Clèves willingly consented to spend a few days at home to avoid going to a place where M. de Nemours would not be present, and he left without having the pleasure of knowing that she was not to go.

He returned the day after the ball and heard that she had not been there; but, as he was unaware that the conversation in the Dauphin's chamber had been repeated in her presence, it never occurred to him that he might have been happy enough to have prevented her from going.

The following day, while he was in the Queen's apartment talking to the Reine Dauphine, Mme de Chartres and Mme de Clèves arrived and approached the young queen. Mme de Clèves was dressed rather carelessly, like someone who had been ill, but her face gave a different impression.

'You look so beautiful', the Reine Dauphine said to her, 'that I cannot believe you have been ill. I think that what the Prince de Condé told you about M. de Nemours's opinion concerning the ball persuaded you that you would be doing the Maréchal de Saint-André a favour in going to his house; that, I believe, is what prevented you from coming to the ball.'

Mme de Clèves blushed because the Reine Dauphine's guess had hit the mark and because she had said this in front of M. de Nemours.

Mme de Chartres saw immediately why her daughter had not wanted to go to the ball; to prevent M. de Nemours seeing it as easily as she had, she broke into the conversation, adopting a manner* that lent her words an air of truthfulness.

'I assure you, Madame,' she said to the Reine Dauphine,

'that your Majesty does my daughter more honour than she deserves. She really was ill; but I am sure that if I had not prevented her she would none the less have gone with you and appeared in public, indisposed as she was, in order to have the pleasure of seeing everything that was exceptional about yesterday evening's entertainment.'

The Reine Dauphine believed what Mme de Chartres told her, while M. de Nemours was most put out to find it plausible; none the less, Mme de Clèves's blushes* made him suspect that what the Reine Dauphine had said was not so far removed from the truth. Mme de Clèves had at first been distressed that M. de Nemours had had reason to believe it was he who had prevented her from going to the Maréchal de Saint-André's ball; but this feeling was followed by a certain regret that her mother had banished the idea from his mind.*

Although the peace talks at Cercamp had been broken off, negotiations had continued uninterrupted, with the result that, towards the end of February,* new talks were held at Cateau-Cambrésis. The same delegates were present. The absence of the Maréchal de Saint-André rid M. de Nemours of his most formidable rival, the one who kept the closest watch on other men who approached Mme de Clèves, and who was most capable of making progress with her on his own account.

Mme de Chartres had not wished to let her daughter see that she was aware of her feelings for the Duc de Nemours, for there were certain things that she wanted to say to her and she feared that her motives might be suspected. One day, she began to talk about him; she spoke in his favour and mingled with her remarks a number of poisoned compliments on his wisdom in not allowing himself to fall in love and on his policy of treating his relations with women as a pleasure rather than as a serious attachment.

'It's not', she added, 'that he hasn't been suspected of having a great passion for the Reine Dauphine. I have even observed that he often visits her, and I advise you as far as possible to avoid speaking to him, especially in private: as the Reine Dauphine treats you so familiarly, it would soon be said that you are their confidante, and you know how disagreeable it is to have that reputation. It is my view that, if these rumours continue, you should visit the Reine Dauphine rather less so that you do not find yourself embroiled in romantic intrigues.'

Mme de Clèves had never heard anyone gossip about M. de Nemours and the Reine Dauphine. She was greatly surprised by what her mother had told her; she thought she now perceived clearly how she had been mistaken in everything she had believed about his feelings, and her face fell. Mme de Chartres saw this. At that moment, some people came in and Mme de Clèves went to her apartments and shut herself in her private room.*

It is impossible to express the pain she felt on discovering,* through what her mother had just told her, her own interest in M. de Nemours; she had not yet dared to confess it to herself. She saw then that the feelings she had for him were those that M. de Clèves had so often asked of her; she realized how shameful it was to have such feelings for a man other than a husband who deserved them. She felt wounded and embarrassed by the fear that M. de Nemours might want to use her as a decoy in his pursuit of the Reine Dauphine, and this thought persuaded her to tell Mme de Chartres what she had so far hidden from her.

The next day she went to her mother's chamber to carry out what she had resolved, but found that she was suffering from a slight fever and thought it better not to speak to her. The illness seemed so trivial, however, that Mme de Clèves made her customary visit to the Reine Dauphine after dinner; she was in her private room with two or three ladies who were on the most familiar terms with her.

'We were talking about M. de Nemours,' she said when she saw Mme de Clèves, 'and we were remarking with astonishment how changed he is since he came back from Brussels. Before he went, he had countless mistresses; it was even a defect in him, because he showed the same consideration to those who had merit and those who had none. Since his return, he no longer recognizes any of them; there has never been such a change. It even seems to me that his humour has altered: he is less spirited than usual.'

Mme de Clèves did not reply. She was thinking with shame that, if she had not already been disabused, she would have taken everything that was being said about the change in M. de Nemours's humour as marks of his passion. She felt a certain bitterness against the Reine Dauphine when she saw her casting about for reasons and feigning astonishment when apparently she knew the truth better than anyone. She could not help giving her some indication of her feeling, and when the other ladies withdrew she came and said to her quietly:

'Was it for me as well as for the others that you said that just now, Madame, and would you wish to hide from me that it was you who brought about this change of behaviour in M. de Nemours?'

'You are not being fair,' said the Reine Dauphine; 'you know that I never hide anything from you. It is true that, before going to Brussels, M. de Nemours wanted, I believe, to give me to understand that he did not hate me;* but since his return it appears to me that he cannot even remember the things he did then, and I confess that I am curious to know what has made him change. I shall have very little difficulty in finding out,' she added; 'the Vidame de Chartres, who is an intimate friend of his, is in love with a woman over whom I have some degree of power and that will enable me to discover what has caused this change.'

The Reine Dauphine spoke in a tone that convinced Mme de Clèves, and she found that, despite herself, her state of mind was calmer and more comfortable than it had been before.

When she went back to see her mother, she found that she was much more unwell than when she had left her. Her fever had increased and continued to do so in the days that followed, to such an extent that it seemed certain that the illness would be a serious one. Mme de Clèves was deeply distressed and remained constantly in her mother's room. M. de Clèves, too, visited her almost every day, both because of his consideration for Mme de Chartres and to prevent his wife from giving herself over entirely to her sorrow, but also to have the pleasure of seeing her: his passion had not diminished.

M. de Nemours, who had always had a friendly regard for him, had not ceased to make this apparent since his return from Brussels. During Mme de Chartres's illness, he contrived to see Mme de Clèves on several occasions by pretending to look for her husband or to come and take him out riding. He would even call on him at times when he well knew that he was not there; on the pretext of waiting for him, he would remain in Mme de Chartres's antechamber, where there were always several persons of quality. Mme de Clèves often appeared there; though sorely afflicted, she seemed none the less beautiful to M. de Nemours. He made sure that she noticed how much concern he felt for her distress, and spoke of it so gently and humbly that he had no difficulty in persuading her that it was not with the Reine Dauphine that he was in love.

She could not help being disturbed at the sight of him, and yet taking pleasure in seeing him; but when he was no longer before her eyes and she reflected that the enchantment she experienced when she saw him was the sign of a new-born passion, she came near to believing she hated him, so sharp was the pain this thought gave her.

Mme de Chartres's condition became so much worse that they began to despair of her life. She accepted what the doctors told her about the danger she was in with a courage worthy of her virtue and piety. After they had gone out, she made everyone else withdraw and had Mme de Clèves called to her side.

'My dear daughter, we must part,' she said, holding out her hand. 'The danger in which I am leaving you and your need of my support increase the regret I feel in abandoning you. You have an inclination for M. de Nemours; I do not ask you to confess it to me: I am no longer in a state to make use of your sincerity in order to guide you. It is already a long time since I noticed your inclination; but I did not wish to speak to you of it at first for fear of making you notice it yourself. You are only too aware of it now; you are on the

edge of a precipice. You will have to make great efforts and
do yourself great violence to hold yourself back. Remember
what you owe to your husband; remember what you owe to
yourself, and reflect that you are on the point of losing the
reputation you have earned for yourself and I so much
desired for you. Have strength and courage, my child, withdraw from the court, persuade your husband to take you
away; have no fear of making the harshest and most difficult
decisions, however dreadful they may appear at first sight:
they will be more benign in their consequences than the
miseries of a love affair. If other reasons than those of your
virtue and your duty could persuade you to do what I desire,
I would say that, were anything capable of troubling the
happiness I hope for in leaving this world, it would be to see
you fall like other women; but, if this misfortune must come
upon you, I embrace death joyfully in order not to witness
it.'

Mme de Clèves burst into tears over her mother's hand,
which she held tightly clasped between her own hands, and
Mme de Chartres, feeling touched herself at the sight, said:

'Farewell, my child; let us put an end to a conversation
that is too distressing for us both, and remember, if you are
able, everything I have just told you.'

She turned away when she had said these words and
ordered her daughter to call her women, refusing to listen to
her or to say anything more. Mme de Clèves left her room
in a state one can easily imagine, and Mme de Chartres now
thought only of preparing herself for death. She lived for two
days longer; during this time she would not see her daughter
again, who was the only thing on earth to which she felt
herself to be attached.

Mme de Clèves's affliction was extreme. Her husband
never left her side and, as soon as Mme de Chartres had
expired, he took her away to the country to remove her from
a place which could only make her grief the more bitter. It
was already beyond all bounds; although love and gratitude
were uppermost in it, her feeling that she needed her mother
to protect her from M. de Nemours also contributed a great
deal. She found herself unfortunate in being left to her own

devices at a time when she was so little in control of her feelings and when she would so much have wished to have someone to pity her and give her strength. The manner in which M. de Clèves behaved to her made her desire yet more strongly than ever to fail in no part of her duty to him. She thus showed him more friendship and affection than hitherto. She would not let him leave her: it seemed to her that if she strengthened her attachment to him he would defend her against M. de Nemours.

This gentleman came to see M. de Clèves in the country. He did his best to pay a visit on Mme de Clèves also, but she refused to receive him and, feeling certain that she could not help being drawn to him, she had made a firm resolution to avoid all the opportunities for seeing him that depended on her.

M. de Clèves went to Paris to make an appearance at court and promised his wife to return the following day. He only came back, however, the day after.

'I waited for you all day yesterday,' Mme de Clèves said to him when he arrived, 'and I must reproach you for not coming back as you promised. I need not tell you that, if a further affliction were capable of touching me in my present state, it would be the death of Mme de Tournon, which I heard about this morning. I should have been moved by it even if I had not been acquainted with her: it is always a cause for pity that a woman as young and beautiful as she should die in two days; but what is more, she was one of the women I liked most of all, and she seemed to combine modesty with merit.'

'I was very sorry not to return yesterday,' replied M. de Clèves, 'but an unhappy man needed the comfort I could bring him and it was impossible for me to leave him. As for Mme de Tournon, I advise you not to be afflicted on her account if you mourn her as a woman of great modesty and worthy of your respect.'

'You astonish me,' returned Mme de Clèves; 'I have heard you say many times that there was no woman at court whom you respected more.'

'That is true,' he replied, 'but women are incomprehensible and, when I look at them all, I consider myself so fortunate to have you as my wife that I cannot but be amazed at my good luck.'

'Your regard for me is higher than I deserve,' responded Mme de Clèves with a sigh, 'and it is too soon to claim that I am worthy of you. Tell me, I beg you, what has disabused you in the case of Mme de Tournon.'

'It is a long time since I was first disabused,' he replied, 'that is to say, since I learnt that she was in love with the Comte de Sancerre, whom she allowed to hope that he might marry her.'

'I can hardly believe', interrupted Mme de Clèves, 'that Mme de Tournon, after showing such an extraordinary aversion to marriage since she became a widow, and after repeatedly declaring in public that she would never remarry, can have raised the hopes of Sancerre.'

'If she had raised only his', replied M. de Clèves, 'there would be no cause for astonishment. What is really surprising is that she was also encouraging Estouteville at the same time. Let me tell you the whole story.'*

PART II

'As you know, Sancerre and I are close friends; yet, when he fell in love with Mme de Tournon about two years ago, he carefully concealed it from me as well as from everyone else. I had not the least suspicion of it. It still seemed that nothing could console Mme de Tournon for the loss of her husband and she lived in austere seclusion from the world. Sancerre's sister was virtually the only person she ever went to see, and it was at his sister's house that he had fallen in love with her.

'One evening, when a play was to be performed at the Louvre and they were only waiting for the King and Mme de Valentinois to arrive in order to begin, news was brought that she was indisposed and that the King would not be coming. It was easy to guess that Mme de Valentinois's indisposition was some kind of disagreement with the King. We knew he had had fits of jealousy over the Maréchal de Brissac while the Maréchal had been at court; but he had returned to Piedmont some days before, and we could not imagine the reason for this particular quarrel.

'Just as I was discussing the question with Sancerre, M. d'Anville appeared in the room and whispered to me that the King was in a pitiable state of anger and distress. In the course of a reconciliation which had taken place a few days earlier between the King and Mme de Valentinois after their disagreements over the Maréchal de Brissac, the King had, it seems, given her a ring and begged her to wear it. While she was getting dressed for the play, he had noticed that the ring was missing and asked her where it was. She appeared to be astonished not to have it and asked her women for it; they replied, whether by mischance or because they had not been told what to say, that they had not seen it for four or five days now.

'"That is exactly how long it is since the departure of the Maréchal de Brissac," continued M. d'Anville; "the King had no doubt that she had given him the ring when they parted. This thought revived so painfully all that jealousy of his, which was not yet fully extinguished, that he lost his temper, contrary to his usual habit, and reproached her bitterly. He has just returned in great distress to his own apartments; but I cannot tell whether he is more upset by the belief that Mme de Valentinois has given his ring away or by the fear that his anger may have displeased her."

'As soon as M. d'Anville had finished telling me this news, I went over to Sancerre to inform him of it; I presented it to him as a secret that had just been entrusted to me and that he should on no account divulge.

'Quite early the next morning, I visited my sister-in-law; I found Mme de Tournon at her bedside. She disliked Mme de Valentinois and was well aware that my sister-in-law had no reason to like her either.* Sancerre had called on Mme de Tournon after the play was over. He had informed her of the King's quarrel with Mme de Valentinois, and Mme de Tournon had come to tell the story to my sister-in-law, without knowing—or without reflecting—that it was I who had communicated it to her lover.

'As soon as she saw me, my sister-in-law said to Mme de Tournon that I could safely be entrusted with what she had just told her and, without waiting for Mme de Tournon's permission, repeated to me word for word everything I had said to Sancerre the previous evening. You may imagine how astonished I was. I looked at Mme de Tournon; I thought she seemed embarrassed. Her embarrassment aroused my suspicions: Sancerre was the only person I had told, and he had left me after the performance without saying why; I remembered having heard him speak of Mme de Tournon in extremely flattering terms. All these circumstances opened my eyes, and I had no difficulty in perceiving that he was having a love affair with her and that he had seen her after leaving me.

'I was so annoyed when I saw that he was hiding his romance from me that I said several things that made Mme de Tournon aware of her indiscretion. I showed her to her carriage and assured her as I took my leave that I envied the happiness of the man who had informed her of the quarrel between the King and Mme de Valentinois.

'I went off at once to find Sancerre. I reproached him and told him that I knew about his passion for Mme de Tournon, without telling him how I had found out. He was obliged to confess. I then let him know what had given him away, and he for his part acquainted me with the details of their romance. He told me that, as the youngest son of his house, he was in no position to aspire to such a good match; yet she was determined to marry him. No one could have been more surprised than I was on hearing this. I told Sancerre to get the marriage concluded as swiftly as possible, saying that he had everything to fear from a woman who had the cunning publicly to sustain a role so far removed from the truth. He replied that her grief had been genuine, but the inclination she felt for him had overcome it, and she had not been able to allow so great a change to become visible all at once. He also gave me several other reasons to excuse her, which made me see how much he was in love with her. He assured me that he would make her consent to my knowing of his passion for her, as it was after all she herself who had revealed it to me. He did in fact oblige her to accept this, albeit with great difficulty, and I was in consequence admitted to their most intimate confidence.

'I have never seen a woman behave so correctly and pleasantly towards her lover; yet I remained shocked by her pretence of appearing still to be in mourning. Sancerre was so much in love and so content with the way she treated him that he scarcely dared urge her to make firm arrangements for their marriage for fear she should believe he desired it rather out of self-interest than because his passion was genuine. He spoke to her about it none the less, and she appeared firmly resolved to marry him; she even began to emerge from the seclusion in which she lived and to take part in social activities once more. She visited my sister-in-law at times when members of the court were present. Sancerre came only on rare occasions, but those who came every evening and often saw her there found her most charming.

'Not long after she had begun to abandon her solitary life, Sancerre thought he discerned some cooling off in her passion for him. He spoke to me about it several times, but his complaints appeared groundless to me at first; eventually, however, when he told me that, instead of bringing their marriage about, she seemed to be putting it off, I began to believe that he was right to feel uneasy. I replied that, even if Mme de Tournon's passion had diminished after lasting two years, that was no cause for astonishment; should it prove that her passion, even undiminished, was not strong enough to constrain her to marry him, he ought not to complain. I reminded him that, in the public view, the marriage would be extremely damaging to her, not only because he was not a good enough match for her, but because of the slur it would cast on her reputation; thus, I told him, all he could legitimately wish for was that she should not deceive him and that she should not encourage him in false hopes. I added that, if she lacked the strength to marry him or confessed to him that she loved some other man, he must not be angry or complain, but should continue to regard her with respect and gratitude.

'"I am giving you", I told him, "the advice I would follow myself;* for sincerity moves me so profoundly that, if my mistress, or even my wife, confessed to me that she was attracted to another man, I believe I should feel distress but not bitterness. I should abandon the role of lover or husband in order to offer her my advice and my compassion."'

These words made Mme de Clèves blush. She saw in them a certain connection with her own position; this disconcerted her and filled her with a disquiet from which she was slow to recover.

'Sancerre spoke to Mme de Tournon', continued M. de Clèves, 'and told her everything I had advised him to; but she took such care to reassure him and appeared so offended by his suspicions that she succeeded in effacing them wholly from his mind. She none the less deferred their marriage until after a journey he was about to make, which was to be quite lengthy; but she behaved so well until his departure and appeared so distressed at the prospect that I was convinced, as he was, that she genuinely loved him. He left about three months ago now; during his absence, I have seen little of Mme de Tournon: I have devoted myself wholly to you, and all I knew was that he was due to return soon.

'The day before yesterday, on arriving in Paris, I heard she was dead. I sent a messenger to Sancerre's house to find out if there was any news of him. I received word that he had arrived just the day before, which was precisely the day Mme de Tournon died. I went to see him at once, fully suspecting the state I should find him in; yet his affliction was far greater than I had imagined.

'I have never seen a grief so profound, so tender. From the moment he saw me, he embraced me, bursting into tears. "I shall never see her again," he said, "I shall never see her again, she is dead! I was not worthy of her; but I shall follow her before long!"

'After that, he fell silent; then, at intervals, continually repeating "She is dead, I shall never see her again!", he would begin to weep and cry out again like a man who had lost his reason. He told me that he had rarely received any letters from her during his absence, but that he had not been surprised by this because he knew her well and was aware how she hated the risk entailed in sending him letters. He had no doubt that she would have married him on his return; he regarded her as the most charming and the most faithful woman who had ever existed; he believed himself tenderly loved by her; and he had now lost her at the very moment when he was expecting to be united to her for ever. All these thoughts cast him into a state of violent affliction: he was utterly overwhelmed, and I confess that I could not help being moved by his plight.

'I was none the less obliged to leave him in order to make an appearance in the King's apartments; I promised him that I would soon return, as indeed I did. I was never so astonished as to find him in a state quite different from the one I had left him in. He was standing in his room with a furious expression, walking up and down, then standing still as if beside himself. "Come," he said, "come and see the very epitome of despair. I am a thousand times more wretched than I was before: I have just heard something about Mme de Tournon that is worse than her death."

'I thought that grief had utterly unhinged his mind. I was unable to imagine that there was anything worse than the death of a mistress whom you love and who returns your love. I told him that, while his distress had been kept within limits, I had given it my approval and shared it with him, but that I would pity him no longer if he gave himself up to despair and lost his reason.

'"I should be only too happy to have lost my reason, and my life as well!" he cried: "Mme de Tournon was unfaithful to me, and I discover her infidelity and treachery the day after hearing of her death, at a moment when my soul is full to overflowing with the sharpest pangs of grief and the most tender love anyone ever felt; at a moment when my heart cherishes her image as the most perfect thing that ever existed, and the most perfect for me in particular,* I find that I have been in error and that she does not deserve my tears. Yet I am as afflicted by her death as if she had been faithful to me, and as wounded by her infidelity as if she were not dead. If I had known of her change of heart before her death, I should have been filled with jealousy, anger, and fury, which would have hardened me in some measure to the pain of losing her; but in my present state I can neither be consoled nor hate her."

'You may judge whether I was astonished at Sancerre's words; I asked him how he had come to know what he had just told me. He recounted how, a moment after I had left his room, Estouteville, who is an intimate friend of his but who even so knew nothing of his love for Mme de Tournon, had come to see him. Estouteville had not sat down before he began to weep and ask his forgiveness for having concealed what he was going to tell him; he begged him to have pity; he had come, he said, to open his heart to his friend, who saw before him the man in all the world most afflicted by the death of Mme de Tournon.

'"When I heard that name," Sancerre said to me, "I was so surprised that, though my first impulse had been to tell him that I was more afflicted by it than he, I nevertheless lacked the strength to speak. He continued, saying that he had been in love with her for six months. He had, it seems, always wanted to tell me, but she had expressly forbidden it, with such authority that he had not dared to disobey her. She had become attracted to him at about the same time as he had fallen in love with her. They had hidden their passion from everyone: he had never visited her publicly, but had had the pleasure of consoling her* for her husband's death. Finally, he had been about to marry her at the time when she had died; but the marriage, which was in reality due to their passion, would have appeared to be an act of duty and obedience: she had persuaded her father to order her to marry Estouteville, so that her conduct, which had previously been so resolutely opposed to a second marriage, would not seem too inconsistent.

'"While Estouteville was speaking to me," Sancerre said, "I believed his words, both because I found them plausible and because the time when he said he had begun to love

Mme de Tournon coincided precisely with the time when I had felt her sentiments change. A moment later, however, I thought him a liar or at least a man suffering from delusions. I nearly said as much to him, then instead I felt a desire to discover the truth; I questioned him, I plied him with doubts, till in the end I worked so hard to become certain of my misfortune that he asked me whether I knew Mme de Tournon's handwriting. He placed on my bed four letters from her and her portrait; just then, my brother came in. Estouteville's face was covered in tears, and he was obliged to go out so that he would not be seen; he told me he would return that evening to take back what he had left with me. I for my part sent my brother away on the pretext of not feeling well, so impatient was I to see the letters Estouteville had left with me; I also hoped to find in them something which would allow me not to believe all that he had just told me. But alas! what did I not find there? What tenderness! What promises! What assurances that she would marry him! What letters! She never wrote such letters to me. And so," he added, "I endure at once the torments of bereavement and of infidelity, two evils which have often been compared but which have never been felt at the same time by the same person. I confess, to my shame, that I am more affected by her death than by her change of heart; I cannot consider her sufficiently guilty to believe she deserved to die. If she were still alive, I should have the pleasure of reproaching her, of taking my revenge by bringing home to her how unjustly she has treated me; but I shall never see her again," he repeated, "I shall never see her again: of all my sufferings, that is the worst. I wish I could give her back her life at the expense of my own. What a thought! If she returned, it would be for Estouteville that she lived. How happy I was yesterday!" he cried. "How happy I was! Of all men, I was the most afflicted, but my affliction was within the bounds of reason, and I found some sweetness in the thought that I was beyond consolation. Today all my feelings are wrong. To her feigned passion for me I pay the same tribute of sorrow that I thought I owed to a genuine passion. I can neither hate nor love her memory; I can neither be consoled nor mourn. At least," he said, turning suddenly towards me, "I beg you to ensure that I never set eyes on Estouteville; his very name fills me with horror. I know well enough that I have no reason to accuse him: it is my fault that he was ignorant of my love for Mme de Tournon; if he had been aware of it, he would perhaps not have become attached to her, she would not have betrayed me. He sought me out to confide his sorrow to me; I feel pity for him. Ah! rightly so," he cried, "since he loved Mme de Tournon, he enjoyed her love, and he will never see her again. Yet I am conscious that I cannot help hating him. I implore you once more to see that he and I never meet."

'Then Sancerre's tears began to flow again: he grieved for Mme de Tournon and spoke to her, saying the most tender things in the world; then his hate returned, and he hurled fresh recriminations, reproaches, imprecations against her. Seeing him in such a violent state, I realized that I needed help if I was to try to calm his mind. I sent for his brother, whom I had just left in the company of the King; I went and spoke to him in the antechamber before he came in, telling him the state Sancerre was in. We gave orders to ensure that he did not meet Estouteville and we spent a considerable part of the night attempting to bring him back to his senses. This morning I found him more distressed than ever; his brother remained with him, and I came back to be with you.'

'No one could be more surprised than I,' said Mme de Clèves at last; 'I believed Mme de Tournon incapable of love and of deception.'

'Cunning and dissimulation', rejoined M. de Clèves, 'can go no further than she took them. But notice that, when Sancerre thought he saw her attitude towards him change, this was true: she had begun to love Estouteville. She told her second lover he was consoling her for the death of her husband; she told him that it was for his sake that she was abandoning her long withdrawal from society; whereas Sancerre thought it was because we had decided that she would no longer pretend to be so deeply in mourning. She persuaded Estouteville that they should hide their mutual understanding and that she should appear obliged to marry him by her father's command, on the pretext that she was concerned for her reputation; whereas it was in order to drop Sancerre without his having any cause for complaint. I must go back', continued M. de Clèves, 'to call on the wretched man, and I think you must return to Paris as well. It is time for you to see people again, and to receive all those countless visits of condolence which you cannot in any case avoid.'

Mme de Clèves agreed to this and returned the next day. She felt calmer about M. de Nemours than before: as a result of everything that Mme de Chartres had said to her on her deathbed, and the sorrow of bereavement, her feelings were in abeyance, and this led her to believe that they had been wholly dispelled.

On the very evening she arrived, Mme la Dauphine came to see her, and after assuring her of all her sympathy on her bereavement, told her that, to distract her from these sad thoughts, she wanted to let her know everything that had happened at court during her absence; after which she acquainted her with certain private matters.

'But what I want to tell you above all', she added, 'is that it is now certain M. de Nemours is passionately in love. Even his most intimate friends are not in his confidence, nor can they guess who it is that he loves. Yet his love is sufficient to make him neglect or—to put it more accurately—abandon the hopes of a crown.'

Mme la Dauphine then recounted everything that had happened in connection with the English affair.

'I heard what I have just told you', she continued, 'from M. d'Anville, who told me this morning that the King sent for M. de Nemours yesterday evening on receiving letters from Lignerolles. Lignerolles is asking to come back, and has written to the King that he can no longer persuade the Queen of England to accept M. de Nemours's constant deferments. He says she is beginning to be offended by them: although she had never given any positive promise, she had surely said enough to make it worth risking a journey. The King read this letter to M. de Nemours, who, instead of talking seriously as he used to at first, only laughed, joked, and made fun of Lignerolles's hopes. He said that all Europe would condemn his imprudence if he risked going to England as a suitor to the Queen without being certain of success. "It also seems to me", he added, "that I should be choosing the wrong moment to make the journey just now, when the King of Spain* is so actively pressing his own suit with Queen Elizabeth. He would perhaps not be a very daunting rival in a love affair, but I don't think that, when it comes to marriage, your Majesty would advise me to dispute any claim he might make." "I should advise it in this instance," rejoined the King; "but there would be no claim for you to dispute: I know that he has other thoughts, and even if he had not, Queen Mary found the yoke of Spain too heavy for anyone to believe that her sister would want to take it up again and allow herself to be dazzled by the brilliance of so many crowns joined in one." "If she doesn't allow herself to be dazzled by that," replied M. de Nemours, "it is likely that she will want to find happiness in love. Some years ago now, she was in love with Lord Courtenay; he was also loved by Queen Mary, who would have married him with the consent of all England had she not perceived that the youth and beauty of her sister Elizabeth made more impression on him than the prospect of a throne. Your Majesty knows that the violent jealousy she conceived led her to put them both in prison, then to exile Lord Courtenay, and finally to decide to marry the King of Spain. It seems to me that Elizabeth, who is now on the throne, will soon recall this lord and will choose a man she has loved, who is most worthy of love, and who has suffered so much for her sake, rather than a man she has never seen." "I should agree with you," said the King, "if Courtenay were still alive; but I discovered a few days ago that he has died in Padua, where he had been living in exile. I can see", he added as he left M. de Nemours's company, "that we shall have to arrange your marriage as if you were the Dauphin and send ambassadors to marry the Queen for you."

'M. d'Anville and M. le Vidame, who were with M. de Nemours in the presence of the King, are convinced that it must be his preoccupation with this new passion that distracts him from so great an enterprise. The Vidame, who is more intimately acquainted with him than anyone, told Mme de Martigues that Nemours is changed beyond recognition; and what astonishes him even more is that he can discern no special dealings, no particular moments when he evades company, so that the Vidame believes he has not established a secret understanding with the person he loves. And that is what makes M. de Nemours unrecognizable—to see him in love with a woman who does not return his love.'

Mme la Dauphine's words were like poison to Mme de Clèves. How could she not recognize herself as the person whose name no one knew? How could she fail to be overwhelmed with gratitude and tenderness on learning, by a route which could not be suspect to her, that M. de Nemours, who had already touched her heart, was hiding his passion from all the world and neglecting the prospect of a crown because he loved her? Thus it is impossible to describe what she felt, the confusion that arose in her soul. If Mme la Dauphine had looked at her carefully, she would easily have perceived that the things she had just said were not indifferent to her; but, as she had not the least suspicion of the truth, she went on talking without giving the matter any thought.

'M. d'Anville,' she added, 'from whom, as I have just told you, I heard these details, believes I know more about them than he does himself: he has such a high opinion of my charms that he is convinced I am the only woman capable of bringing about so great a transformation in M. de Nemours.'

These last words of Mme la Dauphine's produced in Mme de Clèves a confusion very different from the one she had suffered a few moments before.

'I should find it easy to share M. d'Anville's opinion,' she replied; 'it is indeed likely, Madame, that nothing less than a princess such as yourself could make a man disdain the Queen of England.'

'I should confess it if I knew it to be so,' responded Mme la Dauphine, 'and I *should* know if it were true. Such passions cannot escape the notice of the women who cause them; it is they who see them first. M. de Nemours has never shown me any but the slightest attentions, yet there is so great a difference between the manner he adopted with me previously and the one he adopts now that I can assure you I am not the cause of his indifference towards the crown of England.

'I am forgetting myself in talking to you,' added Mme la Dauphine; 'I should have remembered that I must go and see Madame. As you know, the peace treaty* is all but concluded; what you do not know is that the King of Spain has refused to endorse any of its articles except on condition that he himself, instead of his son, Don Carlos, should marry Madame.* Our King has had great difficulty in making up his mind to it, but he has finally given his consent and has just gone to announce the news to Madame. She will, I believe, be inconsolable: to marry a man of the age and character of the King of Spain is not something that can bring any pleasure, especially to Madame, who still has all the joy of early youth and beauty combined, and who was expecting to marry a young prince for whom she felt a certain inclination although she had never seen him. I cannot say whether the King will find her to be as obedient as he wishes; he has given me the task of speaking to her because he knows that she is fond of me and believes that I shall have some influence over her. Afterwards, I shall make another visit, a very different one: I shall go and share the happiness of Madame the King's sister. Everything is settled for her marriage with M. de Savoie, who will be here shortly. Never has a woman of her age been so utterly delighted at the prospect of marriage. The court will be more splendid and more numerous than ever before; despite your sorrow, you must come and help us to show the foreigners that we have beauties who are far from mediocre.'

On these words, Mme la Dauphine left Mme de Clèves; the next day, the news of Madame's marriage was known to all. On the days that followed, the King and the Queens called on Mme de Clèves. M. de Nemours, who had waited for her return with extreme impatience and had a burning desire to speak to her in private, delayed his visit until an hour when everyone would be leaving and when it seemed that no one else would come in. His plan succeeded and he arrived just as the last visitors were leaving.

The princess was lying on her bed.* The day was hot, and the sight of M. de Nemours brought to her features an intenser flush that in no way diminished her beauty. He sat down facing her with that hesitant and timid manner which is the mark of true passion. For some time he remained unable to speak. Mme de Clèves was no less tongue-tied, so that they kept a long silence. Finally, M. de Nemours took the initiative, offering his sympathy on her bereavement. Mme de Clèves, relieved to continue the conversation on this subject, spoke at some length of her loss; she concluded by saying that, even when time had at last diminished the violence of her grief, it would leave behind such a strong impression that her whole nature would be altered.

'Deep sorrows and violent passions', replied M. de Nemours, 'bring about great changes in the spirit. As for me, I hardly recognize myself since my return from Flanders. Many people have noticed this change: even Mme la Dauphine was speaking to me of it only yesterday.'

'It is true', said Mme de Clèves, 'that she has noticed it: I seem to remember her saying something about it.'

'I am not sorry,* Madame,' replied M. de Nemours, 'that she is aware of it, but I wish she were not the only one. There are women to whom one dares give no sign of the passion one feels for them except through matters that do not concern them. Since we dare not let them see we love them, we should at least like them to see that we have no desire to be loved by anyone else. We would have them know that there is no woman of beauty, of whatsoever rank, whom we do not regard with indifference, that there is no crown we would purchase at the price of never seeing them again. Women ordinarily judge the extent of our passion for them', he continued, 'by the care we take to please them and seek them out; but that is not difficult if they have any charm at all. What is difficult is to prevent oneself from surrendering to the pleasure of pursuing them, to avoid them for fear of revealing to others, and even to themselves, one's feelings for them. And what distinguishes a genuine attachment still more clearly is to become the very opposite of what one was before, to renounce all ambitions and all pleasures when one has spent one's whole life in pursuit of these things.'

Mme de Clèves had no difficulty in perceiving that these words were intended for her. She felt she must respond and not allow them to go unchallenged; at the same time she felt she must not listen or give any sign that she had taken them to apply to her. She thought she should speak; she thought she should say nothing. M. de Nemours's remarks pleased and offended her almost equally; they seemed to confirm everything that Mme la Dauphine had made her think. She found in them a note of chivalry and respect, but she also found them a shade too bold and explicit. The attraction she felt for M. de Nemours threw her feelings into a turmoil she was unable to control. The most obscure words of a man one likes are more disturbing than an open declaration from a man one doesn't. And so she made no reply, and M. de Nemours would have noticed her silence—and perhaps thought it a not unpropitious omen—had not the arrival of M. de Clèves put an end to the conversation and to his visit.

The prince had come to bring his wife news of Sancerre; but she had little curiosity to hear the sequel to that adventure. She was so preoccupied by what had just taken place that she could scarcely conceal her distraction. When she was once more at liberty to reflect, she realized she had been mistaken in believing she no longer felt anything but indifference for M. de Nemours. What he had said to her had made exactly the effect he might have desired and wholly convinced her of his passion. His actions were too much in accord with his words to leave her in any doubt. She no longer deluded herself with the hope of not loving him; her only thought was never to give him any sign of her love. It was a thorny enterprise whose difficulties were already familiar to her; she knew that the only way of succeeding was to avoid the presence of M. de Nemours. On the pretext of her mourning, which allowed her to be more retiring than usual, she no longer went to places where he might see her. She was in a state of profound melancholy for which the death of her mother was the apparent cause; no one looked for any other.

M. de Nemours was in despair, so rarely did he now see her. Knowing that he would not find her in any gathering or at any of the entertainments where the whole court assembled, he could not make up his mind to go there himself. He pretended to have a great passion for the chase and arranged hunting parties on the days when there were gatherings in the Queens' apartments. For a long while, a mild illness gave him an excuse for remaining at home rather than going to all the places where he knew very well he would not find Mme de Clèves.

M. de Clèves was ill at about the same time. Mme de Clèves did not leave his chamber during his illness; but when he felt better and began to see people again, including M. de Nemours, who, on the pretext of being still not fully recovered, spent the greater part of the day with him, she saw that she could remain there no longer. None the less, the first few times that he came, she lacked the strength to leave. It was so long since she had last seen him that she could not make up her mind to avoid him. By means of remarks which seemed quite general, but which she understood nevertheless because they bore a relation to what he had said in her chamber, he contrived to let her know that he went hunting to allow himself to daydream, and that he avoided court gatherings because she was not there.

She finally carried out the resolution that she had made to leave her husband's chamber when M. de Nemours was there, but only by doing herself great violence. He noticed that she was avoiding him, and was profoundly touched.

M. de Clèves at first paid no attention to his wife's conduct, but he finally became aware that she refused to remain in his room when there were people there. He spoke to her about it; she replied that she did not believe decorum required her to spend her evenings with the youngest people at court. She begged him to accept that she should live a more retiring life than had been her custom, adding that her mother's virtue and constant presence sanctioned many things that a woman of her age could not undertake alone.

M. de Clèves, who by nature was inclined to treat his wife with kindness and indulgence, showed neither on this occasion and told her flatly that he did not wish her to change her conduct. She was on the point of telling him that she had heard a rumour that M. de Nemours was in love with her; but she lacked the strength to name him. She also felt ashamed of giving a false reason and concealing the truth from a man who had such a high opinion of her.

Some days later, the King was in the Queen's apartments at the hour when her circle gathered there; the talk was of horoscopes and predictions. Opinions were divided over the credence one should give them. The Queen took them very seriously; she maintained that, after all the things that had been predicted and had been proved to be true, it was impossible to doubt that there was some degree of certainty in the science of prophecy. Others argued that so few of these countless predictions turned out to be correct that it was obvious such cases were the result of pure chance.

'I used to have a great deal of curiosity about the future,' said the King; 'but I have been told so many false and implausible things that I have remained convinced one cannot know anything for certain. Some years ago, a man with a great reputation as an astrologer came here. Everyone went to see him; I went, too, but without telling him who I was, and I took M. de Guise and d'Escars with me. I made them go ahead of me. The astrologer nevertheless turned to me first, as if he had judged me to be their master. Perhaps he recognized me; but he told me something which would have been inappropriate had he known who I was. He prophesied* that I should be killed in a duel. Then he told M. de Guise that he would be killed from behind and d'Escars that his head would be broken by a horse's hoof. M. de Guise was rather offended by this prediction, as if he had been accused of having to run away. D'Escars was not greatly satisfied to find that his life was to be ended by such an unfortunate accident. When we finally went out, we were all most displeased with the astrologer. I have no idea what will happen to M. de Guise and to d'Escars, but it is hardly likely that I shall be killed in a duel. The King of Spain and

I have just made peace; even if we had not, I doubt whether we should have fought a duel or that I should have called him out as the King my father called out Charles V.'

After the King's story of the misfortune which had been predicted for him, those who had previously supported astrology abandoned their position and agreed that one should not believe in it at all.

'As for me,' M. de Nemours said audibly, 'I have less reason to believe in it than any man alive,' and, turning towards Mme de Clèves, who was beside him, he added quietly: 'I have been told that I should be made happy by the favours of the person for whom I should have the most violent and the most respectful passion. So you may judge, Madame, whether I ought to believe in prophecies.'

What M. de Nemours had said openly led Mme la Dauphine to believe that this whispered remark concerned some false prophecy he had been given, so she asked him what he was saying to Mme de Clèves. If he had had less presence of mind, this request would have taken him by surprise, but without a moment's hesitation he replied:

'I was telling her, Madame, that it has been foretold that I should be raised to a destiny so elevated that I should not dare even to aspire to it.'

'If the prediction you were given was no more than that,' said Mme la Dauphine with a smile, thinking of the English affair, 'I don't advise you to speak ill of astrology; you could easily find reasons to defend it.'

Mme de Clèves perfectly understood what Mme la Dauphine meant; but she was also well aware that, when M. de Nemours spoke of a high destiny, he did not mean being King of England.

As some time had already elapsed since the death of her mother, she had to begin to appear in society and to perform her court duties as had previously been her habit. She regularly saw M. de Nemours in Mme la Dauphine's apartments; she saw him when he visited M. de Clèves, which he often did in the company of others of his age and rank; but she could not see him now without an agitation which he had no difficulty in discerning.

Try as she might to avoid his gaze and speak to him less
than to others, she could not help making certain instinctive
signs that gave him reason to believe she was not indifferent
to him. A man less acute than he would perhaps not have
noticed them; but so many women had already been in
love with him that he could hardly fail to recognize the
symptoms. He was well aware that the Chevalier de Guise
was his rival, and the Chevalier knew that M. de Nemours
was his. He was the only man at court who had unravelled
this secret; his own interest had made him more clear-sighted
than the others. The two men's mutual knowledge of their
feelings gave a bitter edge to their relations which was
apparent in everything they did. Though they never openly
quarrelled, they were always at odds. They took different
sides in tilting at the ring, in combats at the barrier,* and in
all the entertainments in which the King took part; their
rivalry was so great that it could not be concealed.

The English affair often returned to Mme de Clèves's
thoughts: it seemed to her that M. de Nemours would be
unable to resist the King's advice and the representations of
Lignerolles. It troubled her to see that Lignerolles had not
yet returned, and she awaited him impatiently. If she had
followed her instincts, she would have informed herself
carefully about the progress of the affair; but the same
feeling that made her eager to know also obliged her to
conceal her curiosity, and she only enquired about the
beauty, wit, and temperament of Queen Elizabeth. A portrait
of the English Queen was produced at a gathering in the
King's presence; she found it more beautiful than she would
have liked and could not help saying that it flattered the
Queen.

'I think not,' responded Mme la Dauphine, who was
present. 'She has the reputation of being beautiful and
uncommonly sharp-witted; she has been held up to me as an
example all my life, and I shall not forget it. She must
indeed be attractive if she is like her mother Anne Boleyn.
No woman has ever had such charm, such pleasing qualities
of person and character, as Anne Boleyn. I have heard that
her face had an animated, individual quality, and that she
bore no resemblance to any other English beauty.'

'I also seem to remember hearing', rejoined Mme de Clèves, 'that she was born in France.'

'Those who thought so were mistaken,' replied Mme la Dauphine; 'I will tell you her story* in a few words.

'She came from a good English house. Henry VIII had been in love with her sister and her mother; it was even suspected that she was his daughter. She came here with Henry VIII's sister,* who married King Louis XII. This princess, who was young and amorously inclined, found it hard to leave the court of France after the death of her husband; but Anne Boleyn, who shared her mistress's inclinations, could not make up her mind to leave it at all. The late King was in love with her, and she remained as maid of honour to Queen Claude. When the Queen died, she was taken up by the King's sister Mme Marguerite, Duchesse d'Alençon and later Queen of Navarre, whose stories you will no doubt have seen;* in her society she received the imprint of the new religion. She later returned to England, where she charmed everybody. She had acquired French manners, which people of all nations find pleasing; she sang well, she danced admirably. She became maid of honour to Queen Catherine of Aragon, and King Henry VIII fell hopelessly in love with her.

'Cardinal Wolsey, his favourite and his first minister, had aspired to the papacy; being displeased with the Emperor, who had not supported his claim, he resolved to take his revenge by making an alliance between the King and France. He put it in Henry VIII's mind that his marriage with the Emperor's aunt was null and void, and suggested that he should marry the Duchesse d'Alençon, whose husband had just died. Anne Boleyn, who was ambitious, saw the divorce as a path by which she might make her way to the throne. She began to impress on the King's mind elements of the religion of Luther, and persuaded our late King to give his support in Rome to Henry's divorce in the expectation that he would then marry Mme d'Alençon. Cardinal Wolsey had himself sent to France as an ambassador, on other pretexts, to deal with this affair; but his master could not make up his mind to allow the marriage even to be proposed and, while he was in Calais, sent him an order not to speak of it.

'On returning from France, Cardinal Wolsey was received with honours equal to those the King himself enjoyed: never has a favourite carried pride and vanity to such heights. He arranged an interview between the two kings,* which took place at Boulogne. François I offered his hand to Henry VIII; Henry refused to take it. They treated one another turn and turn about with an extraordinary show of magnificence, and offered each other suits of clothing to match those they had had made for themselves. I remember hearing that the ones the late King sent to the King of England were of crimson satin adorned with pearls and diamonds in a triangular pattern, the robe being of white velvet embroidered with gold. After spending a few days at Boulogne, they went on to Calais. Anne Boleyn was installed in Henry VIII's lodgings with the retinue of a queen, and François I gave her gifts and rendered her honours just as if that was what she was. Finally, after nine years of passion, Henry married her without waiting for the dissolution of his first marriage, which he had been asking Rome to grant for so long. The Pope lost no time in delivering his fulminations against him; Henry was so angered by this that he declared himself head of the Church and dragged all England into the unhappy change of religion that you now perceive.

'Anne Boleyn did not enjoy her lofty position for long. She thought it had become more secure through the death of Catherine of Aragon; but one day when, with the entire court, she was watching her brother Viscount Rochford tilting at the ring, the King was struck with such a violent fit of jealousy that he abruptly left the entertainment, returned to London, and gave orders to arrest the Queen, Viscount Rochford, and several others whom he believed to be her lovers or intimates. Though his jealousy appeared to have broken out on the spur of the moment, it had already been aroused some time before by Viscountess Rochford, who could not bear her husband's close bond with the Queen and induced the King to see it as a criminal attachment. In consequence, Henry VIII, who was in any case in love with Jane Seymour, thought only of how to rid himself of Anne Boleyn. In less than three weeks, he had Anne and her brother tried and executed and married Jane Seymour. He subsequently had several other wives whom he set aside or put to death; one of these was Catherine Howard, who used Viscountess Rochford as her confidante and who was executed together with her. The Viscountess was thus punished for the crimes she had imputed to Anne Boleyn; as for Henry VIII, he eventually died, having become prodigiously fat.'*

All the ladies who were present when Mme la Dauphine told this story thanked her for informing them so thoroughly about the English court; one of these was Mme de Clèves, who could not help questioning her further about Queen Elizabeth.

The Reine Dauphine was having miniatures painted of all the most beautiful women at court in order to send them to the Queen of Scotland.* The day Mme de Clèves's portrait was being completed, Mme la Dauphine came to spend the evening with her after dinner. M. de Nemours did not fail to be present; although he never let it be apparent that he sought out opportunities of seeing Mme de Clèves, he allowed none to pass him by. She looked so beautiful that, if he had not already fallen in love with her, he would have done so that day. However, he dared not keep his eyes on her while she was being painted, and he was afraid that his pleasure in watching her might be too apparent.

Mme la Dauphine asked M. de Clèves for a little portrait he had of his wife, to compare it with the one which was being finished. Everyone gave an opinion on the merits of the two pictures, and Mme de Clèves ordered the painter to adjust a detail in the coiffure of the one that had just been brought in. In order to carry out her command, the painter took the portrait out of its case and, after working on it, replaced it on the table.

M. de Nemours had long desired to have a portrait of Mme de Clèves. When he saw the one belonging to M. de Clèves, he could not resist the temptation to steal it from a husband whom he believed to be dearly loved by his wife; he reflected that, among all the people gathered there, he would not be suspected more than anyone else.

Mme la Dauphine was sitting on the bed* and speaking quietly to Mme de Clèves, who was standing in front of her. Through one of the curtains, which was only half drawn, Mme de Clèves caught sight of M. de Nemours at the end of the bed with his back to the table; she saw that, without turning his head, he was adroitly picking something up from the table. She had no difficulty in guessing that it was her portrait, and she was so disturbed that Mme la Dauphine noticed she was not listening to her and asked her audibly what she was looking at. Hearing this, M. de Nemours turned round; his eyes met Mme de Clèves's, which were still fixed on him, and he realized that it was not impossible that she had seen what he had just been doing.

Mme de Clèves was not a little embarrassed. Her reason told her that she should ask him to return her portrait; but to ask for it publicly would be to inform everyone of his feelings for her, while to ask him privately would amount to inviting him to speak to her of his passion. She judged in the end that it was better to let him keep it, and she was quite content to be able to grant him a favour without his knowledge.* M. de Nemours, who had noticed her embarrassment and who half-guessed the reason, came over to her and said quietly:

'If you saw what I was bold enough to do, Madame, be so kind as to let me believe that you are unaware of it; I dare ask no more of you.' After these words, he withdrew without waiting for a reply.

Mme la Dauphine, followed by all the ladies, went out for a drive.* M. de Nemours went home and shut himself away, for he could not contain in public his delight at possessing a portrait of Mme de Clèves. His feelings were the most enchanting that passion can give rise to: he was in love with the person at court most worthy of love; he was making her love him despite herself, and he could see in all her actions that kind of disquiet and embarrassment which love causes in the innocence of early youth.

That evening, they looked everywhere for the portrait. As the case in which it should have been was found, no one suspected that it had been stolen, and it was generally believed that it had accidentally fallen out. M. de Clèves was distressed by its disappearance, and, after a further search had been made in vain, he said to his wife, though in a way which made it clear he was not in earnest, that she doubtless had some hidden lover to whom she had given the portrait or who had stolen it: anyone other than a lover, he said, would not have been content with the painting without the case.

These words, though spoken in jest, made a sharp impression on Mme de Clèves's mind. They instilled in her a sense of remorse; she gave thought to the violence of the passion that was irresistibly drawing her towards M. de Nemours; she discovered that she was no longer able to master her words or her expression; she reflected on the fact that, since Lignerolles had returned, she need have no more fears about the English affair, and that her suspicions with regard to Mme la Dauphine had been set at rest; she saw, in short, that there was nothing that could protect her now: she would only be safe if she went away. Yet, since she was not in a position to do this of her own free will, she found herself in a desperate plight: she was on the point of falling into what seemed to her the greatest of misfortunes, which was to allow M. de Nemours to perceive her inclination for him. She remembered everything Mme de Chartres had said on her deathbed and how she had advised her to make any resolve, however difficult, rather than to embark on a love affair. She recalled, too, what M. de Clèves had said about sincerity when he had told her the story of Mme de Tournon; it seemed to her that she ought to confess to him her inclination for M. de Nemours. This idea preoccupied her for some time; then she was astonished to have had it at all, it seemed like madness; and so she fell back into the predicament of not knowing what course of action to follow.

The peace had been signed. Mme Elisabeth had finally overcome her reluctance and resolved to obey the King her father. The Duc d'Albe had been appointed to come to France to marry her* in the name of the Catholic King; he was due to arrive soon. The Duc de Savoie was expected, too: he was coming to marry Madame the King's sister, and the wedding was to take place on the same day.* The King's sole concern was to make these weddings illustrious by means of entertainments in which he could display the skill and magnificence of his court. Grandiose proposals were made for ballets and plays, but the King found these entertainments too limited in scope: he wanted something more brilliant. He decided to hold a tournament* in which the foreign visitors could take part and which the common people could attend as spectators. All the princes and young nobles wholeheartedly supported the King's plan, especially the Duc de Ferrare, M. de Guise, and M. de Nemours, who surpassed all others in these kinds of exercise. The King chose them to join with him to make up the four champions of the tournament.

It was advertised throughout the realm that, on 15 June in the city of Paris, a tournament would begin at which His Most Christian Majesty, together with the princes Alphonse d'Este, Duc de Ferrare, François de Lorraine, Duc de Guise, and Jacques de Savoie, Duc de Nemours, would challenge all comers. The tournament would begin with a combat on horseback in the lists, in double armour,* four lances to be broken, and another in honour of the ladies; the second combat to be fought with swords, in single combat or in pairs, as the marshals should direct; the third to be on foot, with three thrusts of the pike and six of the sword. It was announced that the champions would supply lances, swords, and pikes according to the challengers' choice, and that any rider who struck his opponent's horse would be banned from the lists; there would be four marshals to give the orders. Those of the challengers who broke the most lances and swords and performed best would have a prize, its value to be determined by the judges. Shields would be hung up on the platform at one end of the lists and all the challengers, whether Frenchmen or foreigners, would be required to come and touch one of them, or several, as they chose; they would find an officer-at-arms there who would receive them and enrol them according to their rank and according to the shields they had touched. The challengers would be required to have a gentleman bring their own shield, with their coat of arms, and hang it up on the platform three days before the tournament began; otherwise they would not be admitted without the special permission of the champions.

A great field of combat was set up close to the Bastille, running from the Château des Tournelles, crossing the Rue Saint-Antoine, and ending at the royal stables. There were wooden stands and banks of seats on both sides, with covered seating areas in the form of galleries, which made a most pleasing effect on the eye and were capable of containing a very great number of people. The princes and nobles now devoted all their time and care to assembling what they needed in order to appear in the most brilliant light, and to introducing into their monograms and devices some amorous note alluding to the ladies they admired.

Only a few days before the arrival of the Duc d'Albe, the King played a game of tennis with M. de Nemours, the Chevalier de Guise, and the Vidame de Chartres. The Queens came to watch them play, followed by all the ladies of the court, including Mme de Clèves. When the game was over, Chastelart approached the Reine Dauphine as they were leaving the tennis court and told her that chance had placed in his hands a love-letter that had fallen from M. de Nemours's pocket. The Reine Dauphine, who had always been curious about everything that concerned the Duc de Nemours, told Chastelart to give her the letter; she took it and followed the Queen, who was going off with the King to watch the lists being built. After they had been there for a while, the King had some horses brought out* which he had recently sent for. Although they were not yet completely broken in, he wanted to ride them, and gave one to each of his companions. The King and M. de Nemours found themselves on the most headstrong. The horses tried to hurl themselves at one another; M. de Nemours, for fear of injuring the King, backed off abruptly and swung his horse against a pillar of the riding school with such violence that the shock made him lose his balance. People ran to assist him, believing him to be seriously injured. Mme de Clèves thought his injuries even worse than the others did.

Her special interest in him made her feel dismayed and apprehensive, and she gave no thought to hiding these feelings. She accompanied the Queens to his side, with an expression so changed that a more disinterested man than the Chevalier de Guise would have noticed it; he therefore had no difficulty in making it out, and he paid a great deal more attention to Mme de Clèves's state than to M. de Nemours's. The blow Nemours had given himself made him so dazed that he remained for a while with his head leaning on those who were supporting him. When he raised it again, the first thing he saw was Mme de Clèves. He recognized in her face the pity she felt for him and looked at her in such a way that she could easily see how touched he was by her response. Then he thanked the Queens for the kindness they had shown towards him and excused himself for the state they had seen him in. The King ordered him to go and rest.

When Mme de Clèves had recovered from the shock, the signs by which she had betrayed her feelings soon gave her pause for thought. It was not long before the Chevalier de Guise deprived her of any hope that they had not been noticed; taking her hand to escort her from the lists, he said:

'I am more to be pitied, Madame, than M. de Nemours. Forgive me if I abandon the deep respect I have always had for you and allow you to see how grievously I am hurt by the scene I have just witnessed. This is the first time I have been bold enough to speak to you and it will also be the last. Death, or at least eternal exile, will remove me from a place where I can no longer live, for I have just lost the meagre consolation of believing that all those who dare to look at you are as unfortunate as I.'

Mme de Clèves could only utter a few disjointed words in reply, as if she had not understood the meaning of what the Chevalier de Guise had said. On any other occasion she would have been offended that he had spoken to her of his feelings; but at this moment she was only aware of the pain of seeing that he had noticed her feelings for M. de Nemours. The Chevalier was convinced he had guessed the truth and was transfixed with pain; from that day onward he resolved never to entertain the thought of being loved by Mme de Clèves. In order to renounce this ambition, which had seemed to him to be so difficult and so worthy of renown, he needed, however, some other enterprise of equal grandeur to which he might devote himself. He conceived the idea of taking Rhodes,* having already given some consideration to this project previously; and, when death removed him from the world in the flower of his youth, at a time when he had acquired the reputation of being one of the greatest princes of his day, the only regret he displayed in laying down his life was that he had failed to carry through so fine a resolve, for he had devoted to it so much care and attention that he had believed it would infallibly succeed.

On leaving the lists, Mme de Clèves went to call on the Queen, much preoccupied by what had happened. M. de Nemours arrived soon after, magnificently dressed and apparently quite unaffected by his accident. He even seemed to be in better spirits than usual; what he thought he had glimpsed of Mme de Clèves's feelings lent his whole manner an air of delight that increased his charm still further. Everyone was surprised when he came in, and everyone asked him how he was, except Mme de Clèves, who remained standing by the fireplace without giving any indication that she had seen him. The King emerged from an ante-room and, seeing him amid the crowd, called him over to discuss his accident with him. As M. de Nemours passed Mme de Clèves, he whispered:

'Today, Madame, you have shown me signs of pity; but pity is not what I deserve most.'

Mme de Clèves had been quite sure that Nemours had noticed her concern for him, and his words proved she was not mistaken. It was most distressing to her to see that she was no longer sufficiently in command of her feelings to be able to hide them and to know that she had revealed them to the Chevalier de Guise. That M. de Nemours should have recognized them was painful too, but the pain was in this case less unequivocal and was mingled with a kind of sweetness.

The Reine Dauphine, who was extremely impatient to know what was in the letter that Chastelart had given her, came up to Mme de Clèves.

'Go and read this letter,' she said. 'It is addressed to M. de Nemours, and to all appearances it is from the mistress for whose sake he has abandoned all his other mistresses. If you cannot read it just now, keep it; come to my *coucher** this evening to return it and tell me if you recognize the handwriting.'

After these words, Mme la Dauphine departed, leaving Mme de Clèves so astonished and so shaken that it was some time before she was able to move. Her impatience and agitation prevented her from remaining with the Queen; she went to her own apartments, although this was not the hour at which she ordinarily withdrew. She held the letter in a hand that trembled; her thoughts were so confused that not a single one was clear and distinct; and she found herself afflicted by an intolerable pain which she had never felt before and did not recognize. As soon as she was in her private room, she opened the letter and read what follows:

I have loved you too much to allow you to believe that the change you have noticed in me is due to my inconstancy: I wish you to know that your own infidelity is the cause. You may well be surprised to hear me speak of your infidelity; you hid it from me with such skill, and I took such care not to let you see I knew of it, that you have every reason to be astonished that it is in fact known to me. I am myself surprised that I have succeeded in suppressing all sign of it. Nothing can match the pain I have endured. I believed you were violently in love with me; I ceased to hide my own passion from you, and then, at the very moment when I revealed it without reserve, I learnt that you were deceiving me, that you were in love with another woman, and that, to all appearances, you were sacrificing me to your new mistress. I found out on the day of the tilting at the ring; that is what caused me to stay away. I feigned illness in order to conceal my confusion; but my body was unable to bear so violent a disturbance and I became really ill. When I began to recover, I still pretended to be unwell so that I should have a pretext for not seeing you or writing to you. I wanted to have time to decide how to deal with you; I adopted and abandoned the same resolutions over and over again; but finally I judged you to be unworthy to know of my suffering and I determined not to let it be apparent to you. I wanted to wound your pride by making you believe that my passion was diminishing of its own accord. It seemed to me that I should thus reduce the value of what you were sacrificing. I did not wish you to have the pleasure of flaunting my love for you in order to advertise your own powers of attraction. I decided to write you lukewarm, unenthusiastic letters so that the woman you showed them to would think that my love for you was coming to an end. I did not want her to have the pleasure of finding out that I was aware of her victory, nor did I wish that victory to be sweetened by my reproaches and despair. Simply to break with you, as I saw it, would not be sufficient punishment; I should only inflict a superficial wound if I ceased to love you when you no longer loved me. I realized that you would have to love me if you were to feel the pain of not being loved that I suffered so cruelly. The only way to rekindle your feelings for me, I thought, would be to make you see that my own had changed, while at the same time pretending to conceal the fact from you, as if I lacked the courage to confess it. I determined upon this course of action; but how difficult it was for me to adopt, and, when I saw you again, how impossible it seemed to carry through! A hundred times I was on the point of breaking out in reproaches and tears; but my continued ill health helped me to disguise from you my confusion and distress. Later, I was sustained by the pleasure of playing a false role with you, as once you played one with me. None the less, I had to do myself such violence in order to tell you in speech and in writing that I loved you that you realized sooner than I had meant you to that my feelings had changed. I tried to reassure you, but my manner was forced and that convinced you still more effectively that I no longer loved you. In the end, I succeeded in doing precisely what I had intended. The perversity of your heart made you gradually come back to me as you saw me becoming estranged from you. I enjoyed all the pleasure that vengeance can bestow: it seemed to me that you loved me more than you had ever done before and I forced you to see that I no longer loved you. I had reason to believe that you had entirely given up the woman for whom you had left me. I also had grounds for being convinced that you had never spoken to her about me; but your renewed love and your discretion could not make up for your inconstancy. I have shared your heart with another woman, you have deceived me: that is enough to destroy my pleasure in being loved by you as I believed I deserved to be; that is the reason for my irrevocable decision, which you find so surprising, never to see you again.

Mme de Clèves read and reread this letter several times without, however, understanding it at all. She only saw that M. de Nemours was not in love with her as she had thought and that he loved other women whom he deceived as he was deceiving her. For a person of her temperament, who was in the grip of a violent passion, who had just betrayed signs of it to a man she judged unworthy of being loved and to another whom she was ill-treating for his sake—for such a person, to see and to know such things was terrible indeed. Never has pain been so piercing and sharp. It seemed to her that what made the torment most bitter was the incident that had taken place that day: if M. de Nemours had not had grounds for believing that she loved him, she would not, she thought, have cared that he loved another. But she was deceiving herself. This pain that she found so unbearable was in fact jealousy* with all its attendant horrors. The letter showed her that M. de Nemours had long been engaged in a love affair. She judged that the woman who had written it showed both wit and distinction, that she deserved to be loved; she discerned in her more courage than she found in herself and she envied her for having the strength to hide her feelings from M. de Nemours. She saw, from the end of the letter, that the writer believed he loved her; she reflected that his discreet behaviour towards her, which she had found so touching, was perhaps only the effect of his passion for the other woman, whom he was afraid of offending. Her mind fastened on everything, in fact, that could possibly increase her distress and despair. How severely she judged herself, how painfully she recalled her mother's advice! How she repented of her failure to insist on removing herself from society, despite M. de Clèves's objections, or to carry through her idea of confessing to him* her inclination for M. de Nemours! It seemed to her that she would have done better to reveal her passion to a husband of whose kindness she could be assured and who would have had every interest in concealing it, than to allow it to be perceived by a man who was unworthy of it, who was deceiving her, who was perhaps sacrificing her, and who only wanted her love in order to nourish his pride and vanity. She became convinced, in short, that all the evils that might overtake her and all the extremities to which she might be driven were as nothing compared to the fact that she had allowed M. de Nemours to see she loved him, and to the knowledge that he loved another woman. Her only consolation was to reflect that, now she knew the truth, she at least had nothing else to fear from her own feelings, and that she would be wholly cured* of her inclination for Nemours.

The order she had received from Mme la Dauphine to be present at her *coucher* scarcely crossed her mind. She went to bed and pretended she was indisposed. Thus, when M. de Clèves returned from the King's apartments, he was told that she was asleep; yet she was in fact far removed from the tranquillity that leads to sleep. She spent the night doing nothing but torment herself and reread the letter she had been given.

Mme de Clèves was not the only person* whose rest was disturbed by that letter. The Vidame de Chartres—for it was he who had lost it, and not M. de Nemours—was in a state of extreme anxiety because of it. He had spent the whole evening as a guest of M. de Guise, who had given a great supper party for his brother-in-law the Duc de Ferrare and for all the young nobles at court. During supper, the conversation came round by chance to cleverly written letters. The Vidame de Chartres said that he had on his person the cleverest anyone had ever seen. He was pressed to show it; when he refused, M. de Nemours maintained that he had no such letter and that he was only boasting. The Vidame replied that Nemours was pushing his discretion to the limit; he would, however, not show the letter, but would read from it some passages which would convince the company that few men ever received the like. As he said this, he made as if to take the letter out, but it was not there; he looked for it in vain. The others teased him about it, but he appeared so uneasy that the matter was dropped. He withdrew before the rest of the company and returned home impatiently to see whether he had not left the missing letter behind. While he was still looking for it, the Queen's first valet called on him. He announced that the Vicomtesse d'Uzès had thought it necessary to bring urgently to his attention that it had been said, in the Queen's presence, that a love-letter had fallen from his pocket while he had been at tennis; a great deal of what was in the letter had been repeated; the Queen had shown herself most curious to see it and had sent to ask one of her gentlemen-in-waiting for it, but he had replied that he had left it in Chastelart's hands.

The first valet told the Vidame de Chartres many other things that put the final touch to his dismay. He went out at once to call on a gentleman who was an intimate friend of Chastelart's. He had him roused, although it was extra-ordinarily late, to go and ask Chastelart for the letter without saying who wanted it or who had lost it. Chastelart, who had already made up his mind* that it belonged to M. de Nemours and that Nemours was in love with Mme la Dauphine, had no doubt that it was he who was asking for it back. He replied, with malicious pleasure,* that he had passed the letter on to the Reine Dauphine. The gentleman came back to the Vidame de Chartres with this reply, which not only increased his disquiet but also made him see further causes for concern. For a long time, he remained uncertain what to do, but he decided in the end that only M. de Nemours could help him escape from the awkward situation he was in.

So he went to call on him. Day was only just beginning to break as he entered his bedchamber. Nemours was sleeping peacefully: what he had seen of Mme de Clèves the previous day had filled his mind with none but the pleasantest thoughts. He was surprised indeed to find himself roused by the Vidame de Chartres, and he asked him whether it was to take revenge for what he had said to him over supper that he came thus to disturb his rest. The Vidame's face told him clearly enough that the matter that brought him there was entirely serious.

'I have come to entrust to your confidence the most important affair of my life,' he said. 'I know well enough that you have no reason to thank me for it: I come at a time when I need your help. But I also know that, if I had told you what I now have to say without being absolutely compelled to, I should have lost your esteem. I dropped the letter I spoke of yesterday evening; it is of the greatest possible consequence that no one should know it is addressed to me. It has been seen by a number of people who were at the tennis court yesterday when it fell from my pocket; as you were there, too, I beg you to say that it was you who lost it.'

'You must think I have no mistress,' rejoined M. de Nemours with a smile, 'or you would not make such a proposal. You must imagine there is no one with whom, if I let people think I receive that kind of letter, I might risk a quarrel.'

'Please listen to me seriously,' said the Vidame. 'If you have a mistress—and I do not doubt it, although I have no idea who she is—you can easily vindicate yourself: I shall tell you how to do so without fail. Even if you do not succeed, it can only cost you a momentary quarrel, whereas I, by this accident, shall bring dishonour upon a person who has loved me passionately, a woman worthy of the greatest esteem; while, in another quarter, I shall draw upon myself an implacable hatred which will cost me my fortune and perhaps something more.'

'I cannot grasp your meaning entirely,' replied M. de Nemours; 'but what you say seems to suggest that the rumours which have been circulating about the interest a great lady was taking in you are not entirely false.'

'They are not, it is true,' said the Vidame de Chartres; 'would to God they were: I should not now find myself in this awkward situation. But I shall have to tell you the whole story* to bring the extent of my danger home to you.

'Since my arrival at court, the Queen has always shown me great favour and kindness. I had reason to believe she was interested in me, but there was nothing personal in the relationship and I never dreamt of having any feelings for her other than respect. Besides, I was deeply in love with Mme de Thémines; one need only look at her to see that, if she loved you, it would be easy to love her, and she did in fact love me. Some two years ago, when the court was at

Fontainebleau, I found myself on two or three occasions in conversation with the Queen at times when there was hardly anyone else present. It seemed to me that she liked my turn of mind and that she entered into everything I said. On one day in particular, we began to talk about trust. I said that there was no one whom I trusted absolutely: it was my view that one always regretted placing one's confidence in people, and I knew many things I had never spoken about. The Queen told me that she regarded me the more highly for it. She had never, she said, found anyone in France capable of keeping a secret: that was the thing that had always distressed her most, because it had denied her the pleasure of letting someone into her confidence. It was one of life's necessities, she maintained, to have someone to whom one could speak freely, especially for women of her rank. On the days that followed, she repeatedly took up the same conversation again; she even informed me of certain quite private matters that were going on at that time. It became apparent to me, in short, that she wanted to make sure of my ability to keep a secret and to entrust her own secrets to me. This notion drew me to her, I was touched by her favour, and I paid court to her more assiduously than was my custom.

'One evening the King and all the ladies had gone riding in the forest. She did not wish to go so far because she felt rather unwell, and I remained with her. She went down to the edge of the lake and dismissed her equerries so that she could walk* with greater freedom. When she had taken a few turns, she came up to me and ordered me to follow her. "I want to speak to you," she said; "and you will see, from what I have to say, that I am a friend of yours." She stopped after these words and looked at me intently. "You are in love," she continued, "and because you perhaps confide in no one, you believe that your love is a secret; but it is known, even to those whom it most closely concerns. You are being watched, the place where you meet your mistress has been discovered, there is a plan to catch you there unawares. I do not know who she is; I do not ask you and I wish only to protect you from the misfortunes into which you may fall."

You see, no doubt, what a cunning trap the Queen had prepared for me and how difficult it was not to be caught. She wanted to know whether I was in love; by not asking who the lady was and by allowing me to see no other intention but to please me, she banished from my mind any thought that her remarks were prompted by curiosity or by some ulterior motive.

'None the less, against all appearances, I succeeded in unravelling the truth. I was in love with Mme de Thémines, but, although she too loved me, I was not fortunate enough to have any private place where I met her and where there was a danger that I might be taken by surprise. It was thus easy for me to see that Mme de Thémines could not be the person the Queen was referring to. I was well aware too that, as I was conducting a love affair with another woman less beautiful and less severe than Mme de Thémines, it was not impossible that the place where I met her had been discovered; but I cared little for her, so that it was easy to make myself secure against every kind of danger by no longer seeing her. Thus I settled on the following plan: I would admit nothing to the Queen; I would assure her, on the contrary, that I had long since given up the desire to seek the love of other women whom I might expect to attract, because I found them all more or less unworthy of engaging the attention of a gentleman, and because the only thing that might hold me was a prize far above their level. "Your answer is not sincere," replied the Queen; "I know that the reverse is true. The way I am speaking to you puts you under an obligation to hide nothing from me. I should like you to be one of my friends," she continued; "but I do not wish, if I give you that privilege, to be ignorant of your attachments. You must decide whether you are ready to pay the price I am asking for it: namely, to reveal them to me. I give you two days to think it over; but, at the end of that time, consider carefully what you will tell me, and remember that if I later discover that you have deceived me, I shall never in my life forgive you."

'On these words, the Queen left me without waiting for a reply. You may be sure that my mind continued to dwell on what she had said. The two days she had given me to consider her proposal seemed to me by no means too long to reach a decision. I saw that she wanted to know whether I was in love and that she hoped I was not; I saw all the possible consequences of the decision I should have to take. My vanity was immensely flattered by the idea of a private relationship with a queen, and what is more a queen whose personal charms are still considerable. On the other hand, I loved Mme de Thémines, and although I had committed a kind of infidelity towards her with the other woman I mentioned to you, I could not make up my mind to break with her. I also saw the danger I exposed myself to in deceiving the Queen and how difficult it was to deceive her; none the less, I was unable to bring myself to refuse what fortune was offering me, and I decided to risk all the consequences that my misconduct might draw upon me. I broke with the other woman so that my liaison with her could not be discovered, and I hoped to be able to hide my relations with Mme de Thémines.

'At the end of the two days the Queen had given me, just as I was entering the chamber where all the ladies in her circle had gathered, she said to me quite audibly, and in a serious tone that took me by surprise: "Have you given thought to the question I charged you with, and do you have the answer?" "Yes, Madame," I replied; "it is as I told Your Majesty." "Come this evening," she said; "I shall write to let you know the hour. You will then learn the full extent of my commands." I bowed low without replying and did not fail to be present at the time she had designated. I found her in the gallery with her secretary and one or other of her ladies. As soon as she saw me, she came up and led me to the further end of the gallery. "Well!" she said. "Did you need so much reflection to decide that you have nothing to tell me, and does not my conduct towards you deserve a sincere response?" "It is because my response is sincere, Madame," I replied, "that I have nothing to tell you; and I swear to Your Majesty, with all the respect I owe you, that I have no attachment to any woman at court." "I am happy to believe you," rejoined the Queen, "because I wish it to be true; I wish it because it is my desire that you should be exclusively attached to me, and because your friendship would be wholly unacceptable to me if you were in love. One cannot trust people who are in love; one cannot be sure that they will keep a secret. They are too often distracted, too divided in their loyalties, and their mistress has a prior claim on their attention that is not compatible with the way in which I want you to be attached to me. Remember then: it is because you have promised me you have no other commitment that I am singling you out to confide in you absolutely. Remember that, in return, I want your undivided confidence. I want you to have no friend, man or woman, other than those I shall approve, and to renounce every concern except to please me. I shall not expect you to neglect your career: I shall further it more assiduously than you yourself, and, whatever I do for you, I shall consider myself only too well rewarded if your conduct with me is as I hope. I have chosen you as my confidant: I shall tell you all my sorrows and you will help make them more bearable. You may easily guess that they are not trivial ones. It may appear that I tolerate the King's attachment to the Duchesse de Valentinois without too much discomfort; in fact I find it unbearable. She dominates the King, she deceives him, she despises me, all my people are in her pay. My daughter-in-law the Reine Dauphine, who prides herself on her beauty and her uncles' credit, refuses to obey me. The Connétable de Montmorency has the King and the kingdom in his power; he hates me, and has signified his hatred in ways I cannot forget. The Maréchal de Saint-André is an arrogant favourite who treats me no better than the others. A full account of my misfortunes would move you to pity. Until now, I have dared trust no one: I place my trust in you. Make sure that I have no cause to regret it, and be my only consolation." The Queen's eyes reddened as she finished speaking; I felt as if I could throw myself at her feet, so touched was I by her kindness. From that day on, she trusted me absolutely; she no longer did anything without telling me about it; and I have maintained an attachment to her which lasts even now.'

PART III

'YET, constantly preoccupied as I was with my new relations
with the Queen, I could not overcome the instinctive attraction that drew me to Mme de Thémines. I formed the
impression that her love for me was coming to an end, and,
if I had been prudent, I should have made use of this apparent change to help cure myself of love; instead, my feelings
for her became twice as strong and I handled things so
clumsily that the Queen guessed something of my attachment. Jealousy is natural in women of her nation; it may be,
too, that the Queen's feelings for me are stronger than she
herself thinks. At all events, the rumour that I was in love
disturbed and distressed her so much that it seemed to me
time and again that my cause with her was lost. I finally
reassured her by plying her with attentions, protestations of
obedience, and false vows; but I should have been unable
to deceive her for long had not the change in Mme de
Thémines begun to estrange me from her despite myself.
She gave me to believe that she no longer loved me, and she
did it so successfully that I was obliged to leave her in peace
and torment her no more. Some time later, she wrote me
the letter which I have lost. From it I learnt that she had
discovered my liaison with the other woman I spoke to you
of and that it was this that had brought about the change in
her. I now had nothing to divide my allegiance, and the
Queen was reasonably satisfied with my behaviour; but
since my feelings for her are not such as to make me incapable of any other attachment, and since one cannot love
someone simply because one wants to, I have now fallen in
love with Mme de Martigues, to whom I had already been
greatly attracted when she was maid of honour to the Reine
Dauphine and still carried the name Villemontais.* I have
grounds for believing that she for her part does not hate me;
she is pleased that I am so discreet in my relations with her,
although she is not entirely aware of the reasons. The
Queen has no suspicions in that direction, but she has
others which are scarcely less troublesome. As Mme de

Martigues is always in the Reine Dauphine's apartments, I
too go there more often than usual, and so the Queen has
seized on the idea that it is the Reine Dauphine I am in
love with. Her rank, which is equal to the Queen's, and her
beauty and youth, in which she is her superior, have inspired
in the Queen a jealousy bordering on madness, together
with a hatred for her daughter-in-law which she can no
longer conceal. The Cardinal de Lorraine, who has, I believe, long been aspiring to the Queen's favours, and who
sees perfectly well that I occupy a position he would himself
like to fill, has become involved in the quarrel between the
Queen and Mme la Dauphine on the pretext of patching it
up. I have no doubt that he has discovered the real reason
for the Queen's ill humour and I am sure he is doing me
bad turns of every kind without letting the Queen see what
his game is. Such is the present state of affairs. Just imagine
the possible effect of the letter I have lost, which unhappy
chance made me put in my pocket in order to return it to
Mme de Thémines. If the Queen sees it, she will know that
I have deceived her, and that, at almost the same time as
I was being unfaithful to her with Mme de Thémines, I was
being unfaithful to Mme de Thémines with another woman.
Imagine what she is likely to think of me, and whether she
will ever be able to trust my words again. If she does not
see the letter, what shall I tell her? She knows it has been
placed in the hands of Mme la Dauphine; she will think that
Chastelart recognized her writing and that the letter is from
her; she will imagine that she herself is perhaps the person
who is the object of the writer's jealousy; in short, there is
nothing she might not think and I have everything to fear
from her thoughts. Remember, finally, that I have the
strongest feelings for Mme de Martigues, and that Mme la
Dauphine will surely show her the letter, which she will
believe to have been written recently; thus I shall fall out
equally with the woman I love most of all and the woman
from whom I have most of all to fear. After that, consider
whether I am not right to beg you to say the letter is yours,
and to ask you, for pity's sake, to go and retrieve it from
Mme la Dauphine.'

'It is clear to me', said M. de Nemours, 'that it is im-

possible to be in a more awkward situation than yours, and
I cannot help saying you deserve it. I have been accused of
not being a faithful lover and of maintaining several love
affairs at once; but you have gone so much further that I
should not have dared ever to imagine the things you have
tried to do. How could you possibly think you could keep
Mme de Thémines once you had entered into an understanding with the Queen? Did you hope you could preserve
that understanding and deceive her at the same time? She is
Italian and a Queen: it follows that she is full of suspicions,
jealousy, and pride. When your good fortune, rather than
your good behaviour, extricated you from your previous
commitments, you entered into new ones and you imagined
that, in the midst of the court, you could love Mme de
Martigues without the Queen noticing. Nothing you could
have done to relieve her of the shame of having taken the
first step would have been too much. She is violently in
love with you; your discretion prevents you from telling
me so, as mine prevents me from asking you; but in short
she loves you, she distrusts you, and the truth is against
you.'

'What right have you to heap reproaches on me?' the
Vidame interrupted. 'Should not your own experience*
make you indulgent towards my faults? I am certainly willing
to concede that I am in the wrong; but rather give thought,
I implore you, to saving me from the dreadful predicament
I am in. It seems to me that you should see the Reine
Dauphine as soon as she is awake to ask her to give the
letter back, as if you had lost it.'

'I have already told you', said M. de Nemours, 'that what
you are proposing is rather unusual and that my personal
interest could make me hesitate to agree; but, in addition, if
the letter was seen to fall from your pocket, it will surely be
difficult to persuade anyone that it fell from mine.'

'As I believe I said to you before,' replied the Vidame, 'the
Reine Dauphine has been told that it was from your pocket
that the letter fell.'

'What!' M. de Nemours rejoined sharply, seeing at once
the unfortunate effect this error might have on Mme de

Clèves's attitude towards him. 'The Reine Dauphine has been told that it is I who dropped the letter?'

'Yes,' said the Vidame, 'that is what she has been told. The error came about in this way. Your servants and mine went to collect our clothes from one of the rooms in the tennis court. Several of the Queens' gentlemen were there at the time. The letter fell to the ground, and these gentlemen picked it up and read it aloud. Some thought it belonged to you, others to me. Chastelart, who took possession of it and to whom I have just sent to ask for it back, tells me that he gave it to the Reine Dauphine saying it belonged to you; by mischance, those who spoke to the Queen about it said it was mine. So you can easily do as I wish and rescue me from the awkward situation I am in.'

M. de Nemours had always been fond of the Vidame de Chartres, a feeling much enhanced by the Vidame's relationship to Mme de Clèves. None the less, he could not make up his mind to risk her hearing the letter spoken of as something in which he had a personal interest. He began to brood on the question; the Vidame, suspecting more or less what was in his thoughts, said:

'It is obvious that you fear a quarrel with your mistress, and you would even give me grounds for believing that the Reine Dauphine is the lady in question, were not the thought dispelled from my mind by your visible lack of jealousy for M. d'Anville. Whatever the truth of the matter, it is right that you should not sacrifice your peace of mind for the sake of mine. I shall be happy to offer you a way of showing the woman you love that the letter is addressed to me and not to you: here is a note from Mme d'Amboise, a friend of Mme de Thémines, to whom she has confided all her feelings for me. The purpose of the note is to ask me to return her friend's letter which I have lost; my name is on the note; its contents prove beyond doubt that the letter she is asking for is the same as the one that has been found. Take the note: you have my consent to show it to your mistress in order to clear yourself. I beg you to go this very morning, without losing a single moment, to see Mme la Dauphine.'

M. de Nemours promised to do as the Vidame asked and took Mme d'Amboise's note. It was not, however, his intention to see the Reine Dauphine: it seemed to him he had something more urgent to do. He had no doubt that she had already spoken to Mme de Clèves about the letter and he could not bear the thought that someone he so desperately loved should have reasons for believing that he had an attachment to another woman.

He went to visit her at a time when he thought she might be awake and sent a message saying that he would not be asking for the honour of seeing her at such an extraordinary hour if a matter of consequence had not made it imperative. Mme de Clèves was still in bed; her mind was restless, full of the grim and bitter thoughts that had occupied her all night. She was extremely surprised when she was told that M. de Nemours was asking for her; so embittered was her frame of mind that she did not hesitate to reply that she was ill and unable to speak to him.

This refusal caused M. de Nemours little pain: a sign of coldness at a time when she might be suffering from jealousy was by no means a bad omen. He went to M. de Clèves's apartment and told him that he had just left his wife's: he was very sorry, he said, that he had been unable to speak to her, since he had to discuss with her a matter of great importance for the Vidame de Chartres. He explained the significance of the affair to M. de Clèves in a few words, and M. de Clèves took him at once to his wife's room.* If she had not been in darkness, she would have found it hard to hide her confusion and surprise on seeing M. de Nemours brought in by her husband. M. de Clèves told her that there was a difficulty concerning a letter and that her help was needed in the interests of the Vidame; she should, he said, consider with M. de Nemours what was to be done about it, while he himself went to see the King, who had sent for him.

M. de Nemours was left alone with Mme de Clèves; he could have wished for nothing better.

'I have come to ask you, Madame,' he said, 'whether

Mme la Dauphine has not spoken to you about a letter that Chastelart placed in her hands yesterday.'

'She has told me something about it,' replied Mme de Clèves; 'but I cannot see what the letter has in common with the interests of my uncle. I assure you that he is not named in it.'

'It is true, Madame,' rejoined M. de Nemours; 'he is not named in it. None the less, the letter is addressed to him and it is of the utmost importance for him that you should retrieve it from Mme la Dauphine.'

'I find it hard to understand', said Mme de Clèves, 'why it matters to him whether the letter is seen or why I should ask for it back on his behalf.'

'If you will give yourself time to listen to me, Madame,' said M. de Nemours, 'I shall quickly open your eyes to the truth. You will hear things of such consequence for the Vidame that I should not even have confided them to M. le Prince de Clèves had I not needed his assistance in order to have the honour of seeing you.'

'I think it would be pointless for you to go to the trouble of telling me anything,' replied Mme de Clèves drily; 'you would do better to go and find the Reine Dauphine and let her know, without any unnecessary complications, what interest you have in this letter, since she has also been told that it came from you.'

The bitter note M. de Nemours detected in Mme de Clèves's attitude gave him the most palpable pleasure he had ever enjoyed, almost outweighing his impatience to vindicate himself.

'I have no idea, Madame,' he pursued, 'what may have been said to Mme la Dauphine; but the letter does not concern my interests. It is addressed to M. le Vidame.'

'Doubtless,' replied Mme de Clèves; 'but the Reine Dauphine has been told the opposite, and she will not think it likely that M. le Vidame's letters should fall from your pocket. So, unless you have some reason of which I am unaware for hiding the truth from Mme la Dauphine, I advise you to confess it.'

'I have nothing to confess to her,' he rejoined; 'the letter is not addressed to me and, if there is anyone I wish to convince of that fact, it is not Mme la Dauphine. But, Madame, as M. le Vidame's career is at stake in this matter, please allow me to tell you certain things which even you may find worthy of interest.'

Mme de Clèves indicated by her silence that she was ready to listen, and M. de Nemours recounted to her as succinctly as he could everything he had just heard from the Vidame. Although the tale was such as to arouse astonishment and demand close attention, Mme de Clèves heard it with unremitting coldness: she seemed to give it no credence or at least to be wholly indifferent to it. She maintained this attitude until M. de Nemours spoke of Mme d'Amboise's note to the Vidame de Chartres, which proved everything he had just said. As Mme de Clèves knew that she was a friend of Mme de Thémines's, she found a semblance of truth in what M. de Nemours was telling her, which made her think that the letter was perhaps not addressed to him. This thought at once made her shake off, despite herself, the cold attitude she had preserved until that moment. Nemours, after reading to her the note that exonerated him, gave it to her to read, telling her that she might well recognize the handwriting. She could not help taking it, looking at the top of the page to see if it was addressed to the Vidame de Chartres, and reading it through in order to determine whether the letter the writer was asking him to return was the one she herself had in her possession. M. de Nemours continued to say everything he could to persuade her and, as it is easy to persuade someone of a truth they want to believe, he convinced her that he had no part in the letter.

She now began to discuss with Nemours the Vidame's embarrassing and dangerous predicament. She condemned his misconduct; she considered ways of helping him; she expressed astonishment at the Queen's behaviour; she admitted to Nemours that she had the letter; in short, as soon as she believed him innocent, she openly and calmly entered into a discussion of the very things that she had at first appeared to regard as unworthy of her attention. They

agreed that it would be better not to return the letter to
the Reine Dauphine in case she showed it to Mme de
Martigues, who knew Mme de Thémines's writing and
whose own interest in the Vidame would have enabled her
to guess without difficulty that the letter was addressed to
him. They also decided that they should not tell the Reine
Dauphine the part of the story concerning the Queen. Mme
de Clèves, on the pretext that this was her uncle's business,
happily agreed to keep all the secrets that M. de Nemours
entrusted to her.

Nemours would have spoken to her of other things than
the Vidame's interests, and the freedom he now enjoyed in
her company would have made him bolder than he had
hitherto dared to be, had not a message arrived from the
Reine Dauphine ordering Mme de Clèves to come at once.
M. de Nemours was obliged to withdraw. He went to
find the Vidame to tell him that, after leaving him, he had
thought it more appropriate to seek the help of Mme de
Clèves, given that she was his niece, than to go straight to
Mme la Dauphine. He was not at a loss for reasons why the
Vidame should approve his way of handling the matter and
why a happy outcome might be expected.

Meanwhile, Mme de Clèves hastily dressed for her visit
to the Reine Dauphine. Hardly had she appeared in her
chamber than Mme la Dauphine called her over and said
to her in a low voice:

'I have been waiting for you for two hours, and never
have I found it so awkward to disguise the truth as I have
this morning. The Queen has heard about the letter that
I gave you yesterday. She thinks it was the Vidame de
Chartres who dropped it; you are aware that she takes a
certain interest in him. She gave orders to find the letter;
she sent to Chastelart for it; he said he had given it to me; I
have been asked for it on the pretext that the Queen was
curious to see such a clever letter. I dared not say you had it:
I thought she would imagine that I had passed it on to you
because the Vidame is your uncle, and that there was some
deep understanding between him and me—I have already
noticed that she can hardly bear it if he sees me frequently.

So I said that the letter was in the clothes I was wearing yesterday and that the people who had the key to my wardrobe had gone out. Give me the letter without delay,' she added, 'so that I can send it to her; I must also read it before I send it to see whether I cannot recognize the handwriting.'

Mme de Clèves found herself even more embarrassed than she had expected.

'I am at a loss to know what you can do, Madame,' she replied; 'for M. de Clèves, to whom I gave it to read, has passed it on to M. de Nemours, who came first thing this morning to beg him to ask you for it back. M. de Clèves was unwise enough to tell him he had the letter, and weak enough to give in to M. de Nemours's insistent requests to return it to him.'

'You have put me in the most awkward position it is possible to imagine,' said Mme la Dauphine. 'It was wrong of you to pass the letter on to M. de Nemours; since it was I who gave it to you, you ought not to have given it to anyone else without my permission. What do you expect me to say to the Queen? What is she going to think? She will believe, with good reason, that the letter concerns me and that there is something between the Vidame and me. She will never be persuaded that the letter belongs to M. de Nemours.'

'I am mortified', replied Mme de Clèves, 'by the embarrassment I am causing you. I see how serious it is; but the fault is M. de Clèves's, not mine.'

'It is your fault,' rejoined Mme la Dauphine. 'You gave him the letter, and you are the only woman in the world who confides to her husband* all the things she knows.'

'No doubt I am wrong, Madame,' said Mme de Clèves; 'but it would be better to think how to correct my mistake than to subject it to examination.'

'Do you not remember more or less what is in the letter?' the Reine Dauphine then said.

'Yes, Madame,' she replied, 'I remember: I read it more than once.'

'In that case,' continued Mme la Dauphine, 'you must go and have it written out immediately in an unknown hand. I shall send it to the Queen; she will not show it to the people who have seen it. Even if she did, I shall continue to maintain that it is the one Chastelart gave me; he won't dare contradict me.'

Mme de Clèves assented to this device. She did so the more willingly because it came to her that she could send for M. de Nemours to get the letter itself back: it could then be copied word for word and the handwriting imitated as closely as possible. She thought the Queen would then be deceived without fail. As soon as she returned home, she informed her husband of Mme la Dauphine's awkward situation and asked him to send for M. de Nemours. He was summoned and came with all haste. Mme de Clèves told him everything she had already told her husband and asked him for the letter; M. de Nemours replied, however, that he had already given it back to the Vidame de Chartres, who had been so delighted to get it and to have escaped from the danger he would have been in that he had sent it back immediately to Mme de Thémines's friend. Mme de Clèves thus found herself in yet another predicament. Finally, after a great deal of discussion, they decided to write out the letter from memory. They shut themselves away to work on it, giving orders to the servants at the door not to let anyone in, and dismissed all M. de Nemours's people. This atmosphere of mystery and secrecy had no small charm for Nemours and even for Mme de Clèves. The presence of her husband and the aim of protecting the Vidame's interests helped to silence her scruples. She felt only the pleasure of seeing M. de Nemours, a pure, unmixed delight that was new to her, and from this delight came a mood of gaiety and freedom which M. de Nemours had never before seen in her and which increased his love many times over. As he had never experienced such pleasant moments, he was even more sparkling than usual: when Mme de Clèves wanted to start remembering and rewriting the letter, Nemours, instead of helping her seriously, did nothing but interrupt her and make amusing remarks to her. Mme de Clèves entered into the same light-hearted mood, with the result that they had already been closeted for some time, and two messages had arrived from the Reine

Dauphine telling Mme de Clèves to make haste, before they had composed half of the letter.

M. de Nemours was quite happy to spin out an hour that was so delightful to him, and forgot his friend's interests. Mme de Clèves was herself by no means bored; she too forgot her uncle's interests. Finally, the letter was only just finished by four o'clock, and it was so ill done, and the writing in which they had it copied was so unlike the one they had intended to imitate, that the Queen would have had to be very careless in her enquiry in order to fail to discover the truth. And in fact she was not deceived, however much trouble they took to persuade her that the letter was addressed to M. de Nemours. She remained convinced not only that it belonged to the Vidame to Chartres but also that the Reine Dauphine was a party to it and that there was some understanding between them. Her belief so increased the hatred she felt for the Reine Dauphine that she never forgave her and persecuted her until she had forced her to leave France.*

As for the Vidame de Chartres, his position in her eyes was utterly destroyed. Whether the Cardinal de Lorraine had already taken possession of her mind, or whether the letter incident, making her see she had been deceived, led her to unravel all the Vidame's other deceptions, it is certain that he was never able to achieve a genuine reconciliation with her. Their liaison came to an end, and she eventually brought about his ruin at the time of the Amboise conspiracy,* in which he was involved.

After the letter had been sent to Mme la Dauphine, M. de Clèves and M. de Nemours left and Mme de Clèves remained alone. As soon as she was no longer sustained by the joy of being with a person one loves, she awoke as from a dream. She contemplated with astonishment the immense difference* between the way she had felt the previous evening and the way she felt now. She recalled the cold and bitter manner she had adopted with M. de Nemours while she had believed that Mme de Thémines's letter was addressed to him; how calm and gentle her manner had been, by contrast, as soon as he had persuaded her that the letter had nothing to do with him! When she reflected that, the previous day, she had reproached herself, as if it were a crime, because she had let him see she was touched by an emotion that might have been no more than pity, whereas her display of bitterness had shown him feelings of jealousy that were a certain proof of passion, she could scarcely recognize herself. Again, when it came to her that M. de Nemours, who was perfectly well aware that she knew he loved her, had seen that this made her treat him none the worse, even in her husband's presence—that, on the contrary, she had never looked on him so favourably; when she remembered that it was at her own bidding that M. de Clèves had sent for him and that they had just passed the afternoon together in private; when she reflected on all this, she concluded that she was in league with M. de Nemours and that she was deceiving the husband who least of all deserved to be deceived. She felt ashamed to appear, even in the eyes of her lover, so unworthy of esteem. But what was more intolerable to her than anything was the memory of the state in which she had passed the night, the dreadful pain she had suffered at the thought that M. de Nemours was in love with another woman and that he was unfaithful to her.

She had been ignorant until then of the deadly torments that spring from distrust and jealousy. She had thought only of preventing herself from falling in love with M. de Nemours and she had not yet begun to fear that he might love someone else. Although the suspicions the letter had given her had been set at rest, they none the less opened her eyes* to the risk of being deceived and gave her intimations of distrust and jealousy that she had never known before. She was astonished never to have thought how unlikely it was that a man like M. de Nemours, who had always displayed such a superficial attitude towards women, was capable of a sincere, lasting attachment. She felt that it was almost impossible for her to find happiness in his love. But even if I could, she said to herself, what can I want with it? Do I really want to tolerate it? respond to it? Am I ready to embark on a love affair? to be unfaithful to M. de Clèves?

to be unfaithful to myself? Do I wish to expose myself to the cruel remorse and mortal sufferings that love gives rise to? I am conquered and overcome by an inclination that carries me with it in spite of myself. All my resolutions are of no avail; my thoughts yesterday were no different from what I think today, yet today I do the very opposite of what I decided yesterday. I must tear myself away from M. de Nemours's presence; I must go to the country, however strange my journey may appear; and if M. de Clèves persists in preventing it or wanting to know the reasons for it, perhaps I shall give him, and myself, the pain of telling him. She remained firm in this resolution and spent the evening at home without going to find out from Mme la Dauphine what the effect of the false letter had been.

When M. de Clèves returned, she told him that she wished to go to the country: she was feeling unwell, she said, and needed fresh air. She looked so extraordinarily beautiful to M. de Clèves that he could not believe her illness was serious, and at first he mocked her idea of going away and replied that she was forgetting that the princesses' weddings and the tournament were about to take place. She needed all the time at her disposal, he said, to prepare herself so that she could appear at these events with as much splendour as the other women. Her husband's arguments failed to make her change her mind. She begged him to allow her, while he himself went to Compiègne with the King, to go to Coulommiers. This was a fine house, only a day's journey from Paris,* that they were having built: they were devoting the greatest care to its construction. M. de Clèves gave his consent and she departed, meaning not to return for some time; meanwhile, the King went to Compiègne, where he was due to stay for only a few days.

It had been very painful for M. de Nemours not to see Mme de Clèves again since the afternoon which he had spent so pleasantly with her and which had increased his hopes. His impatience to see her allowed him no rest, and so, when the King returned to Paris, he resolved to visit his sister the Duchesse de Mercœur, whose house was in the country not far from Coulommiers. He suggested to the

Vidame that he should go with him, and the Vidame readily accepted; M. de Nemours had conceived this idea in the hope of seeing Mme de Clèves and visiting her in the company of the Vidame.

Mme de Mercœur was delighted to receive them and gave herself up to entertaining them and offering them all the pleasures of the countryside. While they were out stag-hunting,* M. de Nemours lost his way in the forest. Enquiring which path he should take to find his way back, he learnt that he was close to Coulommiers. As soon as he heard the name, without reflecting on what he was doing and with no precise intention, he went off at full gallop in the direction that was pointed out to him. He found himself in the forest* and allowed himself to be guided at random by well-marked paths, guessing that they would lead him to the château. At the end of these paths he came across a pavilion, the lower part of which was occupied by a large room with a smaller room on either side. One of these looked out on a flower garden which was only separated from the forest by a fence; the second opened on to a broad avenue in the park. He went into the pavilion, and he would have stopped to admire its beauty had he not seen M. and Mme de Clèves coming down the avenue accompanied by a large number of servants. As he had not expected to find M. de Clèves there, having left him in the company of the King, his first instinct was to hide: he entered the side room next to the flower garden, intending to escape through a door that was open in the direction of the forest. But, seeing that Mme de Clèves and her husband had sat down in the pavilion and that their servants were still in the park and could not come his way without passing through the room where M. and Mme de Clèves were sitting, he was unable to deny himself the pleasure of seeing the princess, nor to resist the temptation of listening to her conversation with a husband who caused him more jealousy than any of his other rivals.

He heard M. de Clèves saying to his wife:*

'But why will you not come back to Paris? What makes you stay in the country? For some time now you have had a taste for solitude that astonishes and distresses me because it keeps us apart. I even find you more melancholy than usual and I am afraid something may be troubling you.'

'I have nothing disagreeable on my mind,' she replied, looking embarrassed; 'but the court is so crowded and noisy and there are always so many people in your house that body and mind inevitably become tired and one longs for rest and tranquillity.'

'Rest and tranquillity', he rejoined, 'are hardly what a woman of your age needs most: the life you lead at home and at court is not such as to be unduly burdensome to you. My fear would rather be that it suited you to be separated from me.'

'It would be most unjust of you to think that,' she replied with an ever-increasing air of embarrassment; 'but I implore you to leave me here. If you could yourself remain, I should be delighted, provided that you remained alone, and that you would agree to dispense with the company of all those countless people who seem never to leave your side.'

'Ah! Madame,' cried M. de Clèves, 'I see from your expression and your words that you have reasons for wishing to be alone of which I am unaware. I beg you to tell me what they are.'

He continued for some time to press her for her reasons, but without success. After she had resisted in a way that made her husband ever more curious, she fell into a profound silence, her eyes cast down. Then she suddenly looked up at him and said:

'Do not force me to confess something I am not strong enough to confess, although the thought has occurred to me on more than one occasion. Only consider that it is not prudent for a woman of my age, a woman whose behaviour is in her own hands,* to remain exposed in the midst of the court.'

'What ideas are you putting into my mind, Madame!' cried M. de Clèves. 'I should not dare tell you for fear of offending you.'

Mme de Clèves made no reply, and her silence finally confirmed her husband's suspicions.

'You say nothing,' he continued, 'which is as much as to say that I am not mistaken.'

'Well then, Monsieur,' she replied, throwing herself at his feet, 'I will make you a confession which no woman has ever made to her husband. Only the innocence of my conduct and my intentions gives me the strength to do it. It is true that I have my reasons for staying away from court and that I wish to avoid the dangers to which women of my age sometimes find themselves exposed. I have never shown any sign of weakness and I should have no fear of showing any if you gave me the liberty of withdrawing from the court, or if I still had Mme de Chartres to guide my conduct. However dangerous the decision I am taking now, I take it gladly if it ensures that I remain worthy to be your wife. I ask you a thousand pardons if I have feelings which are displeasing to you: at least I shall never displease you by my actions. Reflect that, in order to do what I am doing, it is necessary to have a greater affection and esteem for one's husband than any wife has ever had before. Be my guide, have pity on me, and continue to love me if you can.'

Throughout this speech, M. de Clèves sat with his head in his hands. He was quite beside himself: it had not even occurred to him to raise his wife to her feet. When she stopped speaking, when he cast his eyes on her and saw her at his feet, her face covered in tears, wonderfully beautiful, he thought he would die of grief. Raising her up and embracing her, he said:

'Have pity on me yourself, Madame, for I deserve it; and forgive me if, in the first moments of a distress as violent as mine is, I do not respond to your gesture as I ought. No woman has ever been as worthy of esteem and admiration as you are in my eyes; yet I feel I am the unhappiest man in the world. I loved you passionately from the very first moment I saw you; neither your refusals nor your eventual capitulation have been able to extinguish my passion; it continues unabated. I have never been able to inspire love in you, and I see that you are afraid of loving another man. Who is he, then, Madame, this happy man who can make you thus afraid? How long have you been attracted to him? What has he done to attract you? What means has he devised to find the way to your heart? I consoled myself in some measure for not having moved you by the thought that you could never be moved; now another man succeeds where I failed. I am jealous both as a husband and as a lover;* yet it is impossible to feel a husband's jealousy after a gesture such as yours. Your behaviour is too noble for me not to be entirely reassured; it consoles me even in my role as lover. Your sincerity, your trust in me, are of infinite worth: you respect me enough to believe that I shall not abuse your confidence. You are right, Madame: I shall not abuse it and I shall not love you any the less because of it. You have made me unhappy by the greatest proof of fidelity that a woman has ever given her husband. But, Madame, you must now finish your story and tell me who it is that you wish to avoid.'

'I beg you not to ask me that,' she replied. 'I have made up my mind not to tell you, and I believe that prudence forbids me to name him.'

'Have no fear, Madame,' pursued M. de Clèves. 'I know the world too well to be unaware that respect for the husband does not prevent a man from being in love with the wife. One should hate such a man, not complain about him. So, once again, Madame, I implore you to tell me what I desire to know.'

'It will be useless for you to press me any further,' she replied; 'I have the strength to keep to myself what I believe I must not reveal. It was not weakness that made me confess:* it needs more courage to admit such a truth than to seek to hide it.'

No word of this conversation was lost on M. de Nemours, and what Mme de Clèves had said made him scarcely less jealous than her husband. He was so desperately in love with her that he believed everyone else had the same feelings. It was certainly true that he had several rivals, but he imagined still more, and he became quite distraught wondering which of them Mme de Clèves was referring to. He had often thought that he was not displeasing to her, yet he had come to this conclusion on evidence that now seemed to him slight in the extreme: he could not imagine he had succeeded in inspiring a passion violent enough to prompt her to seek such an extraordinary remedy. He was so carried away that he could scarcely grasp what he was witnessing, and he could not forgive M. de Clèves for not pressing his wife hard enough to divulge the name she was hiding.

M. de Clèves was none the less making every effort to find out. After he had questioned her in vain, she replied:

'It seems to me that my sincerity should be enough for you. Ask for nothing more and do not give me cause to repent of what I have just done. Be content with this assurance, that none of my actions has revealed my feelings and that no one has ever said anything to me that could offend me.'

'Ah! Madame,' M. de Clèves burst out, 'I cannot believe you.* I remember how embarrassed you were the day your portrait was lost. You made a present of it, Madame, you made a present of that portrait, which was so dear to me and which was my legitimate property. You were unable to hide your feelings; you are in love, he knows it; only your virtue has preserved you, up to now, from the consequences.'

'Is it possible', cried the princess, 'that you can think there was any duplicity in a confession such as mine, which nothing compelled me to make? Do not doubt my words: I am paying a high enough price for the trust I ask of you. Please believe, I implore you, that I did not give my portrait away. It is true that I saw someone take it, but I did not want to let it be seen that I had, lest I expose myself to the risk of having things said to me that no one yet has dared to say.'

'By what means then did this man show you that he loved you,' M. de Clèves pursued, 'and what tokens has he given you of his passion?'

'Spare me the pain', she replied, 'of repeating to you details which make me ashamed to have noticed them and which have brought my weakness home to me all too clearly.'

'You are right, Madame,' he said. 'I am unjust. Refuse to answer every time I ask you such things, but do not be offended if I ask them.'

At this moment several of their servants, who had re-

mained outside in the avenues, came to inform M. de Clèves
that a gentleman was looking for him, sent by the King, to
order him to be back in Paris that evening. M. de Clèves
was obliged to leave. He was able to say nothing further to
his wife except that he begged her to join him the next day;
he also urged her to believe that, distressed as he was, he
felt a tenderness and esteem for her which ought to give her
some comfort.

When the prince had left, when Mme de Clèves found
herself alone and contemplated what she had just done, she
was so horrified that she could hardly imagine it was true. It
seemed to her that she had deprived herself of the love and
esteem of her husband and that she had dug for herself a
deep pit from which she would never escape. She asked
herself why she had done something so perilous, and she
concluded that she had embarked on it almost without
thinking. The singular nature of such a confession, for
which she could find no parallel, brought home to her all
the risks it entailed.

Yet when she went on to consider that this remedy,
violent as it might be, was the only one that could protect
her against M. de Nemours, she decided that she ought to
have no regrets and that she had not taken too great a risk.
She spent the whole night tormented by uncertainty, confusion, and fear, but in the end her mind recovered its
tranquillity. She even felt a certain sweetness in the idea
that she had given such a token of fidelity to a husband who
deserved it so much, who regarded her with such affection
and esteem, and who had just given her further proof of
these feelings by the manner in which he had received her
confession.

Meanwhile, M. de Nemours had left the place where he
had overheard a conversation that moved him so profoundly,
and had wandered far into the forest. What Mme de Clèves
had said about her portrait had brought him back to life by
revealing to him that he was the man she loved. At first, he
abandoned himself to this happy thought; but it did not last
long when he reflected on the fact that the very thing which
had told him he had touched Mme de Clèves's heart ought

also to persuade him that he would never be offered any sign of her feelings and that it was impossible to obtain the favours of a woman who had recourse to such an unprecedented remedy. None the less, he felt a marked pleasure at having reduced her to this extremity. It flattered his pride that he had inspired love in a woman so different from all others of her sex. In short, he was at once deliriously happy and unspeakably miserable. Night caught him unawares in the forest, and he had great difficulty in finding his way back to Mme de Mercœur's house. He arrived there at dawn. He found it quite awkward to give an account of what had detained him; he extricated himself as well as he could and returned to Paris that same day with the Vidame.

M. de Nemours was so preoccupied with his passion and so surprised by what he had heard that he fell into an error of judgement* which is common enough: he talked about his personal feelings in general terms and told his own story under assumed names. Once back in Paris, he turned every conversation towards love and spoke extravagantly of the pleasure of being in love with a woman worthy of being loved. He talked of the strange effects of passion and finally, unable to keep to himself his astonishment at Mme de Clèves's action, he recounted it to the Vidame. He neither named the person nor said to the Vidame that he himself was involved in any way, but he told the story with such warmth and such a tone of wonderment that the Vidame had no difficulty in suspecting that it concerned Nemours. He urged him most pressingly to confess that it was so. He told him that he had long known he was violently in love; it was unjust, he said, to hide it from a man who had entrusted him with the greatest secret of his life. M. de Nemours was too much in love to confess; he had always hidden his feelings from the Vidame, although he was his closest friend at court. He replied that one of his friends had told him this story and had made him promise not to speak of it; he implored the Vidame also to keep the secret. The Vidame assured him that he would say nothing; yet M. de Nemours regretted having told him so much.

Meanwhile, M. de Clèves had gone to visit the King. A

mortal sorrow pierced his heart through and through. Never had a husband been so violently in love with his wife nor held her in such high regard. What he had discovered did not lessen his esteem; rather, it gave him a new kind of respect for her. What most occupied his mind was the desire to guess who it was who had been able to win her love. M. de Nemours occurred to him at once, since he was the most attractive man at court; also the Chevalier de Guise and the Maréchal de Saint-André, both of whom had paid court to her and still surrounded her with attentions. Thus he concluded that it must be one of these three. He arrived at the Louvre and the King led him into his private room to tell him he had been chosen to escort Madame the King's daughter to Spain.* It was his belief, he said, that no one would perform this duty better than he, and no one, in addition, would be such a credit to France as Mme de Clèves. M. de Clèves accepted the honour this choice conferred on him as he was bound to, and even saw it as a means of taking his wife away from court without any change in her conduct being apparent. None the less, the date of their departure was still too far removed for this to provide a remedy for the predicament he was in. He wrote to Mme de Clèves instantly to inform her of what the King had just told him, adding that he absolutely insisted that she return to Paris. She came as he commanded; when they met, they were both overcome by an extraordinary sadness.

M. de Clèves's words were those of the most perfect gentleman in the world, the man most worthy of what she had done.

'I have no anxiety with regard to your conduct,' he said to her; 'you are stronger and more virtuous than you think. I am also not tormented by fears of the future, only by the knowledge that you have feelings for another man that I have not been able to inspire in you.'

'I do not know what to say,' she said; 'just to speak of it makes me die of shame. Spare me, I implore you, a conversation that hurts me so cruelly; dispose of my conduct; ensure that I never see anyone. That is all I ask. But please allow me never again to speak to you of something that makes me appear so unworthy of you and that I find so unworthy of myself.'

'You are right, Madame,' he replied; 'I am abusing your kindness and trust; but please have some compassion, too, for the state you have put me in, and remember that, despite everything you have told me, you are hiding a name that arouses in me a curiosity I cannot live with. Even so, I do not ask you to satisfy it; but I cannot prevent myself from telling you my supposition: the man whom I must envy is either the Maréchal de Saint-André, the Duc de Nemours, or the Chevalier de Guise.'

'I shall not reply,' she said with a blush, 'and I shall make sure that my answers never give you grounds for increasing or diminishing your suspicions; but if you attempt to resolve them by observing me, you will make me so embarrassed that everyone will notice. In God's name,' she continued, 'please allow me, on the pretext of some illness or other, to see no one.'

'No, Madame,' he replied; 'people would soon realize that it was a mere pretence; furthermore, I wish to place my trust in no one but you: that is the path my heart tells me to take, and reason too. I know that, with your character, I give you stricter limits in leaving you your liberty than I myself could possibly prescribe.'

M. de Clèves was not mistaken: the trust he displayed towards his wife greatly strengthened her against M. de Nemours and had the result that she regulated her conduct with greater austerity than any constraint could have done. And so she went to the Louvre and called on the Reine Dauphine as was her habit; but she avoided M. de Nemours's presence and his gaze with such care that she deprived him of almost all the joy he took in believing himself to be loved by her. He saw nothing in her actions, indeed, that did not persuade him of the contrary. He was no longer certain whether what he had heard was not a dream, so implausible did it seem to him. The only thing that assured him that he had not been mistaken was Mme de Clèves's extreme sadness, hard as she tried to conceal it: indulgent words and glances would not, perhaps, have increased M. de Nemours's love as effectively as this austere conduct.

One evening when M. and Mme de Clèves were in the Queen's apartments, someone said there was a rumour that the King was going to appoint another court nobleman to escort Madame to Spain, adding that the choice would perhaps fall on either the Chevalier de Guise or the Maréchal de Saint-André. M. de Clèves was watching his wife at that moment, and he noticed that she was not moved by the mention of these two names, nor by the proposal that they might make the journey with her. He therefore came to the conclusion that neither was the man whose presence she feared and, wishing to clear up his suspicions, he went into the Queen's private room, where the King was. After staying there a while, he came back to his wife's side and said to her quietly that he had just heard it was to be M. de Nemours who would go with them to Spain.

The name of M. de Nemours and the prospect of being exposed to the danger of seeing him every day during a long journey, in the presence of her husband, disturbed Mme de Clèves so deeply that she could not conceal her feelings. In an attempt to explain them away, she replied:

'The choice is a disagreeable one for you. He will share all the honours. It seems to me that you should try to have someone else chosen.'

'It is not the desire for glory, Madame,' pursued M. de Clèves, 'that makes you fear the prospect of M. de Nemours's company. The distress you feel comes from a different source. It tells me what I should have learnt from any other woman by the joy she felt. But have no fear. What I told you is not the truth: I invented it in order to be certain of something of which I was already all too convinced.'

On these words, he went out, not wishing to increase by his presence his wife's extreme confusion.

M. de Nemours came in at that moment and immediately noticed the state Mme de Clèves was in. He approached her and quietly told her that he had too much respect for her to dare ask why she was more pensive than usual. At the sound of M. de Nemours's voice, she came to herself. Looking at him without hearing what he had just said, still full of her own thoughts and the fear that her husband might see them together, she cried:

'In God's name, leave me in peace!'

'Alas, Madame!' he replied. 'I do little but leave you in peace. What grounds have you for complaint? I dare not speak to you, I dare not even look at you; I tremble when I come near you. What have I done to deserve that remark, and what makes you suggest that I have anything to do with the distress I see you in?'

Mme de Clèves was sorry indeed that she had given M. de Nemours cause to speak more openly than he had ever done before. She left him without replying and returned home in a state of the utmost mental agitation. Her husband noticed at once how much more confused and embarrassed she now was. He saw that she was afraid he might speak to her of what had happened. She had gone into a private room, and he followed her there.

'Do not avoid me, Madame,' he said; 'I shall say nothing disagreeable to you, and I beg you to forgive me for having taken you by surprise just now. I am sufficiently punished for that by what I found out. M. de Nemours was of all men the one I most feared. I see the danger into which you have fallen; try to master your feelings for your own sake and even, if possible, for mine. I do not ask you this as a husband but as a man whose happiness depends on you and who loves you more passionately, more tenderly, more violently than the man your heart prefers.'

M. de Clèves broke down as he uttered these last words and could hardly bring them out. His wife was profoundly touched: she burst into tears and embraced him with such tenderness and sorrow that his own state was soon little different from hers. They remained for some time in silence and parted without having the strength to speak to one another again.

The preparations for Madame's wedding were now complete. The Duc d'Albe arrived to marry her* for the King of Spain. He was received with all the pomp and

ceremony imaginable on an occasion like this. To meet
him, the King sent the Prince de Condé, the Cardinal de
Lorraine and the Cardinal de Guise, the Ducs de Lorraine,
de Ferrare, d'Aumale, de Bouillon, de Guise, and de
Nemours. They were accompanied by a number of gentlemen and a host of pages wearing their liveries. The King
himself awaited the Duc d'Albe at the first gate of the
Louvre with two hundred gentlemen-in-waiting led by the
Connétable. When the Duc d'Albe met the King, he made
as if to embrace his knees,* but the King prevented him and
made him walk at his side until they arrived in the apartments of the Queen and of Madame, to whom the Duc
d'Albe presented a magnificent gift on behalf of his master.
He then went to the apartments of Mme Marguerite, the
King's sister, to pay her M. de Savoie's compliments and
to assure her that he would arrive in a few days. Great
assemblies were held at the Louvre to show off the court
beauties to the Duc d'Albe and to the Prince d'Orange, who
had accompanied him.

Mme de Clèves did not dare be absent, much as she
desired to be, for fear of displeasing her husband, who
ordered her unconditionally to be there. What made the
decision a great deal easier was the absence of M. de
Nemours. He had gone to meet M. de Savoie and, after his
arrival, was obliged to stay almost constantly by his side to
assist him with everything that had to do with his wedding
ceremony. The consequence was that Mme de Clèves met
M. de Nemours less often than usual, and this gave her
something resembling peace of mind.

The Vidame de Chartres had not forgotten his conversation with M. de Nemours. The idea had remained with
him that the tale Nemours had told him was his own, and he
observed him so closely that he might easily have fathomed
the truth, had not the arrival of the Duc d'Albe and M. de
Savoie created a change of climate at court and a general
distraction that prevented him from seeing the signs that
might have enlightened him. His curiosity, or rather the
natural inclination to tell everything one knows to one's
beloved, made him repeat to Mme de Martigues the extra-

ordinary behaviour of the woman who had confessed to her husband her passion for another man. He assured her that M. de Nemours was the man who had inspired this violent passion and he begged her to help him observe Nemours. Mme de Martigues was very glad to hear what the Vidame told her; she had always been aware of Mme la Dauphine's curiosity about everything concerning M. de Nemours, and this made her still more anxious to get to the truth of the matter.

Only a few days before the one chosen for the wedding ceremony, the Reine Dauphine was giving a supper party for the King and the Duchesse de Valentinois. Mme de Clèves had been preoccupied with her toilet and set out for the Louvre later than usual. On her way, she met a gentleman whom Mme la Dauphine had sent to fetch her. As she entered the room, the Reine Dauphine, who was on her bed, called out that she was waiting impatiently for her.

'I hardly think, Madame,' she replied, 'that I need thank you for your impatience: it is doubtless caused by something other than the desire to see me.'

'You are right,' said the Reine Dauphine; 'nevertheless you will be grateful, for I am going to tell you a story that I am certain you will be very glad to hear.'

Mme de Clèves knelt down beside her bed; fortunately for her, her face was in shadow.

'You know', the Reine Dauphine began, 'how much we all wanted to guess what caused the change we have seen in M. de Nemours. I think I know the answer, and it is something that will surprise you. He is desperately in love and much loved in return by one of the most beautiful women at court.'

Mme de Clèves could not apply these words to herself since she did not believe that anyone knew she loved Nemours; it is easy to imagine how painful they were to her.

'I see nothing surprising in that,' she replied, 'for a man of M. de Nemours's age and as handsome as he is.'

'No, indeed, that isn't the surprising part,' continued Mme la Dauphine. 'It is that this woman who loves M. de

Nemours has never given him any sign of her love and that her fear of not being able to remain always in control of her passion has made her confess it to her husband so that he would take her away from court. What is more, M. de Nemours himself is the source of this story.'

If Mme de Clèves had at first been hurt by the thought that she played no part in the story, Mme la Dauphine's last words brought her close to despair, for she now saw that her part was all too evident. She was unable to reply; she remained kneeling with her head bowed down on the bed while the Reine Dauphine continued to speak, so full of what she was saying that she was unaware of Mme de Clèves's confusion. When Mme de Clèves had recovered somewhat, she said:

'The story hardly sounds plausible to me, Madame; I should dearly like to know who you got it from.'

'From Mme de Martigues, who heard it from the Vidame de Chartres,' replied Mme la Dauphine. 'As you are aware, he is in love with her; he told it her as a secret, and he got it from the Duc de Nemours himself. It is true that M. de Nemours did not tell him the name of the lady and did not even admit that he was the man she loved; but the Vidame de Chartres is quite certain of it.'

As the Reine Dauphine finished speaking, someone came up to the bed. Mme de Clèves's position prevented her from seeing who it was; but she did not remain ignorant for long, for Mme la Dauphine cried out in delight and astonishment:

'Here he is himself: let us ask him for the truth.'

Without turning to face him, Mme de Clèves recognized that it was indeed the Duc de Nemours. She made a hasty movement towards Mme la Dauphine and whispered to her that she must at all costs not speak to him about the story. He had confided it to the Vidame de Chartres, she said, and to make it public might easily lead to a quarrel between them. Mme la Dauphine replied with a laugh that she was being too cautious and turned towards M. de Nemours. He was finely dressed for the gathering that evening; with the charm that came so naturally to him, he said:

'I think I may without temerity guess that you were

speaking of me when I came in; you wanted to ask me something, but Mme de Clèves is against it.'

'That is true,' replied Mme la Dauphine; 'but I am not going to be as indulgent to her as I usually am. I want to know from your lips whether a story I have heard is true: are you not the man who is in love with and loved by a woman at court who takes care to hide her passion from you but has confessed it to her husband?'

Mme de Clèves's confusion and embarrassment were greater than it is possible to imagine: if death had come to her rescue at that moment, she would have greeted it with joy. But M. de Nemours was even more disconcerted, if that is possible. He had reason to believe that Mme la Dauphine's feelings for him were far from hostile; to hear what she had just said in the presence of Mme de Clèves, who was the person at court whom she most trusted and who most trusted her, filled his mind with such a confused mixture of strange thoughts that he was unable to control his expression. Seeing the awkward position he had put Mme de Clèves in and realizing that he had given her good reason to detest him, he was overcome by shock and could not reply. Mme la Dauphine saw his deep embarrassment and said to Mme de Clèves:

'Look at him, look at him, and judge for yourself whether or not that story is his own.'

However, M. de Nemours, recovering from his initial confusion and seeing how important it was to find a way out of this dangerous situation, succeeded at a stroke in gathering his wits and mastering his expression.

'I confess, Madame,' he said, 'that it would be difficult to be more astonished and distressed than I am that the Vidame de Chartres has betrayed my trust by divulging the story of one of my friends which I had told him as a secret. I shall be able to take my revenge,' he continued, smiling so calmly that Mme la Dauphine's suspicions were all but set at rest; 'he has told me in confidence various things that are of no small importance. But I have no idea, Madame, why you do me the honour of drawing me into this story. The Vidame cannot say that it has anything to do with me, since

I told him the contrary. I may reasonably have the reputation of being a man in love, but I do not think, Madame, that you can possibly regard me as a man whose love is requited.'

M. de Nemours was very glad to be able to say something to Mme la Dauphine that had some connection with his behaviour towards her in the past: he hoped in this way to distract her mind from other thoughts. She indeed believed she had taken his point; but, without replying directly, she continued to tease him about his embarrassment.

'I was upset, Madame,' he replied, 'on behalf of my friend, and troubled by the reproaches he might justly heap upon me for repeating something that is dearer to him than life itself. However, he only told me part of the secret, and he never named the person he loves. I only know that there is no one more deeply in love and more worthy of pity.'

'Is he, do you think, so worthy of pity,' rejoined Mme la Dauphine, 'seeing that his love is requited?'

'Do you really believe it is, Madame?' he said. 'Could a woman whose passion was genuine reveal it to her husband? She is doubtless ignorant of love, and merely has some slight feeling of gratitude to him for his attachment to her. My friend cannot flatter himself with any hopes; and yet, unhappy as he is, he considers himself happy to have at least made her afraid of falling in love with him, and he would not exchange his state with the happiest lover in the world.'

'Your friend's passion is an easy one to satisfy,' said Mme la Dauphine; 'I am beginning to be convinced that you cannot be talking about yourself, and it would take little to make me share Mme de Clèves's view that the story must be a fiction.'

'That is indeed my view,' rejoined Mme de Clèves, who had not spoken so far; 'and even if it were possible that the story could be true, how could anyone ever have come to know of it? It is hardly likely that a woman capable of something so extraordinary would be weak enough to talk about it; to all appearances, her husband would not have talked about it either, unless he was wholly unworthy of the gesture she had made.'

M. de Nemours, who saw that Mme de Clèves was be-

ginning to harbour suspicions towards her husband, was
very glad to confirm them. He knew that M. de Clèves was
his most dangerous rival and the hardest to eliminate.

'Jealousy,' he replied, 'and curiosity to know more perhaps
than he has been told, can make a husband commit many an
imprudence.'

Mme de Clèves had reached the extreme limits of her
strength and courage and could sustain the conversation no
longer. She was about to say that she felt unwell when,
happily for her, the Duchesse de Valentinois came in and
told Mme la Dauphine that the King was about to arrive.
The Reine Dauphine went into her private room to dress.
M. de Nemours approached Mme de Clèves as she made
to follow her.

'I would give my life, Madame,' he said, 'to speak to you
for a moment; but of all the things I might say, I see none
more important than to beg you to believe that, if I just now
said something which Mme la Dauphine might apply to
herself, I did so for reasons that have nothing to do with
her.'

Mme de Clèves gave no sign that she had heard M. de
Nemours. She left him without looking at him and began to
follow the King, who had just come in. A great many people
were present: in the crush, she tripped on her dress and
stumbled. She made use of this pretext to leave a place
where she no longer had the strength to stay and, pretending
she could not stand unaided, went home.

M. de Clèves came to the Louvre and was astonished not
to find his wife there. He was told about her accident and
went home at once to see how she was. He found her in bed
and soon discovered that her injury was only slight. When
he had been with her a little while, he was surprised to
observe that she was overcome by sadness.

'What is wrong, Madame?' he asked. 'It seems to me
that the pain you complain of is not the only one you are
suffering from.'

'I could not be more sorely afflicted,' she replied. 'How
have you used the extraordinary, or rather the foolish, trust
that I placed in you? Did I not deserve that you should keep

my secret? Even if I did not deserve it, was it not in your own interests to do so? Was it necessary for you to be so curious to discover a name which I must not tell you, that you confided in someone in an attempt to find it out? It can only be curiosity that made you commit such a cruel imprudence. The consequences are as appalling as they could possibly be. The story is out: someone has just repeated it to me, without knowing that I was the person it most concerned.'

'What are you saying, Madame?' he cried. 'You accuse me of having repeated what happened between the two of us, and you tell me the story is known? I refuse to defend myself against the charge of having passed it on: you cannot possibly believe that. You must doubtless have applied to yourself something that was said about another woman.'

'No, no, Monsieur,' she pursued; 'there could be no other story like mine in the world, no other woman capable of doing such a thing! Chance cannot have made someone invent it; no one has ever imagined it, the thought has never come into anyone's head but mine. Mme la Dauphine has just told me the full story; she got it from the Vidame de Chartres who got it from M. de Nemours.'

'M. de Nemours!' cried M. de Clèves, with a gesture of wild despair. 'What! M. de Nemours knows that you love him, and that I know?'

'You always seem to single out M. de Nemours,' she replied. 'I have told you that I would never confirm or deny your suspicions. I have no idea whether M. de Nemours is aware of the part I played in the story, or of the part you attribute to him; but he repeated it to the Vidame de Chartres, telling him that he had got it from one of his friends, who had not named the person concerned. This friend of M. de Nemours must be a friend of yours, and you must have confided in him in an attempt to find out the truth.'

'Is there any friend in the world to whom one would want to tell such a secret?' returned M. de Clèves. 'Who would wish to set his suspicions at rest at the cost of revealing to someone else what he would like to be able to hide from himself? It is rather for you, Madame, to ask yourself whom you have told. It is more likely that the secret has been let out by you than by me. You were unable to bear on your own the terrible predicament in which you found yourself, and you sought the relief of telling your woes to some confidante who has betrayed you.'

'Would you destroy me utterly?' she cried. 'Can you be harsh enough to accuse me of a fault you yourself have committed? Can you possibly suspect me of it? Since I was capable of speaking to you, could I be capable of speaking to anyone else?'

The confession Mme de Clèves had made to her husband was so convincing a proof of her sincerity and she so forcefully denied having confided in anyone that M. de Clèves did not know what to think. On the other hand, he was quite sure he had repeated nothing; it was a story that could never have been guessed; yet it was known, therefore it must have been revealed by one or other of them. What, however, caused him the sharpest pain was to know that the secret was in the hands of someone else and that it would apparently soon be made public.

Mme de Clèves was thinking much the same things: she found it equally impossible to believe that her husband had spoken and that he had not spoken. M. de Nemours's observation that curiosity can lead a husband to commit imprudences seemed to her to fit M. de Clèves's position so exactly that she could not believe the telling of the story to be a coincidence; the plausibility of this explanation inclined her to believe that M. de Clèves had abused her confidence in him. They were both so preoccupied with their own thoughts that they fell into a long silence, from which they only emerged to repeat the things they had already said several times before. Their hearts and minds remained more deeply estranged and more grievously altered than they had ever been.

It is easy to imagine in what state they passed the night. All M. de Clèves's fortitude had been exhausted by having to endure the misery of seeing a wife whom he adored in love with another man. His courage was at an end; it even seemed to him that none was required of him in an affair where his honour and self-esteem were so deeply wounded. He no longer knew what to think of his wife; he no longer saw how he should require her to behave, nor how he should behave himself: he saw nothing but precipices and chasms on every side. Finally, after a long period of agitation and uncertainty, realizing that he would soon have to leave for Spain, he decided to do nothing that might increase suspicions or allow more to be known of his unhappy state. He went to see Mme de Clèves and told her that what was important was not to establish which of them had failed to keep the secret, but rather to make people think that the story they had been told was a fiction which had nothing to do with her. It was up to her, he said, to convince M. de Nemours and everyone else of this: she need only treat him with the coldness and severity that it was her duty to adopt towards a man who showed her that he loved her; in this way, she would easily stop him believing that she had any feelings for him. Thus, he concluded, there was no reason to be distressed by what M. de Nemours might have thought: if in future she gave no sign of weakness, all his suppositions would easily be destroyed. Above all, it was essential for her to go to the Louvre and attend court functions as usual.

Having said this, M. de Clèves left his wife without waiting for an answer. She found a good deal of sense in everything he had said, and she was so angry with M. de Nemours that she thought it would also be easy to put his suggestions into effect, except that she saw some difficulty in appearing in public at all the wedding ceremonies with composed features and a mind at ease. None the less, as she had been chosen in preference to several other princesses to carry Mme la Dauphine's train, there was no way of withdrawing without causing people to gossip and question her motives. She resolved, then, to make every effort to suppress her feelings; but she allowed herself the rest of the day to prepare for the ordeal and to give free rein to the turmoil of her thoughts. She shut herself away, alone, in her private room. Of all her troubles, the one that presented itself most violently to her mind was that she had reason to complain of

M. de Nemours's behaviour and that she could find no way
of exonerating him.* She could not doubt that he had told
the story to the Vidame de Chartres: he had confessed as
much. Nor could she doubt, given the way in which he had
spoken, that he knew it concerned her. How could such a
grave imprudence be excused? What had become of the
extreme discretion that had so touched her in Nemours?

'He was discreet', she said to herself, 'while he thought
he had nothing to hope for; but the prospect of possible
success, however uncertain, put an end to his discretion. He
was not capable of imagining that his love was returned
without wanting to tell other people about it. He told everything he could tell: I never confessed that he was the one I
loved, but he guessed it and let it be seen that he guessed. If
he had had certain proof, he would have acted in the same
way. I was wrong to believe that any man alive was capable
of hiding something that flattered his self-esteem. And yet it
is for this man, whom I believed so different from other
men, that I have become like other women, I who resembled
them so little. I have lost the love and esteem of a husband
with whom I ought to have been happy. I shall soon be
regarded publicly as a woman who has given way to a wild
and violent passion; he himself knows it already. Yet it was
in order to avoid these very misfortunes that I risked my
peace of mind and even my life!'

These bitter reflections were followed by a flood of tears;
but, crushed as she was by her sorrows, she knew in her
heart that she would have had the strength to bear them if
she had had no cause for complaint against M. de Nemours.

As for Nemours himself, his state was hardly more
tranquil. His indiscretion in speaking to the Vidame and
its cruel consequences threw him into a profound gloom.
Whenever he recalled the sight of Mme de Clèves's embarrassment, confusion, and distress, he was appalled. He
could not forgive himself for saying things to her about
the incident which, although in themselves witty enough
allusions to his love for her, now seemed to him coarse and
impolite, since they had conveyed to Mme de Clèves that he
knew the identity of the woman with the violent passion, and

that he also knew he was the object of that passion. The best he could have hoped for was a further conversation with her, but he could not help feeling that such a conversation was to be feared rather than desired.

'What could I say to her?' he cried to himself. 'Should I make plain to her once more what I have only too clearly let her know already? Shall I show her that I know she loves me, I who have never even dared tell her that I loved her? Shall I begin to speak openly to her of my passion, so that she sees me as a man whom hope has made bold? Can I even think of approaching her? Dare I give her the embarrassment of being forced to set eyes on me? How could I justify my behaviour? I have no excuse; I am unworthy that she should look favourably on me and I cannot expect that she ever will. Through my own fault, I have only given her more effective arms with which to protect herself against me than any she herself sought, and might have sought in vain. My indiscretion has cost me the proud and happy claim to be loved by a woman more worthy of love and esteem than any other. And yet, if I had lost that good fortune without causing her to suffer, without inflicting on her such mortal distress, it would be a consolation: I am more sensible now of the harm I have done her than of the harm I have done myself in her eyes.'

M. de Nemours long continued to torment himself, going over these same thoughts again and again. The desire to speak to Mme de Clèves returned incessantly to his mind. He reflected on ways of arranging it, he thought of writing to her; but he finally concluded that, after the fault he had committed, and taking her character into account, the best he could do would be to show his deep respect by a sorrowful silence, even to let her see that he dared not appear in her presence, and to await whatever time, chance, and her inclination for him might do in his favour. He resolved, too, not to reproach the Vidame de Chartres for having betrayed him, lest he should reinforce his suspicions.

Preparations for Madame's betrothal, which was to take place the next day, and for the wedding on the day after that, so preoccupied the court that Mme de Clèves and M. de

Nemours had no difficulty in hiding their unhappiness and confusion from the public gaze. Even Mme la Dauphine only spoke to Mme de Clèves in passing about the conversation they had had with M. de Nemours, and M. de Clèves made a point of not saying anything further to his wife about what had happened, with the result that she found her situation less embarrassing than she had imagined.

The betrothal took place at the Louvre. After the banquet and the ball, all the members of the royal house went to spend the night at the Bishop's Palace, as was the custom. In the morning, the Duc d'Albe, who always dressed simply on other occasions, put on a coat of cloth of gold interwoven with fiery red, yellow, and black, and covered in jewels, and wore a closed crown on his head. The Prince d'Orange, no less magnificently dressed, with his servants in livery, and all the Spaniards followed by theirs, came to fetch the Duc d'Albe from the Hôtel de Villeroi where he was lodged, and left, marching four by four, to make their way to the Bishop's Palace. As soon as he had arrived, a procession was formed and made its way to the church. The King escorted Madame, who was also wearing a closed crown; her train was carried by Mlles de Montpensier and de Longueville. The Queen came next, but without a crown. After her came the Reine Dauphine, Madame the King's sister, Mme de Lorraine, and the Queen of Navarre, their trains carried by princesses. All the maids of the Queens and princesses were magnificently dressed in the same colours as themselves, so that one could recognize whom the maids belonged to by the colour of their gowns. The procession mounted the stand which had been erected in the church and the wedding ceremonies were held. Then everyone returned to the Bishop's Palace to dine; at five o'clock, they left for the Palais de Justice where a banquet was to be held, to which the Parlement, the Crown Courts, and the Maison de Ville* were invited. The King, the Queens, the princes, and the princesses ate at the marble table in the great hall of the palace, the Duc d'Albe being seated next to the new Queen of Spain. The marble table was on a raised dais; at the bottom of the steps, on the King's right hand, was a table for the ambassadors, the archbishops, and the knights of the Order,* on the other side a table for the gentlemen of the Parlement.

The Duc de Guise, wearing a robe of gold frieze,* served the King as Chamberlain of the Household, M. le Prince de Condé as chief steward, and the Duc de Nemours as cupbearer.* After the tables had been cleared, the ball began. It was interrupted by ballets and by spectacular scenic effects.* Then the ball began afresh, until at last, after midnight, the King and the whole court returned to the Louvre. Unhappy as Mme de Clèves was, she none the less appeared incomparably beautiful to everyone present, and especially to M. de Nemours. He dared not speak to her, even though the general confusion of the ceremony gave him various opportunities; but such was the sorrowful expression he showed her and his respectful hesitation to come near that she no longer found him quite so guilty, although he had said nothing to exonerate himself. He adopted the same conduct on the following days, with the same effect on Mme de Clèves's heart.

The day of the tournament finally arrived. The Queens made their way to the galleries and stands which had been prepared for them. The four champions appeared at the end of the lists, accompanied by a large number of horses and attendants in livery: it was the most magnificent spectacle ever seen in France.

The King's only colours were white and black: he always wore them for Mme de Valentinois, who was a widow. M. de Ferrare and his retinue wore yellow and red; M. de Guise appeared in rose-pink and white: at first, no one could think why he wore those colours, but then someone recalled that they were the colours of a beauty whom he had loved before she was married and still loved, although he no longer dared to let her see it. M. de Nemours wore yellow and black,* no one could discover why. Mme de Clèves had no difficulty in guessing: she remembered having said in his presence that yellow was a colour she loved and that it vexed her to have fair hair because she could not wear it. Nemours believed he could appear in this colour without indiscretion, because as Mme de Clèves never wore it no one could suspect that it was hers.

The skill displayed by the four champions was incomparable. Although the King was the best horseman in the land, it was impossible to decide which of the four was superior. M. de Nemours's movements had such grace and elegance that ladies whose personal interest was less than Mme de Clèves's might easily have been led to give him the advantage. As soon as she saw him appear at the end of the lists, she was overcome by an extraordinary emotion, and each time he jousted, she found it hard to conceal her joy when he had successfully completed his course.

Towards evening, when almost all the events were over and everyone was on the point of leaving, the King decided, to the great ill fortune of the state, that he wanted to break one more lance. He sent a message ordering the Comte de Montgomery, who was an extremely accomplished horseman, to enter the lists. Montgomery begged the King to excuse him, citing all the reasons he could think of; but the King replied, almost angrily, that he absolutely insisted. The Queen sent a messenger to the King to ask him not to ride: he had performed so well, she said, that he ought to be content with his success, and she implored him to return to her side. He replied that it was for love of her that he was going to ride again, and he passed through the barrier.* She sent M. de Savoie to beg him once more to return, but to no avail. He ran his course; the lances broke, and a splinter from Montgomery's lance entered his eye and lodged there. He instantly fell from his horse; his squires and M. de Montmorency, one of the marshals, ran to assist him. They were dismayed to see him so badly wounded; but the King remained unmoved. He said that it was of no account, and that he forgave the Comte de Montgomery. It is easy to imagine what confusion and distress this fateful accident brought upon a day that seemed destined for joy. As soon as the King had been carried to his bed, the surgeons examined his wound. They found it to be very serious.

M. le Connétable remembered then the prophecy* that the King would be killed in single combat, and he had no doubt that it would be fulfilled.

The King of Spain, who was in Brussels at the time, heard of the accident and sent his doctor, who was a man of great reputation; but he judged that the King's case was hopeless.

A court so divided and so full of opposed interests could not but be in a state of extreme agitation with the prospect of such a great event; yet all these seething thoughts were kept hidden and everyone gave the appearance of being anxious only about the King's health. The Queens, the princes, and the princesses hardly left his antechamber.

Mme de Clèves knew that she could not avoid being present, that she would see M. de Nemours there, and that she would not be able to conceal from her husband the embarrassment she would feel. She was aware, too, that his mere presence would suffice to exonerate him in her eyes and ruin all her good resolutions. And so she decided to pretend to be ill. The court was too busy to pay attention to her conduct and find out whether her illness was genuine or false. Only her husband was in a position to know the truth, but she was not sorry that he should know. She therefore stayed at home, hardly thinking of the great change that was about to take place: her mind was full of thoughts of her own, and she was now free to give her undivided attention to these. Everyone was in the King's apartments. M. de Clèves came regularly to bring news of his condition. He continued to behave towards her as he had always done, except that, when they were alone, there was something a little colder and more constrained in his manner. He had not spoken to her again of what had taken place; she for her part had not had the strength to take up that particular subject again, nor had she even felt it to be appropriate.

M. de Nemours, who had expected to find a few moments to speak to Mme de Clèves, was most surprised and distressed not to have the pleasure even of seeing her. The King's wound proved so serious that, on the seventh day, the doctors gave him up for lost. The fortitude he showed on hearing that he must die was extraordinary, and all the more admirable because he was losing his life through such an unfortunate accident, in the prime of life, happy, adored by his subjects, and loved by a mistress whom he loved passionately. The day before he died, he had his sister, Madame, married to M. Savoie without any ceremony. It is easy to imagine the state the Duchesse de Valentinois was in. The Queen did not permit her to see the King and sent to ask her for his seals and the crown jewels, which she had in her keeping. Mme de Valentinois enquired whether the King was dead, and when the answer came that he was not, she replied:

'No one, then, can give me orders yet, and no one can oblige me to give back what he has entrusted to my keeping.'

As soon as he had breathed his last at the Château des Tournelles, the Duc de Ferrare, the Duc de Guise, and the Duc de Nemours escorted the Queen Mother, the King, and his Queen to the Louvre. M. de Nemours was accompanying the Queen Mother.* As they set off, she fell back a few steps and told her daughter-in-law the Queen that it was for her to go first; but it was easy to see that she made this gesture with more ill humour than courtesy.

PART IV

THE Cardinal de Lorraine* had gained absolute ascendancy over the mind of the Queen Mother.* The Vidame de Chartres no longer received any favours from her, but he was so much in love with Mme de Martigues and with his freedom that he was less conscious of what he had lost than he ought to have been. During the ten days of the King's illness, the Cardinal had had time to make his plans and persuade the Queen Mother to take measures that furthered them. Thus, as soon as the King was dead, she ordered the Connétable to remain at the Château des Tournelles, where the late King lay, and arrange the usual ceremonies. This duty kept him away from everything that was happening and removed his freedom of action. He sent a messenger to the King of Navarre asking him to come with all speed so that they could together oppose what he saw to be the inevitable rise to power of the Guise brothers. The Duc de Guise was placed in command of the army while the Cardinal de Lorraine was given control of the finances. The Duchesse de Valentinois was driven out of the court; the Cardinal de Tournon, a declared enemy of the Connétable, and the Chancelier Olivier, a declared enemy of the Duchesse de Valentinois, were brought back. In short, the court was completely transformed. The Duc de Guise adopted the same rank as the princes of the blood in carrying the King's mantle at the funeral ceremony; he and his brothers were entirely in control, not only because of the Cardinal's credit with the Queen Mother, but also because she believed she could remove them if they displeased her, whereas she could not remove the Connétable, who was supported by the princes of the blood.

When the mourning ceremonies were over, the Connétable came to the Louvre, where the King received him with the utmost coldness. He wanted to speak to him in private, but the King called the Guise brothers and told him in their presence that he advised him to take a rest. The army and the finances were already in hand, he said; if he should ever need his advice, he would summon him. The Queen Mother received him still more coldly than the King; she even reproached him for having said to the late King that his children did not look like him. The King of Navarre arrived and was received no better. The Prince de Condé, who was less patient than his brother, complained publicly, but his complaints were of no avail: he was sent away from court on the pretext of a mission to Flanders to sign the ratification of the peace treaty. The King of Navarre was shown a forged letter from the King of Spain accusing him of having designs on his fortresses; he was made to feel that his own lands were under threat and was given every encouragement to go back to Béarn. The Queen Mother expedited his return by appointing him escort to Mme Elisabeth; she even made him leave in advance. Thus no one remained at court who was capable of counterbalancing the power of the house of Guise.

Although it was a blow to M. de Clèves to find that he was no longer to escort Mme Elisabeth, he could not complain, given the rank of the man who had been given preference over him. He regretted this mission less for the honour it would have brought him than as a means of removing his wife from court without it seeming that he wanted to remove her.

Only a few days after the death of the King, it was decided that the court should go to Reims for the coronation. As soon as this journey was mentioned, Mme de Clèves, who had continued to remain at home pretending to be ill, asked her husband to allow her not to accompany the court but rather to go away to Coulommiers: the fresh air, she said, would be good for her health. He replied that he had no desire to know whether it was really for the sake of her health that she was obliged to miss the coronation; he gave his consent none the less. This was easy for him, since he had already decided she should not go: although he had a high opinion of his wife's virtue, he was well aware that it would hardly be prudent for him to expose her any longer to the gaze of a man she loved.

M. de Nemours soon discovered that Mme de Clèves was not to accompany the court. He could not make up his mind to leave without seeing her and, on the eve of his departure, he called on her at as late an hour as decorum allowed in the hope of finding her alone. Fortune favoured his plan. As he entered the courtyard, he met Mme de Nevers and Mme de Martigues, who were leaving and who told him that she had been alone when they left her. He went up in a state of agitation and confusion which can only be compared with Mme de Clèves's own confusion when she was told that M. de Nemours had come to see her. Her fear that he might speak to her of his passion and that she might reply too favourably, the anxiety that his visit might cause her husband, the embarrassment of either reporting it to M. de Clèves or concealing it, all crowded at once into her mind; so great was her perplexity that she resolved to avoid the very thing she perhaps most desired in all the world. She sent one of her women to M. de Nemours, who was in her antechamber, to tell him that she had just been taken ill and that she was very sorry not to be able to accept the honour he wished to do her. How painful it was for him not to see Mme de Clèves, and not to see her because she did not wish him to see her! He was leaving the next day; there was nothing more now that he could expect from chance. He had not spoken to her since the conversation at Mme la Dauphine's, and he had reason to believe that his error in speaking to the Vidame had destroyed all his hopes. He was leaving, in short, in circumstances that could only sharpen a pain that was already hard enough to bear.

As soon as Mme de Clèves had somewhat recovered from the confusion into which she had been thrown by the thought of his visit, all the reasons why she had turned him away vanished; she even felt that she had committed an error, and if she had dared or if it had not been too late, she would have recalled him.

On leaving Mme de Clèves's house, Mme de Nevers and Mme de Martigues went to the Queen's apartments; M. de Clèves was there. The Queen asked them where they had been. They said they had come from Mme de Clèves's, where they had spent part of the evening together with a good many other people; when they had left, only M. de Nemours was there. These words, which seemed so innocent to them, were not so to M. de Clèves. Although he must have realized that M. de Nemours could often find opportunities for speaking to his wife, none the less the thought that he was with her now, alone, and that he was free to speak to her about his love, appeared to him at this moment as something so new and intolerable that jealousy blazed up in his heart more violently than ever before. It was impossible for him to remain in the company of the Queen, and he returned home, not even knowing why he was doing so or whether it was his intention to interrupt M. de Nemours's tête-à-tête. As soon as he came to his house, he looked to see if there were any signs which might indicate that Nemours was still there; he felt some relief when he saw that he had left, and the thought that he could not have remained long was sweet to him. He wondered whether it was perhaps not of M. de Nemours that he ought to be jealous, and although he did not doubt it, he made every effort to do so. Yet so many things were there to persuade him of it that he could not long remain in this comforting state of uncertainty. He went at once to his wife's room. For a while, he spoke to her about indifferent matters, but eventually he could not help asking her what she had done and whom she had seen. She told him. When he saw that she had not mentioned M. de Nemours, he asked her, trembling with anxiety, if she had seen no one else: he wanted to give her the opportunity to name Nemours and spare himself the pain of seeing her try to deceive him about it. As she had not seen him, she did not name him. Then M. de Clèves continued in a voice that betrayed his distress:

'And what about M. de Nemours? Did you not see him or have you forgotten him?'

'No,' she replied, 'I did not see him; I felt ill and sent one of my women to make my excuses to him.'

'So you only felt ill for his sake?' rejoined M. de Clèves. 'As you saw everyone else, why make an exception for M. de Nemours? Why is he not the same to you as other men? Why do you have to be afraid of the very sight of him? Why let him see that you are afraid? Why make him aware that you are exercising the power over him that his passion confers on you? Would you dare refuse to see him if you did not know very well that he can tell the difference between your affectation of severity and mere discourtesy? But why must you be so severe towards him? From a woman like you, Madame, everything but indifference is a favour.'

'However suspicious you may be of M. de Nemours,' said Mme de Clèves, 'I never thought you would be capable of reproaching me for not seeing him.'

'But I do reproach you, Madame,' he replied, 'and with good reason. Why not see him if he has said nothing to you? But it is clear, Madame: he has spoken to you. If the only sign of his passion had been his silence, it would not have made such a great impression on you. You were unable to tell me the whole truth, you hid the greater part of it; you even regretted the little you did confess to me and lacked the force to carry it through. I am unhappier than I thought, indeed I am the unhappiest man in the world. You are my wife, I love you as if you were my mistress; yet I am forced to recognize that you love another man, the most attractive man at court, who sees you every day and knows you love him. Ah!' he cried. 'I was capable of believing that you would overcome your passion for him. I must have lost my reason to believe such a thing.'

'Perhaps you were wrong', Mme de Clèves sadly replied, 'to approve of a gesture as extraordinary as mine; perhaps I was wrong to believe you would be fair to me.'

'Have no doubts on that score, Madame,' rejoined M. de Clèves; 'you were wrong. What you expected of me was as impossible as what I expected of you. How could you hope that I should remain capable of rational judgement? Had you forgotten, then, that I was desperately in love with you and that I was your husband? Even one of those conditions can drive a man to extremities: what might not both together be capable of? What indeed are they doing to me?' he continued. 'I have fallen prey to violent, shifting emotions which I cannot master. I no longer consider myself worthy of you; you no longer seem worthy of me. I adore you, I hate you, I offend you, I beg your forgiveness; I admire you, I am ashamed of my admiration. There is, in short, no last shred of tranquillity or reason in me. I cannot think how I have survived since you spoke to me at Coulommiers, or since the day you heard from Mme la Dauphine that your story was known. I am wholly unable to fathom how it was divulged, or what passed between M. de Nemours and you on the subject. You will never explain it to me, and I do not ask you to explain it. I ask you only to remember that you have made me the unhappiest of men.'

M. de Clèves went out of his wife's room after these words and left the next day without seeing her, but he wrote her a letter full of sorrow, courtesy, and kindness. The reply she wrote him was infinitely touching and abounded in assurances with regard to her conduct both in the past and in the future; as these assurances were founded on the truth and the feelings she expressed were genuine, the letter made its mark on M. de Clèves and brought him some degree of tranquillity. Furthermore, M. de Nemours was going to join the King just as he himself was, so that he had the relief of knowing that he would not be in the same place as Mme de Clèves.

Every time she spoke to her husband,* the passion he showed her, the courteous way he dealt with her, the friendly regard she felt for him, and what she owed him, all affected her deeply and partly effaced the image of M. de Nemours. But this effect lasted only a little while; then the image rapidly returned, more vivid and real than ever.

The first few days after he left, she was hardly aware of his absence; then she felt it cruelly. Since she had been in love with him, not a day had passed without her fearing or hoping to meet him, and she found it painful to think that chance could no longer bring them together.

She went away to Coulommiers, taking care to give instructions that a set of large paintings should go with her: these were copies she had had made from originals that Mme de Valentinois had commissioned for her fine house at Anet.* All of the noteworthy events that had taken place during the reign of the late King were represented in these paintings. One of them depicted the siege of Metz, with lifelike renderings of all those who had distinguished themselves there, including M. de Nemours: this was perhaps* what had made Mme de Clèves want to have the paintings.

Mme de Martigues, who had been unable to leave with the court, promised to come and spend a few days with her at Coulommiers. The fact that they both enjoyed the Queen's favour had not made them envious or wary of one another; they were friends, but did not tell each other about their intimate feelings. Mme de Clèves knew that Mme de Martigues loved the Vidame; but Mme de Martigues was not aware that Mme de Clèves loved M. de Nemours, nor that he loved her. Mme de Clèves was the dearer to Mme de Martigues because she was the niece of the Vidame, while Mme de Clèves was fond of her too as a woman who, like her, was passionately in love—in love, what was more, with the close friend of her own admirer.

Mme de Martigues came to Coulommiers as she had promised and found Mme de Clèves living a life of great solitude. She had even sought ways of isolating herself completely, spending her evenings in the gardens unaccompanied by her servants. She would go to the pavilion where M. de Nemours had overheard her, entering the little room which opened on to the garden. Her women and her servants remained in the other side room or in the central room,* and did not disturb her unless she called them. Mme de Martigues had never seen Coulommiers; she was astonished by its many beauties and especially by the charm of the pavilion. She and Mme de Clèves spent every evening there. Free of all other constraints, alone together at night in the most beautiful place imaginable, the two young women, each of whom hid in her heart a violent passion, talked endlessly; although they told each other no secrets, their conversations gave them great pleasure. Mme de Martigues would have found it difficult to leave Coulommiers had she not been obliged to leave it for a place where the Vidame happened to be. She left, then, to join the court, which was just then at Chambord.

After the coronation had been celebrated at Reims by the Cardinal de Lorraine, it was agreed in fact that the court should spend the rest of the summer at the recently built château of Chambord.* The Queen seemed delighted to see Mme de Martigues again; after giving her many tokens of her pleasure, she asked her for news of Mme de Clèves and what she was doing in the country. M. de Nemours and M. de Clèves were also with the Queen just then. Mme de Martigues, who had thought Coulommiers splendid, described all the beauties of the place, dwelling at length on the details of the forest pavilion and on the pleasure Mme de Clèves took in walking there alone until late at night. M. de Nemours, who knew the spot well enough to understand what she was saying, reflected that it might not be impossible for him to see Mme de Clèves there without being seen by anyone but her. He asked Mme de Martigues some questions to be more certain. M. de Clèves had watched him closely while Mme de Martigues was speaking and thought he saw what was going through his mind at that moment. The questions M. de Nemours asked further confirmed his impression, with the result that he had no doubt he was planning to go and see his wife. His suspicions were not mistaken. The plan took such a hold on M. de Nemours's mind that, after spending the night thinking about ways of carrying it out, he asked leave of the King the very next morning to go to Paris on some invented pretext.

M. de Clèves did not doubt what the purpose of this journey was, but he resolved to inform himself of his wife's conduct and not to remain in such a cruel state of uncertainty. He wanted to leave at the same time as M. de Nemours and to go there himself, in secret, to discover what the outcome of the journey would be, but he was afraid that his departure might seem unusual and that M. de Nemours would hear of it and change his plans. He therefore resolved to confide in one of his gentlemen whose loyalty and presence of mind were well known to him. He informed him what a predicament he found himself in; he told him how virtuous Mme de Clèves had been until then and ordered him to follow M. de Nemours's tracks, to keep him under close observation, to see whether he went to Coulommiers and whether he entered the garden at night.

The gentleman, who was fully capable of such a mission, carried it out to the very last detail. He followed M. de Nemours to a village half a league from Coulommiers, where Nemours stopped, and the gentleman had no difficulty in guessing that he intended to stay there until nightfall. He did not think it appropriate to wait there himself, so he went past the village into the forest at the point where he thought it likely that M. de Nemours would go by. He was not mistaken in these conjectures. As soon as night had fallen, he heard someone coming, and although it was dark, he easily recognized M. de Nemours. He saw him go round the garden, as though he wanted to hear whether anyone was there and choose the place where he could most easily get in. The fences were very high,* and there were others behind to prevent anyone entering, so that it was quite difficult to find a way. M. de Nemours succeeded nevertheless, and as soon as he was in the garden, he could easily make out where Mme de Clèves was. He saw many lights in the side room; all the windows were open and, slipping silently along the garden fence, he approached the pavilion in a state of trepidation and emotion which one may readily imagine. He took up a position behind one of the french windows to see what Mme de Clèves was doing. He saw that she was alone, and looked so wonderfully beautiful that he could scarcely control his rapture at the sight. It was hot,* and on her head and breast she wore nothing but her loosely gathered hair. She was reclining on a day-bed with a table in front of her on which there were several baskets full of ribbons. She picked out some of these, and M. de Nemours noticed that they were of the very colours he had worn at the tournament. He saw that she was tying them in bows on a very unusual malacca cane which for a while he had carried around with him and which he had then given to his sister; it was from her that Mme de Clèves had taken it* without showing that she recognized it as having belonged to M. de Nemours. She completed this task with such grace and gentleness that all the feelings in her heart seemed reflected in her face. Then she took a candlestick and went over to a large table in front of the painting of the siege of Metz that contained the likeness of M. de Nemours. She sat down and began to gaze at it with a musing fascination that could only have been inspired by true passion.

It is impossible to express what M. de Nemours felt at this moment. To see a woman he adored in the middle of the night, in the most beautiful place in the world, to see her, without her knowing he was there, entirely absorbed in things connected with him and with the passion she was hiding from him—what lover has ever enjoyed or even imagined such delight?

He was so beside himself that he remained transfixed, watching Mme de Clèves without reflecting that every passing moment was precious to him. When he had recovered a little, he thought he should wait to speak to her until she went into the garden. He believed this would be safer, since she would be further from her women; but, seeing that she remained inside the room, he made up his mind to go in. When he came to put this plan into effect, how troubled he found he was! How afraid of displeasing her, of changing that gentle look on her face and seeing it become severe and angry!

He felt that it had been madness, not to come to see Mme de Clèves without her seeing him, but to imagine that he could reveal himself to her. Everything he had so far failed to realize now presented itself to his mind. His bold plan to come unawares, in the middle of the night, upon a woman to whom he had never yet spoken of his love, seemed foolhardy to the point of extravagance. He had no right, he now saw, to expect her to listen to him, and she would justifiably be angry that he was exposing her to such danger, given the accidents that might easily happen. All his courage abandoned him, and he was several times on the point of deciding to go back without letting himself be seen. Driven nevertheless by the desire to speak to her and reassured by the hopes raised in him by everything he had seen, he took a few steps forward, but in such a state of confusion that a scarf he was wearing became caught in the window so that he made a noise. Mme de Clèves turned her head. Whether because her mind was full of his image, or because he was in a spot where the light carried sufficiently for her to make him out, she thought she recognized him and, without hesitating or turning back in his direction, went to join her women in the other room. She was visibly so disturbed that she was obliged to say she felt unwell, both for the sake of appearances and to keep her people occupied, thus giving M. de Nemours time to withdraw. On further reflection, however, she decided that she had been mistaken and that it was only a flight of the imagination which had led her to believe she had seen him. She knew he was at Chambord, and she thought it most unlikely that he had ventured on such a hazardous undertaking. Several times, the desire came over her to go back into the side room and thence into the garden to see if anyone was there. Perhaps she wanted to find M. de Nemours there no less than she feared it. But at last good sense and prudence triumphed over all her other feelings, and she decided that it was better to remain in her present state of doubt than to take the risk of discovering the truth. It was long before she could bring herself to leave a place where she believed M. de Nemours might perhaps be so near, and day was almost breaking when she returned to the château.

M. de Nemours had remained in the garden as long as he saw lights in the pavilion. He had not been able to abandon the hope of seeing Mme de Clèves again, even though he was convinced that she had recognized him and that she had only gone out in order to avoid him. But when he saw that they were closing the doors, he realized he had nothing more to hope for. He went back to the place where he had left his horse. M. de Clèves's gentleman was waiting nearby, and followed him to the village he had left the previous evening. M. de Nemours resolved to spend the whole day there and to go back to Coulommiers at night. He wanted to know whether Mme de Clèves would again be cruel enough to flee his presence, or to avoid exposing herself to the possibility of being seen. Although he was overcome with joy at finding her so preoccupied with thoughts of him, he was also deeply dismayed to have seen in her such a natural impulse to take flight.

Never has passion been so tender or so violent as M. de Nemours's was then. He walked out beneath the willows, by a little stream that flowed behind the house where he was hiding. He went as far away as possible so that he would be seen or heard by no one; he gave himself up to the transports of love, and his heart was so full that he was constrained to let fall a few tears; yet they were not the kind that sorrow alone gives rise to: they were mingled with sweetness and with the charm that only love can bring.

He began to go over in his mind everything Mme de Clèves had done since he had been in love with her—how, though she too loved him, she had always shown him a firmness tempered with courtesy and modesty. 'For, after all, she does love me,' he said to himself: 'she loves me, I cannot doubt it; not even the most solemn vows and the greatest favours are such certain proof as the signs I have been given. Yet I am treated as severely as if she hated me; I hoped that time might make her kinder, but now I can expect it no longer; I see that she always protects herself equally against me and against her own feelings. If she did not love me, I could give thought to ways of pleasing her; but I do please her, she loves me, yet hides it from me. What then can I hope for, what change in my destiny? Can it be that I am loved by the most charming woman in the world, that I feel the intenser passion that comes with the first certainty of being loved, only to suffer more grievously the pain of being ill-treated? Allow me to see that you love me, my beautiful princess,' he cried; 'show me your feelings; if you grant me that just once in my life, you may with my consent put on again for ever that mask of severity with which you have been tormenting me. At least look at me as I saw you look last night at my portrait. Your gaze then was so gentle and loving: after that, how could you so cruelly run away when you saw my real self? What are you afraid of? Is my love so dreadful to you? You love me, it is useless to try to hide it; you have yourself given me unwitting proof of it. I am sure of my good fortune: let me enjoy it, and do nothing more to make me unhappy. Is it possible', he went on, 'that Mme de Clèves loves me and that I am unhappy? How beautiful she was last night! How did I resist the desire to throw myself at her feet? If I had, I should perhaps have prevented her from running away; my respect would have reassured her. But perhaps she did not recognize me; I am tormenting myself more than I need; perhaps the mere sight of a man at such an extraordinary hour terrified her.'

M. de Nemours's mind was full of these thoughts the whole day long. He waited impatiently for night to fall; then he retraced his steps to Coulommiers. M. de Clèves's gentleman, who had disguised himself so that he would not be so easily noticed, followed him to the same spot as the previous evening and saw him enter the garden. M. de Nemours soon discovered that Mme de Clèves had not wanted to risk his making another attempt to see her: every door was closed. He went all round the pavilion to discover whether there were any lights, but in vain.

Mme de Clèves, suspecting that M. de Nemours might return, had remained in her room; she feared she might not always have the strength to run away, and had not wanted to expose herself to the risk of speaking to him in a manner that so contradicted the rule she had adopted up to then.

Although M. de Nemours had no hopes of seeing her, he could not bring himself yet to leave a place where she so often came. He spent the whole night in the garden, finding some consolation at least in seeing the very objects that she saw every day. The sun had risen before he thought of taking his leave, but finally the fear of being discovered forced him to go.

He found it impossible to depart without seeing Mme de Clèves, so he went to visit Mme de Mercœur, who was at that time in her house near Coulommiers. She was extremely surprised at the arrival of her brother. He invented a reason for his journey that was sufficiently plausible to deceive her, and in the end he handled the situation so cleverly that she herself was prompted to suggest that they should call on Mme de Clèves. The suggestion was put into effect the very same day, and M. de Nemours told his sister that he would take his farewell from her at Coulommiers so that he could return in haste to join the King. He devised this plan with the idea of letting her leave first: he thought he had found an infallible device for arranging a private conversation with Mme de Clèves.

When they arrived, she was taking a walk along a great avenue beside the flower garden. She was more than a little disconcerted to see M. de Nemours and could no longer doubt that he was the man she had seen the other night. The certainty made her feel angry, for it seemed to her that what he had ventured to do was bold and imprudent. M. de Nemours noticed a touch of coldness in her expression which caused him much pain. They conversed of indifferent matters; none the less, he contrived to display such wit, such an obliging manner, and such admiration for Mme de Clèves that, much as she tried to resist, he succeeded in dissipating some of the coldness she had at first assumed.

Once his initial fears had been set at rest, he showed himself extremely curious to go and see the forest pavilion. He spoke as if it were the most delightful place in the world and even described it in such detail that Mme de Mercœur said he must have been there several times, so well was he acquainted with all its charms.

'And yet I do not believe', said Mme de Clèves, 'that M. de Nemours has ever been inside it; it was only built a little while ago.'

'It is not long, in fact, since I was there,' rejoined M. de Nemours, glancing at her; 'perhaps I should be flattered that you have forgotten you saw me.'

Mme de Mercœur was admiring the gardens and paid no attention to what her brother was saying. Mme de Clèves blushed; lowering her eyes without looking at M. de Nemours, she said:

'I cannot remember having seen you; if you were there, it was without my knowledge.'

'It is true, Madame,' replied M. de Nemours, 'that I went without your permission, and spent in that spot the sweetest and cruellest moments of my life.'

Mme de Clèves understood all too well what he was saying, but she made no reply. She gave thought rather to preventing Mme de Mercœur from going into the side room, for the portrait of M. de Nemours was there and she did not want her to see it. She succeeded so well that the time passed imperceptibly, and Mme de Mercœur spoke of going back. But when Mme de Clèves saw that M. de Nemours and his sister were not leaving together, she realized what she was to be exposed to. She found herself in the same awkward situation she had been in previously in Paris, and she decided on the same way out; the fear that M. de Nemours's visit might further confirm her husband's suspicions made no small contribution to her choice. To avoid being left alone with him, she told Mme de Mercœur that she would accompany her to the edge of the forest, and she ordered her carriage to come up behind. The pain M. de Nemours felt when he saw that Mme de Clèves continued to be as unrelenting as before was so violent that he immediately turned pale. Mme de Mercœur asked him if he felt ill, but he looked at Mme de Clèves without anyone noticing and his eyes told her that his illness was nothing other than despair. All the same, he was obliged to let them leave without daring to follow them; after what he had said, he could no longer return with his sister, so he went back to Paris and travelled on from there the following day.

M. de Clèves's gentleman, who had been keeping him under observation, also returned to Paris and, seeing that M. de Nemours had left for Chambord, took the post in order to arrive there first and give an account of his journey. His master was waiting for his return in the knowledge that his whole life might be ruined by what he heard.

As soon as he saw him, he guessed, from his silence and the expression on his face, that his news could only be bad. For a while he remained transfixed with pain, his head bowed, unable to speak; finally, he gestured to him to take his leave, saying:

'Go now; I see what you have to tell me, but I cannot bear to hear it.'

'I have nothing to tell you', answered the gentleman, 'on which any firm conjecture can be based. The truth is that M. de Nemours went into the forest garden on two successive nights and spent the following day at Coulommiers with Mme de Mercœur.'

'That is enough,' replied M. de Clèves; repeating his signal to withdraw; 'that is enough: I need no further enlightenment.'

The gentleman was obliged to abandon his master to a despair so violent that there has perhaps never been any like it. Few men as courageous and as passionate of heart as M. de Clèves have experienced in a single moment the pain caused by a mistress's infidelity and the shame of being deceived by a wife.

M. de Clèves was unable to resist the crushing sorrow that overcame him. That very night he was struck down by a fever, with so many alarming symptoms that his life appeared at once to be in great danger. Mme de Clèves was informed and came with all haste. By the time she arrived, he was still worse; she detected something so cold, so icy in his manner towards her that she was extremely surprised and hurt. It even seemed to her that the services she rendered him were unwelcome to him, but she decided in the end that this was perhaps only an effect of his illness.

As soon as she arrived at Blois, where the court now was, M. de Nemours could not help feeling a certain joy in the knowledge that they were both in the same place. He tried to see her and called on M. de Clèves every day on the pretext of getting news of him, but in vain. She never left her husband's room and was terribly distressed to see him in such a state. Her suffering threw M. de Nemours into despair: he had no difficulty in guessing how far it might reawake her affection for M. de Clèves, and how far that affection threatened to distract her from the passion hidden in her heart. These thoughts tormented him for a while, but the extreme gravity of M. de Clèves's illness gave him fresh hopes.* He saw that Mme de Clèves would perhaps be free to follow her inclination, and that he might be able to look forward to a sustained happiness and lasting pleasures. This thought so disturbed and delighted him that he could not dwell on it too long, and he put it out of his mind for fear of being too unhappy if his hopes proved to be unfounded.

Meanwhile, M. de Clèves had almost been given up for lost by the doctors. On one of the last days of his illness, after spending a particularly troubled night, he said as morning came that he wanted to rest. Mme de Clèves remained alone with him. It seemed to her that, instead of resting, he was extremely agitated. She came to his bedside and knelt down, her face covered in tears. M. de Clèves had resolved to give her no sign of the terrible bitterness he felt towards her, but the care she lavished on him, together with her distress, which at times appeared to him to be genuine but which at others he interpreted as evidence of hypocrisy and treachery, gave rise in him to feelings so contradictory and painful that he was unable to contain them.

'You shed many tears, Madame,' he said, 'for a death

which you yourself have caused and which cannot be as painful to you as you pretend. I am no longer in a condition to reproach you,' he continued in a voice weakened by illness and pain; 'but I am dying of the cruel blow you have struck me. How could an action as extraordinary as your confession to me at Coulommiers have had such meagre consequences? Why reveal to me your passion for M. de Nemours if your virtue was not better equipped to resist it? I loved you so much that I should have been glad to be deceived; I confess it to my shame. I wish I had never lost the peace of mind, false as it was, from which you awoke me. Why did you not leave me in that happy state of blindness so many husbands enjoy? I should perhaps have been unaware my whole life long that you loved M. de Nemours. I shall die,' he added; 'but you should know that you have made me welcome death: now you have taken away all the tenderness and esteem I felt for you, life would be repugnant to me. What use would life be if I were to spend it with a woman whom I loved so much and who so cruelly deceived me, or live apart from her, causing a public scandal and angry scenes that would be so out of keeping with my character and my passion for you? That passion went far beyond what you saw of it, Madame; I concealed the greater part of it for fear of upsetting you, or of losing your respect by behaving in a way ill suited to a husband. In short, I deserved your love; since I was unable to win it and can no longer desire it, I say once more: I die without regrets. Farewell, Madame; some day you will be sorry to have lost a man whose passion for you was both genuine and legitimate. You will feel the bitter sorrow that women of sense eventually experience in such attachments; you will learn the difference between being loved as I loved you and the attentions of those who, while making a show of love, think of nothing but the honour of seducing you. But then, of course, my death will leave you free to do as you wish,' he added, 'and you will be able to make M. de Nemours happy without having to commit any crimes. What do I care what will happen when I am gone? How weak I am even to think of it!'

Mme de Clèves was so far from imagining that her husband might have any grounds for suspecting her that she listened to this speech uncomprehendingly; her only thought was that he was reproaching her for her attraction to M. de Nemours. But at last the scales fell from her eyes.

'I, commit crimes!' she cried. 'Nothing was ever further from my mind. The most austere virtue could not have dictated conduct more correct than mine. I have never performed any act which I would not have been happy for you to witness.'

'Would you have wished', replied M. de Clèves, with a glance of contempt, 'that I had witnessed the nights you spent with M. de Nemours? Ah! Madame, when I speak of a woman spending nights with a man, can you really be that woman?'

'No, Monsieur,' she rejoined; 'no, I am not that woman. I have never passed any nights nor even any moments with M. de Nemours. He has never seen me in private; I have never let him, I have never listened to him, and I swear to you on my honour . . .'

'Say no more,' interrupted M. de Clèves. 'Hypocritical oaths or an open confession, both would be equally painful to me.'

Speechless with weeping and misery, Mme de Clèves was unable to reply. Finally, she made an effort:

'At least look at me, listen to me,' she said. 'If this concerned no one but me, I should bear your reproaches patiently. But it is your life that is at stake. Listen to me, for your own dear sake: it is impossible that, with truth on my side, I shall not be able to persuade you of my innocence.'

'Would to God that you could!' he cried. 'But what can you say? Was not M. de Nemours at Coulommiers with his sister? Did he not spend the two previous nights with you in the forest garden?'

'If that is my crime,' she replied, 'I can easily exonerate myself. I do not ask you to believe me, but at least believe your servants: ask them whether I went into the forest garden the evening before M. de Nemours's visit to Coulommiers, and whether I did not leave it the previous evening two hours earlier than usual.'

She went on to tell him how she thought she had seen someone in the garden, confessing that she had believed it was M. de Nemours. She spoke with such assurance, and the truth is so persuasive, even where it is improbable, that M. de Clèves was all but convinced of her innocence.

'I do not know', he said, 'whether I ought to allow myself to believe you. I feel I am close to death, and I want to hear nothing that might make me sorry to die. Your explanation comes too late; but it will at least be some relief to me if I can die thinking that you are worthy of the esteem I had for you. Please grant me also the consolation of believing that my memory will be dear to you and that, if you could have willed it so, you would have loved me as you love him.'

He wanted to go on, but a faintness overtook him and deprived him of speech. Mme de Clèves called the doctors. They found that life was almost gone; yet he lingered a few days more. He met his death at last with wonderful fortitude.

Mme de Clèves was left in a state of such violent grief that it was as if she had lost the use of her reason. The Queen made it her duty to visit her and personally took her to a convent without her being conscious of where she was going. When her sisters-in-law brought her back to Paris, she was still not capable of discerning the true nature of her affliction. Gradually, however, she began to have the strength to look it in the face. When she realized what a husband she had lost, when she reflected that she herself had caused his death and that she had caused it by her passion for another man, she was overcome by an indescribable horror both for herself and for M. de Nemours.

In these first stages of her mourning, Nemours dared pay her no respects other than those required by decorum. He knew Mme de Clèves well enough to guess that she would be displeased if he showed too much attentiveness; but he then heard something that made him realize he would have to adopt the same behaviour for a long time to come.

One of his equerries was a close friend of M. de Clèves's gentleman. He told him that this man, in his grief at his master's death, had said that it had been caused by M. de Nemours's visit to Coulommiers. M. de Nemours was extremely surprised by this remark, but after some reflection he guessed at least a part of the truth. It was clear to him what Mme de Clèves's response would be at first, what repugnance she would feel towards him, if she believed that her husband's illness had been caused by jealousy. He decided that he should do nothing to make her even recall his name for the time being, and he followed this course, painful as it was.

He made a journey to Paris; despite his resolution, he could not prevent himself from going to her door to ask for news of her. He was told that she was seeing no one and that she had even forbidden her servants to inform her who had called; such exact orders had perhaps been given because she wished to hear nothing of Nemours himself. He was, however, too much in love to bear to be deprived so absolutely of the sight of Mme de Clèves. He resolved to find the means, difficult though that might be, to escape from a situation which he found so intolerable.

Mme de Clèves's grief went beyond the bounds of reason. Her dying husband, dying because of her and so tenderly in love with her, haunted her imagination. She brooded endlessly over what she owed him, and she blamed herself for not having loved him passionately enough, as if it had been in her power to do so. Her only consolation was to feel that she regretted him as he deserved and that, for the rest of her life, she would do nothing he would not have wished her to do had he lived.

She had often wondered how he had discovered that M. de Nemours had come to Coulommiers. She did not suspect Nemours of having told anyone about it; she indeed cared little whether he had or not, for she believed herself entirely cured, once and for all, of the passion she had felt for him. It was none the less deeply painful to her to imagine that he was the cause of her husband's death, and she recalled with distress how, at the last, M. de Clèves had expressed the fear that she might marry him. Yet all these different feelings became indistinctly mingled in the sorrow of losing her husband, so that she believed she had no other.

After several months, the violence of her affliction passed and she fell into a state of languid melancholy. Mme de Martigues made a journey to Paris and visited her regularly while she was there. She spoke of everything that was going on at court; the fact that Mme de Clèves showed no interest did not prevent Mme de Martigues from talking about it in the hope of distracting her.

She told her the latest stories about the Vidame, M. de Guise, and various others who attracted attention because of their personal appearance or their outstanding qualities.

'As for M. de Nemours,' she said, 'I cannot tell whether public affairs have dispelled all thoughts of love from his heart; but he is in much poorer spirits than he used to be, and he seems to have withdrawn altogether from the society of women. He often comes to Paris; indeed, I believe he is here just now.'

The name of M. de Nemours took Mme de Clèves by surprise and made her blush. She changed the subject, and Mme de Martigues did not notice her confusion.

The next day, Mme de Clèves, wanting to find an occupation appropriate to her present state, went to see a man* whose house was close to hers and who did a special kind of work in silk; she was thinking she might do something similar herself. After he had shown her some samples, she noticed the door of a room where she thought there were some more; she asked him to open it. He replied that he did not have the key; the room was used, he said, by a man who sometimes came during the day to sketch the fine houses and gardens that could be seen from the windows.

'He is an extraordinarily handsome man,' he added; 'he hardly looks as if he could be reduced to earning a living. Every time he comes here, I see him gazing endlessly at the houses and gardens, but I have never seen him at work.'

Mme de Clèves listened to these remarks with the closest attention. What Mme de Martigues had said to her about M. de Nemours's visits to Paris became connected in her imagination with this handsome man who came to a house so close to hers; it brought to her mind's eye a picture of

M. de Nemours, of a M. de Nemours intent on seeing her,
which bewildered and disturbed her, though she could not
even say why. She went over to the windows to see where
they looked out; she found that her whole garden and the
front of her apartment were visible. And indeed, when she
was at home in her own room, she had no difficulty in
making out the window to which she had been told the
unknown visitor came. The idea that it was M. de Nemours
changed her state of mind entirely. The melancholy yet
tranquil mood that she was beginning to enjoy gave way to a
sense of unease and agitation. Finally, unable to find peace
within herself, she went out to take the air in a garden
outside the limits of the city where she thought she would
be alone. When she arrived, this supposition seemed to be
confirmed: she saw no sign of anyone, and she walked for
some considerable time.

As she came out of a little wood, she noticed, at the end
of an avenue in the most remote part of the garden, a kind
of summer-house open at the sides, to which she directed
her steps. As she drew near, she saw a man reclining on
some benches, deeply absorbed as it seemed in reverie,
and she recognized that it was M. de Nemours. The sight
brought her up short, but her people, who were following
her, made a noise of some kind which aroused M. de
Nemours from his reverie. Without looking to see who
had made the noise, he stood up in order to avoid these
intruders and turned away into another avenue, with a bow
so low that he was even unable to see* who it was that he
was greeting.

If he had but known what he was avoiding, one can
imagine how ardently he would have retraced his steps; but
he continued down the avenue, and Mme de Clèves saw
him go out by a rear gate where his carriage was waiting.
What a turmoil this momentary glimpse aroused in Mme de
Clèves's heart! How violently her slumbering passion was
rekindled! She went and sat down in the very place M. de
Nemours had just left and remained there as if stunned. His
image came to her mind, more desirable than anything else
in the world, the image of a man who had loved her long

and passionately yet faithfully and with respect, scorning all else for her sake, honouring even the grief of her bereavement, seeking to see her without being seen, abandoning the court, where he was adulated, to go and gaze at the walls in which she was enclosed, to dream the day away in places where he could not expect to meet her; a man, in short, worthy of being loved simply for the strength of his attachment, and for whom she had such a violent inclination that she would have loved him even if he had not loved her; but, what is more, a man whose quality and rank matched her own. No duty, no virtue could now stand in the way of her feelings; all obstacles were removed; nothing remained of their past circumstances but M. de Nemours's passion for her, and hers for him.

All these ideas were new to the princess. Her bereavement had sufficiently occupied her mind to prevent her considering such things. M. de Nemours's presence brought them crowding back until it seemed there was no room for more; but then she remembered too that this same man who she now thought could marry her was the one she had loved during her husband's lifetime, the one who had caused his death; she remembered that, as he lay dying, he had even expressed the fear that she might marry him; and, in the austerity of her virtue, she was so wounded by this thought that she now felt it to be scarcely less of a crime to marry M. de Nemours than it had seemed to love him while her husband was alive. She gave herself up to these reflections, fatal as they were to her happiness, and reinforced them still further with other reasons—the need to preserve her peace of mind and the troubles she foresaw if she were to marry Nemours. Finally, after spending two hours in the same place, she returned home, convinced that to see him was something quite contrary to her duty and that she should do everything possible to avoid it.

Yet this conviction, inspired as it was by her reason and virtue, failed to carry her heart with it. Her feelings remained attached to M. de Nemours, and their violence, allowing her no respite, made her state a pitiable one: that night was one of the cruellest she had ever known. In the morning, her first impulse was to go and see whether there was anyone at the window overlooking her house; she went, and saw M. de Nemours. Taken by surprise, she withdrew so promptly that Nemours guessed he had been recognized, as he had often wished to be ever since his passion had made him devise this means of seeing Mme de Clèves; when he had no hopes that his wish might be gratified, he would go and dream in that same garden where she had found him.

Weary of a situation so unhappy and uncertain, he resolved at last to venture upon some course that would decide his destiny. 'What am I waiting for?' he said to himself. 'I have long known that she loves me; she is free; her duty can no longer be an obstacle. Why reduce myself to seeing her without being seen or speaking to her? Can love have deprived me so absolutely of reason and courage? Can it have made my behaviour so different from what it used to be in my other attachments? I had to respect Mme de Clèves's mourning, but I have been respecting it too long and giving her time to extinguish her feelings for me.'

These reflections led him to consider how he might contrive to see her. Judging that he was no longer under an obligation to hide his passion from the Vidame de Chartres, he decided to speak to him about it and tell him of his intentions towards his niece.

The Vidame was in Paris at the time; everyone was there, preparing their retinue and wardrobes for the journey with the King, who was to escort the Queen of Spain. So M. de Nemours called on the Vidame and openly confessed to him everything he had so far hidden, except for Mme de Clèves's own feelings, of which he wished to appear ignorant.

The Vidame was delighted at the news. He assured him that, since Mme de Clèves had become a widow, he had often thought she was the only woman worthy of him, though he had known nothing of Nemours's feelings. His friend begged him to make an opportunity for him to speak to her and discover what her attitude might be.

The Vidame suggested he might take him to visit her, but Nemours thought she might find this shocking as she was not receiving yet. They decided it would be best for the

Vidame to invite her on some pretext to visit him; M. de Nemours would then come up by a hidden staircase so that no one would see him. All went according to plan: Mme de Clèves arrived; the Vidame went to receive her and took her into a large room at one end of his apartment. A little later, M. de Nemours came in as if by chance. Mme de Clèves was extremely surprised to see him; she blushed, then tried to hide her embarrassment. The Vidame spoke for a while of various matters, then went out, pretending to have some orders to give. He asked Mme de Clèves to entertain his guest, saying that he would be back in a moment.

It is impossible to express what M. de Nemours and Mme de Clèves felt when they found themselves alone and able to talk to one another for the first time. For a while, they remained speechless, but finally M. de Nemours broke the silence:

'Will you forgive M. de Chartres, Madame,' he said, 'for giving me the opportunity to see you and converse with you which you have always so cruelly denied me?'

'I cannot forgive him', she replied, 'for forgetting my present situation and putting my reputation at risk.'

Having said this, she made as if to go, but M. de Nemours would not let her.

'You have nothing to fear, Madame,' he replied; 'no one knows I am here and there is no risk. Listen to me, Madame, only listen, if not out of kindness to me, then at least for your own sake, to spare you the excesses to which I should be irresistibly driven by a passion I can no longer control.'

Mme de Clèves yielded for the first time to the attraction she felt for M. de Nemours. Throwing him a look at once gentle and charming, she said:

'But what do you hope to gain if I give my consent? You may well regret having obtained it and I shall certainly regret having granted it. Your fate has not been a happy one up to now, and you are unlikely to find greater happiness in the future unless you look for it elsewhere. You deserve better.'

'Look for happiness elsewhere!' he exclaimed. 'What other could there be but to be loved by you? Although I have never spoken openly, I cannot believe that you are ignorant of my passion or that you could fail to recognize it as the truest and most violent anyone will ever feel. Has it not been thoroughly put to the test in ways you know nothing of? Has it not been put to the test, again and again, by your refusals?'

'You wish me to speak, and I will,' replied Mme de Clèves. She sat down, and went on: 'Indeed, I have made up my mind to answer you with a sincerity you will rarely find in persons of my sex. I shall not say I have not noticed your interest in me; perhaps you would not believe me if I did. I confess, then, not only that I have noticed it, but that I have seen it exactly as you would have wished.'

'Then if you have, Madame,' he interrupted, 'is it possible that you were not touched? Dare I ask whether it did not make some impression on your heart?'

'You must have been able to judge by my conduct,' she said; 'but I should very much like to know what conclusion you came to.'

'I could only bring myself to tell you if my position were a happier one than it is,' he answered; 'my fate bears so little relation to what I should have to say. All I can say is this: I wished with all my heart that you had not confessed to M. de Clèves what you concealed from me, and that you had concealed from him what you might have allowed me to discover.'

Mme de Clèves blushed and replied: 'How were you able to discover that I had confessed anything to M. de Clèves?'

'I learnt it from your own lips, Madame,' he replied; 'but you will forgive me for having had the audacity to listen to you if you ask yourself whether I ever made improper use of what I overheard, whether my hopes were in any way increased by it, or whether it gave me greater licence to speak to you.'

He began to tell her how he had overheard her conversation with M. de Clèves; but she interrupted him before he had finished.

'Say no more,' she said; 'I see now by what means you were so well informed. You already seemed to know all too much on that occasion at Mme la Dauphine's: she had heard the story from the people to whom you had divulged it.'

M. de Nemours then told her how this had come about.

'Make no excuses,' she responded; 'I have long since forgiven you without any explanation from you. But since you have heard from my lips something I meant to hide from you for the rest of my life, I confess that you have aroused in me feelings I knew nothing of, indeed scarcely knew existed, before I saw you. I was thus taken entirely by surprise at first, which greatly increased the state of confusion that always accompanies feelings of that kind. I make this confession with no great sense of shame because no crime attaches to it any longer, and you have ample evidence that my conduct has not been governed by my emotions.'

'Can you say such things, Madame,' exclaimed M. de Nemours, falling to his knees, 'and not believe that I shall die of joy and rapture here at your feet?'

'I have only told you', she replied with a smile, 'what you already knew well enough.'

'Ah! Madame,' he rejoined, 'what a difference there is between knowing it by chance and seeing that you wish me to know!'

'It is true', she said, 'that I wish you to know and that I find it sweet to tell you. I cannot even say whether I am not telling you more for my own sake than for yours. For my confession will have no consequences: I shall continue to follow the austere principles my duty imposes on me.'

'You can be thinking of no such thing, Madame,' replied M. de Nemours; 'no duty ties your hands now, you are free; and if I dared, I should even go so far as to say that it depends on you to make sure that your duty one day obliges you to preserve your feelings for me.'

'My duty', she rejoined, 'forbids me ever to think of anyone, and of you less than any man alive, for reasons of which you are unaware.'

'I am perhaps not so unaware of them, Madame,' he said; 'but those are not genuine reasons. I have grounds for believing that M. de Clèves thought me happier than I was:

he imagined you had given your approval to excesses that were prompted by my passion alone, without your consent.'

'Let us not speak of that episode,' she said; 'I cannot bear even to think about it. It makes me feel ashamed and I also find it too painful because of what happened as a result. The truth is that you are the cause of M. de Clèves's death; the suspicions your thoughtless behaviour aroused in him cost him his life no less than if you had killed him with your own hands. Imagine what my duty would have been had you and he agreed to put your quarrel to the ultimate test,* with the same outcome. Yes, I am aware it is not the same thing in the eyes of the world; but in my eyes there is no difference, since I know that he died because of what you did and that it happened because of me.'

'Ah! Madame,' said M. de Nemours, 'would you allow some phantom of duty to stand in the way of my happiness? Will a vain, groundless fancy prevent you from making a man happy you clearly do not hate? What! Can it be that I have conceived the hope of spending my life with you; that fate has willed that I should love the woman who of all women is worthiest of esteem; that she for her part should not hate me; that I should see in her all the qualities of a charming mistress together with the conduct one would most desire in a wife—for you are perhaps the only woman, Madame, who has ever possessed these two qualities in such a high degree: when a man marries a mistress who loves him, he trembles once the marriage vows are made, fearing that she will behave with others as she behaved with him, but you, Madame, give no cause for such fears, everything you do commands admiration—can it be, then, that I have glimpsed such bliss only to see you yourself put obstacles in its way? Ah! Madame, you forget that you singled me out from the rest of mankind—or perhaps you never did at all: you were mistaken, and I have been flattering myself.'

'You have not flattered yourself,' she replied; 'the reasons my duty dictates would perhaps not seem so persuasive were it not that I do indeed see in you qualities superior to those of other men, as you have guessed: that is what makes me see only unhappiness if I attach myself to you.'

'What can I say, Madame,' he continued, 'when you tell me you are afraid of being unhappy? However, I confess that, after everything you have been so kind as to tell me, I did not expect to be given such a cruel reason.'

'The reason is so far from being offensive to you,' rejoined Mme de Clèves, 'that I even find it hard to say what it is.'

'Alas! Madame,' he replied, 'after the things you have just told me, what could you be afraid of saying that would flatter me too much?'

'I feel I must speak to you once more as sincerely as I have already spoken,' she said. 'I shall leave aside all the discretion and reticence I ought to show in a first conversation with you; but I implore you to listen to me without interrupting.

'It seems to me that your attachment to me deserves at least this meagre reward, that I should not hide from you any of my feelings and that I should show them to you as they are. This will no doubt be the only time in my life when I shall give myself the liberty of revealing them to you, yet I must confess to my shame that what I fear is the certainty that one day the love you feel for me now will die. That certainty seems to me so dreadful that, even if the reasons imposed by my duty were not insurmountable, I doubt whether I could bring myself to face such unhappiness. I know that you are free, that I am free also, and that, in all the circumstances, the world would perhaps have no reason to blame either of us if we were to bind ourselves together for life. But how long does men's passion last when the bond is eternal? Can I expect a miracle in my favour? If not, can I resign myself to the prospect that a passion on which my happiness depended must infallibly come to an end? M. de Clèves was perhaps the only man in the world capable of remaining in love with the woman he had married.* I was fated not to be able to take advantage of my good fortune; perhaps, too, his passion only endured because he found no answering passion in me. But I should not be able to keep yours alive in this way: it seems to me, indeed, that your constancy has been sustained by the obstacles it has encountered. There were enough of them to arouse in you the desire for victory, while my involuntary actions, together with what you discovered by chance, gave you enough hope not to be deterred.'

'Ah! Madame,' exclaimed M. de Nemours, 'I can no longer keep the silence you imposed on me. Your words are too unjust and you make it too plain how far you are from being predisposed in my favour.'

'I confess', she replied, 'that my passions may govern me, but they cannot blind me. Nothing can prevent me from recognizing that you were born with a great susceptibility to love and all the qualities required for success in love. You have already had a number of passionate attachments; you would have others. I should no longer be able to make you happy; I should see you behaving towards another woman as you had behaved towards me. I should be mortally wounded at the sight and I cannot even be sure I should not suffer the miseries of jealousy. I have already said too much to be able to hide from you now that you once made me feel those cruel sufferings. It was the evening the Queen gave me Mme de Thémines's letter, the one they said was addressed to you: what I felt then has remained with me, convincing me that it is the greatest of all evils.

'There is not a woman who does not wish, whether through vanity or true inclination, to have you at her feet. There are very few who do not like you; my experience tells me that there are none who would not like you if you wanted them to. I should always believe you to be in love, and loved in return, and I should not often be mistaken. Yet in that predicament, I should have no other choice but to suffer: I cannot tell if I should even dare complain. A woman may reproach a lover, but can she reproach a husband who has merely stopped loving her? Even if I could accustom myself to misery of that sort, there is another to which I could never become inured: I should always hear M. de Clèves accusing you of his death, reproaching me for loving you and marrying you, and reminding me of the difference between his devotion and yours. It is impossible to set aside such powerful reasons: I must remain in my present state and stand by the resolution I have taken never to abandon it.'

'But do you think you can succeed?' cried M. de Nemours. 'Do you believe your resolutions will hold firm against a man who worships you and who is fortunate enough to have aroused your feelings? It is harder than you think, Madame, to resist someone who both attracts you and who loves you. You have succeeded so far, thanks to a virtue so austere that is almost without parallel, but your virtue is no longer opposed to your feelings and it is my hope that you will follow those feelings in spite of yourself.'

'I am well aware that there is nothing more difficult than what I propose to do,' replied Mme de Clèves. 'I put little faith in my own powers, despite all the reasons I can muster. What I believe I owe to the memory of M. de Clèves would be a feeble resource were it not sustained by self-interest, namely my desire for tranquillity of mind; likewise, the reasons that speak in favour of tranquillity need to be supported by those that duty prescribes. Little as I trust myself, however, I believe that I shall never be able to vanquish my scruples, nor can I hope to overcome my attraction to you. It will make me unhappy, and I intend to remove myself from your sight, however violent the pain of separation. I implore you, by all the power I have over you, not to seek any opportunity to see me. My present state makes what might be legitimate at other times a criminal offence; decorum alone forbids all commerce between us.'

M. de Nemours threw himself at her feet and surrendered himself utterly to the feelings that shook his soul. In his words and tears she saw revealed the most ardent and tender passion that has ever touched a human heart. Mme de Clèves's own heart was not insensible; she gazed at Nemours, her eyes brimming with tears, and exclaimed:

'Why must I be obliged to accuse you of M. de Clèves's death? Why could I not have met you after I became free, or rather before I gave myself away? Why has fate put such an insuperable obstacle between us?'

'There is no obstacle, Madame,' protested M. de Nemours.

'You alone stand in the way of my happiness; you alone have made for yourself a law that virtue and reason could never impose.'

'It is true', she replied, 'that I am sacrificing a great deal to a duty that exists only in my imagination. Wait and see what time may do. M. de Clèves has only just died, and that grim spectacle is still so close that I can as yet see nothing clearly and distinctly. Meanwhile, you may at least enjoy the pleasure of having won the heart of a woman who would have loved no one if she had never seen you; do not doubt that my feelings for you will exist eternally and unchangeably whatever I do. Farewell,' she said; 'I am ashamed of this conversation. Tell M. le Vidame everything: you have my consent, it is what I wish.'

On these words she went out; M. de Nemours could not make her stay. She found M. le Vidame in the next room. He saw how distressed she was and dared not speak to her; he took her to her carriage in silence. Then he came back to see M. de Nemours, who was out of his senses with joy and sadness, confusion and wonder—all the feelings, in short, that a passion fraught with fear and hope is capable of. It was a long while before the Vidame could extract from him a report of their conversation, but finally he succeeded; though he was not himself in love with Mme de Clèves, he marvelled at her virtue, her wit, and her other remarkable qualities no less than M. de Nemours himself. They considered what hopes Nemours might legitimately have, and he finally agreed with M. le Vidame, despite all the fears his love aroused in him, that Mme de Clèves's present resolve could not possibly last. They recognized, none the less, that it would be better to obey her orders: if his attachment to her was noticed in society, there was a risk that she might make public declarations and denials to which she would later feel bound, for fear that people would believe she had loved him during her husband's lifetime.

M. de Nemours resolved to accompany the King. It was an obligation he could in any case hardly avoid, and he made up his mind to go without even attempting to see Mme de Clèves again from the place where he used to watch her. He asked M. le Vidame to speak to her, and plied him with messages, with endless reasons that might persuade her to overcome her scruples. It was already far into the night before M. de Nemours would finally consent to leave him in peace.

For Mme de Clèves, too, peace was not easy to find. To be free from her self-imposed constraints, to have allowed someone, for the first time in her life, to tell her he was in love with her, to have said she loved him, was something entirely new to her, and she scarcely recognized herself. She was amazed at what she had done; she felt both regret and delight; her heart was full of a passionate turmoil. She reviewed the reasons that duty placed in the way of her happiness; it was painful to her to find that they were so strong and she regretted having represented them so forcefully to M. de Nemours. Although the thought of marrying him had come into her mind as soon as she had seen him in the garden, it had not made such a lively impression on her as the conversation she had just had with him, and there were moments when she found it hard to comprehend that she might be unhappy if she married him. She would have liked to be able to tell herself that she was mistaken, both in her scruples about the past and in her fears for the future. At other moments, reason and duty put arguments in her mind that were quite the opposite of these and brought her swiftly to the conclusion that she should neither remarry nor ever see M. de Nemours again. Yet this resolve could not be established without great violence in a heart so profoundly touched and so freshly acquainted with the charms of love. Finally, in order to bring some calm into her thoughts, she told herself that she did not yet need to force a final decision upon herself; decorum allowed her some considerable time to make up her mind. She remained absolutely determined, however, to have no dealings with M. de Nemours. The Vidame came to see her and defended his friend's cause with the utmost wit and perseverance, but he could not make her change her mind about her own conduct or about the rule she had imposed on M. de Nemours. She told him that it was her intention to remain in her present state; that she realized how difficult this would be; but that she hoped to be strong enough. She made him see how far the idea that M. de Nemours had caused her husband's death had taken hold of her mind, how convinced she was that to marry him would be contrary to her duty, and she argued so well that the Vidame feared it would not be easy to persuade her otherwise. He omitted to say this to Nemours: when he reported the conversation, he left him the hopes that a man who knows himself to be loved can reasonably have.

The two men left the next day and went to join the King. M. de Nemours prevailed upon the Vidame to write a letter to Mme de Clèves speaking of him; in a second letter which followed close upon the first, M. de Nemours wrote a line or two in his own hand. But Mme de Clèves, who did not wish to disobey the rules she had imposed on herself and who was afraid of the accidents that letters can give rise to,* sent word to M. le Vidame that she would refuse to receive his letters if he continued to speak to her of M. de Nemours; she expressed herself so strongly that Nemours himself begged the Vidame to mention him no more.

The court escorted the Queen of Spain as far as Poitou. During their absence, Mme de Clèves kept to herself; as M. de Nemours became more remote, together with everything that might remind her of him, she increasingly recalled M. de Clèves, making it a point of honour to preserve his memory. Duty seemed to her a powerful reason for not marrying M. de Nemours, her peace of mind an insurmountable one. The eventual cooling of Nemours's passion, together with the ills of jealousy, which she believed to be inevitable in marriage, presented an image of the certain misery that awaited her if she took that step; yet she also saw that she could not possibly hope to resist the most desirable man in the world, who loved her and whom she too loved, to resist him, what is more, on grounds that contravened neither virtue nor decorum—she could never do this if she continued to see him. She judged that only absence and distance could give her the strength she needed, not only to maintain her resolve not to enter into any commitment, but even to avoid seeing M. de Nemours. Thus she decided to make a lengthy journey to occupy all the time that decorum required her to spend in retirement. A large estate of hers near the Pyrenees seemed to her the most appropriate place she could find. She set out only a day or two before the court returned, leaving a letter for M. le Vidame in which she begged him to see that no one sought news of her or wrote to her.

This journey caused as much grief to M. de Nemours as the death of a mistress would to another man. The thought of being deprived of the sight of Mme de Clèves for a long time was agony to him, especially as he had recently had the pleasure of seeing her, and of seeing her touched by his passion. There was nothing he could do, however, but suffer, and his suffering increased immeasurably. Mme de Clèves, after so much mental turmoil, became violently ill as soon as she arrived at her estate; the news reached the court, and M. de Nemours was inconsolable: his grief turned to a wild despair. The Vidame had great difficulty in preventing him from making a public spectacle of his passion; he could also scarcely hold him back and dissuade him from going in person to seek news of her. The fact that the Vidame was both her uncle and her friend gave him a pretext for sending several messengers, and they finally heard that she was no longer in extreme peril of her life, though she continued to suffer a lingering malady which left little hope of recovery.

This long, close look at death made Mme de Clèves see the things of this life differently from the way they appear when one is in full health. Knowing she must soon die, she grew used to detaching herself from the world, and as her illness continued the habit became ingrained. None the less, when she recovered a little, she found that M. de Nemours had not been erased from her heart; she summoned to her aid, in order to defend herself against him, all the reasons she had marshalled for never marrying him. A great combat took place within her. At last she overcame the remains of a passion already weakened by the sentiments her illness had inspired. Thoughts of death had brought home to her the memory of M. de Clèves, which, being in harmony with her duty, imprinted itself deep in her heart. The passions and attachments of the world now appeared to her as they do to those whose vision is more elevated and more detached. Her state of health, which remained very weak, helped her to preserve these sentiments, but, having learnt the power of chance events over the most virtuous of resolutions, she was unwilling to put hers at risk by returning to a place frequented by the man she had loved. On the pretext of a change of air, she retired to a house of religion, although without announcing any firm intention of abandoning the court for good.

As soon as M. de Nemours heard of this move, he felt its full weight and saw its significance. It seemed to him at that moment that his hopes were at an end; yet this did not prevent him from doing everything possible to secure the return of Mme de Clèves. He got the Queen to write, he got the Vidame to write, he sent the Vidame in person, but all was in vain. The Vidame saw her: she did not say she had made any final decision, but he nevertheless formed the view that she would never return. Finally, M. de Nemours went himself on the pretext of taking the waters. She was extremely disturbed and surprised to hear of his arrival. She asked a woman of superior qualities, whom she was fond of and who was with her at that time, to speak to him on her behalf. She begged him not to find it strange if she did not expose herself to the danger of seeing him and destroying, by the effect of his presence, sentiments that she was obliged to preserve. She wished him to know, she added, that, since she had found her duty and peace of mind to be irreconcilable with her desire to belong to him, all other things of this world had appeared so indifferent that she had renounced them for ever: she thought of nothing now but the life hereafter, and the only sentiment that remained to her was the desire to see him adopt the same view.

M. de Nemours thought he would die of pain and grief in the presence of the woman who spoke these words. He begged her a hundred times to go back to Mme de Clèves and prevail on her to let him see her; but she said that Mme de Clèves had forbidden her not only to bring her any message from him, but even to give her an account of their conversation. In the end, he was obliged to depart, over-whelmed by grief as only a man could be who had now lost all possible hope of ever seeing again a woman whom he loved with the most violent, the most natural, and the most well-founded passion in the world. And yet he still would not give up: he did everything he could think of to make her change her mind. Finally, after years had gone by, time and absence diminished his pain and quenched his passion. Mme de Clèves adopted a way of life which dispelled any thought that she would ever return. She spent part of the year in the convent; the rest she spent at home, though in profound retreat and in occupations more saintly than those of the most austere houses of religion. Her life, which was quite short, left inimitable examples of virtue.

The Princesse de Montpensier

Publisher's Note to the Reader

The respect due to the illustrious name* which appears in the title of this book, and the consideration one owes to the eminent descendants of those who have borne that name, requires me to say, if I am to avoid offending them in presenting this story to the public, that it has not been taken from any manuscript that has survived from the time of the persons who figure in it. The Author wished to amuse himself by composing entirely imaginary adventures, but he thought it better to take familiar names from our history than to use those one finds in romances; he judged that Mme de Montpensier's reputation could not be damaged by a story which was in effect a fiction. If such was not his intention, allow me to make good the lapse by means of this notice, which will be to the Author's advantage and at the same time mark my respect towards the Dead who have an interest in the matter and towards the Living who might share that interest.

IN the reign of Charles IX, when France was torn apart by civil war, Love continued to conduct his affairs* amid the disorder and to cause many disorders in his own kingdom. The only daughter of the Marquis de Mézières,* a most notable heiress both because of her great wealth and because she was a descendant of the illustrious house of Anjou, had been promised to the Duc du Maine,* the younger brother of the Duc de Guise,* who was later known as Scar-Face. As she was extremely young, her marriage was delayed, and in the meantime the Duc de Guise,* who often saw her and who discerned in her the early promise of great beauty, fell in love with her and was loved in return. They concealed their love with the greatest care. The Duc de Guise, who was not yet as ambitious as he was later to become, passionately desired to marry her; but he was so much in awe of the Cardinal de Lorraine,* who had taken the place of his dead father, that he dared not make an open declaration. This was how matters stood when the house of Bourbon,* which could only feel envy on seeing the house of Guise elevated, perceived the advantage the Guises would obtain by the marriage and resolved to destroy that advantage and profit by it themselves by marrying the heiress to the young Prince de Montpensier.* They pursued this aim with such success that Mlle de Mézières's relatives, breaking the promises they had made to the Cardinal de Lorraine, agreed to give her in marriage to the young prince. The whole Guise family was extremely surprised by this manœuvre, but the Duc de Guise was overwhelmed with grief: being in love, and thus self-interested, he regarded the broken promise as an intolerable affront. His resentment soon broke out publicly, despite the stern injunctions of his uncles the Cardinal de Lorraine and the Duc d'Aumale,* who did not wish to persevere in a matter which they saw was beyond repair; and he became so violently angry, even in the presence of the young Prince de Montpensier himself, that a hatred was born between them that only ended with their lives. Mlle de Mézières was being harassed by her parents in their efforts to make her marry the Prince. She saw that she could not in any event marry the Duc de Guise; her virtue told her that it was dangerous to have as a brother-in-law a man she would have wanted as a husband; and she finally decided to obey the wishes of her family and implored M. de Guise to place no further obstacle in the way of her marriage.

Thus she married the Prince de Montpensier,* who shortly afterwards took her with him to Champigny,* the usual residence of the princes of his house, to remove her from Paris, which seemed likely to bear the whole brunt of the war.* The capital was under threat of siege by the Huguenot army, led by the Prince de Condé; the Huguenots had just declared war on the King for the second time. In his earliest youth, the Prince de Montpensier had formed an especially close friendship with the Comte de Chabannes,* who was a great deal older than he and a man of the rarest qualities. The Comte de Chabannes valued the trust and esteem of the young prince and could not bring himself to oppose in any way someone so dear to him; he therefore broke the promises he had made to the Prince de Condé, who was tempting him with the prospect of high office in the Huguenot party, and declared himself in favour of the Catholics. As there was no other reason for this change of sides, people doubted whether it was genuine, and the Queen Mother, Catherine de Médicis,* became so suspicious that, when the Huguenots declared war, she wanted to have him arrested; but the Prince de Montpensier prevented her and took Chabannes with him when he left for Champigny with his wife. As he had a most gentle and pleasant manner, Chabannes soon acquired the esteem of the Princesse de Montpensier; it was not long before she liked and trusted him as much as her husband did. Chabannes, for his part, marvelled at the young princess's great beauty, wit, and

virtue, and made use of the friendship she showed him to
instil in her a consciousness of the exalted virtue to which
she should aspire in order to be worthy of her illustrious
birth; in this way, he soon made her one of the most accomplished women in society. The prince returned to court,
where he was called by the continuation of the war. The
Comte de Chabannes remained alone with the Princesse de
Montpensier; he did not cease to feel for her a respect
and friendship commensurate with her rank and her merits.
Their mutual trust increased, so much so indeed on her side
that she told him of her former inclination for M. de Guise;
but she also told him at the same time that it was now almost
extinguished, all that remained being just enough to allow no
other inclination to enter her heart. Virtue, she said, had
joined forces with this lingering impression so that she was
capable of feeling only contempt for anyone who dared to
love her. The Comte de Chabannes, who knew how sincere
this beautiful young princess was and who saw that she had
adopted principles quite opposed to any kind of amorous
weakness, did not doubt the truth of what she said. Yet he
found himself unable to resist the daily sight, at such close
quarters, of so many charms. He fell passionately in love
with the princess; ashamed as he was of allowing his feelings
to get the better of him, there was nothing he could do but
love her with the most violent and sincere passion in the
world. He succeeded, however, in mastering his actions if
not his heart. The change in his soul brought none in his
conduct, so that no one suspected his love. For a whole year,
he took the greatest care to hide it from the princess, and he
believed that his desire to hide it would never waver. Yet
love wrought in him what it does in every other lover:* it
made him long to speak, and at last, after all the inner
struggles that usually take place on such occasions, he dared
to tell her that he loved her, having fortified himself in
advance against the stormy scenes with which her pride
threatened him. Her cool, calm reply was, however, a
thousand times worse than all the severity he had expected.
She did not so much as take the trouble to be angry with
him. She briefly reminded him of their difference in rank

and age, of his personal knowledge of her virtue, of her
former inclination for the Duc de Guise, and above all of
how much he owed to her husband's friendship and trust.
The Comte de Chabannes thought he would die of shame
and grief at her feet. She tried to console him by assuring
him that she would completely forget what he had just said,
that she would never allow herself to believe something that
placed him in such a poor light, and that she would never
regard him otherwise than as her best friend. Whether these
assurances consoled the Comte de Chabannes may easily be
imagined. He felt the whole weight of the princess's scorn
in her words; when she received him the next day with
her usual candour, his pain greatly increased. Her conduct
towards him did nothing to lessen it. She continued to show
him her customary good nature. She spoke to him again,
when chance brought the subject up, of her earlier inclination
for the Duc de Guise, whose noble qualities were just then
beginning to be publicly noticed; and she confessed to the
Comte de Chabannes that she was delighted to hear of them
and that it pleased her to see he merited the feelings she
had had towards him. All these indications of trust, which
had once been so welcome, became intolerable to the Comte
de Chabannes. He dared not, however, show the princess
that this was so, although he did venture to remind her
sometimes of what he had been bold enough to tell her.

Peace was made,* and the Prince de Montpensier returned to his wife after two years of absence, covered in the
glory he had won at the siege of Paris and at the Battle of
Saint-Denis. He was astonished to see that her beauty had
reached such a degree of perfection; since he was naturally
inclined to jealousy, he was not altogether pleased, for he
foresaw that he would not be the only man who found her
beautiful. He was very glad to see the Comte de Chabannes
again, for whom his friendship had not diminished. He
asked him in confidence for an account of the present state
of his wife's mind and character; he had lived with her for so
short a time that she was almost a stranger to him. His
friend told him, with as exact a fidelity as if he had not
been in love, of all the qualities he recognized in her that

might make the prince love her; he also advised Mme de Montpensier of all the things she should do to complete her conquest of her husband's love and esteem.

In other words, the Comte de Chabannes's passion naturally led him to give thought only to what might increase the princess's happiness and reputation, and in the end it was easy for him to forget that lovers have an interest in preventing the women they love from being on the best terms with their husbands.

The peace proved to be illusory. War broke out again* immediately as a result of the King's plan to have the Prince de Condé and the Amiral de Châtillon arrested at Noyers. The plan was discovered, preparations for war were renewed, and the Prince de Montpensier had no choice but to leave his wife in order to go where his duty called him. The Comte de Chabannes followed him to the court, having fully cleared his name with the Queen.* The pain he felt on leaving the Princesse de Montpensier was extreme; she, for her part, remained in melancholy contemplation of the perils to which the war would expose her husband. The Huguenot leaders had retreated to La Rochelle.* The provinces of Poitou and Saintonge being on their side, war broke out violently in that region and the King assembled all his troops there. His brother the Duc d'Anjou,* who was later to become Henri III, won great renown by his glorious deeds in this campaign, especially at the Battle of Jarnac, where the Prince de Condé was killed. It was in this war that the Duc de Guise began to be assigned to positions of high command and to show that he could go far beyond even the great things that had been predicted of him.* The Prince de Montpensier, who hated him both as his private enemy and as the enemy of his house, was not happy to see the Duc de Guise covered in glory, nor was he pleased by the Duc d'Anjou's friendship towards him.

After the two armies had worn themselves out in a series of minor engagements, the troops were disbanded for a while by common consent. The Duc d'Anjou stayed in Loches* in order to prepare all the strongholds which were likely to be attacked. The Duc de Guise remained there with

him, while the Prince de Montpensier, accompanied by the
Comte de Chabannes, returned to Champigny, which was
not far away.

The Duc d'Anjou often went to visit the places he was
having fortified. One day when he was returning to Loches
by a road little known to those in his company, the Duc de
Guise, who boasted that he knew it, went in front to act as a
guide; but, having ridden for some time, he lost his way and
found himself on the bank of a little river which he himself
did not recognize. The Duc d'Anjou teased him* for having
been such a poor guide. While they lingered on this spot, as
ready for enjoyment as one would expect young princes* to
be, they noticed a little boat which was anchored in the
middle of the river; and, as the stream was not broad, they
could easily make out three or four women in the boat. One
of these seemed to them remarkably beautiful. She was
magnificently dressed, and was closely watching two men
who were fishing beside her. This adventure* delighted the
princes and all their companions still more. They thought it
something out of a romance. Some told the Duc de Guise
that he had deliberately led them astray to show them this
beautiful woman; others said that, now chance had played its
part, he would have to fall in love with her; and the Duc
d'Anjou maintained that it was he who was to be her lover.

Finally, wishing to bring the adventure to its climax, they
ordered some of their servants on horseback to ride as far
out into the river as possible, in order to call out to the lady
that M. d'Anjou was here, that he would like to cross to the
other side, and that he would be grateful to be carried over.
The lady, who was the Princesse de Montpensier, heard
them say that the Duc d'Anjou was there and did not doubt,
seeing how many servants there were on the bank, that it was
he; she therefore gave orders for her boat to be directed
towards the spot where he was standing. She soon distinguished him from the others by his fine appearance; but
she was even quicker to distinguish the Duc de Guise. The
sight of him produced in her a confusion which made her
blush a little,* so that she was presented to the gaze of
the princes clothed in what seemed to them a supernatural

beauty. The Duc de Guise recognized her at once, although she had changed greatly, and for the better, during the three years* since he had last seen her. He told the Duc d'Anjou who she was. The Duc d'Anjou was at first ashamed of the liberty he had taken, but he found Mme de Montpensier so beautiful and the adventure so delightful that he made up his mind to carry it through. After endless excuses and compliments, he invented an important matter which he claimed to have to attend to on the other side of the river and accepted her offer to take him across in her boat.

Only he and the Duc de Guise entered the boat; he ordered all the rest of their company to go and cross the river at another point and meet them at Champigny, which Mme de Montpensier told them was only two leagues off. As soon as they were in the boat, the Duc d'Anjou asked her to what they owed such a pleasant meeting and what she was doing in the middle of the river. She replied that she had left Champigny with her husband, intending to accompany him on the hunt, but had felt too tired and had come down to the river's edge; curious to watch a salmon being caught which had swum into a net, she had entered the boat. M. de Guise took no part in the conversation; but he felt everything that the princess had once awakened in his heart being kindled there anew, and he told himself* that he would find it hard to emerge from this adventure without having once more become her captive.

They soon reached the bank, where they found Mme de Montpensier's horses and equerries waiting for them. The Duc d'Anjou and the Duc de Guise helped her to mount her horse, where her bearing was wonderfully graceful. As they rode along, she conversed with them most agreeably on various subjects. They were no less astonished by the charm of her wit than they had been by her beauty; and they could not help letting her see how exceedingly astonished they were. She replied to their words of praise with all the modesty imaginable, but rather more coldly to the Duc de Guise's, since she wished to maintain an aloofness which would prevent him from founding any hopes on the inclination she had had for him.

When they arrived in the first courtyard of Champigny, they met the Prince de Montpensier, who had just returned from the hunt. He was greatly surprised to see two men walking beside his wife; but his surprise became extreme when, on coming closer, he recognized that it was the Duc d'Anjou and the Duc de Guise. The hatred he felt for the latter, together with his jealous nature, caused him to find something so disagreeable in the sight of the princes with his wife, without knowing why they were there or what they were doing in his house, that he could not hide his displeasure. He skilfully found a pretext in his fear of being unable to receive so great a prince in a manner fitting to his rank and as he would have wished. The Comte de Chabannes was even sorrier to see M. de Guise with Mme de Montpensier than M. de Montpensier was. The chance which had brought these two people together seemed to him a bad omen, and he foresaw all too easily that this first chapter of the romance would not lack a sequel.

That evening, Mme de Montpensier played her part as hostess no less charmingly than she did everything else. In short, she pleased her guests all too well. The Duc d'Anjou, who was amorously inclined and extremely handsome, was unable to contemplate a gift of fortune so worthy of him without feeling a passionate desire to enjoy it. He was infected by the same malady as M. de Guise and, maintaining his pretext of an unusually important matter which he had to attend to, he remained at Champigny for two days without any other reason for staying than Mme de Montpensier's charms, for her husband made no effort to detain him forcibly. The Duc de Guise did not leave without conveying to Mme de Montpensier that his feelings for her were as they had been in the past; and, as his passion had been known to no one, he told her several times in public, without being understood by any but her, that his heart had not changed.

Both he and the Duc d'Anjou left Champigny with great regret. They rode for some time, neither saying a word.* But at last the Duc d'Anjou, suddenly guessing that his daydream might have the same cause as the Duc de Guise's, asked him abruptly if he was thinking about Mme de Montpensier's charms. This blunt question, together with what the Duc de Guise had already observed of the Duc d'Anjou's feelings, made it clear to him that they would infallibly be rivals, and that it was of the utmost importance that he should not reveal his love to the prince. To remove any such suspicion from his mind, he laughingly replied that he himself appeared to be so immersed in the daydream of which he was accusing him that he had not judged it appropriate to interrupt. The Princesse de Montpensier's charms, he added, were not new to him: his eyes had become accustomed to their brilliance in the days when it was thought she would become his sister-in-law; but he could see very well that not everyone was so little dazzled as he. The Duc d'Anjou confessed that he had never before seen anything comparable to the young princess and that he was well aware that the sight of her might be dangerous to him if he were frequently exposed to it. He wanted to make the Duc de Guise agree that he felt the same, but Guise, who was beginning to take his own love very seriously indeed, would admit nothing of the kind. They returned to Loches; their conversation often reverted pleasurably to the adventure in which they had happened upon the Princesse de Montpensier.

The subject was regarded as less entertaining at Champigny. The Prince de Montpensier was not pleased by what had happened, although he could not say why. He thought it a bad thing that his wife had been in the boat. It seemed to him that she had made the princes much too welcome; and what displeased him the most was to have noticed that the Duc de Guise had looked at her with particular attention. From that moment on, he became violently jealous of him, and his jealousy reminded him of the anger the Duc de Guise had shown when they were married; he began to suspect that even then he had been in love with her. The annoyance these suspicions inspired in him gave the Princesse de Montpensier many an uncomfortable hour. The Comte de Chabannes, as was his custom, took care to prevent them from falling out altogether, in order to persuade the princess how sincere and disinterested his passion for her was. He could not help asking her what effect the sight of the Duc de Guise had had on her. She told him that it had disturbed her because she was ashamed to remember the inclination she had once let him see. She had, she said, found him a good deal more handsome than he had been in those days, and she had even formed the impression that he wanted to persuade her that he still loved her; but she assured the Comte de Chabannes at the same time that nothing was capable of shaking the resolution she had made never to become entangled. Chabannes was delighted to hear of this resolution; yet nothing could reassure him where the Duc de Guise was concerned. He let the princess see that he was extremely apprehensive lest her earlier feelings should soon return; and he impressed on her how deeply dismayed he would be, for both their sakes, were he one day to see her attitude change. The Princesse de Montpensier, adopting her usual manner with him, scarcely replied to what he was saying about his passion and insisted on paying attention to him only as the very best friend in the world, without doing him the honour of noticing his claims as a lover.

The armies had been mobilized again and all the princes returned to their posts. The Prince de Montpensier thought it best to send his wife to Paris so that she would no longer be so close to the theatre of war. The Huguenots laid siege to the town of Poitiers.* The Duc de Guise rushed to its defence and performed deeds that would have sufficed on their own to bring glory to any other man's life. Then the Battle of Moncontour* was joined. The Duc d'Anjou, having taken Saint-Jean-d'Angély, fell ill* and immediately quitted the army, whether because his sickness was so violent, or because he wanted to return to savour the tranquillity and the pleasures of Paris, where the presence of the Princesse de Montpensier was not the least tempting prospect. The army remained under the command of the Prince de Montpensier. Not long after, when peace was made,* the whole court gathered in Paris. The princess's beauty outshone all those that had been admired until then.

All eyes were upon her,* such was the charm of her wit and her person. The feelings the Duc d'Anjou had conceived for her at Champigny did not change in Paris. He made sure that she noticed this, plying her assiduously with all kinds of attention, while taking care not to give her any sign that was too public for fear of making her husband jealous. If the Duc de Guise had not been violently in love with her before, he became so now; as he wanted, for several reasons, to keep his passion secret, he resolved to make his declaration to her at once, in order to spare himself all those opening manœuvres that always give rise to gossip and public attention. One day when he was in the Queen's apartment,* at a time when there were very few people there and the Queen herself had withdrawn to discuss matters of state with the Cardinal de Lorraine, the Princesse de Montpensier came in. He resolved to seize the opportunity to speak to her. He went up to her and said:

'I shall surprise and displease you, Madame, when I tell you that my passion for you, which was known to you in the past, has never ceased. Indeed it has become so much greater on seeing you again that neither your severity, nor M. de Montpensier's hatred, nor the rivalry of the first prince in the kingdom, could lessen its violence by one iota. It would have been more respectful to let my deeds inform you of it rather than my words; but, Madame, my deeds would have disclosed it to others as well as yourself, and I wish you to be the only one who knows that I am bold enough to adore you.'

At first, the princess was so surprised and disturbed by this speech that it did not occur to her to interrupt; but then, just as she had recovered and was beginning to reply, the Prince de Montpensier entered. Her face was a portrait of confusion and agitation; the sight of her husband added the final touch to her embarrassment, so that she allowed him to perceive even more than the Duc de Guise had just told her. The Queen came out from her private room and the Duc de Guise withdrew in an attempt to allay the prince's jealousy. That evening, the Princesse de Montpensier found her husband's mind full of the most extreme displeasure imaginable. His anger towards her broke out with a terrible violence and he forbade her ever to speak to the Duc de Guise again. She withdrew to her apartment in great sadness, absorbed in the adventures which had befallen her that day. She saw the Duc de Guise again the next day in the Queen's apartment; but he did not come near her and contented himself with leaving shortly after her, to let her see that he had nothing more to do there when she was no longer present. Not a day passed without her receiving countless secret indications of his passion, although he never attempted to speak to her of it except when no one could see him. As she was entirely convinced that he loved her, she began, despite all the resolutions she had made at Champigny, to feel* in the depths of her heart something of what had been there in the past.

The Duc d'Anjou,* for his part, who neglected no opportunity to show her his love wherever he could set eyes on her and who was always at her side when she visited his mother the Queen and his sister Marguerite de Valois,* was treated with such singular severity that any other passion than his would have been cured by it. It was discovered at that time that the Princesse Marguerite, who later became Queen of Navarre, had some degree of inclination for the Duc de Guise; what made it yet plainer was a visible cooling in the Duc d'Anjou's relations with the Duc de Guise. The Princesse de Montpensier heard the rumour; it was not a matter of indifference to her, and it made her aware* that her interest in the Duc de Guise was greater than she thought. M. de Montpensier,* her father-in-law, then married Mlle de Guise, the Duc de Guise's sister, so that she was obliged to see him frequently in the places where the wedding ceremonies required both her presence and his. The Princesse de Montpensier could no longer bear the thought that a man whom all France believed to be in love with Madame* should dare to tell her he loved her; she felt offended, even distressed at having deceived herself; so that, one day when the Duc de Guise met her in his sister's house, somewhat apart from the others who were there, and wanted to speak to her of his passion, she abruptly forestalled him. In a tone of voice which conveyed her anger, she said:

'I cannot think why, on the pretext of a weakness one was capable of at the age of 13, a man should have the audacity to play the lover to a woman like me, and especially when he is recognized by the whole court as the lover of another woman.'

The Duc de Guise, who was a man of no little wit and very much in love, needed to consult no one in order to understand the full significance of her words. He replied with great respect:

'I confess, Madame, that I was wrong not to scorn the honour of being the King's brother-in-law rather than to let you suspect for one moment that I could desire any woman's heart but yours; but, if you will be so gracious as to listen to me, I can easily justify myself in your eyes.'

The Princesse de Montpensier made no answer; but she did not move away, and the Duc de Guise, seeing that she was giving him the audience he desired, told her that, without his having attracted Madame's favour by any special attentions, she had granted it herself. Having no passion for her, he went on, he had made a very poor response to the honour she was doing him until she had given him some hope of marrying her. Then, indeed, the high position to which such a marriage was capable of raising him had obliged him to court her favour more assiduously, and this was what had made the King and the Duc d'Anjou suspicious. Their opposition, he said, would not dissuade him from proceeding with the plan, but, if it displeased the Princesse de Montpensier, he would abandon it that very moment and never think of it again. The sacrifice that the Duc de Guise was making for her sake caused her entirely to forget the severity and the anger with which she had spoken to him at first. She adopted a different tone and began to discuss with him the weakness Madame had shown in declaring her love before he did, and the considerable advantages that would come to him if he married her. In short, without saying anything flattering to the Duc de Guise, she allowed him to see once again all the countless pleasing qualities he had earlier seen in Mlle de Mézières. Although they had not spoken together for a long time, they discovered that they were in sympathy with one another and their hearts soon found themselves following a familiar path.

When this pleasant conversation was over, it left a lively sense of delight in the Duc de Guise's mind. The Princesse de Montpensier's own delight in seeing that he truly loved her was also great; but when she was in her private room, how deeply she reflected on the shame of having allowed herself to yield so easily to the Duc de Guise's explanations, on the predicament into which she would now fall if she became entangled in something that she had regarded with such horror, and on the appalling miseries into which her husband's jealousy was capable of throwing her! These thoughts caused her to make new resolutions, which were, however, dissipated the very next day by the sight of the Duc de Guise. He did not fail to give her an exact account of what was happening between Madame and himself. The new alliance between their houses gave him frequent opportunities to speak to her. But he had no little difficulty in curing her of the jealousy aroused in her by Madame's beauty, against which there was no oath that could reassure her. The Princesse de Montpensier used her jealousy to defend what remained of her heart against the attentions of the Duc de Guise, who had already conquered the greater part of it.

The King's marriage to the daughter of the Emperor Maximilian filled the court with celebrations and festivities.* The King offered a ballet in which Madame and all the princesses danced. Only the Princesse de Montpensier could dispute Madame's claim to the prize for beauty. The Duc d'Anjou was dancing a Moorish entry; the Duc de Guise, with four others, was to dance it with him. Their costumes were all alike, as is usual for those dancing the same entry. The first time the ballet was danced, the Duc de Guise, before putting on his mask for the dance, said a few words in passing to the Princesse de Montpensier. She saw that her husband had noticed, and this made her anxious. Some time after, she saw the Duc d'Anjou in his mask and his Moorish costume coming to speak to her; confused by her anxiety, she thought it was the Duc de Guise again and, going up to him, she said:

'Look at no one this evening but Madame; I shall not be jealous; it is what I command; I am being watched; do not come near me again.'

She withdrew as soon as she had said these words. The Duc d'Anjou remained as if struck by a thunderbolt. At that moment, he perceived that he had a successful rival. The mention of Madame told him that this rival was the Duc de Guise; and he could not doubt that his royal sister was the sacrifice by means of which the Princesse de Montpensier had been persuaded to look kindly upon his rival's protestations of love. Jealousy, vexation, and rage, mingling with the hatred he already felt for the Duc de Guise, produced the most violent effect imaginable in his soul: his despair would have shown itself forthwith in some bloody act, had not his natural tendency to dissimulation come to his aid and forced him, for reasons that were compelling in the circumstances, to undertake nothing against the Duc de Guise. He could not, however, deny himself the pleasure of informing him that he knew the secret of his love. Approaching him as they left the room where they had been dancing, he said:

'You go too far in daring to lift your gaze to my sister while at the same time taking my mistress from me. Respect for the King prevents me from showing my anger; but remember that the loss of your life* will perhaps be the least punishment that I will exact for your temerity.'

The Duc de Guise's self-esteem was not accustomed to such threats. Although he could not respond because the King, who was coming out at that moment, called both of them to him, the Duc d'Anjou's words engraved on his heart a desire for vengeance which he was to work all his life to satisfy. From that very evening, the Duc d'Anjou did him all kinds of disservice with the King. He persuaded him that Madame would never consent to be married to the King of Navarre, as was being proposed, while the Duc de Guise was allowed to come near her; and that it was shameful to permit one of his subjects, merely to satisfy his own vanity, to place obstacles in the way of an arrangement which was intended to bring peace to France. The King's feelings towards the Duc de Guise were already bitter, and the Duc d'Anjou's remarks made them so much the more so that, when he saw him arrive the next day for the ball in the Queen's apartment, dazzling the eye with countless precious stones but even more with his handsome looks, he placed himself at the entrance and asked him abruptly where he was going. Without flinching, the Duc de Guise told him that he was coming to offer him his most humble services; the King replied that he had no need of any services he might offer, and turned away without looking at him. The Duc de Guise entered the room none the less, his heart full of fury against both the King and the Duc d'Anjou. But his pain fortified his natural self-esteem and, as a gesture of defiance, he approached Madame much more than was his custom; besides, what the Duc d'Anjou had said to him about the Princesse de Montpensier prevented him from looking at her. The Duc d'Anjou observed both of them with care. The Princesse de Montpensier's eyes betrayed a certain annoyance, despite herself, when the Duc de Guise was speaking to Madame. The Duc d'Anjou, who had realized that she was jealous from what she had said when she had mistaken him for the Duc de Guise, had hopes of causing a quarrel between them; placing himself next to her, he said:

'I wish you to know, Madame, in your own interest rather than mine, that the Duc de Guise does not deserve the preference you have given him at my expense. Do not interrupt me, I pray, to tell me the contrary of a truth of which I am all too sure. He is deceiving you, Madame, and sacrificing you to my sister just as he sacrificed her to you. He is a man capable of nothing but ambition, but, since he has had the good fortune to please you, that is enough. I shall not stand in the way of a happiness which I doubtless deserved better than he. I should show myself to be unworthy of it if I persisted any longer in attempting the conquest of a heart which is possessed by another. It is already too much that I have only been able to attract your indifference. I have no wish to turn that indifference into hatred by continuing to press upon you the most faithful passion that ever was.'

The Duc d'Anjou, who was genuinely moved by love and sorrow, could hardly finish these words. Even though he had begun his speech in a spirit of rancour and vengeance, his heart melted when he considered the princess's beauty and how much he must lose in losing the hope of her love; and, without waiting for her to reply, he left the ball, pretending to be ill, and went to his own apartment to muse over his misfortune. The Princesse de Montpensier remained, as one may well imagine, in a state of distress and confusion. To see her reputation and the secret of her life in the hands of a prince whom she had ill-treated and to learn from him, with no possibility of doubt, that she was deceived by her lover—these were things which did not afford her that freedom of spirit necessary to enjoy a place where pleasure was offered on all sides. She was, however, obliged to remain there and to go on to supper afterwards at the house of the Duchesse de Montpensier, her mother-in-law, who took her with her. The Duc de Guise, who was dying of impatience to tell her what the Duc d'Anjou had said to him the previous day, followed her to his sister's house. But what was his astonishment when he sought to converse with the beautiful princess and found that she would only address him the most terrible reproaches! And her vexation made her express them in such a confused manner that he could understand nothing of them, except that she accused him of infidelity and treachery. Overcome with despair at finding his pain so much magnified when he had hoped to have consolation for all his troubles, and full of a passion which would no longer allow him to live without being certain that the princess loved him, he suddenly made up his mind.

'You will be satisfied, Madame,' he said. 'I am going to do for you what the whole authority of the crown could not have made me do. It will cost me my fortune, but that is a mere trifle if it will satisfy you.'

Without staying longer in his sister's house, he went that very hour to find the cardinals, his uncles, and, on the pretext of the ill-treatment he had received from the King, he told them that it was absolutely necessary to his fortune to demonstrate publicly that he had no thought of marrying Madame, and thus persuaded them to conclude his marriage with the Princesse de Portien,* this having been spoken of previously. The news of the marriage immediately spread through the whole of Paris. Everyone was surprised, and the Princesse de Montpensier, when she heard of it, was moved by joy and sorrow. She was glad to see this proof of the power she had over the Duc de Guise; at the same time, she was sorry to have made him abandon something so much to his advantage as marriage with Madame. The Duc de Guise, who at least wanted love to compensate him for what he was losing on the side of fortune, urged the princess to hear him in private so that he could defend himself against her unjust reproaches. He persuaded her to agree to be at the Duchesse de Montpensier's house at a time when his sister would not be present and he could speak to her in private. The Duc de Guise there had the luxury of being able to throw himself at her feet, of speaking freely to her of his passion, and of telling her what her suspicions had made him suffer. The princess could not remove from her mind what the Duc d'Anjou had told her, although the Duc de Guise's behaviour was such as to reassure her completely. She informed him of the good reason she had for believing that he had betrayed her, seeing that the Duc d'Anjou knew something he could only have learnt from the Duc de Guise himself. He could not see how to defend himself and was as much at a loss as the Princesse de Montpensier to guess how their mutual understanding had been found out. Finally, as their conversation proceeded and as she was arguing that he had been wrong to settle his marriage to the Princesse de Portien so hastily and to abandon the chance of marrying Madame, which would have been greatly to his advantage, she said that it was easy for him to judge that she had not been at all jealous of Madame, since, on the day of the ballet, she herself had implored him to have eyes only for her. The Duc de Guise told her that she had no doubt intended to give him this order, but that she certainly had not done so. She maintained the contrary. Finally, after much argument and reflection, they came to the conclusion* that she must have been misled by the similarity of the costumes and that she herself must have let the Duc d'Anjou know what she was accusing the Duc de Guise of telling him. The Duc de Guise, whose marriage had almost justified him in her eyes, was now wholly vindicated by this conversation. The beautiful princess could not refuse her heart to a man who had possessed it in the past and who had just sacrificed everything for her. She consented therefore to accept his protestations of love and allowed him to believe that she was not insensible to his passion. The arrival of the Duchesse de Montpensier, her mother-in-law, put an end to the conversation and prevented the Duc de Guise from displaying to her his transports of delight.

Some time afterwards,* the court left for Blois, where the marriage of Madame with the King of Navarre was agreed, and the Princesse de Montpensier went there also. The Duc de Guise, who no longer recognized any advancement or good fortune but that of being loved by the princess, was delighted to see this marriage settled, even though it would earlier have reduced him to utter misery. He was incapable of concealing his love so successfully that the Prince de Montpensier did not catch a glimpse of it; the prince, who was no longer master of his jealousy, ordered his wife to leave for Champigny. This command was harsh indeed, but she was obliged to obey. She managed to say farewell in private to the Duc de Guise, but she was at a loss to know how to ensure that he could safely write to her. Finally, after exploring many possibilities, she thought of the Comte de Chabannes, whom she still regarded as her friend, without considering that he was her suitor. The Duc de Guise knew how close a friend of the Prince de Montpensier the Comte de Chabannes was, and was horrified that she should have chosen him as her confidant; but she gave him such a good account of his trustworthiness that he was reassured. He parted from her with all the pain that the absence of a person one loves passionately is capable of causing.

The Comte de Chabannes, who had been ill in Paris during the whole of the Princesse de Montpensier's stay in

Blois and who knew that she was going to Champigny, went
to meet her on her way in order to accompany her. She
treated him to endless flattering looks and friendly words,
and manifested a quite unusual impatience to speak to him
in private, which he at first found charming. How astonished
and how hurt he was, then, to find that she was only
impatient to tell him that the Duc de Guise was passionately
in love with her and that she loved him equally! His pain and
surprise made it impossible for him to reply. The princess,
whose thoughts were full of her passion and who found it an
extreme relief to speak to him about it, did not notice his
silence and began to recount her adventure to him in the
minutest detail. She told him how she had made a plan with
the Duc de Guise to use him as a go-between for the letters
they would write to one another. It was the final blow for the
Comte de Chabannes to see that his mistress wanted him to
serve his rival and that she was proposing this to him as
something he ought to find agreeable. He was so absolutely
in possession of himself that he concealed from her everything he felt. He only made plain how surprised he was to
see such a great change in her. He hoped at first that this
change, which destroyed all his hopes, would also destroy his
passion; but he found her so charming, her natural beauty
having been further enhanced by a certain grace she had
acquired from court manners, that he felt he loved her
more than ever. She confided to him all the tenderness and
delicacy of her feelings towards the Duc de Guise, and this
showed him how precious her love was and made him desire
to possess it. His passion being the most extraordinary in
the world, it produced the most extraordinary effect:* it
persuaded him to deliver to his mistress the letters of his
rival. The absence of the Duc de Guise cast the Princesse
de Montpensier into a state of great anguish; since her
only hope of relief was through his letters, she continually
tormented the Comte de Chabannes, asking him whether he
had not received any and almost blaming him for not having
them soon enough. Finally, one of the Duc de Guise's
gentlemen gave him some and he took them to her instantly,
in order not to delay her joy for one moment. When she

received them, her joy was indeed extreme. She made no effort to hide it from him, and made him swallow deep draughts of every imaginable kind of poison by reading the letters to him, together with her tender, amorous reply. He delivered the reply to the gentleman as faithfully as he had brought the letter to the princess, but more painfully. He was, however, somewhat consoled by the thought that the princess would take some notice of what he was doing for her and show her gratitude to him. Finding that as the days went by she treated him more harshly because of her own sorrows, he took the liberty of begging her to give some thought to what she was making him suffer. The princess, who could think of nothing but the Duc de Guise and who considered that only he was worthy to adore her, found it so unacceptable that anyone other than he should dare to think of her that she treated the Comte de Chabannes much worse* on this occasion than the first time he had spoken to her of his love. Although his passion, no less than his patience, was extreme and proof against all trials, he left the princess and went to stay with one of his friends not far from Champigny. From there he wrote to her with all the fury that such strange behaviour could well provoke, yet with all the respect that was due to her rank; and in his letter he said farewell to her for ever. The princess began to feel sorry that she had failed to humour a man over whom she had so much power. She could not make up her mind to let him go, not only because she regarded him as her friend, but also in the interests of her love, to which he was indispensable; she therefore sent him a message saying that she absolutely must speak to him once more, after which she would leave him free to do as he pleased. We are very weak when we are in love. The Comte de Chabannes returned and in less than an hour the beauty of the Princesse de Montpensier, her wit, and a few flattering words made him a more abject servant than he had ever been; he even gave her some letters from the Duc de Guise which he had just received.

Meanwhile, the terrible plot which was carried out on St Bartholomew's Day* was being conceived at court. The plan was to summon the leaders of the Huguenot party to court, and, in order better to deceive them, the King sent away all the princes of the house of Bourbon and all those of the house of Guise. The Prince de Montpensier returned to Champigny; his presence there made his wife's misery complete. The Duc de Guise went to visit his uncle the Cardinal de Lorraine in the country. Love and idleness bred in his mind such a violent desire to see the Princesse de Montpensier that, without considering what was at stake for her and for himself, he pretended to set out on a journey. He left all his retinue in a little town, took as his sole companion the gentleman who had already made several journeys to Champigny, and went there post-haste. As he had no other address than the Comte de Chabannes's, he instructed the gentleman to write a note asking him to meet the gentleman in a place he indicated to him. The Comte de Chabannes, believing that this was only so that he could receive letters from the Duc de Guise, went to meet him; but he was extremely surprised—and no less distressed—when he saw the Duc de Guise. Being preoccupied with his plan, the Duc de Guise no more noticed the Comte de Chabannes's embarrassment than the Princesse de Montpensier had noticed his silence when she had told him of her love. He began to describe his passion in the most extravagant terms and to insist that he would perish without fail if he did not obtain for him the princess's permission to see her. The Comte de Chabannes coldly replied that he would tell the princess everything he wanted him to say and that he would come back with her reply. He returned to Champigny, hard pressed by his own feelings, whose violence sometimes deprived him of all consciousness. Time and again he made up his mind to send the Duc de Guise away without telling the Princesse de Montpensier; but the exact fidelity he had promised her immediately changed his resolve.

He arrived at her house without knowing what he should do; learning that the Prince de Montpensier was out hunting, he went straight to the princess's apartment. Seeing how agitated he was, she at once ordered her women to withdraw so that she could discover the cause of his agitation. He told her, with as much restraint as he could manage, that the Duc de Guise was only a league away from Champigny and that he passionately desired to see her. The princess uttered a great cry when she heard this news, and her confusion was almost equal to the Comte de Chabannes's. She was at first persuaded by love how delightful it would be to see a man for whom she had such tender feelings. But when she reflected how contrary to her virtue such a meeting would be, and that she could only see her lover by letting him into her apartment at night without the knowledge of her husband, she found herself in a terrible dilemma. The Comte de Chabannes waited for her reply as if his life depended on it. Judging by the princess's silence that she was uncertain, he took it upon himself to represent to her all the perils to which she would expose herself if she agreed to the rendezvous. Wishing to show her that it was not in his own interests that he was speaking to her thus, he said:

'If, Madame, after everything I have just said, your passion proves too strong and you wish to see the Duc de Guise, let consideration for me not prevent you, if your own interests cannot. I do not want to deprive a woman I adore of such a great satisfaction, nor to cause her to look for persons less trustworthy than I am in order to procure it. Yes, Madame, if you wish, I shall seek out the Duc de Guise this very evening—for it is too dangerous to leave him any longer where he is—and I shall bring him to your apartment.'

'But how will he get in?' the princess interrupted.

'Ah! Madame,' cried the Comte de Chabannes, 'the question is decided, if you are thinking of nothing now but the means. He shall come, your most fortunate lover, Madame: I shall bring him through the grounds; only order the most trustworthy of your women, on the stroke of midnight, to lower the little drawbridge* which leads from your antechamber into the garden, and have no care for the rest.'

As he finished these words, he stood up; without waiting for any further consent from the Princesse de Montpensier, he mounted his horse again and went to find the Duc de Guise, who was waiting for him with extreme impatience. The Princesse de Montpensier remained in such a state of

confusion that it was some time before she came to herself.
Her first impulse was to have the Comte de Chabannes
recalled in order to forbid him to bring the Duc de Guise,
but she lacked the strength. She reflected that, without
recalling him, she need only fail to lower the drawbridge.
She believed that she would be able to hold to this resolution. When the time for the assignation came near, she
could no longer resist her desire to see a lover whom she
believed to be so worthy of her, and she explained to one of
her women everything that needed to be done in order to
admit the Duc de Guise to her apartment.

Meanwhile, the Duc de Guise and the Comte de
Chabannes were both coming towards Champigny, but in
very different states of mind. The Duc de Guise abandoned
his soul to joy and to all the pleasant thoughts that hope
gives rise to, while the Comte de Chabannes was so consumed with despair and rage that he was often prompted to
thrust his sword through the body of his rival. Finally they
arrived at the grounds of Champigny, where they left their
horses in the care of the Duc de Guise's equerry; passing
through a gap in the wall, they found themselves in the
garden. The Comte de Chabannes, in the midst of his
despair, had some hope that the Princesse de Montpensier
would recover her reason and resolve not to see the Duc de
Guise. When he saw the little bridge lowered, he could no
longer doubt that the contrary was true: it was then that he
felt ready to take matters to an extreme conclusion. But,
reflecting that, if he made any noise, he would probably
be heard by the Prince de Montpensier, whose apartment
opened on to the same garden, and that all the ensuing
trouble would fall on the person he loved most, his rage was
immediately calmed, and he completed the task of leading
the Duc de Guise to the feet of his princess. He could not
bring himself to witness their conversation, although the
princess said she wished him to and he would very much
have wished it himself. He withdrew into a little passage
leading towards the Prince de Montpensier's apartment, his
mind occupied by the most melancholy thoughts a lover has
ever had.

Meanwhile, although they had made very little noise in crossing the bridge, the Prince de Montpensier, who unfortunately was awake at that moment, heard it and roused one of his valets to see what it was. The valet looked out of the window and made out, through the darkness of the night, that the bridge was lowered. He informed his master, who at once ordered him to go out into the grounds to find out what was happening. A moment later, he himself rose, being alarmed by what seemed to him to be the sound of someone moving, and he went straight to his wife's apartment, which was directly opposite the bridge. At the moment when he was approaching the little passage where the Comte de Chabannes was, the Princesse de Montpensier, who was somewhat ashamed to find herself alone with the Duc de Guise, was begging the Comte de Chabannes insistently to come into her room. He rejected all her pleas, and, as she continued to press him, overcome with rage and fury, he replied so loudly that he was overheard by the Prince de Montpensier, yet so indistinctly that the prince heard only the voice of a man, without recognizing the Comte de Chabannes's. Such an extraordinary occurrence* would have provoked the anger of a calmer and less jealous man; it therefore filled the prince from the outset with the utmost rage and fury. He at once knocked impetuously at the door and shouted out for it to be opened. The princess, the Duc de Guise, and the Comte de Chabannes had the cruellest of surprises. The Comte de Chabannes heard the prince's voice and understood immediately that it was impossible to prevent him from believing that there was someone in the princess's room. His own great passion told him at that moment that, if the Duc de Guise were found there, Mme de Montpensier would have to bear the pain of seeing him killed before her eyes, and that her own life would not be safe. He therefore resolved, with an unparalleled generosity of spirit, to expose his own life in order to save an ungrateful mistress and a successful rival. While the Prince de Montpensier was knocking incessantly at the door, he went to the Duc de Guise, who could not decide what to do, and put him in the hands of the woman who had brought him in by the bridge; his plan was to have him taken out by the same route, while he exposed himself to the prince's fury. Hardly was the Duc de Guise out of the antechamber than the prince, having broken down the door leading into the passage, came into the room like a man mad with rage, seeking someone on whom to vent it. But when he saw only the Comte de Chabannes, leaning motionless on the table, his face a picture of sadness, he remained motionless himself; and his astonishment on finding the man he liked best in the world alone at night in his wife's room made him wholly incapable of speech. The princess had half fainted away on the tiled floor, and fortune has perhaps never brought together three people in such a pitiful state. Finally, the Prince de Montpensier, who could not believe he was seeing what he saw and who wanted to make sense of the chaos into which he had fallen, spoke thus to the Comte de Chabannes, in a tone which made it plain that he still had feelings of friendship towards him:

'What do I see here? Is it an illusion or the truth? Is it possible that a man whom I have loved so dearly should choose to seduce my wife of all the women in the world? And you, Madame,' he said, turning to the princess, 'was it not enough for you to rob me of your heart and my honour, without taking from me the only man who could console me for such ills? Answer me, one or other of you,' he said to them, 'and tell me the meaning of an occurrence so strange* that I cannot believe it to be as it appears.'

The princess was not capable of replying and the Comte de Chabannes opened his mouth several times without being able to speak.

'I have indeed acted criminally towards you,' he said at last, 'and I am unworthy of the friendship you have had for me; but not in the way you may imagine. I am unhappier than you and in deeper despair. I cannot tell you more than this. My death will be your revenge, and if it pleases you to give it to me at once, you will give me the only thing I desire.'

These words, uttered in accents of mortal pain and with an expression that spoke of innocence, instead of enlightening the Prince de Montpensier, persuaded him all the more that there was some mystery in this scene* that he could not unravel. His despair was greatly increased by this uncertainty and he said:

'Take my life yourself, or tell me the meaning of your words; they are wholly obscure to me. You owe this explanation to my friendship; and you owe it to my moderation, for any other man than I would already have avenged on your life so palpable an affront.'

'Things are not at all as they appear,'* interrupted the Comte de Chabannes.

'Ah! this is too much,' replied the prince; 'I must take my revenge and discover the truth afterwards* at my leisure.'

As he said this, he approached the Comte de Chabannes with the attitude of a man overcome by rage. The princess, fearing some unfortunate consequence (which could, however, not occur since her husband had no sword), rose from the floor and placed herself between them. In her weakened state, this effort was too much for her: as she came near her husband, she fell in a swoon at his feet. The prince was still more touched by her fainting than he had been by the Comte de Chabannes's calmness when he had threatened him. No longer able to bear the sight of two people who caused in him such deep feelings of sadness, he turned his head away from them and fell on to his wife's bed, struck down by a pain and sorrow beyond belief. The Comte de Chabannes, overwhelmed by repentance at having abused a friendship of which he had received so many tokens, and believing that he could never set right what he had just done, left the room abruptly; passing through the prince's apartment, of which he found the doors open, he went down into the courtyard. He obtained horses and went out into the country, guided only by his despair. Meanwhile, the Prince de Montpensier, who saw that the princess was not recovering from her faint, left her in the hands of her women and withdrew into his own room in mortal distress.

The Duc de Guise had successfully made his way out of the grounds. Almost without knowing what he was doing, so confused was he, he left Champigny several leagues behind him; but he could not go further without obtaining news of the princess. He stopped in a forest and sent his equerry to learn from the Comte de Chabannes what the outcome of that terrible event had been. The equerry did not find the Comte de Chabannes, but he learnt from others that the Princesse de Montpensier was extremely ill. The Duc de Guise's disquiet was increased by what his equerry told him, but he was unable to assuage it, as he was obliged to return to his uncles in order not to arouse suspicion by a longer journey. The equerry had reported the truth when he told him that Mme de Montpensier was so ill; for it was true that, as soon as her women had carried her to her bed, she was so violently overcome by fever, accompanied by terrible hallucinations, that by the second day her life seemed to be in danger.

The prince pretended to be ill so that no one would be astonished that he did not enter his wife's chamber. He then received an order to return to court, where all the Catholic princes were being recalled to exterminate the Huguenots, and this enabled him to escape from his predicament. He left for Paris without knowing what he had to hope or fear* from his wife's illness. Hardly had he arrived when the Huguenots began to be attacked in the person of one of their leaders, the Amiral de Châtillon; and two days later the horrible massacre was carried out of which the notoriety has spread through the whole of Europe. The poor Comte de Chabannes, who had come to hide on the outskirts of one of the suburbs of Paris in order to abandon himself to his sorrow, was engulfed in the ruin of the Huguenots. The people in whose house he was staying, having recognized him and remembered that he had been suspected of belonging to the Protestant party, murdered him on the very night that was fatal to so many others. In the morning, the Prince de Montpensier, on his way to give some orders outside the town, passed through the street where the body of Chabannes was lying. At first, he was profoundly shaken by this piteous sight; then, as his feelings of friendship reawoke in him, they brought him pain and sorrow; but the memory of the offence he believed he had received from the Comte de Chabannes finally gave him joy, and he was glad to find that he had been avenged by the hand of fortune.

The Duc de Guise, preoccupied by the desire to avenge the death of his father* and, shortly afterwards, exulting in his vengeance, gradually allowed the wish to hear news of the Princesse de Montpensier to fade from his mind; and, having made the acquaintance of the Marquise de Noirmoutier,* a woman of great wit and beauty who gave him more to hope for than the princess, he became wholly attached to her and loved her with an inordinate passion that lasted until death.

Meanwhile, after Mme de Montpensier's illness had almost proved fatal, it began to diminish. Her reason returned and, finding herself somewhat relieved by her husband's absence, she gave some hopes that she might live. She recovered her health, however, with great difficulty, owing to her wretched state of mind; and her thoughts were tormented afresh when she remembered that she had had no news from the Duc de Guise throughout her illness. She enquired of her women whether they had seen anyone, whether they had received any letters; and, finding nothing she would have wished for, she thought herself the un-happiest woman in the world to have risked everything for a man who had abandoned her. It was yet another cruel blow to her to hear of the Comte de Chabannes's death, of which her husband soon took care to inform her. The ingratitude of the Duc de Guise made her more sharply aware of the loss of a man whom she knew to be so faithful. All these afflictions, pressing her from all sides, soon caused her to fall back into a state as dangerous as the one from which she had just recovered. And, as Mme de Noirmoutier was a woman who took as much care to advertise her love affairs as others take to hide them, her relations with M. de Guise became widely known, and the Princesse de Montpensier, although ill and far removed from public life, heard of them from so many quarters that she could have no doubts. This was the blow that proved fatal to her. She could not hold out against the pain of having lost the esteem of her husband, the heart of her lover, and the most perfect

friend that ever was. She died within a few days, in the
flower of her youth: she was one of the most beautiful
princesses in the world, and would doubtless have been the
happiest, if virtue and prudence had guided all her actions.

The Comtesse de Tende

IN the first year of the regency of Queen Catherine de Médicis,* Mademoiselle de Strozzi,* the daughter of the Maréchal and a close relation of the Queen, married the Comte de Tende* of the house of Savoy. He was rich and handsome; he lived with greater magnificence than any other nobleman at court, though more in a manner to attract esteem than to give pleasure. His wife none the less loved him passionately at first.* She was very young; he regarded her as a mere child, and he soon fell in love with another woman. The Comtesse de Tende, who was spirited and of Italian descent, became jealous. She allowed herself no rest; she gave none to her husband; he avoided her presence and ceased to live with her as a man lives with his wife.

The beauty of the Comtesse de Tende increased; she showed that she was well endowed with wit; she was regarded in society with admiration; she busied herself with her own affairs and gradually recovered from her jealousy and passion.

She became the intimate friend of the Princesse de Neufchâtel,* the young and beautiful widow of the prince of that house. On his death, he had bequeathed her a sovereign position that made her the most high-ranking and brilliant match at court.

The Chevalier de Navarre,* a descendant of the former monarchs of that kingdom, was also at that time young, handsome, full of wit and nobility; but fortune had endowed him with no other goods than his illustrious birth. His glance fell on the Princesse de Neufchâtel—with whose character he was acquainted*—as a woman capable of a passionate attachment and well suited to making the fortune of a man like himself. With this in mind, he paid court to her and attracted her interest: she did not discourage him, but he found that he was still very far from the success he desired. His intentions were known to nobody except one of his friends, to whom he had confided them; this friend was also an intimate of the Comte de Tende. He made the Chevalier de Navarre consent to entrust the Comte de Tende with his secret, in the hope that he might be persuaded to further his cause with the Princesse de Neufchâtel. The Comte de Tende already liked the Chevalier de Navarre; he spoke of the matter to his wife, for whom he was beginning to have greater consideration, and persuaded her, in fact, to do what was wanted.

The Princesse de Neufchâtel had already told her in confidence about her inclination for the Chevalier de Navarre, and she gave her friend her support and encouragement. The Chevalier came to see her; they established connections and made arrangements together; but, on seeing her, he also conceived a violent passion for her. At first, he refused to give himself up to it; he saw the obstacles that would be put in the way of his plans if he were subject to conflicting feelings of love and ambition; he tried to resist; but, in order to succeed, he would have had to avoid seeing the Comtesse de Tende frequently, whereas in fact he saw her every day when he visited the Princesse de Neufchâtel. In this way, he fell hopelessly in love with her. He was unable to hide his passion from her entirely; this flattered her self-regard and she began to feel a violent love for him.

As she was speaking to him one day of his good fortune in marrying the Princesse de Neufchâtel, he gave her a look in which his passion was fully declared and said:

'Do you then believe, Madame, that there is no good fortune I would prefer to that of marrying the princess?'

The Comtesse de Tende was struck by his expression and his words; she returned his look, and there was a moment of troubled silence between them more eloquent than words. From that time on, she was in a state of constant agitation and could find no rest; she felt remorse at depriving her friend of the heart of a man she intended to marry solely for the sake of his love, amid universal disapproval, and at the expense of her high rank.

The treachery horrified her. The shame and misery of a

love affair presented themselves to her imagination; she saw the abyss into which she was about to cast herself, and resolved to avoid it.

Her resolutions were ill kept. The Princesse de Neufchâtel was almost persuaded that she should marry the Chevalier de Navarre; however, she was not satisfied that he loved her sufficiently and, despite her own passion and the care he took to deceive her, she discerned that his feelings were no more than lukewarm. She complained of it to the Comtesse de Tende, who reassured her; but Mme de Neufchâtel's complaints added the final touch to her disquiet, making apparent to her the extent of her treachery, which might perhaps cost her lover his fortune. She warned him of the Princesse de Neufchâtel's suspicions. He declared that he was indifferent to everything except her love for him; none the less, he mastered his feelings at her command and succeeded in reassuring the princess, who indicated to her friend that she was now entirely satisfied with the Chevalier de Navarre.

Then jealousy took possession of the Comtesse de Tende. She feared that her lover really did love the princess;* she perceived all the reasons he had for loving her; their marriage, which she had earlier desired, horrified her; yet she did not wish him to break it off, and she found herself in a state of cruel uncertainty. She allowed the Chevalier de Navarre to see the remorse she felt towards the princess; but she resolved to hide her jealousy from him and believed she had in fact done so.

The Princesse de Neufchâtel's passion finally triumphed over her hesitations; she determined upon marriage, but resolved that it should be consecrated in secret and only made public afterwards.

The Comtesse de Tende felt she would die of grief. On the day the wedding was to take place, there was also a public ceremony; her husband attended. She sent all her women there; she let it be known that she was receiving no one and shut herself in her private room, where she lay on a couch* and gave herself up to the most cruel torments of remorse, love, and jealousy.

The room had a secret door. While she was in this state,

she heard the door open and saw the Chevalier de Navarre, finely dressed and more elegant and charming than she had ever seen him.

'Chevalier! What are you doing here?' she cried. 'What do you want? Have you lost your reason? What has become of your marriage? Do you care nothing for my reputation?'

'Have no fear for your reputation, Madame,' he replied; 'no one can know I am here; there is no question of my marriage; I care no longer for my fortune, I care only for your heart, Madame; all the rest I willingly renounce. You have allowed me to see that you did not hate me; yet you have tried to conceal from me that I am fortunate enough to have caused you pain by marrying the Princesse de Neufchâtel. I have come to tell you, Madame, that I will not proceed with the marriage, that it would be a torment to me, and that I want to live only for you. They are waiting for me as I speak to you now, everything is ready, but I shall break it all off, if, in doing so, I do something that is pleasing to you and that convinces you of my passion.'

The Comtesse de Tende fell back on her couch, from which she had half risen, and looked at the Chevalier with eyes full of love and tears.

'Do you then wish me to die?' she said. 'What heart could contain everything you make me feel? That you should abandon for my sake the fortune that awaits you! I cannot even bear to think of such a thing. Go to the Princesse de Neufchâtel, go to the high position destined for you; you will have my heart as well. I shall deal with my remorse, my hesitations, and my jealousy—since I am forced to admit it—in whatever way my feeble reason dictates; but I shall never see you again if you do not go immediately and consecrate your marriage. Go, don't hesitate an instant; but, for my sake and yours, give up this unreasoning passion you have revealed to me; it could lead us into terrible misfortunes.'

The Chevalier was at first enraptured to see how genuinely the Comtesse de Tende loved him; but the horror of giving himself to another woman presented itself anew to his gaze. He wept, he lamented, he promised her everything she wanted, provided that she would agree to see him again in this same place. She asked him, before he left, how he had found his way in. He told her that he had entrusted himself to an equerry in her service who had once been in his own; this man had brought him through the stable yard and up a little staircase that led to the private room as well as to the equerry's own room.

Meanwhile, the time for the wedding was drawing near and the Chevalier, urged on by the Comtesse de Tende, was at last obliged to go. He went to the greatest and most desirable gift of fortune to which a penniless younger son has ever been raised up; but he went as if to the scaffold. The Comtesse de Tende passed the night, as may well be imagined, in a state of agitation and disquiet. When morning came, she called her women; not long after her room was open, she saw her equerry approach her bed and put a letter on it without anyone noticing. The sight of this letter disturbed her, both because she recognized it as coming from the Chevalier de Navarre and because it was so improbable that, during a night which was supposed to have been his wedding night,* he had had the opportunity to write to her—so improbable was it, indeed, that she feared he or others might have put obstacles in the way of his marriage. She opened the letter with deep emotion and read these words, or something like them:

'I think only of you, Madame, I care for nothing else: in the first moments of legitimate possession of the highest-born match in France, when the day has hardly begun to break, I have left the chamber where I spent the night in order to tell you that I have already repented a thousand times of having obeyed your will and of failing to renounce everything to live for you alone.'

The Comtesse de Tende was much moved by this letter and by the circumstances in which it was written. She went to dine at the house of the Princesse de Neufchâtel, who had invited her. The princess's marriage had now been made public. The Comtesse de Tende found the room full of people; but as soon as the Princesse de Neufchâtel caught sight of her, she left the gathering and asked her to come with her to her private room. Hardly had they sat down before the princess's face was covered in tears. Her friend believed the cause to be the public declaration of her marriage: she must be finding this more difficult to bear than she had imagined. She soon saw, however, that she was wrong.

'Ah! Madame,' the Princesse de Neufchâtel said to her, 'what have I done? I have married a man for love; I have entered into an unequal match which is universally disapproved of and which drags me down; and the man I have placed above everything else loves another woman!'

The Comtesse de Tende thought she would faint when she heard these words; she did not believe that the princess could have fathomed her husband's passion without having also unravelled its cause. She was unable to reply. The Princesse de Navarre, as she was now called, noticed nothing and continued thus:

'The Prince de Navarre, Madame, far from showing the impatience one would have expected once the wedding was over, kept me waiting yesterday night. When he came, he was joyless, distracted, and preoccupied. At dawn, he left my room on some pretext or other. But he had been writing: I saw it on his hands. To whom could he have been writing if not to a mistress? Why did he keep me waiting, and what was it that preoccupied him?'

At that moment the conversation was interrupted because the Princesse de Condé* was arriving; the Princesse de Navarre went to receive her and the Comtesse de Tende remained, beside herself. That very evening, she wrote to the Prince de Navarre to warn him of the suspicions of his wife and to urge him to restrain his behaviour.

Their passion was in no way diminished by the perils and obstacles they faced. The Comtesse de Tende could not rest, and sleep no longer came to alleviate her distress. One morning, after she had called her women, her equerry approached and told her quietly that the Prince de Navarre was in her private room and that he begged her to let him tell her something it was absolutely necessary for her to know. It is easy to yield to what gives pleasure:* the Comtesse de Tende knew that her husband had gone out; she said that she wished to sleep, and told her women to close her doors again and not to return unless she called them.

The Prince de Navarre came in from the private room and fell on his knees by her bed.

'What have you to tell me?' she said.

'That I love you, Madame, that I adore you, that I cannot live with Mme de Navarre. This morning, I was overcome by such a violent desire to see you that I was unable to resist it. I have come here at the risk of all the consequences that might follow and without even hoping to be able to speak to you.'

The Comtesse de Tende rebuked him at first for compromising her so heedlessly; then their passion drew them into such a long conversation that the Comte de Tende returned from town. He went to his wife's apartment; he was told that she was not yet awake. It was late; he insisted on entering her room and found the Prince de Navarre on his knees by her bed, as he had been from the start. Never was a man so astonished as the Comte de Tende; never was a woman so dismayed as his wife. The Prince de Navarre alone retained some presence of mind; without losing his poise or getting up, he said to the Comte de Tende:

'Come, I beg you, and help me to obtain a favour: I have gone down on my knees to ask for it, yet it has not been granted.'

The tone and manner of the Prince de Navarre allayed the astonishment of the Comte de Tende. 'I am not sure', he replied in the same tone as the prince, 'that a favour that you ask of my wife on bended knees, when she is said to be asleep and I find you alone with her, and with no carriage at my door, is likely to be of the kind that I would wish to grant.'

The Prince de Navarre, who had overcome the embarrassment of the first moments and regained his assurance, rose from his knees and sat down with the greatest self-possession. The Comtesse de Tende, trembling and distraught, was able to hide her confusion because her bed was in shadow.* The Prince de Navarre addressed her husband thus:

'I shall surprise you: you will no doubt blame my conduct, but you will none the less be obliged to help me. I love and am loved by the person at court most worthy of love. Yesterday evening, I slipped away from the company of the Princesse de Navarre and all my servants in order to go to an assignation with this lady. My wife, who has already fathomed that I have something other than herself on my mind and who is keeping my conduct under observation, found out from my servants that I was no longer with them; her jealousy and despair are beyond bounds. I told her that I had spent the time that gave her anxiety as a guest of the Maréchale de Saint-André,* who is unwell and who is seeing hardly anyone; I told her that only Mme la Comtesse de Tende was there and that she could ask her if it were not true that she had seen me there the whole evening. I decided to come and place myself in your wife's hands. I went to the house of La Châtre,* which is only a few steps away from here; I left the house without my servants seeing me and was told that Mme la Comtesse was awake. I found no one in her antechamber and made so bold as to enter. She is refusing to tell lies on my behalf; she protests that she is unwilling to betray her friend and is very properly rebuking me, as I have vainly rebuked myself. It is imperative to relieve Mme la Princesse de Navarre of her anxiety and jealousy so that I may be spared the mortal embarrassment of her reproaches.'

The Comtesse de Tende was hardly less surprised by the Prince de Navarre's presence of mind than by the arrival of her husband; she recovered her composure, and the Comte de Tende's doubts were entirely set at rest. He joined his wife in pointing out to the Prince de Navarre the depths of misfortune and misery into which he was about to cast himself, and what he owed to the princess; the Comtesse de Tende promised to tell her whatever her husband wanted.

As the Prince de Navarre was about to leave, the Comte de Tende stopped him. 'To reward us', he said, 'for the service we are to perform for you at the expense of the truth, at least tell us who this charming mistress is. She cannot be a person worthy of any esteem, since she loves you and maintains a liaison with you when you are committed to a woman as beautiful as the Princesse de Navarre, married to her, and deeply in her debt. This person can have neither wit, nor courage, nor delicacy; the truth is that it is not worth spoiling for her sake such great good fortune as yours and making yourself guilty of such ingratitude.'

The Prince de Navarre could find nothing to say; he pretended to be in a hurry. The Comte de Tende showed him out personally so that he would not be seen.

The Comtesse de Tende remained deeply distressed by the risk she had run, by the thoughts her husband's words inspired, and by her perception of the misfortunes to which her passion left her exposed; but she lacked the strength to withdraw from it. She continued her relations with the Prince de Navarre; she saw him sometimes through the offices of her equerry La Lande. She considered herself, and was indeed, one of the most unhappy women in the world. Every day, the Princesse de Navarre confided to her a jealousy of which she was the cause and which filled her with remorse; when the Princesse de Navarre was satisfied with her husband's behaviour, she was herself consumed with jealousy in her turn.

A new torment was added to those she already suffered: the Comte de Tende became as much enamoured of her* as if she had not been his wife; he no longer left her alone and tried to avail himself of all the rights he had previously despised.

She refused him forcefully, bitterly, even scornfully. Her feelings being already committed to the Prince de Navarre, she was wounded and offended by any passion but his. The Comte de Tende was sensitive to the full severity of her behaviour. Cut to the quick, he assured her that he would never trouble her again: he left her, in fact, in the abruptest manner possible.

The campaign was about to begin: the Prince de Navarre had to leave to join the army. The Comtesse de Tende began to feel the pain his absence would cause and to be fearful for the perils to which he would be exposed. She resolved to evade the necessity of hiding her affliction and

made a plan to spend the summer on an estate she owned
thirty miles from Paris.*

She put this plan into effect. Their farewell was so painful
that they could only consider it a bad omen for them both.
The Comte de Tende remained with the King, to whom he
was attached by virtue of his office.

The court was to move closer to the army; Mme de
Tende's house was not far removed from it; her husband
told her that he would visit the house for a single night to
see to some building work that he had set in train. He did
not wish her to have any reason to believe that the purpose
of the visit was to see her; his resentment towards her was of
the kind that only passion brings. Mme de Tende had found
the Prince de Navarre so respectful at first, and she had felt
herself capable of so much virtue, that she had mistrusted
neither him nor herself. But time and opportunity had
triumphed over her virtue and his respect, and, not long
after she had arrived at her house, she realized that she was
pregnant.* One need only reflect on the reputation she had
acquired and preserved, and on the state of her relations
with her husband, in order to measure her despair. She
came near several times to making an attempt on her life;
yet she conceived some slight hope* on the basis of her
husband's impending visit, and resolved to await its outcome. While thus oppressed, she endured the further pain
of knowing that La Lande, whom she had left in Paris to
pass on her lover's letters and her own, had died after a
short illness, and she found herself deprived of all help at
a time when she needed it most.

Meanwhile the army had undertaken a siege. Because of
her passion for the Prince de Navarre, she was subject to
incessant fears, even amidst the mortal horrors that racked
her.

Her fears proved to be only too well founded. She received letters from the army informing her that the siege was
over; but they informed her at the same time that the Prince
de Navarre had been killed on the last day. She lost her
senses and her reason; both, at times, deserted her entirely.
There were moments when this extreme misery seemed to

her a kind of consolation. She no longer feared for her peace of mind, her reputation, or her life. Death alone seemed desirable to her. She hoped her grief would bring it about; if not, she was resolved to make an end of herself. A last trace of shame persuaded her to say that she was suffering severe pains as a pretext for her cries and tears. When her many afflictions forced her gaze to turn inward, she saw that she had deserved them, and her natural feelings as well as her Christian ones* dissuaded her from becoming her own murderer and suspended the execution of her resolve.

She had not long been a prey to these violent torments when the Comte de Tende arrived. She believed she had experienced all the feelings her unhappy state could inspire in her; but the arrival of her husband brought with it a further agitation and confusion that she had not felt before. He learned on his arrival that she was ill and, as he had always maintained proper forms of behaviour in the eyes of the public and of his household servants, he came at once to her room. She seemed, when he saw her, like a woman beside herself, a woman distracted; she was unable to hold back her tears, attributing them as before to the pains that tormented her. The Comte de Tende, touched by the state he found her in, felt compassion for her and, believing that he might thereby divert her mind from her pain, spoke to her of the death of the Prince de Navarre and of his wife's grief.

Mme de Tende's own grief could not withstand these remarks; her tears became so copious that the Comte de Tende was taken aback and almost guessed the truth. He left the room in a state of great turmoil and agitation; it seemed to him that his wife's condition was not one caused by physical pain; the way she had wept still more bitterly when he had spoken to her of the death of the Prince de Navarre had struck him, and all at once the singular incident when he had found him kneeling by her bed presented itself to his imagination. He remembered how she had treated him when he had wanted to come back to her, and, in the end, thought he saw the truth; yet there still remained in his mind

that trace of doubt which our self-regard always allows us*
in cases where belief exacts too high a price.

His despair was extreme, and all his thoughts were violent;
but he was wise enough to master his first reactions and
resolved to leave the next day at dawn without seeing his
wife, trusting that time would bring him greater certainty
and enable him to determine his course of action.

Deeply immersed in her misery as Mme de Tende was,
she had not failed to notice her own lack of self-possession
and the manner in which her husband had left her room; she
guessed a part of the truth and, feeling only horror now for
her mortal life, she resolved to end it in a way that might not
cost her the hope of salvation.

She considered carefully what she should do; then, shaken
to the depths of her soul and overwhelmed by a sense of her
misfortunes, repenting of her very life, she finally brought
herself to write these words to her husband:

'This letter will cost me my life; but I deserve death and
desire it. I am pregnant. The man who caused my misfortune is no longer on this earth, nor is the only other
person who knew of our liaison; the world at large has never
suspected it. I had resolved to put an end to my life by my
own hand, but I offer it instead to God and to you in
expiation of my crime. I had no wish to dishonour myself in
public, since my reputation concerns you also; preserve it for
your own sake. I shall reveal the state I find myself in; you
must conceal its shameful cause and bring about my death
when you wish and by what means you wish.'

Day was beginning to break as she finished this letter,
perhaps the most difficult to write that has ever been written.
She sealed it, went to the window, and, seeing the Comte de
Tende in the courtyard about to get into his carriage, sent
one of her women to take it to him and tell him that there
was no hurry and that he could read it at his leisure. The
Comte de Tende was surprised to receive the letter; it gave
him a kind of presentiment, not of everything he would
in fact find in it, but of something connected with his reflections the day before. He got into his carriage alone, full

of disquiet and not even daring to open the letter, impatient as he was to read it. Finally, he did read it and discovered his misfortune. It is difficult to imagine the thoughts that came into his mind at that moment. The violent state he was in would have led anyone who had been present to believe that he had lost his reason or was about to die. Jealousy and well-founded suspicions ordinarily prepare husbands for their misfortunes; it may even be that they always have their doubts;* yet they are spared the certainty afforded by an open confession,* which it is beyond our capacity to comprehend.

The Comte de Tende had always found his wife worthy of love, even though he had not loved her constantly himself; but, of all the women he had ever known, she had always appeared to him to be also the most worthy of esteem. Thus, he felt no less astonishment than rage, and through these emotions he still felt, despite himself, a pain in which tenderness had its part.

He stopped at a house that happened to be on his road and passed several days there in a state of agitation and affliction, as one can well imagine. His first reflections were those it was natural to have on such an occasion. He thought only of killing his wife, but the death of the Prince de Navarre and La Lande, whom he recognized without difficulty as the confidant, gave his fury some pause. He had no doubt that his wife had told him the truth in claiming that her liaison had never been suspected; he judged that the marriage of the Prince de Navarre could easily have deceived the world at large, since he had himself been deceived. Now that he had been made so palpably aware of the truth, the fact that everyone else was wholly ignorant of his misfortune was a consolation; but the circumstances, making evident to him how far and in what way he had been deceived, pierced his heart, and his only desire was for vengeance. Yet he reflected that, if he killed his wife and it was noticed that she was pregnant,* people would easily guess the truth. As he was the proudest of men, he decided on the course of action which would best protect his reputation and resolved to let nothing emerge in public. With this in mind, he sent a gentleman to the Comtesse de Tende with this note:

'The desire to prevent my shame from becoming a public spectacle must have precedence for the time being over my vengeance; I shall consider later how to dispose of your worthless life. Conduct yourself as if you had continued to be what you ought to have been.'

Mme de Tende received this message with joy; she believed it to be her death sentence and, when she saw that she had her husband's consent to make her pregnancy known, she became keenly aware that shame is the most violent of the passions. She discovered a kind of peace in believing herself sure to die and to see her reputation safeguarded; her sole thought now was to prepare herself for death; and, as she was a woman whose every feeling was lively, she embraced virtue and penitence as ardently as she had followed the dictates of her passion. Besides, her soul was disabused and steeped in affliction; she could turn her gaze on nothing in life that was not more harsh than death itself, so that she saw no other remedy for her misfortunes than the ending of her unhappy life. She spent some time in this state, appearing more dead than alive. Finally, in about the sixth month of her pregnancy, her body succumbed, a continuous fever took hold of her and the very violence of her illness caused her to give birth. She had the consolation of seeing her child alive, of being certain that he could not live and that she would not give her husband an illegitimate heir. She herself died a few days later, receiving death with a joy no mortal has ever felt; she instructed her confessor to deliver to her husband the news of her death, to ask his pardon on her behalf, and to beg him to forget her memory, which could only be odious to him.

The Comte de Tende received the news without inhumanity, and even with some sentiments of pity, but none the less with joy. Although he was very young, he never had the desire to marry again,* and he lived to a very advanced age.*

EXPLANATORY NOTES

References are to page numbers.

The Princesse de Clèves

PART I

2 *he will nevertheless declare himself*: a promise which was of course to remain unfulfilled. This Publisher's Note indicates that the question of anonymity was not a routine one: it was used, no doubt for publicity reasons, to arouse the reader's curiosity (identifying fictional characters with real personalities was another similar game often played in the seventeenth century).

3 *Never has France seen*: the tense here creates the fiction of a narrator contemporary with the action of the novel: for the novel's first readers, it was the court of Louis XIV rather than that of Henri II that had achieved an unprecedented splendour. The advantage of the *nouvelle historique* is precisely that it combines a degree of historical distancing with a familiar—and thus plausible—setting.

courtly magnificence and manners: the French phrase is 'La magnificence et la galanterie'. The word *galanterie* has a range of meanings extending from 'politeness' to 'amorous conduct', 'love affair', and even 'flirtation'. It recurs in the following sentence in the adjectival form 'galant', where it is rapidly followed by the more explicit 'amoureux' (here translated as 'chivalrous' and 'amorously inclined' respectively) and then by a reference to Henri II's celebrated love affair with Diane de Poitiers. In this way, the opening of the novel introduces the theme of love, but in association with the almost legendary splendour of court life, which will provide the backdrop for many of the central events of the story. The private and the public worlds are already closely—and explosively—linked.

monogram: two D's interlaced. The monogram was used a great deal in contemporary art and architecture celebrating Diane de Poitiers.

The Queen: Catherine de Médicis.

4   *in her apartments*: this phrase is used here and elsewhere to translate the vaguer French expression 'chez (la Reine, etc.)'. The leading figures of court society each had their own suite of rooms where they entertained their circle.

Marie Stuart: her presence and influence throughout the novel add an important element of historical and romantic colouring. Note that she was only 16–17 years old at the time when the novel is set.

the Cardinal de Lorraine: a figure who plays a significant—and often sinister—role in the novel as a master of political intrigue. He was one of several brothers of the house of Guise (see 'Glossary of Names'), which became immensely powerful, especially after the death of Henri II, adopting a militantly Counter-Reformation position.

5   *which the reformers*: movements of religious reform in France began to gather momentum as early as the 1520s; by the late 1550s, when the events of the novel take place, France was on the verge of the 'wars of religion', which were to last for some thirty years.

the Prince de Clèves: a historical figure, the future husband of the fictional Princesse de Clèves.

The Vidame de Chartres: a significant figure in the main story, and the protagonist of the last of the secondary narratives.

the Duc de Nemours: the parade of handsome and powerful men culminates in the figure who will play the male lead in the novel. As Valincour points out, his sexual exploits are very much toned down in the novel by comparison with its source, Brantôme's *Hommes illustres*.

6   *mistresses*: this word should be taken in its older, less explicitly sexual sense.

exile: banishment to his family's estates at Chantilly.

8   *the Battle of Saint-Quentin*: this and the following battles mentioned represent the last phase of the long-standing wars between France and the Holy Roman Empire, which were resolved by the Treaty of Cateau-Cambrésis (see below).

the English had been driven out of France: Calais was recaptured from the English in 1558.

at the time of the marriage of M. le Dauphin: the marriage of the future François II to Marie Stuart took place in April 1558.

Cercamp: these negotiations began on 13 October 1558 and continued until the end of November (see below).

that Queen Mary of England had died: in November 1558.

Elizabeth: born in 1533, she was 25 years old when she succeeded her half-sister Mary. Her succession was contested because some refused to recognize the divorce of Henry VIII from Catherine of Aragon and thus the legitimacy of his marriage to her mother Anne Boleyn. The story of her interest in Nemours is based on a passage in Brantôme's sixteenth-century *Dames galantes*, one of the major sources for the novel's 'historical' materials.

9 *There appeared at court*: the delayed entrance of the heroine is criticized by Valincour, who suggests that the description of the court and its personalities could have been more skilfully introduced by having Mme de Chartres impart this essential knowledge to her daughter on her arrival at court. But Mme de Lafayette's sequence not only creates a kind of suspense and allows the heroine to appear against a sumptuous backcloth (part historical, part legendary), it also ensures that the narrative proper, once it begins, moves forward without major digressions to the marriage of Mlle de Chartres and her first encounter with Nemours.

it aroused wonder and admiration: the single word 'admiration' had both these senses in seventeenth-century French. It is used frequently in the novel, notably when the Prince de Clèves first sees Mlle de Chartres (p. 10, 'gazed at her in amazement') and at the first meeting of the Princesse de Clèves and Nemours (p. 24, 'he could not help betraying his admiration'). The English equivalent has been selected in each case with regard to factors such as the use in the context of other words from the same semantic area.

wealth: some translators and editors interpret the French word ('bien') in a moral sense; the relationship of the word to the other two in the phrase makes that reading implausible. The language of high society in Louis XIV's day often equivocates between moral and social qualities, or implies that, if you have one sort, you will have the other, too. Mme de Chartres's means, her social standing, and her respectability are emphasized here rather than her innate moral goodness.

9 *wit and beauty*: the French word translated here as 'wit'
   ('esprit') could mean 'mind'; but it is not plausible to imagine
   that Mme de Chartres subjects her daughter to lengthy aca-
   demic study. She teaches her to have presence of mind, to
   have her wits about her, and (no doubt) to be well-informed.

10 *brilliance and distinction*: once again, Mme de Chartres's advice
   to her daughter links moral injunctions inextricably to reputation, social standing, and security. The last sentence of this
   paragraph shows how far love itself may be considered a
   principle of outward behaviour rather than an inward impulse.

   in her sixteenth year: one should bear in mind that Mlle de
   Chartres will be no more than 16 to 17 years old when the
   action of the novel takes place.

   she went to match some stones: Valincour tells us that many
   readers found it implausible that Mme de Chartres should let
   her daughter go alone to choose jewels; and that the Prince de
   Clèves should be so overcome that he neither speaks to her
   nor even asks who she is after she leaves.

11 *at Nice at the interview*: the King and the Pope had met in
   1538 (i.e. some twenty years earlier) to arrange a truce in the
   wars between France and the Empire.

   Mlle de Chartres's wit and beauty: readers from the seventeenth
   century onwards have found it hard to imagine what the
   Prince de Clèves could have known of her wit after such a
   brief encounter in which no word was exchanged between
   them. The example shows how far 'wit' ('esprit') was a social
   quality, an alertness and self-possession which could be
   rapidly identified by an attentive observer.

13 *the marriage of one of her daughters*: this allusion is obscure.

   the Vidame's niece: Mlle de Chartres.

15 *the marriage of younger sons*: aristocratic families preferred their
   wealth to be passed down intact from eldest son to eldest son
   rather than dividing it up between several children. The same
   rule was applied to daughters: a large settlement could normally only be provided for the eldest daughter.

   The Cardinal nourished a hatred for the Vidame: see p. 81.

16 *the son of the Duc de Montpensier*: François de Bourbon, who
   was called the 'Prince Dauphin' because the Dauphiné of
   Auvergne had been granted to his father. This is the Prince de

Montpensier whose marriage to Mlle de Mézières forms the subject of *The Princesse de Montpensier*.

17   *the ill-fated passion*: after the death of François II, Chastelart followed Marie Stuart to Scotland, where he was found hiding in her chamber and executed.

the Queen my mother: this brief explanatory story is the first of the secondary narratives, related by one of the characters, which play an important part in the structure of the novel. It provides a historical example of the clash of love and politics, as well as of ill-starred passion.

18   *three kings*: Henri II of France, James V of Scotland, Henry VIII of England.

19   *The death of his father the Duc de Nevers*: this actually occurred in 1562; the author changes it to 1558 in order to solve the narrative problem she has created (the father's objection).

he flattered himself: the sense of the French word *flatter* here is very strong, and could be translated as 'persuaded' or even 'deceived'. This is an early example in the novel of self-deception: the prince believes what his emotional self-interest makes him want to believe.

20   *was troubled by no fear*: see above, note on p. 10 ('brilliance and distinction'). Mme de Chartres's view of love is not romantic, and she is only doing what most aristocratic mothers of the sixteenth or seventeenth century would have done. Yet this sentence, with its sinister undertones, seems designed to show how dangerously inadequate such moral and psychological perceptions can be.

neither impatient, nor restless, nor troubled: because he is in love, the prince sees what her mother could not—or would not—see. Yet, precisely because he *is* in love, he cannot take advantage of this knowledge.

22   *The wedding had been fixed for February*: it in fact took place on 22 January 1559. Since Mlle de Chartres only arrives at court in November 1558 at the earliest, the fictional period that elapses before her first meeting with Nemours (at the betrothal celebrations) is at most three months. Valincour makes no comment on this, but he queries the length of Nemours's unbroken absence from court, which is necessary if the Princesse de Clèves is to meet him for the first time at the ball.

23 *the ball began*: it has often been remarked that this episode has
    a fairy-tale quality; the meeting of 'heroine' and 'hero' takes
    place in a sumptuous royal setting and is accompanied by
    superlatives. Yet there are other elements, too. The narrator is
    unusually careful to note circumstantial detail (the noise by the
    door, Nemours seen stepping over a chair), which produces an
    effect of almost hallucinatory intensity given the absence of
    such detail elsewhere; there is a slightly sinister and porten-
    tous note in the way in which the King stage-manages their
    meeting, as if he knew what effect he would produce; and the
    constant reference to surprise, astonishment, amazement,
    'admiration' (in both senses: see above, note to p. 9), signals
    the initial emotional shock which, according to seventeenth-
    century psychology, undoes rational judgement and leaves the
    heart vulnerable. It is here that the author uses the feminine
    ending for 'surpris' ('not to be *taken aback*') where, as Valin-
    cour insists, the uninflected form would have been expected
    (see Introduction, p. xxi).

24 *it is even quite flattering*: the Reine Dauphine perceives the
    princess's tell-tale *evasion* here.

    Whether her face . . . inner turmoil: the Chevalier de Guise, who
    has a personal interest in the matter, catches the first signs of
    the princess's 'inclination' for Nemours even more perspica-
    ciously than the Reine Dauphine. But, precisely because he is
    self-interested, there remains the possibility that he is over-
    interpreting. Emotional disturbance creates uncertainty.

26 *what is said of all women of my age*: the characterization of a
    female narrator who 'loves telling stories of her own day' is
    commonplace enough, but may serve to reinforce the argu-
    ments in favour of regarding the novel as a whole as a woman's
    narrative.

    I should explain to you the beginnings: a further historical *récit*
    (see above, note to p. 17; it has in fact become a critical
    convention to regard the story of Diane de Poitiers as the first
    of the major secondary narratives). Valincour attacks it as
    irrelevant, but Diane de Poitiers's presence is felt throughout
    the novel, and her relationship with Henri II embodies the
    interplay between passion and power which will affect so many
    of the characters. It is also, from the Princesse de Clèves's
    view, a striking example of an illicit passion which succeeds
    and endures, and in which a woman wields exceptional power.

if she ever has any power: see the opening passage of Part IV.

while he was in prison: he was taken prisoner at Saint-Quentin (1557) by the Imperial forces; see also the allusion to his 'exile', above, p. 6.

27 *the affair of the Connétable de Bourbon*: this Connétable (not to be confused with Montmorency) was convicted of plotting against François I in favour of the Emperor Charles V.

the King's imprisonment: after François I was taken prisoner by Charles V at the battle of Pavia (1525), he was held in Spain. His mother, Louise de Savoie, acted as regent during his absence (see the following sentence).

28 *When the Emperor passed through France*: this incident occurred in 1539. Charles V was given permission to cross France to the Low Countries, where he had to deal with a rebellion.

29 *the seventeen provinces*: the Spanish Netherlands.

in this way saved their entire army: the story of Mme d'Étampes's secret manœuvre, which has a major effect on historical events, is just one of a striking series of exemplary narratives illustrating the subversive effects of passion.

By chance: disguising an illegitimate feeling by transferring it to a legitimate object is a device frequently used by characters in the novel.

30 *the first thing his son did*: the revolution in the fortunes of these historical characters on the death of François I prefigures (with an almost tragic irony) the more cataclysmic change described towards the end of the novel. Structurally, then, as well as thematically, this secondary narrative is of crucial importance.

32 *She found herself to be less disposed*: Valincour praises this passage, saying that 'it expresses wonderfully well the nature of certain movements which are formed in our hearts, which we hide from our most intimate friends, and which we attempt to hide from ourselves lest we should be obliged to fight against them'. This comment, and others like it, demonstrate that seventeenth-century readers found it natural to read the novel in the light of such works as La Rochefoucauld's *Maximes* (see Introduction, p. xviii).

The Maréchal was also gratified: the Maréchal de Saint-André, to whom the novel seems to refer here, was distinctly older than one might expect of a possible pretender to the affections of the princess (he would have been about 52 when these events take place). The author has probably confused the figure described by Brantôme with his son.

33 *They are arguing*: this conversation, with its formal if not stilted language and its sophisticated analysis of the psychology of love, reflects the seventeenth-century phenomenon loosely known as 'preciosity'. Whether anyone actually talked quite like that in the salons is immaterial; the seventeenth-century reader would have regarded it as perfectly plausible. The author cleverly allows a significant development in the princess's passion to be prompted by what appears to be only light-hearted chatter. Appearances, as usual, are deceptive.

34 *she was gratified*: the princess's double-think is now explicitly, even ironically, brought out by the narrator. The later part of this paragraph, which is even more convoluted in the original than in the translation given here, brilliantly conveys the twists and turns of her attempts at deception and self-deception.

35 *adopting a manner*: Mme de Chartres, for all her virtue, is clearly a good liar when she needs to be.

36 *M. de Nemours was most put out . . . Mme de Clèves's blushes*: an example of the way in which the most careful construction of verbal appearances may be undermined by involuntary physical signs, a device that Mme de Lafayette shares with dramatists of the period, especially Racine.

Mme de Clèves had at first . . . idea from his mind: a particularly elegant and subtle instance of psychological ambivalence.

towards the end of February: the talks in fact began on 6 February 1559. The Treaty of Cateau-Cambrésis was concluded on 27 March and signed on 3 April 1559. In addition to putting an end to the Imperial wars, it prescribed a series of dynastic marriages which will be described below.

37 *private room*: the French word is 'cabinet', a small room, often leading off a bedroom, to which the occupant can withdraw for private reflection or conversation; it is also used, for example, for the 'side rooms' of the pavilion in the garden at Coulommiers (see below, Part III).

the pain she felt on discovering: an important stage in the princess's groping and hesitant progress towards an understanding of her own feelings; it is this progress, rather than a sequence of striking external events, that constitutes the central narrative interest of the novel. It should be noted that her 'discoveries' are often prompted indirectly and by quasi-accidental circumstances rather than by simple introspection.

38   *he did not hate me*: this litotes is a common feature of *précieux* language and has been preserved in the translation for that reason, stilted as it may sound to a modern ear.

42   *Let me tell you the whole story*: a new secondary narrative. Historical *récit* has now given way to straightforward amorous intrigue: Mme de Clèves will have her eyes opened to just what may go on behind appearances of modesty and respectability. Valincour once again thinks that this story is irrelevant and too long: the reader, he says, isn't interested in Mme de Tournon.

PART II

43   *my sister-in-law had no reason to like her either*: the Prince de Clèves's sister-in-law was Anne de Bourbon, daughter of the Duc de Montpensier, who was an enemy of Diane de Poitiers. It was Diane de Poitiers who had prevented the marriage of Mlle de Chartres to Anne's brother (see above, p. 17).

46   *the advice I would follow myself*: this comment, together with the reaction of the princess mentioned in the following paragraph, is an instance of prolepsis or narrative anticipation. It provides a powerful justification for the inclusion of the Sancerre 'digression'.

47   *the most perfect for me in particular*: the point of this second phrase is not wholly clear. It perhaps suggests that Mme de Tournon's image is perfect in general, but particularly so in the eyes of Sancerre himself.

48   *consoling her*: see above, the opening paragraph of Part II. The consolation that Mme de Tournon has in fact availed herself of proves to be quite concrete.

52   *the King of Spain*: Philip II, who had previously been married to Mary Tudor (see the King's reply, below), entertained for a while the idea of marrying Elizabeth.

54   *the peace treaty*: the Treaty of Cateau-Cambrésis.

he himself... should marry Madame: 'Madame' is Elisabeth, Henri II's daughter, as opposed to 'Madame the King's sister', below, who is Marguerite de France.

55 *The princess was lying on her bed*: it was normal in seventeenth-century high society for a hostess to receive visitors while reclining on a bed. This might be only a couch or day-bed (but see below, note on p. 64); nevertheless, this passage, with its delicately managed suggestion of intimacy and sensuality, is one of a handful of such passages that stand out amid the prevailing abstract style.

I am not sorry: this speech is a masterly example of confession by indirection.

58 *He prophesied*: all three prophecies came true (of course). The King's accidental death provides a focal point in the novel.

60 *combats at the barrier*: the barrier is normally the wooden fence separating the combatants when jousting; occasionally it appears to refer to the wooden fence encircling the lists (see p. 117).

61 *I will tell you her story*: a third historical *récit*, again showing the connection between love and politics, and the violence arising from jealousy.

Henry VIII's sister: Mary, known as Marie d'Angleterre after her marriage to Louis XII of France (1514). Louis died in 1515.

whose stories you will no doubt have seen: Marguerite de Navarre wrote a celebrated collection of stories, the *Heptameron*, in the manner of Boccaccio's *Decameron*; first published posthumously in 1558, they were still remembered in the seventeenth century (see Introduction). Marguerite was a patroness of moderate, non-schismatic reformers in France.

62 *an interview between the two kings*: this is the famous 'Field of the Cloth of Gold' (1520).

63 *prodigiously fat*: this detail constitutes an interesting breach of the decorum that normally governs neoclassical style. It may be explained simply as a commonplace, but perhaps also as an irony against the English, whom the French were inclined to regard as coarse.

the Queen of Scotland: the widow of James V; see above, p. 18.

64 *was sitting on the bed*: it is clear in this instance that the bed is not merely a couch or day-bed but a proper bed with curtains, these providing the opportunity for private conversations. There is no reason to assume that this is not the one on which

the princess was lying when Nemours managed to speak to her alone (above, p. 55).

it was better to let him keep it . . . knowledge: another instance of self-interested casuistry.

went out for a drive: the French expression 'se promener' used here may mean 'to take a walk', but may also cover excursions on horseback or by carriage; the last of these seems the most plausible in the context.

65   *to marry her*: by proxy, as often happened with royal marriages between different nations (see the King's joke, above, p. 52).

66   *on the same day*: both royal weddings took place on 9 July 1559.

a tournament: this set-piece is a rare instance of historical 'local colour' in the novel; it is of course reminiscent of the tradition of chivalric romance. One should bear in mind, however, that tournaments were still held in Mme de Lafayette's day, even though they were becoming an archaic survival of feudal times. Thus the seventeenth-century reader would not be in the same position as the reader of, say, *Ivanhoe*, for whom the tournament was only a romantic legend.

in double armour: the sense of the French expression here ('en double pièce') is not wholly clear; most commentators interpret it as armour covering both the lower and the upper part of the body.

67   *had some horses brought out*: as indicated in the previous paragraph, the lists are next to the royal stables (see also the subsequent reference to the 'riding school').

69   *Rhodes*: the Knights Hospitaller had been ousted from Rhodes by the Turks in 1523. The pathos of this brief narrative is touched with irony: the Chevalier seems, appropriately, to fulfil a chivalric destiny in which a quest for love is replaced by a quest for crusading glory; yet he fails in both, and the chivalric myth is in any case not a part of *this* story.

70   *coucher*: the last royal reception of the day. The Reine Dauphine is so constantly exposed to the public eye that she is unable to find a moment during the day to read the letter for herself.

72   *jealousy*: the princess has been touched by jealousy before— for example, when she thought Nemours was in love with the

Reine Dauphine—but her passion is now fully established and the attack is critical. It is of course significant that the letter which provides the immediate occasion for her jealousy is also *about* jealousy and its effects.

72 *her idea of confessing to him*: another preparatory (proleptic) reference.

73 *that she would be wholly cured*: the princess has not yet learnt enough about the workings of passion to see that the reverse is the case.

was not the only person: the change of narrative viewpoint here is striking, and reminds one that the princess has been, if not always the protagonist, at least the implied observer of most narrative events since her marriage (she also listens to all the secondary narratives). In this instance, Mme de Lafayette needs to correct the error for the reader while leaving the princess in suspense. Thus the Vidame will tell his story first to Nemours; the princess will only hear the correct version later, from Nemours himself.

74 *who had already made up his mind*: Chastelart, like the princess, has jumped to the wrong conclusion, and for similar reasons, namely that he is himself in love (with the Reine Dauphine).

with malicious pleasure: he thinks the letter will spoil Nemours's chances with her.

75 *I shall have to tell you the whole story*: the second non-historical narrative 'digression', and the last of the secondary narratives. It turns on the question of secrecy, trust, and sincerity, and in this way indirectly prepares the 'confession' scene in Part III.

76 *so that she could walk*: it is conceivable that the French word used here ('marcher') could mean 'ride'; this would be consistent with her dismissing the equerries, who seem to have been leading her horse.

PART III

80 *still carried the name Villemontais*: i.e. before her marriage to the Comte de Martigues.

82 *your own experience*: the emphasis on Nemours's inconstancy in this sharp exchange is one of a series of such clues strategically placed for the reader to pick up; it is one of the ways in which the secondary narrative makes its point for the main narrative.

84 *took him at once to his wife's room*: this time she clearly is still in bed, or just out of it.

88 *who confides to her husband*: another dramatic irony.

90 *forced her to leave France*: after the death of her husband François II in 1560.

the Amboise conspiracy: a Huguenot conspiracy in 1560, one of the first incidents in what was to become the wars of religion.

the immense difference: the shift in the princess's perceptions and responses in this episode as a whole is one of the most brilliant inventions in the novel; it was praised by Valincour for its depiction of the elusive workings of the human heart. The ensuing internal monologue anticipates in form and style certain passages in Jane Austen.

91 *they none the less opened her eyes*: this development anticipates and prepares the denouement of the novel.

92 *a day's journey from Paris*: about twenty-five miles east of Paris.

93 *stag-hunting*: this episode is in certain respects reminiscent of a fairy-tale (the handsome prince lost in the forest and finding his way to the enchanted castle where a princess lives under a spell).

lost his way in the forest . . . found himself in the forest: it seems that, after becoming lost, Nemours eventually emerges from the forest and asks the way. He then rides off towards Coulommiers, which is itself surrounded by forest.

He heard M. de Clèves saying to his wife: the accidental presence of Nemours at what is itself a highly unusual scene creates a problem of plausibility which was vigorously discussed in the seventeenth century. See Introduction, p. xiv.

94 *a woman whose behaviour is in her own hands*: no doubt a further reference to the death of Mme de Chartres, which has left the princess without a guide and companion.

96 *both as a husband and as a lover*: the separation of these roles is crucial to the novel's effect. The Prince de Clèves remains a lover even when he becomes a husband because his love is unrequited (see below, note on p. 148).

It was not weakness that made me confess: we need not take the princess at her word here; she is never fully aware of her motives at the moment when she acts.

97   *I cannot believe you*: what she has just said is in fact at best a half-truth.

99   *he fell into an error of judgement*: this indiscretion will be doubly disastrous, since it will destroy the understanding reached between the prince and his wife and will also undermine the princess's own faith in Nemours.

100   *he had been chosen to escort Madame . . . to Spain*: history has been adjusted here to suit the fiction. In 1559, the real Prince de Clèves was only 15 years old, and it was the King of Navarre who accompanied Elisabeth to Spain after her marriage to Philip II.

103   *to marry her*: by proxy for the King of Spain, as indicated earlier.

104   *to embrace his knees*: a traditional gesture of homage.

113   *she could find no way of exonerating him*: it is of course ironic that she should wish to exonerate him (see also below, paragraph beginning 'These bitter reflections'). Her awareness of his indiscretion is, however, an important stage in the development of her increasingly complex and problematic feelings towards him.

115   *the Parlement, the Crown Courts, and the Maison de Ville*: in other words, all the secular dignitaries of Paris. The Parlement was primarily a judicial rather than a legislative body; the Crown Courts (*Cours souveraines*) were courts of appeal; the Maison de Ville was the assembly of municipal officers.

116   *the Order*: the Order of the Knights of Malta (of which the Chevalier de Guise was Grand Prieur).

   gold frieze: like the Duc d'Albe (above, p. 115), the Duc de Guise is wearing a robe of cloth of gold, but this time it is specified that the gold is 'frisé', i.e. the texture has been roughened by pulling out the ends of the gold thread (this technique is more usually associated with velvet). The extravagant opulence of such garments was fashionable in the sixteenth century (cf. the Field of the Cloth of Gold, mentioned earlier in the novel).

   Chamberlain of the Household . . . chief steward . . . cupbearer: these were honorific duties assumed on ceremonial occasions. They are approximately equivalent to head waiter, waiter, and wine waiter.

spectacular scenic effects: the French word 'machines' used here denotes mechanical devices of a kind which were especially popular in the later seventeenth century, although they were already used in the sixteenth century at court entertainments. They often accompanied mythological tableaux, as in English court masques.

M. de Nemours wore yellow and black: after the emotional drama of the preceding scenes, these references may seem frivolous. It is certainly the case that the royal wedding and the tournament provide a breathing space in the narrative; but the symbolism of the tournament, in which passion is mingled with conflict, aggression, and death, is wholly appropriate to the themes of the novel, and the long tradition of 'wearing colours' was by no means only a piece of quaint medieval lore for seventeenth-century readers. The evocation of the spectacle, with its mood of celebration and its shimmering surface colours, also prepares the dramatic shift into darkness when the King is wounded.

117   *the barrier*: see above, note on p. 60.

118   *the prophecy*: see above, note on p. 58.

119   *the Queen Mother*: Catherine de Médicis. The new King is François II; the Queen is Marie Stuart, previously the Reine Dauphine.

PART IV

119   *The Cardinal de Lorraine*: the opening pages of Part IV describe the struggle for power that followed the death of Henri II, and in particular the rise to power of the house of Guise at the expense of the house of Bourbon. François II was still only 15 years old and in poor health; the Queen Mother thus began to play a central role.

    the Queen Mother: Catherine de Médicis is occasionally referred to as the Queen in the following lines. Likewise the new Queen is sometimes called the Reine Dauphine. All such inconsistencies have been removed in the translation.

125   *Every time she spoke to her husband*: since M. de Clèves is away, this passage must be construed as referring to the situation in general terms, reaching back perhaps to the 'confession'.

125   *Anet*: a château built for Diane de Poitiers by Henri. It was famous for its art and architecture; little of it has been preserved.

this was perhaps: since Mme de Clèves will later be seen gazing at the painting in which Nemours is depicted, the 'perhaps' here is mildly ironic. It also, however, suggests a motive of which the person concerned is herself not conscious, and which is thus—at least at the moment when she chooses to take the paintings—still inscrutable. Similarly, La Rochefoucauld's *Maximes* often include words and expressions which suggest uncertainty in the ascription of motives.

126   *in the central room*: the French phrase 'sous le pavillon' is not particularly clear, since the word 'pavillon' seems to denote the building as a whole. If the two side rooms are thought of as extraneous to the main structure, the phrase may be taken to refer to the 'large room' (French 'salon') mentioned in the earlier passage (above, p. 93).

Chambord: one of the most magnificent châteaux of the Loire valley.

127   *The fences were very high*: these obstacles again recall a fairy-tale setting. Note the shift of viewpoint in this passage from M. de Clèves's gentleman to Nemours himself.

128   *It was hot*: again the note of slight fever, or passion; again the princess is on a day-bed.

it was from her that Mme de Clèves had taken it: another pointer to Mme de Clèves's undeclared motivation.

135   *the extreme gravity of M. de Clèves's illness gave him fresh hopes*: Nemours's single-minded self-interest here is so openly emphasized by the narrator that it is hard not to read the passage as a moral demolition of his behaviour, if not of his character.

140   *went to see a man*: there is a fine structural balance between this scene, in which the princess visits a merchant and discovers the hidden gaze of Nemours, and the scene in Part I where the Prince de Clèves sees her for the first time in the house of a merchant. It is as if her preoccupation with jewels and fine silks was in some way connected with a predatory male gaze. Valincour, who admires the handling of Mme de Clèves's response to her husband's death, finds that this episode, and the ensuing one where the princess sees

Nemours accidentally in a public garden, is intrusive and superfluous. But he adds, with a typically seventeenth-century moral emphasis: 'perhaps they were included in order to show us how insubstantial human resolutions may be, since a trifle can cause such disorder in the most prudent and virtuous mind'.

141 *Without looking to see . . . he was even unable to see*: Nemours's failure to see who the newcomers were is somewhat strained; the double reference merely draws attention to the difficulty.

147 *the ultimate test*: a duel.

148 *M. de Clèves was perhaps the only man . . . married*: this sentence reflects the well-established tradition of courtly love according to which true love is only possible outside marriage; this literary convention is itself based on the social reality of arranged marriages and the psychological observation that passion increases in proportion to the obstacles placed in its way (see the princess's subsequent remarks).

153 *the accidents that letters can give rise to*: an echo of the trouble over Mme de Thémines's letter.

The Princesse de Montpensier

158 *the illustrious name*: Montpensier. The Montpensier family was extremely powerful in the seventeenth century. There is in fact evidence that the bearers of such names were liable to be offended if dubious fictional exploits were attributed to their ancestors. On the other hand, the Publisher's Note shows how the *nouvelle historique*—explicitly distinguished here from the romance—was designed to attract the reader by the lure of prestigious historical names.

159 *when France was torn apart by civil war, Love continued to conduct his affairs*: *The Princesse de Montpensier* begins during the wars of religion, several years after the events referred to in *The Princesse de Clèves*. Charles IX was the son of Henri II and the younger brother of François II, who died in 1560. Metaphorical parallels between love and war are a commonplace of both the romance tradition and the courtly love tradition. None the less, the way in which *The Princesse de Montpensier* establishes at the outset the correspondence between historical backdrop and amorous intrigue anticipates the much more extensive opening section of *The Princesse de Clèves*.

159 *The only daughter of the Marquis de Mézières*: Renée d'Anjou, daughter of Nicolas d'Anjou, Marquis de Mézières (two other daughters seem to have died young). She was born in 1550 and married François de Bourbon, Prince de Montpensier, in 1566.

the Duc du Maine: Charles de Lorraine, born 1554, son of François de Lorraine, Duc de Guise, and Anne d'Este; better known as the Duc de Mayenne.

the Duc de Guise: Henri de Lorraine, born 1550, nicknamed Scar-Face because of a face wound received in 1575; note that his father, François de Lorraine, was given the same nickname, having received a similar wound in 1545. Note that these brothers are sons and nephews respectively of the 'Guise brothers' frequently referred to in *The Princesse de Clèves* (see 'Glossary of Names'): the principal characters of this *nouvelle* belong to the younger generation.

As she was extremely young, her marriage was delayed, and in the meantime the Duc de Guise: a manuscript variant reads 'They were both extremely young, and the Duc de Guise'. The Duc du Maine was over three years younger than Renée d'Anjou. The story presents her as being 13 years old at the time (see her remark to the Duc de Guise, p. 171); this suggests that the period between her initial engagement to the Duc du Maine and her eventual marriage in 1566 lasted some three years. The Duc de Guise was himself two months younger than Renée d'Anjou.

the Cardinal de Lorraine: one of the Duc de Guise's uncles; see *The Princesse de Clèves*, note on p. 4, and 'Glossary of Names'. François de Lorraine, the Duc de Guise's father, had been killed early in 1563 (presumably not long before the events of the story begin).

the house of Bourbon: the rivalry between Guise and Bourbon is central to the political struggles of the period and is frequently alluded to in *The Princesse de Clèves*.

the young Prince de Montpensier: François de Bourbon, born 1542, died 1592; referred to in *The Princesse de Clèves* as the Prince Dauphin (the title is mentioned in a manuscript variant of this passage).

the Duc d'Aumale: see 'Glossary of Names'.

160   *Thus she married the Prince de Montpensier*: in 1566, her six-
      teenth year. This was also the year in which the Duc de
      Nemours married Anne d'Este, the widow of François de
      Lorraine and the mother of the Duc de Guise; the event is
      not mentioned in this story, but is chronicled immediately
      before the marriage of the Prince de Montpensier by the
      seventeenth-century historian Mézeray, whose work Mme de
      Lafayette certainly knew. The Duc de Guise, who plays the
      role of lover in this story, was thus historically the stepson of
      the Duc de Nemours—a link between history and fiction, but
      also between *The Princesse de Montpensier* and *The Princesse de
      Clèves*.

      Champigny: Champigny-sur-Veude, in the *département* of
      Indre-et-Loire.

      the whole brunt of the war: the second of the wars of religion
      began in September 1567. The Prince de Condé, the leader
      of the Huguenots, laid siege to Paris; the indecisive Battle of
      Saint-Denis followed.

      the Comte de Chabannes: there is no historical evidence for
      a friendship between the Prince de Montpensier and any
      Comte de Chabannes. The role of the Princesse de Mont-
      pensier's confidant and unrequited lover is thus entirely
      fictional.

      Catherine de Médicis: the widow of Henri II and a central
      figure in *The Princesse de Clèves*; see also 'Glossary of Names'.

161   *love wrought in him what it does in every other lover*: one of the
      maxim-like generalizations that are frequently found in these
      stories. The inability to suppress one's feelings, however
      dangerous these may be, is a frequent motif in late seven-
      teenth-century French literature (Racine's tragedies provide
      a number of celebrated examples); 'confession' is also a
      central theme of *The Princesse de Clèves*.

162   *Peace was made*: the Peace of Longjumeau, March 1568. The
      war had lasted only some six months; the reference here
      to 'two years of absence' (not to mention the Comte de
      Chabannes's year of silence) is thus a fictional dilation.

163   *War broke out again*: the third war of religion, which lasted
      until August 1570.

      cleared his name with the Queen: the Queen Mother had sus-
      pected him of being a Protestant (see above, p. 160).

163 *La Rochelle*: this became a major Huguenot stronghold, supported by the surrounding provinces.

the Duc d'Anjou: born in 1551, the Duc d'Anjou became Henri III, the last king of the house of Valois, on the death of his brother Charles IX in 1574; he was assassinated in 1589. The Battle of Jarnac took place in March 1569; Condé was murdered when he was about to surrender.

It was in this war ... great things that had been predicted of him: the manuscripts omit the reference to the Duc de Guise and attach the subsequent part of this sentence to the previous one as a further elaboration of the Duc d'Anjou's qualities. However, as it is quite clear that the object of the Prince de Montpensier's hate in the following sentence must be the Duc de Guise, who has not otherwise been mentioned for some considerable time, the printed version makes much better sense.

Loches: a small fortified town south of Tours.

164 *The Duc d'Anjou teased him*: a manuscript variant reads: 'The whole band teased him'.

young princes: the Duc d'Anjou was 17 years old, the Duc de Guise 18, at the time when these events are said to have occurred.

adventure: the French word 'aventure' used here is frequently repeated throughout the story. Unlike its English equivalent, it may be used of a single incident or situation. It marks the movement of the narrative into a special imaginative world, a movement immediately confirmed by the ensuing reference to 'something out of a romance' ('une chose de roman'; see above, Introduction, pp. viii–ix).

made her blush a little: the manuscripts omit 'a little' and thus make her response less unambiguous.

165 *three years*: they had presumably not met since her marriage in 1566. Both are now 18 years old.

he told himself: after this phrase, a manuscript variant reads: 'that he might be as thoroughly trapped by the beautiful princess as the salmon was in the fisherman's net.' This conceit shows that the details of the setting are not mere 'background': they are figuratively potent.

166 *neither saying a word*: compare the discomfort of the Prince de Clèves and the Chevalier de Guise as potential rivals in *The Princesse de Clèves*, p. 12.

168 *The Huguenots laid siege to the town of Poitiers*: the siege of Poitiers took place during the summer of 1569; the Duc de Guise is indeed said to have performed valiant deeds in its defence.

the Battle of Moncontour: the battle was won by the Duc d'Anjou on 3 October 1569.

The Duc d'Anjou . . . fell ill: December 1569.

when peace was made: the Peace of Saint-Germain, August 1570.

168–9 *The princess's beauty . . . All eyes were upon her*: the impact of the Princesse de Montpensier's beauty when she comes to court is described in terms that anticipate Mlle de Chartres's first appearance at court in *The Princesse de Clèves* (see above, p. 9).

169 *the Queen's apartment*: here as elsewhere, the Queen Mother (Catherine de Médicis) is referred to simply as the Queen.

170 *she began, despite all the resolutions she had made . . . to feel*: the gradual progress of the princess's love, against her best intentions, makes the story an early example of the theme of involuntary passion which will dominate many of the most celebrated works of later seventeenth-century France, and not least *The Princesse de Clèves*.

The Duc d'Anjou: the version of the sentence given here is that of the manuscripts and most modern editions. The 1662 printed text contains the 'appalling mistake' which Mme de Lafayette refers to in a letter to her friend Ménage: it divides the sentence into two and suggests that Marguerite de Valois was in love with her brother.

his sister Marguerite de Valois: daughter of Henri II, born 1553. In 1572, she married Henri de Bourbon, King of Navarre and later King of France (Henri IV).

it made her aware: the discovery of love through jealousy is another aspect of the motivation of this story which anticipates *The Princesse de Clèves*.

M. de Montpensier: Louis de Bourbon was married for the second time in February 1570 to Catherine de Lorraine, the

Duc de Guise's sister. Catherine was born in 1552, and was thus nearly two years younger than her daughter-in-law.

170 *Madame*: Marguerite de Valois is so called from this point on.

172 *The King's marriage... celebrations and festivities*: Charles IX married Elizabeth of Austria by proxy. The contract was signed on 14 January 1570; the wedding celebrations took place in the autumn of that year. The reference to court festivities as the context for amorous 'adventures' anticipates (on a small scale) *The Princesse de Clèves*.

173 *the loss of your life*: this threat was eventually carried out when the Duc de Guise was assassinated on the orders of Henri III (formerly the Duc d'Anjou) at Blois in 1588; the motivation is, however, fictitious.

176 *the Princesse de Portien*: Catherine de Clèves, born in 1548, widow of the Prince de Portien.

177 *they came to the conclusion*: there are similarities between this episode and the mysterious divulgation of the Princesse de Clèves's confession, except that the Princesse de Montpensier and the Duc de Guise are more successful than the Prince and Princesse de Clèves in guessing how it came about.

Some time afterwards: the court left for Blois in August 1571. Negotiations for the marriage of Marguerite de Valois with Henri de Navarre continued throughout the winter and the contract of marriage was signed as part of a peace treaty in April 1572. The religious ceremony did not take place until August 1572.

178 *it produced the most extraordinary effect*: towards the end of the story, the exceptional nature of the Comte de Chabannes's predicament and behaviour is frequently emphasized in a way which is again reminiscent of the romance tradition: the author's skill—and the reader's interest—is invested in the contrivance of implausible situations.

179 *she treated the Comte de Chabannes much worse*: the Comte de Chabannes's uncomfortable position here anticipates that of Antiochus in Racine's *Bérénice* (1670).

St Bartholomew's Day: 23–4 August 1572, when a large number of Huguenots who had come to Paris for the wedding of Marguerite de Valois and Henri de Navarre were assassinated; the carnage subsequently spread to the provinces. The author follows the account given by historians of her period not only for the circumstantial details but also for the negative judgement. One should perhaps recall that the Edict of Nantes (1598), by which Henri IV gave limited freedom of worship to the Protestants, was to be revoked by Louis XIV in 1685.

181 *to lower the little drawbridge*: the Duc de Guise's penetration into the Princesse de Montpensier's garden at night anticipates Nemours's nocturnal visits to Coulommiers. In both instances, it may be argued that the scene enacts a drama of (unconsummated) sexual invasion at one remove. The position of the Comte de Chabannes as go-between becomes increasingly fraught here: his role is markedly voyeuristic and masochistic.

183 *Such an extraordinary occurrence*: the noun used here in French is 'aventure'; it connects this episode generically with the romance-like episodes of the earlier part of the story.

184 *an occurrence so strange*: as above, p. 183, the word used here in French is 'aventure'.

185 *some mystery in this scene*: 'scene' is a rendering, once again, of 'aventure'.

Things are not at all as they appear: the theme of deceptive appearances is to be found everywhere in later seventeenth-century literature and will be central to *The Princesse de Clèves*.

discover the truth afterwards: the prince here proposes to follow the model of an Aristotelian recognition tragedy in which the deed is performed in ignorance of the circumstances and the truth discovered afterwards. However, as the following paragraph makes clear, the threat lacks tragic edge since the prince has no sword.

186 *what he had to hope or fear*: as in *The Comtesse de Tende*, the wronged husband fears that his wife's illness may be fatal, but also hopes that it will be, since her death would avenge him and relieve him of embarrassment.

187 *the desire to avenge the death of his father*: this is the motivation for the Duc de Guise's role in the St Bartholomew's Day massacre provided by seventeenth-century historians; his father had been murdered by a Huguenot in 1563.

187   *the Marquise de Noirmoutier*: Charlotte de Beaune, born in
      1551, was in fact not married to the Marquis de Noirmou-
      tiers (the name is normally spelt thus) until 1584.

The Comtesse de Tende

191   *the regency of Queen Catherine de Médicis*: this story begins
      immediately after the historical events recounted in *The Prin-
      cesse de Clèves*, i.e. in 1559–60.

      Mademoiselle de Strozzi: the daughter of Pierre Strozzi, Maré-
      chal de France; her mother was a member of the Medici
      family, and thus related to the Queen Mother. In 1560, she
      married Honorat de Savoie, Comte de Tende; she died in
      1564.

      the Comte de Tende: born in 1538, Honorat de Savoie fol-
      lowed his father as governor of Provence.

      at first: the French expression used here ('d'abord') could
      also mean 'from the very beginning' in seventeenth-century
      French. Both readings are plausible: she is young, impression-
      able, and susceptible to instant passion; at the same time, her
      passion for her husband will not last long.

      the Princesse de Neufchâtel: the most likely historical candidate
      for this role is Jacqueline de Rohan, the wife of François
      d'Orléans-Longueville. However, although the date of her
      birth is unknown, she was married in 1536 and widowed in
      1548, so that the phrase 'the young and beautiful widow'
      must be regarded as a fictional adjustment.

      The Chevalier de Navarre: apparently a fictional character.

      with whose character he was acquainted: the French word
      translated as 'character' is 'esprit'; the sense seems too broad
      in this instance to be covered by 'wit'.

193   *She feared that her lover really did love the princess*: the situation
      is not unlike that in Racine's *Bajazet* (1672), where Atalide,
      in love with Bajazet, fears that he may really love Roxane,
      whom he is obliged to court in order to protect himself
      against the threat of violent death.

      private room . . . couch: this scene has more than one pre-
      cedent in *The Princesse de Clèves*; the 'couch' is a 'lit de repos'
      or day-bed.

195   *wedding night*: the narrative here is more melodramatic than
      anything in *The Princesse de Clèves* or *The Princesse de Mont-
      pensier*, although nocturnal visits take place in both.

196   *the Princesse de Condé*: Eléonor de Roye, born 1535, married
      in 1551 to Louis I de Bourbon, Prince de Condé, died in
      1564.

      It is easy to yield to what gives pleasure: a maxim-like state-
      ment, but one which, unlike many of those in *The Princesse
      de Clèves*, does not draw markedly on the psychology of
      self-deception.

197   *her bed was in shadow*: compare *The Princesse de Clèves*, pp. 84
      and 105.

198   *the Maréchale de Saint-André*: Marguerite de Lustrac, married
      to Jacques d'Albon, a favourite of Henri II and Maréchal de
      France from 1547 (the 'Maréchal de Saint-André' who plays
      a not insignificant role in *The Princesse de Clèves*).

      La Châtre: possibly Gaspard de La Châtre, who in 1570
      married a cousin of the Comte de Tende.

199   *the Comte de Tende became as much enamoured of her*: in this
      (though in little else) he resembles the Prince de Clèves; his
      uxorious desires are a good deal more baldly expressed.

200   *thirty miles from Paris*: about the same distance from Paris as
      the Princesse de Clèves's residence at Coulommiers.

      she realized that she was pregnant: the fact that the Comtesse
      de Tende's love is consummated sets this story apart from
      the other two: the sexual references become more explicit
      and the outcome more lurid and violent.

      some slight hope: i.e. that her pregnancy could be 'covered' by
      a renewal of relations with her husband.

201   *her natural feelings as well as her Christian ones*: this explicitly
      Christian moralizing element is absent from the other two
      stories.

202   *our self-regard always allows us*: this maxim, with its emphasis
      on self-deception and *amour-propre*, is strongly reminiscent of
      La Rochefoucauld, and is the closest this story comes to the
      psychological principles on which much of *The Princesse de
      Clèves* is based.

203   *it may even be that they always have their doubts*: the French is
      awkward and unclear here.

203   *an open confession*: this 'confession' is of course very different
       from the famous one in *The Princesse de Clèves*; it is, however,
       at least a distant relation.

       if he killed his wife and it was noticed that she was pregnant: the
       brutality of the Comte de Tende's attitude is particularly
       striking here. It is clear that one is looking at a sensibility very
       different from our own; it is more difficult, however, to assess
       exactly the range of responses that contemporary readers
       might have made to the denouement of the story (applause
       and sympathy for the Comte de Tende? sympathy for his
       wife?). The fear that the Comtesse de Tende might give him
       an illegitimate heir, mentioned below, indicates the social and
       economic importance of lineage for a well-born family.

204   *he never had the desire to marry again*: in the anonymous
       edition of 1718, the final sentence reads: '... marry again, he
       had a horror of women, and he lived ...'. The omission
       (suppression?) of such a striking phrase in the attributed
       edition of 1724 suggests that it cannot be regarded as a
       standard authorized response to a woman's sexual transgres-
       sion. The censorship exercised by the 1724 editor implies
       that the waters here are troubled indeed.

       he lived to a very advanced age: Honorat de Savoie in fact died
       in 1572 at the age of 34. The fictional extension of his life is
       clearly designed to emphasize the traumatic impact of his
       wife's infidelity.

GLOSSARY OF NAMES IN
THE PRINCESSE DE CLÈVES

THE relatively few historical names in *The Princesse de Montpensier* and *The Comtesse de Tende* are glossed in the notes to those stories, with reference to this glossary where appropriate.

ALBE, DUC D', the Spanish Duke of Alva, 1508–82, proxy to Philip II in his marriage to Elisabeth de France.

AMBOISE, MME D', an unidentified character.

ANNEBAULD, AMIRAL D'. Claude d'Annebault, Maréchal de France from 1538.

ANVILLE, M. D', 1534–1614, younger son of the Connétable de Montmorency, married Mlle de La Marck.

AUMALE, DUC D', Claude de Lorraine, 1526–73, younger brother of the Duc de Guise and the Cardinal de Lorraine, married Louise de Brézé.

BOLEYN, ANNE, 1507–36, married Henry VIII (1533), mother of Queen Elizabeth I.

BOUILLON, DUC DE, Robert de La Marck, married Françoise de Brézé.

BOURBON, CONNÉTABLE DE, Charles de Bourbon, 1490–1527 (the *connétable* was the commander of the king's armies).

BRÉZÉ, M. DE, Louis de Brézé, married Diane de Poitiers (later Mme de Valentinois) (1514).

BRÉZÉ, FRANÇOISE DE, and LOUISE DE, daughters of Mme de Valentinois.

BRISSAC, COMTE DE, Charles de Cossé, 1506–63, Maréchal de France.

CARLOS, DON, Infante of Spain, 1546–68, son of Philip II.

CATHERINE DE MÉDICIS, Queen of France, later Queen Mother, 1519–89, wife of Henri II.

CATHERINE OF ARAGON, Queen of England, first wife of Henry VIII.

CHARLES V, Holy Roman Emperor (1519–56).

CHARLES IX, King of France (1560–74), born 1550, son of Henri II.

CHARTRES, MLLE DE, later Princesse de Clèves. fictitious niece of the Vidame de Chartres.

CHARTRES, MME DE, fictitious character, mother of Mlle de Chartres.

CHARTRES, VIDAME DE, François de Vendôme, 1524–62, uncle of the fictitious Mlle de Chartres.

CHASTELART, PIERRE DE BOSCOSEL DE, escorted Marie Stuart on her return to Scotland in 1561.

CLAUDE, QUEEN, born 1499, daughter of Louis XII of France, married François I (1514).

CLAUDE DE FRANCE, 1547–75, daughter of Henri II, married Charles, Duc de Lorraine (1558).

CLÈVES, PRINCE DE, born 1544, married Diane de La Marck, granddaughter of Mme de Valentinois (not the fictitious Mlle de Chartres), died 1564 (not 1560(?) as in the novel).

CLÈVES, PRINCESSE DE, see Chartres, Mlle de.

CONDÉ, PRINCE DE, Louis de Bourbon, 1530–69, leader of the Protestants during the wars of religion until he was assassinated.

CONNÉTABLE, THE, see Bourbon *or* Montmorency.

COURTENAY, LORD, Edward Courtenay, Earl of Devonshire, Marquis of Exeter, died in exile in 1556.

DAMPIERRE, MME DE, Jeanne de Vivonne, wife of the Baron de Dampierre, lady-in-waiting to Marguerite de France, died 1583.

DAUPHIN, THE, or M. LE DAUPHIN, see François, eldest son of François I, or François, later François II.

DAUPHIN, THE PRINCE, see Prince Dauphin, the.

DAUPHINE, THE REINE, or MME LA DAUPHINE, see Marie Stuart.

DIANE, MME, illegitimate daughter of Henri II.

DIANE DE POITIERS, see Valentinois, Mme de.

ELISABETH DE FRANCE, MME, 1545–68, daughter of Henri II, betrothed to Don Carlos, married Philip II of Spain (1559).

ELIZABETH, Queen of England, born 1533, daughter of Henry VIII and Anne Boleyn.

ESCARS, JEAN D', Prince de Carency, Comte de La Vauguyon, favourite of Henri II, died 1595.

ESTE, ALPHONSE D', Duc de Ferrare (Duke of Ferrara), 1533–97, brother of Anne d'Este (wife of (1) the Duc de Guise, (2) M. de Nemours).

ESTOUTEVILLE, a name found in sixteenth-century memoirs; no positive identification possible.

ÉTAMPES, DUCHESSE D', Anne de Pisseleu, born 1508, mistress of François I.

EU, COMTE D', François de Clèves, elder brother of the Prince de Clèves.

FERRARE, DUC DE, see Este, Alphonse d'.

FRANÇOIS I, King of France (1515–47), born 1494.

FRANÇOIS, eldest son of Henri II, born 1544, Dauphin, later François II, King of France (1559–60).

FRANÇOIS, 'Monsieur le Dauphin', eldest son of François I, 1517–36 (he was said to have been poisoned).

GUISE, CHEVALIER DE, François de Lorraine, 1534–63, younger brother of the Duc de Guise (whose name he shares and who died in the same year), the Cardinal de Lorraine, and the Duc d'Aumale.

GUISE, DUC DE, François de Lorraine, the eldest and historically the most renowned of the Guise brothers, born 1519, assassinated 1563.

HENRI II, King of France (1547–59), born 1518.

HENRY VIII, King of England (1509–47), born 1491.

HOWARD, CATHERINE, Queen of England, fifth wife of Henry VIII, executed 1542.

JAMES V, King of Scotland (1512–42).

LA MARCK, MLLE DE, Antoinette de La Marck, daughter of the Duc de Bouillon, granddaughter of Mme de Valentinois.

LIGNEROLLES, PHILIPPE DE, said to have been a friend of Nemours, assassinated 1571.

LONGUEVILLE, DUC DE, first husband of Marie de Lorraine.

LORRAINE, CARDINAL DE, Charles de Guise, 1524–74, younger brother of the Duc de Guise.

LORRAINE, DUC DE, Charles, born 1543, married Claude de France (1558).

LORRAINE, DUCHESSE DE, born 1521, mother of Charles, Duc de Lorraine.

LOUIS XII, King of France (1498–1515).

MADAME, see Elisabeth de France.

MADAME THE KING'S SISTER, see Marguerite de France.

MAGDELEINE, MME, Madeleine de France, daughter of François I, first wife of James V of Scotland.

MARGUERITE DE FRANCE, known as 'Madame the King's sister', born 1523, sister of Henri II, married Emmanuel-Philibert, Duc de Savoie (1559).

MARGUERITE DE NAVARRE, 1492–1549, sister of François I, married Henri, King of Navarre, mother of Jeanne d'Albret ('the Queen of Navarre'), author of the *Heptameron*.

MARIE DE LORRAINE, 1515–60, elder sister of the Duc de Guise and the Cardinal de Guise, married James V of Scotland, mother of Marie Stuart.

MARIE STUART, Queen of Scots, 'the Reine Dauphine' or 'Mme la

Dauphine', born 1542, daughter of James V of Scotland and Marie de Lorraine, married the Dauphin François (later François II) (1558).

MARTIGUES, MME DE, Marie de Beaucaire, married the Comte de Martigues, lady-in-waiting to Marie Stuart.

MARY, Queen of England (1553–8), Mary Tudor, daughter of Henry VIII and Catherine of Aragon, born 1516, married Philip II of Spain (1554).

MARY, known as 'Marie d'Angleterre', sister of Henry VIII, married to Louis XII.

MERCŒUR, DUCHESSE (MME) DE, 1532–68, Jeanne de Savoie, sister of the Duc de Nemours, married Nicolas de Lorraine, Duc de Mercœur (1555).

MONTGOMERY, COMTE DE, captain of Henri II's Scottish Guards.

MONTMORENCY, CONNÉTABLE DE, 1492–1567, exiled from court by François I, brought back by Henri II, falls from favour after the death of Henri II.

MONTMORENCY, FRANÇOIS DE, elder son of the Connétable de Montmorency.

MONTPENSIER, DUC DE, Louis de Bourbon, father of the Prince Dauphin.

NAVARRE, KING OF, Antoine de Bourbon, 1518–62, becomes King of Navarre as a consequence of marrying Jeanne d'Albret (see Navarre, Queen of) (1548).

NAVARRE, QUEEN OF, Jeanne d'Albret, 1528–72, daughter of Marguerite de Navarre, mother of the future Henri IV of France.

NEMOURS, DUC DE, Jacques de Savoie, 1531–85, married Anne d'Este (widow of the Duc de Guise) (1566).

NEVERS, DUC DE, François de Clèves, 1516–62, father of the Prince de Clèves.

NEVERS, MME DE, (1) wife of the Duc de Nevers and mother of the Prince de Clèves, (2) wife of the Comte d'Eu.

OLIVIER, CHANCELIER, 1497–1560, Chancelier de France from 1545, removed from power under Henri II, restored after the death of Henri II.

ORANGE, PRINCE D', William of Nassau, 1533–84.

ORLÉANS, DUC D', 1522–45, third son of François I, brother of the future Henri II.

PHILIP II, King of Spain (1558–98), son of Charles V, married Mary Tudor, then Elisabeth de France.

PISSELEU, MLLE DE, see Étampes, Duchesse d'.

PRINCE DAUPHIN, THE, François de Bourbon, later Duc de Montpensier (see also *The Princesse de Montpensier*).

QUEEN, THE, usually refers to Catherine de Médicis, but later to Marie Stuart (the expression 'the Queens' refers to both).

RANDAN, COMTE DE, Charles de La Rochefoucauld, died 1562.

REINE DAUPHINE, THE, see Marie Stuart.

ROCHFORD, VISCOUNT, brother of Anne Boleyn.

SAINT-ANDRÉ, MARÉCHAL DE, 1506(?)–62, Maréchal de France from 1547.

SAINT-VALLIER, father of Diane de Poitiers.

SANCERRE, no positive identification.

SAVOIE, M. DE, Emmanuel-Philibert, Duc de Savoie, 1528–80, cousin of the Duc de Nemours, married Marguerite de France (1559).

SEYMOUR, JANE, Queen of England, third wife of Henry VIII, died 1537.

TAIX, COMTE DE, died in action 1553.

THÉMINES, MME DE, Anne de Puymisson, wife of Jean de Lauzières de Thémines.

TOURNON, CARDINAL DE, François de Tournon, 1497–1562.

TOURNON, MME DE, mistress of the obscure Sancerre and Estouteville, probably an invented character.

VALENTINOIS, MME DE, 1499–1566, married Louis de Brézé (1514), widowed in 1531, mistress of future Henri II, created Duchesse de Valentinois (1547), known as Diane de Poitiers.

VILLEROY, perhaps Nicolas de Neufville, an official under Henri II.

WOLSEY, CARDINAL, Lord Chancellor under Henry VIII, fell from power after taking issue with the King over his divorce from Catherine of Aragon, died 1530.

The Oxford World's Classics Website

www.worldsclassics.co.uk

- Browse the full range of Oxford World's Classics online

- Sign up for our monthly e-alert to receive information on new titles

- Read extracts from the Introductions

- Listen to our editors and translators talk about the world's greatest literature with our Oxford World's Classics audio guides

- Join the conversation, follow us on Twitter at OWC_Oxford

- Teachers and lecturers can order inspection copies quickly and simply via our website

www.worldsclassics.co.uk

American Literature

British and Irish Literature

Children's Literature

Classics and Ancient Literature

Colonial Literature

Eastern Literature

European Literature

Gothic Literature

History

Medieval Literature

Oxford English Drama

Poetry

Philosophy

Politics

Religion

The Oxford Shakespeare

A complete list of Oxford World's Classics, including Authors in Context, Oxford English Drama, and the Oxford Shakespeare, is available in the UK from the Marketing Services Department, Oxford University Press, Great Clarendon Street, Oxford OX2 6DP, or visit the website at www.oup.com/uk/worldsclassics.

In the USA, visit www.oup.com/us/owc for a complete title list.

Oxford World's Classics are available from all good bookshops. In case of difficulty, customers in the UK should contact Oxford University Press Bookshop, 116 High Street, Oxford OX1 4BR.

ANTON CHEKHOV   **Early Stories**
                         Five Plays
                         The Princess and Other Stories
                         The Russian Master and Other Stories
                         The Steppe and Other Stories
                         Twelve Plays
                         Ward Number Six and Other Stories

FYODOR DOSTOEVSKY   **Crime and Punishment**
                         Devils
                         A Gentle Creature and Other Stories
                         The Idiot
                         The Karamazov Brothers
                         Memoirs from the House of the Dead
                         Notes from the Underground and
                             The Gambler

NIKOLAI GOGOL   **Dead Souls**
                         Plays and Petersburg Tales

ALEXANDER PUSHKIN   **Eugene Onegin**
                         The Queen of Spades and Other Stories

LEO TOLSTOY   **Anna Karenina**
                         The Kreutzer Sonata and Other Stories
                         The Raid and Other Stories
                         Resurrection
                         War and Peace

IVAN TURGENEV   **Fathers and Sons**
                         First Love and Other Stories
                         A Month in the Country

	Women's Writing 1778–1838
WILLIAM BECKFORD	Vathek
JAMES BOSWELL	Life of Johnson
FRANCES BURNEY	Camilla
	Cecilia
	Evelina
	The Wanderer
LORD CHESTERFIELD	Lord Chesterfield's Letters
JOHN CLELAND	Memoirs of a Woman of Pleasure
DANIEL DEFOE	A Journal of the Plague Year
	Moll Flanders
	Robinson Crusoe
	Roxana
HENRY FIELDING	Joseph Andrews and Shamela
	A Journey from This World to the Next and The Journal of a Voyage to Lisbon
	Tom Jones
WILLIAM GODWIN	Caleb Williams
OLIVER GOLDSMITH	The Vicar of Wakefield
MARY HAYS	Memoirs of Emma Courtney
ELIZABETH HAYWOOD	The History of Miss Betsy Thoughtless
ELIZABETH INCHBALD	A Simple Story
SAMUEL JOHNSON	The History of Rasselas
	The Major Works
CHARLOTTE LENNOX	The Female Quixote
MATTHEW LEWIS	Journal of a West India Proprietor
	The Monk
HENRY MACKENZIE	The Man of Feeling
ALEXANDER POPE	Selected Poetry